DISENCHANTED

HEIDE GOODY
IAIN GRANT

Paperback ISBN: 978-0-9957497-0-2

Ebook ISBN: 978-0-9933655-8-4

ONCE UPON A TIME...

There was a little girl called Ella Hannaford who loved to visit her Granny Rose.

Granny Rose's house smelled of fruit cake and beef gravy and the little cigarettes that Granny smoked. And the beds in Granny's house were big and bouncy (although Granny Rose would give Ella a clip round the ear if she was ever caught bouncing on them). And in Grandma's living room — the living room she kept for 'best', not the one for everyday — there was a glass-fronted sideboard full of treasures, like Granddad Doug's darts tankard and a pair of little silver peacocks and Granny Rose's delicate crystal bell and a painted plate of the most beautiful sunny beach with the message 'A gift from Bournemouth'. And in the garden there were chickens. Sometimes one of the chickens would lay an egg and Ella was allowed to carry it into the kitchen if she was careful. And Granny would ask her if she had spoken to the chicken or if the chicken had spoken to her and Ella would always say no. And then there would be egg sandwiches for tea or fried egg for breakfast and Granny Rose's fried eggs would taste better than the ones Ella's mum cooked because Granny used a secret ingredient in all her cooking and that secret ingredient was lard.

In short, a visit to Granny Rose's was a visit to the most magical place in all the world.

On this summer's afternoon, the sun was warm in Grandma Rose's garden and Ella was wearing her favourite yellow sun dress. She sat with her dollies on the lawn and made sure that they were all looking at her as she organised the picnic. Grandma had given her a cloth to put upon the grass and she smoothed it under her hands as she arranged the tea set.

"Who wants a cup of tea an' a sammidge?" she asked the dollies.

Dance Sensation Barbie and Malibu Barbie each had an arm up, so Ella knew what they wanted. Baby Chuckles had eyes that were meant to open and close when she was laid down or picked up but one of the eyes was stuck closed in a permanent wink. Ella knew what that wink meant and today it meant, 'I'd like a cup of tea an' a sammidge, please'.

Ella realised that there was a dolly in their little circle that had not been there before. This new dolly was taller than the Barbies, and she had wings that were as shiny and inviting as sweet wrappers. Ella didn't remember putting her there, and wasn't sure how she was standing up; the Barbies always toppled over. She reached out to touch the fabric of the dolly's dress. It was soft, like a rose petal or maybe the toilet paper that some of her friends had in their houses. Her other dollies' clothes were shiny and a bit scratchy.

"Pretty, isn't it?" said the dolly, smiling at her.

Ella snatched her hand back. One of her friends had a doll with a string that you could pull to make it talk but this one was smiling, and looked as if it was waiting for Ella to answer.

"Want a sammidge?" she asked in a small, uncertain voice.

"We can do better than sandwiches," said the dolly in a voice that reminded Ella of the crystal bell that she wasn't supposed to play with. "How would you like some cake?"

The dolly swept a dainty arm over the cloth and the tiny tea set tinkled as cakes appeared on it. Ella stared. These were not the sort of cakes that Granny might cut her a slice of. These weren't ginger cakes or scones or fruit cakes or any of the 'good and honest cakes' that Granny Rose made. These cakes looked dainty and fluffy and were decorated with colourful icing and Ella reckoned that they didn't have any lard in them, not even an ounce. These swirling colourful bites were even more beautiful than Mr Kipling French Fancies, which was what posh people had for their teas.

Ella reached out for one and then she stopped. There was a rule about this, wasn't there? The rules were important. Her mum and Granny Rose had told her many times. She started to sing quietly, to remind herself.

Don't let fairies come and play
Tell an adult right away

SHE LOOKED SOLEMNLY at the new dolly. "Are you a fairy?"

The dolly shook her head. Ella continued with the song.

Eating or drinking a fairy's food
Will never do you any good.

SHE LOOKED AT THE CAKES. Maybe she should just try one? They did look very nice, and they were so small that one couldn't matter, surely? The Barbies hadn't come to any harm. And besides, 'food' didn't really rhyme with 'good' so she shouldn't take the song seriously.

Ella looked round. There was no one about. Ella's dad, Gavin, was in the front room, sleeping off his Sunday lunch in Granddad Doug's old chair (which Granny Rose kept even though she never sat in it herself and Granddad Doug had been dead a long time). Ella's mum, Natalie, had gone to the shed with a big jar to do some tidying up or something. And Granny Rose was in the kitchen and, although the back door was open, Ella couldn't see her inside.

"Ella?"

Granny Rose was looking at her through the kitchen window.

Ella jumped up, but the new dolly tugged at her dress. "Why don't you just have a bite of cake?"

"Granny called."

"You can go in a moment," said the dolly.

Ella paused, but Grandma Rose could not be ignored, not even for a short while. She ran down the garden path and into the kitchen.

Granny shook her wet hands and dried them on her apron. She took a bowl of apple trimmings from the side and passed them to Ella.

"Take these for t'chickens," Granny said, talking with her Park Drive cigarette wedged in the corner of her mouth.

Ella took the bowl.

"Is everything all right out there?" said Granny.

"Yes, Granny."

"Tha looked a mite discombobulated, lass."

"I gotta new dolly," said Ella.

"Oh aye?" said Granny with a frown. "And where did that come from?"

"It was just there," said Ella. "And cake as well!"

Granny advanced, a worried look on her face (although a worried look on Granny Rose's face meant that others should be doing the worrying because she was what dad called a 'tough old bird' with arm muscles like Popeye the sailor man and hands that could pick up scalding hot pans without getting hurt).

"Did tha eat any of the cake?" she asked, taking hold of Ella's hand.

"S'all right Granny," said Ella. "I know she's not a fairy. She told me."

"Oh, did she now? Right, tha needs to sit down at t'table so's I can deal with yonder missy who's not a fairy."

She sat Ella down with the bowl of apple trimmings on her lap.

"But my dollies are out there," said Ella. The gloomy kitchen seemed like a punishment.

"I'll fetch them shortly," said Granny. "We'll have that apple pie with t'dollies when I'm done." She stubbed out her cigarette, went to the cleaning cupboard and got out a bucket, a bottle of bleach and a plastic carrier bag. "How big?"

"What, Granny?" Ella asked.

"How big is t'dolly that's not a fairy?"

Ella held her hands apart. Granny swapped the carrier bag for a larger bin liner and then went out into the garden.

Ella sighed and opened the story book that was on the table beside Ella's crayons and colouring pad. The book was called *Magical Kingdoms for Small Children.*

Ella loved the exotic stories, which were set in exciting places and featured dragons, giants and unicorns. Her mum and dad would read them to her at night. Ella couldn't read many of the words for herself yet, so she flipped through the book looking at the pictures. She found a picture of a pretty lady with wings.

"*That's* a fairy," said Ella.

The differences were clear to Ella. The pretty lady in the book was sitting comfortably inside a buttercup, which meant that she was smaller than Ella's thumb. The dolly she'd seen outside had been much bigger than that. The lady in the book had delicate wings, like a butterfly, and stood on her tiptoes. The new dolly had stood more like Wonder Woman, from the television.

Eventually Granny Rose came back into the kitchen. She no longer had the bleach or the bin liner but she did have Ella's toys. Ella jumped down from her chair.

"Let's play dollies now, Granny!"

"Let me see to t'pie." Granny had gathered up the dollies, the tea set and the cloth into a basket and she put them onto the table before she turned to the oven.

Ella examined the basket. "Where's the new dolly, Grandma?"

Granny put the pie on the counter to cool. Its crust was crisp and golden and steam wafted from the slits cut in its centre.

"That were a fairy, love. It had to go," said Granny.

Ella's disappointment made her eyes prick with the threat of tears. "But it didn't look like a fairy, Granny. Fairies are smaller."

"Is that so? And how would tha know that?"

She turned the book to show Granny the illustration. The old woman stabbed the picture with a finger and looked at Ella. "I reckon tha's learned a useful lesson about being tricked. Fairies will pop up in all manner o' guises. Asking 'em's no good, they'll not be truthful. If tha's thought to ask the question, it's probably a fairy."

The afternoon had started off so exciting. She knew the rules were important but they were no fun sometimes.

"What is this, anyroad?" said Granny, flipping disdainfully through Ella's book.

"Fairy tales, Granny."

Granny stopped at a page. "*The Good Buttercup Fairy*? Blummin' heck. Stuff and nonsense. Good fairies? Ha! Let's feed t' dollies and then we'll see about reading summat else."

Granny and Ella sat the dollies at the table and served up some apple pie. Granny put a jug of double cream on the table and didn't mind when Ella poured nearly all of it on her slice. It really was very good, and Ella nearly forgot about the new dolly who was a fairy.

"This un'll catch her death o' cold in them clothes," said Granny, indicating Malibu Barbie in her swimsuit.

Ella laughed. "She's from 'merica, Granny. Like Wonder Woman. Ev'ryone dresses like that, I think."

Granny gave Ella a yellow duster to fashion into something warmer for Malibu Barbie, and Ella busied herself silently while Granny washed up. Ella flipped through the book to find the picture she had in mind, then she found an elastic band from Granny's kitchen table to finish the job.

"Granny, look!" Ella held up Malibu Barbie wearing her yellow cloak. "It's like this one!"

Granny came round and looked at the illustration. It was *Red Riding Hood*, and Ella jigged in her seat full of excitement at how closely Malibu Barbie's yellow cloak, fastened at the neck with the elastic band, resembled the red one worn by the young heroine in the story.

Granny nodded, but Ella saw that she had a small frown on her face as she did so.

"Don't you like it?"

"Aye, it's grand enough. You know, a smart girl would do better than going off into t'woods and consorting with wolves and that. And certainly not running around in her unmentionables like Wonder Woman. Give me a girl who can mend a broken fence or fix up a chicken coop any day."

"Is your fence broken, Granny?"

Granny Rose stood up and took down a book from the dark shelf above the fridge freezer. The yellow cover showed a line drawing of a house with images of various tools and decorating equipment within.

"What is it?" said Ella.

"The *Reader's Digest Complete Do-it-yourself Manual*," said Granny Rose, pointing at each word in turn. "Tha can have it."

"Thank you," said Ella who didn't really want it but even at the age of four knew that you always said thank you when you were given something.

Granny stroked Ella's hair. "Now I reckon it's about time to pack tha things away and go wake tha dad."

Ella busied herself putting away the toys and crayons until she heard her mum come round through the garden. Then she ran out to meet her. Her mum had a stern expression on her face and an oily rag wrapped around her left hand, which she held in place with her right hand.

"What's tha done?" said Granny Rose without much in the way of sympathy.

"Bloody thing bit me," said Ella's mum.

"What did tha think it were going to do? Let's get it under the tap."

"What have you done, mum?" asked Ella.

Granny Rose gave her a *look*. It was the same *look* Ella's mum gave her sometime. Ella's mum was good at the *look* but Granny Rose was a world champion. One day, Ella's mum would be world champion and Ella herself would have learned the secret of the *look*.

"I told thee to go wake tha father, Ella. And none of your questions."

Ella scurried to do as she was told. Her dad was sprawled in Granddad Doug's old chair, his head back and his mouth wide. An empty wine glass dangled precariously between his fingertips, inches above the carpet. His hairy nostril quivered as he snored.

"Daddy, it's time to wake up."

He didn't stir. Ella poked him sharply in the knee and attempted to give him the *look*. He snorted and came awake, peering at Ella.

"Are you trying to go cross-eyed, squozzle?" he asked.

Ella tried the *look* again but it made her cheeks hurt so she gave up. From the kitchen, came the restrained but sharp sounds of Granny Rose and mum arguing at low volume.

"Are the Thorn girls having a *word* with each other?" said Ella's dad. "Then it must be time to go home."

Ella's dad scooped her up in his arms, blew a raspberry on her belly and then carried her kicking and laughing into the kitchen. The argument between Ella's mum and grandma stopped instantly. Ella's mum had a large plaster across her left hand.

"Had a bit of an accident?" said Ella's dad.

"Playing silly buggers," said Granny Rose.

"Ah, I used to be able to play that," said Ella's dad, "but I forgot the rules."

Granny Rose tutted at the ridiculous man and Ella giggled.

Shortly after, bundled up in the back of the family's Austin Metro with Malibu Barbie in her yellow cloak in her hands, Ella waved goodbye to Granny Rose. Ella's dad put the car into gear and pulled away. Ella knelt up on the seat and waved faster.

"And what was that one about?" said her dad.

"Oh, the usual," said her mum.

"Oh, the usual," said dad in a daft and pompous voice.

And that, Ella already understood, was her parents in a nutshell. Her dad's love was silliness and cuddles and smoothing the edge between the jagged people in his life. And her mum's love was sharp looks and hard attitudes and a fierceness that both frightened and protected Ella.

"Granny Rose has got my book," said Ella, looking back at Granny Rose with *Magical Kingdoms for Small Children* in the crook of her arm. The trade for the *Reader's Digest Complete Do-it-yourself Manual* hardly seemed fair.

"We'll get you a different one," said Ella's mum. "No more fairy tales anymore."

And that was that.

1

The years bleached the colour from the cover and scuffed its edges but, thirty years after Granny Rose had presented it to her, Ella Hannaford still owned the *Reader's Digest Complete Do-it-yourself Manual.* It sat on the shelf in her office, between Geoff Hamilton's *Cottage Gardens* and Buckminster Fuller's *Operating Manual for Spaceship Earth.* The office in question was a cabin built from responsibly-sourced spruce and reclaimed slate tiles, sited in the expansive grounds of the "Diggers and Dreams" garden centre and only occasionally mistaken for a display shed by confused customers. From this hi-tech nerve centre, Ella ran her one-woman, environmentally friendly home improvement and eco building business.

However, today, the environment had to take care of itself as Ella was faced with a different task, one that was slowly driving her potty.

Nearly a hundred scraps of card and paper were pinned to her office noticeboard in a labyrinthine pattern. Each scrap had a name copperplated on it. Most of the scraps were pages torn from a security company's promotional calendar — from the firm where Myra used to work — and they featured cartoon illustrations of the application of handcuffs, leg irons, waist chains, Hannibal Lector-style body boards, muzzles and more. It was surprising, and more than a little disturbing to know that there was such a variety of ways to incapacitate a human, and look cheerful while doing it. A smaller proportion of scraps — those from Ella's dad, Myra's fiancé — were written on the backs of old Bordeaux labels. It had amused him to soak them off the bottles and dry them out so that he could comply with Ella's demand that he used only recycled notepaper. He told her that if he was going to be environmentally aware, it might as well be fun.

The noticeboard as a whole presented an image of middle-class, socially acceptable alcoholism besieged by the forces of totalitarianism and hardcore bondage. For all Ella knew, that was probably an accurate description of her father and future step-mother's personal relationship. What it was slowly turning into was a map of Ella's own increasingly deranged mind. With this evidence, Ella could probably take up her trowel on a murderous rampage through "Diggers and Dreams" garden centre and expect a verdict of not guilty by way of insanity.

Of course, what the board was *meant* to represent was a seating plan for the wedding reception after the marriage of her dad to one Myra Whuppie. And it didn't work.

Ella's phone rang.

She speculatively moved an obscure aunt on Myra's side from one position to another and back again. She looked at her trowel (currently serving as a paperweight for a stack of invoices) and considered the relative attractiveness of a murderous rampage followed by a long quiet stretch at Her Majesty's pleasure.

She turned to pick up her phone and saw, for the first time, that two garden gnomes had been deposited by the door of her office.

"Just because this place looks like a shed, doesn't mean you can use it like one," she said to no one and then answered the phone. "Green Dwellings, eco-buildings, general insanity and gnome depository."

"Do you answer your phone like that all the time?" said Myra disapprovingly.

"Um. Hi Myra."

"Ella, I assume you've worked through the seating plan by now."

"I'm finalising it right now," she lied.

"I haven't seen it ticked off yet on the group to-do list."

"No, but..." Ella was unable to finish.

"The wedding is only eleven days away, you know."

"I do know," said Ella. "I'm working on it, or at least I was trying to."

"Well what could possibly be stopping you?"

"Well, nothing. I mean someone's stuck a pair of garden gnomes in my office and —"

Ella choked mid-sentence as one of the gnomes, the one in the bright red hat, moved. It stood with its hands on its hips, cleared its throat and growled at her in a voice that seemed *too big* for a two-foot gnome.

"We're dwarfs, bab."

Ella wasn't sure whether to be amused or horrified. This was an enormously clever piece of kit, no doubt about it, but who decided that gnomes needed a voice? It was consumerism gone mad, and one of the things about the garden centre that slightly depressed her. You could walk a considerable way through it before you found a plant. She'd pointed this out to Roy on more than one occasion but Roy, garden centre owner and heir to the Avenant fortune, remained unabashed and told her he was simply giving people what they wanted.

"No. I can't believe people want talking gnomes," she said out loud, shaking her head.

"Who wants gnomes?" said Myra.

"Not gnomes. Dwarfs," the little bearded fellow on the floor said. "Hate fucking fishing for a start. Now, we've got a bastard warning for you, duck."

Ella stared in horror as the other one, who wore a hat of unpleasantly stain-like yellow raised his head and gave her a brief unfocused look — a small but oh so sincere expression of apology in his eyes — before his head went forward again and he vomited copiously on the floor.

"That's not the warning," said the red-capped one. "Ignore Shitfaced."

"Shitfaced?"

"I beg your pardon!" said Myra on the line.

Ella cupped her hand over the phone and stared at the tiny man.

"She's gonna try to kill you," the dwarf informed her.

"Shitfaced?" said Ella. "That's his name?"

The very sorry looking Shitfaced tried to shake the vomit off his boots, mumbled something and pointed at his companion.

"Pardon?" said Ella.

"Fuck's sake. He said I'm Psycho," huffed the red-hatted one.

"Psycho?"

"Yes," said Psycho and head-butted a solar panel display to make his point.

Ella's brain was still in the utterly-bewildered stage and had not yet moved onto the freaked-out-and-terrified stage. These were dwarfs. Pointy little hats. Stout little boots. Fat little belts. Little white beards (which one of them was using to wipe sick off his tunic).

"Shitfaced and Psycho? Seriously?" she said.

"Thought you'd be quicker on the uptake than this, if I'm honest," said Psycho. "Anyway, I'd better go and get some brekkie down this lad, and you'll be wanting to get a mop I'm sure."

Ella put the phone back to her ear, dazed.

"Sure... I don't understand," said Myra, most put out. "I don't see why you would be going on about gnomes and getting shi— drunk when there are important matters to discuss. Which is why I popped down even though I have far too much to do as it is."

"Popped down?"

"Regard the fences if you would."

Still utterly baffled by what was happening, Ella looked out of the office window towards the fencing display. A figure waved at her from behind a lattice-work fence.

"Stay there," she said to the dwarfs. And before they could stop her, she was out of the door and striding toward where her future step-mother lurked. Myra Whuppie wasn't one of life's lurkers. She was about as demure and subtle as a rhinoceros. And as thick-skinned.

"What are you doing, Myra?" said Ella.

"Keeping a low profile," said the fifty-something bride-to-be, as she emerged cautiously onto the path, glaring at the world around her and daring it to comment.

"Please make sense."

"Says the woman wittering on about gnomes and wotnot."

"Dwarfs," said Ella. "Not gnomes."

"Ah I see!" there was an abrupt change in Myra's tone. "A little non-PC treat for the hen do tonight! Well in that case carry on. Can't have anything spoiling our girly evening."

"Girly evening. Can't wait."

"Which is why I want you to check that Petunia has booked the limo for tonight."

"Couldn't you ask her yourself?"

Myra tutted. "What? Do I want to look like a helicopter parent, checking up on my little girl all the time?"

"Um."

There were any number of points in that sentence Ella could

have disagreed with. Myra was less a helicopter parent than a helicopter gunship parent. And Petunia was far from little, either age-wise or width-wise, although in the mental capacity stakes, one might argue Petunia was a tad undersized...

"That's why I'm keeping the low profile," said Myra. "Can't have my little girl thinking I'm dropping in on her place of work snooping on her. Besides, if you tell her, it saves me a phone call."

"You phoned me, didn't you?" said Ella. "That was the phone call you would have made to Petunia."

"So very smart," said Myra. "You should have been a barrister instead of a hippy hut constructor —"

"Eco builder. One whose services are very much sought-after."

"Oh, I can see that by the way you're taking a stroll round the garden centre rather than eco-building," smirked Myra.

Ella knew she shouldn't rise to it. Knew she should stick to the moral high ground. She considered steering Myra towards the hothouse where the cactuses were displayed, just in case she needed an environmentally friendly weapon.

"But, fear not. I'm going to stretch your thinking muscles by giving you some of your father's wedding tasks," said Myra.

"What? Why?" asked Ella.

"Because he's off gallivanting again with work," said Myra. "At the beck and call of that shifty European chap."

"Mr Dainty."

"Whatever he calls himself. New money. No manners. No taste."

"I'll have a word with dad later. He's got to stop."

Myra humphed.

"He doesn't listen to *me*," she said, silently challenging Ella to suggest that Gavin Hannaford paid more attention to his daughter than to his bride-to-be.

"Well, I'll try," said Ella.

"Good. And when you do, try to get him to make a final decision on the cake."

Myra dipped into her capacious handbag and produced three laminated sheets. Ella looked from image to image.

"Yes, they're all wedding cakes," said Ella.

"But which one?" said Myra.

Ella looked at them again. They all had three tiers. Each of the layers in all of them was wrapped in silk. Stylised bride and groom figures stood atop each cake. It was like looking at a spot the difference competition.

"They're all the same," she said.

Myra snorted. "I would have thought someone in the building trade would have a finer appreciation of the details. Just show your father."

"What kind of cakes are they?" asked Ella.

"Wedding cakes," said Myra, as though Ella was somehow mentally deficient.

"I meant, what's in them."

"I'm not bothered with what's inside them," said Myra shirtily. "Which looks the best? It's all about appearances, Ella."

Ella sighed. "A cake's a cake."

"Well, my girl, at least your father understands the importance of creating a magical fairy tale wedding, even if he is too preoccupied to actually pull his weight on the tasks in hand."

Ella heard the click of the Green Dwellings office door swinging closed. She looked round in time to see a booted foot disappear behind a display of potted plants.

"Fine," said Ella, snatching the photos from Myra. "I will show them to dad. He will pick one. And, yes, I'll ask Petunia about the limo. But a cake is just a cake. And a wedding day is just another day. In the long run, it really doesn't matter, Myra."

"Oh, that's the attitude you're taking, is it?"

"Speaking as 'someone in the building trade' I'd say it's all about the foundations and the bricks and mortar. This…" — She waved the cake pictures violently. — "is window dressing. And I'm sorry but I just don't see why you're getting worked up about it. Now I must go. I need to catch up with things. Two things in particular."

She turned and left Myra among the trellises while she went off through Diggers and Dreams garden centre in pursuit of dwarfs or gnomes or whatever they were. It shouldn't be too hard to catch up, her own legs were at least twice the length of theirs.

"Maybe I am going mad," she told herself.

Whether it was her subconscious telling her to take a break, or actually some freaky animatronic toy, she was unimpressed. She did not need this right now. Or ever. Maybe this was all just a prelude to the trowel-themed murder rampage.

"The dwarfs told me to do it, your honour," she said and went inside the main building.

Petunia, her soon-to-be stepsister, was at her post at the Natural Beauty counter, which was enveloped, as always, in an aromatic fog of scent. Ella had long suspected that it would be possible to find your way there blindfolded, which was handy as the overpowering clouds of perfume that hung over the place weren't just gagging but occasionally blinding.

"There's my big sis," shouted Petunia.

Lily, Petunia's assistant, 'bestie' and all-round partner in crimes against cosmetics waved at her but did not speak, sat back as she was, mouth closed, her face slick with oil.

"Come to get dolled up for the big night out?" asked Petunia.

Ella forced a smile. She wasn't happy with the 'big sister' label. Ella's dad and Petunia's mum weren't even married yet. And, yes, they were both only children but Ella wasn't ready to sign up to sisterhood — particularly if, as she feared, it involved doing each other's nails and spending quality time waxing God knows where, quaffing chardonnay and generally acting like footballers' wives.

Having said that, Ella was a few years older than Petunia (and both of them on the wrong side of thirty), and whenever Ella was around Petunia and Lily, who acted like a pair of vain pre-teens hyped up on sugar, she always seemed to drop into the role of embittered babysitter.

"We were just discussing wardrobes." Petunia looked Ella up and down. "What are you wearing tonight?"

"Clothes?" said Ella.

Lily looked surprised at Ella's sarcastic response although that might have been because her hair was tied back so tight that her face was as taut as stretched rubber.

"What are you two up to?" said Ella.

"We've had a delivery," said Petunia.

Ella looked at the opened boxes that surrounded the pair.

"We're trying Tincture of Himalayan Rose so that we glow with spiritual beauty for the hen do." mumbled Lily through closed lips. "Want a go?"

Ella picked up a box. "This is pretty concentrated stuff."

"It's organic," said Petunia, "and the — er — monks or eunuchs or whatever gather the petals in the first hour of daylight so that the oils are more concentrated. Lily did me first and now I'm doing her."

"Did you have that rash before Lily did yours?" Ella asked, pointing to the livid eruptions on Petunia's face.

"Rash?" Petunia, grabbed a mirror. "Oh!"

"Ah, and it's coming up on Lily now."

"What is it? What is it?" warbled Lily, panicked.

"Chemical burns I should think," said Ella.

Petunia and Lily howled in unison and grabbed tissues to wipe their rapidly reddening faces.

"I'm disfigured," Petunia howled.

"Just wash your faces and don't put any make-up on," said Ella.

She helped Lily as she flailed for the face wipes below the counter.

"Call an ambulance!" cried Petunia.

"You'll be fine," said Ella. "But that reminds me. Taxi tonight?"

"What?"

"Did you book it?"

Petunia was apparently in no fit state to answer and was now blotting E45 cream all over her red face and turning it into a passable facsimile of a raspberry pavlova.

A considerable crowd of shoppers had drawn around and Ella was about to do a spot of "move along, nothing to see here," when Buster, the tireless pet dog of Roy, the owner, came bounding by. Ella was aghast to see a dwarf — the red hatted one, Psycho — was riding on Buster's back, holding onto his floppy spaniel ears. To make matters worse, Buster was frolicking merrily, his tail wagging, as if he were enjoying the attention.

"Go on, go faster you furry bastaaaaard!" came the vanishing cry of the dwarf.

Ella stared. She looked to the crowd. "Did any of you see that?"

"Yes, love." An old dear with a handbag pointed at the two hysterical beauty consultants. "Do they do children's parties?"

"No, I meant the dwarf on the..." She trailed off. Had no one else seen the red-hatted miniature jockey?

"Fine," she said and stomped off in pursuit.

"No makeup? Does she mean like *nude shades only*?" she heard before she stepped outside once more.

She heard the distant sound of barking again and hurried on. Dwarves. Jesus. When this wedding was finally over, she might need to get away from work and family for a bit. It was obvious that the stress was taking its toll on her. What was she even doing? If nothing else, she wanted to catch up with Buster and, dwarf or no dwarf, check that Roy's hunting buddy was okay.

She slowed her pace, spotting a coloured hat between the fronds of a potted fern.

"Stay there, you foul mouthed pest!" she muttered and crept around the fern to get a better view.

She sighed.

It was a display of garden gnomes. Each wore the same outfit and the same expression of idiotic glee while frozen in the inane acts of pushing wheelbarrows, sitting on toadstools, even those sticking their heads in buckets probably had the same expression.

"You're mad, Ella," she told herself, irritated on every level that she had clearly hallucinated the whole dwarf thing after seeing these ridiculous ornaments at some point — "Wait. Head in a bucket? Shitfaced?" she said, advancing.

"Well, it's a little early in the day but I *could* do with a sherry now you come to mention it," said a voice from behind her.

"Roy!" She turned quickly, but not so quickly that she didn't spot a gnome with a wheelbarrow barging forward and scooping up his friend with the bucket. "I was just looking for Buster. Have you seen him?"

Roy, handsomely bespectacled and allegedly four-hundred-and-something-th in line to the English throne, was wearing his tweediest tweeds. Both Roy and Ella appreciated a fine tweed, she principally because it was handmade in Britain and used natural materials and dyes making it a locally-sourced, carbon-friendly and all round environmentally amicable product. She knew, however, that when Roy was kitted out with his tweed hat, his tweed jacket, his Hunter wellies and whatever those ridiculous trousers were then he'd probably been shooting, which wasn't quite so good for the environment, at least the parts of it that sported fur or feather.

"Seen him? He's helping me carry my things," said Roy.

Buster appeared holding a pheasant in his mouth.

Had she earlier mistaken the pheasant for a brightly coloured dwarf? Perhaps. She once mistook a black plastic bag for an injured kitten (which she'd insisted her dad turn the car around to rescue). The mind did play such tricks.

But a dwarf who came with monosyllabic threats and a nauseated companion? That would be an impressive feat of impersonation for any dead pheasant.

"Are you walking up to The Bumbles," asked Ella.

"Care to join me?" said Roy.

"Mmm. I could do with a change of scene."

THE AVENANT FAMILY residence was called The Bumbles. It sat in the rolling fields of the prettiest bit of Warwickshire, almost at the dead centre of England and as far from the sea as it was generally possible to get. The land had been gifted to the first lord of the manor in the middle ages, probably for doing something nasty to the French with the pointy end of a sword. The Bumbles was a ridiculously modest and twee name for a farmhouse that was only a couple of bedrooms and a peacock short of being a stately home. Roy's family owned not only the house and the garden centre, but also every bit of farmland in sight.

Buster trotted obediently alongside Ella and Roy as they walked up past the yew that bordered the rear gardens, every inch of him a good and obedient dog, with no sign of his earlier silliness. She slipped Buster one of the bone-shaped dog biscuits she always kept in her pockets and he snaffled it up.

"Crikey O'Reilly, Ella. It's just a seating plan, isn't it?" said Roy.

"Ha!" scoffed Ella. "*Just* a seating plan? As in '*just* the bubonic plague' or '*just* a nuclear meltdown.'"

Roy held open the door to the orangery, a stunningly light and spacious glasshouse and, thanks to Roy's generosity, the reception venue for the forthcoming wedding of Mr Gavin Hannaford to Ms Myra Whuppie.

"It's the one thing everyone will moan about if I get it wrong," said Ella.

"Really?" said Roy. "Look, they're having the ceremony and disco in the marquee. They're only coming in here for the meal and speeches. What can they possibly complain about?"

"Who sits with who and where and how close to the top table..."

"Well, yes." Roy followed Ella in, "I can imagine it's a particular problem when your side of the family's so thin on the ground."

"Tell me about it. The Hannafords are an endangered species. Friends of the family aside, it's just the pair of us now. It's a good job dad's not precious about such things."

"No, he'll just be thrilled that you're there to give him away," said Roy, settling into an easy chair while Ella wove through the dining tables that had already been placed in the room.

"Give him away?" Ella looked at him askance.

Roy gave her a raffishly charming grin and, for a moment, she remembered how attractive he was — as attractive as a gun-toting hedgerow-demolishing member of the landed gentry could be.

"You know, as the responsible adult in the family," he said.

Ella laughed. "It's not quite that bad, honestly!"

Roy fixed her with a serious look.

"Don't forget, I've known you for a long time. I know how things have been for you two. It's not easy. Single dad. Growing up without a mum."

"She died when I was five. I've not known any different."

"But that experience is what's made you the formidable adult that you are now."

Ella started to count chairs and tables, slightly embarrassed. There was a scratching sound off to one side. She looked round, expecting to find Buster as the source of the noise but Buster was sat at Roy's feet and gazing lovingly up at his master.

"Don't you still have a grandma somewhere?"

Ella stopped and creased her brow. "Yes, as far as I know. Mum's mum actually. Rose. Nobody ever mentions her."

"Black sheep of the family, was she?"

"I think she was some sort of hippy or something. Does that qualify as a black sheep? She lives in some place called Rushy Glen."

"Is that like a commune or a kibbutz?" Roy asked.

Ella shrugged. "It might be. I don't remember. Dad sounded a bit wary of it, wherever it is."

"Well even if you are going to be horribly outnumbered by the ugly sisters and the rest of the —"

"Shh, you can't call them that!"

"Sorry. I meant one ugly stepsister and her piggish best mate —"

"Roy!"

"I can't believe you convinced me to employ those two. Now, what was I saying?"

"You were insulting my future family, Roy Avenant."

"Right," he grinned. "I was saying that despite being the last of your line I *hope* that you'll make some time to enjoy yourself at this wedding, and not just end up in the background, being their lackey."

"Enjoy is a strong word." Ella inspected the azure satin of one of the chair covers. "For weddings generally, I mean. Surely we just endure them, you know? We hope that they go well for the bride and groom and that nobody will actually throw up on us." Ella's mind went back to her office. Was there really a puddle of vomit on the floor? She half expected to go back there and find that she had imagined the whole thing.

"Nonsense!" said Roy, lolling in his chair. "Where else can you bust crazy dance moves with small children into the small hours?

Eating and drinking too much is more or less expected and everybody gets to dress up nicely."

"Exactly my point," said Ella. "Absolute hell and utterly frivolous."

"Ella, you are a practical woman to the point of masochism."

"Oh, I just live in the real world, Roy."

The scratching noise came again, and this time she placed it. Two birds perched on the outside of a window pane and knocked the glass, tapping and twittering as though trying to gain entrance.

"Blimey!" exclaimed Roy. "Would you look at those birds?"

"I'm just surprised that you can see them too," said Ella.

"Pardon?"

"It's been that sort of day. Signs and portents. Bird stalkers were bound to happen sooner or later."

"They're entirely blue."

"Bluebirds?" suggested Ella.

"In the UK?"

"Well, what are they then?"

I have no idea." Roy was already on his feet. "Never saw anything like it. We'll soon look them up once I've got 'em though."

"Got them?" said Ella and then, "You are not shooting them, Roy."

"Back in a jiffy."

Ella approached the glass as Roy went off. The two birds fluttered into the air, about six inches above their previous position. They were indeed bright blue, and even more remarkably, they held between them something the size and shape of a paper napkin. On it was scrawled a message:

Go! she wont to kil yo

IT WAS WRITTEN in lettering that might very well have been executed by a bird, or some other creature lacking opposable thumbs.

"She? Who?" she said.

The birds began a bizarre and involved pantomime that conveyed absolutely no meaning whatsoever. Ella heard the sound of Roy returning with his gun, so she tapped the glass and gave the birds a thumbs-up.

"Go away," she hissed, "or it's a trip to the taxidermist for you."

They dropped the note and flew off just as Roy re-entered with a break-action shotgun open over his arm.

"Gone have they?" he said, disappointed.

"Maybe that's for the best," said Ella. "Roy, can I ask you something?"

"Shoot," he said.

"What would you say if I told you that those birds were trying to tell me that my life is in danger?"

Roy had the decency to give it some thought.

"I'd say, you ought to go home, Ella, and have a bit of a lie down."

"Good answer," said Ella.

ELLA DID GO HOME with every intention of having a lie down.

Home was a detached house in nearby Nether-cum-Studley on a patch of land that didn't belong to the Avenants but was fairly surrounded by land that did.

She didn't expect to find her dad in the kitchen, making a hamper lunch.

The kitchen was a mixture of modern equipment and antique kitchenalia, much of which hung down from an old fashioned wooden clothes airer, suspended from the ceiling. An inexperienced guest had multiple opportunities to give themselves a concussion, but Gavin ducked expertly between them as he prepared his food.

"Myra said you had gone again," said Ella.

"Not gone, but going," he told her with a smile that made his little red cheeks all the redder.

Gavin Hannaford considered himself a bon viveur and took the life of a bon viveur very seriously, so his packed lunch used several different types of bread, and he carefully filled a set of small storage boxes with olives, pate and a hardboiled egg. He folded a linen napkin onto the top and made sure that he had a china plate and silver cutlery as well. She didn't need to ask him about salt and pepper, as he always carried a tiny Edwardian cruet set with him, in case of emergencies.

"You're back at Mr Dainty's again?" she asked, popping an olive into her mouth.

"Again," he agreed.

"That man's taking all of your time."

"It does seem that way, but there's a lot to do," he replied. "More antiques to value and catalogue than you could imagine. And he's a difficult man to please."

"Myra thinks he's Yugoslav mafia or something."

"No, but he likes it that people think he is. I need to build his trust. He's a tricky client. You know about tricky clients."

"Tell me about them," laughed Ella. "I had a voicemail from Mrs Jubert in Little Wangford, the one where I replaced all the rendering on her cottage."

"Oh yes?"

"She says it's gone soft. I can't understand how she can think that, it dried perfectly and it's completely weatherproof, but she insists it's gone so soft that the local kids are pulling it off. She's pretty angry, so I need to go out there and check it out."

Her father gave her a sympathetic smile.

"We must keep our customers happy, Ella. Here."

He pulled a book out from under his hamper, a battered thing bound in red leather which he opened to an obviously well-viewed page. There was a picture, a Victorian woodcut image of a multi-layered and turreted monstrosity built onto and into a rocky cliff. Waves pounded the cliffs and the lower levels.

"Thornbeard House," said Gavin Hannaford.

"House? That's a castle."

"It's Dainty's place on the south Devon coast. Imagine having to do the rendering on that behemoth. Our clients might be wrong or crazy — Mr Dainty thinks I've been moving his furniture round for goodness sake — but we must do our best to put their minds at rest. Happy clients pay their bills on time. Crazy clients..."

"Yeah, crazy," said Ella and, at that moment, heard a small voice. It sounded as if it was coming from the pantry.

"Have you got a radio on somewhere?" she asked him.

Her father shook his head and gathered up his book and hamper.

"I'm going to load up the car."

"Sure," she said and then, once he was gone, went to the pantry to investigate. She stopped outside the door.

"Pickled herring. Would you place it under *p* or *h*?" a voice said.

"I wouldn't," said a different, throatier voice.

"Or shall we have pickles as a special category, organised alphabetically *within* that category?"

"There's no point," said the second voice, accompanied by a flatulent squeak.

"No point? Where would we be without some order?"

"I mean I've eaten them."

"All of them?"

Ella whisked the door open and looked inside to see two more dwarfs.

"What are you doing here? Do I have an actual dwarf infestation? You're not the same ones I saw already are you? They had yellow and red hats."

"Colour co-ordination," said the one wearing the green hat and holding an antique Filofax. "That was my idea. Simple code for fast recognition. Nobody else has my organisational skills."

Ella rolled her eyes. "And you are?"

"Oh. I'm the Judicious Application of Systems and Measures," said the dwarf. "This here is Uncontrollably Flatulent."

The dwarf in the brown hat looked up guiltily from the jar of gherkins that he was guzzling. He looked as though he was searching for the correct words of greeting, but, failing to find them, he farted instead.

"I'm Windy," he said, stifling a belch. "He's OCD."

"I don't care," snapped Ella. "I want to know what you're doing in my house."

"Eating your pickles," said Windy.

"Saving your life," said OCD.

"By eating your pickles." Windy looked into the now empty jar.

"Not by eating your pickles," said OCD, "although they were perilously close to being out of date."

"Shut up!" said Ella. "I've got enough going on in my life without having to deal with a pair of pint-sized pickle inspectors. I've got a hen do that I don't want to go to, an irate customer with soft rendering and a wedding reception plan that —. What's this?"

OCD had presented her with a sharply folded rectangle of paper. Ella opened it up.

"I did notice that your seating plan for the wedding was not properly symmetrical and did not conform to Vitruvius's dictums on harmony, proportion and ratio," said OCD. "This is a proposed layout that I knocked up."

"You were snooping in my office!"

"For your own good," belched Windy.

"Your life is in danger and we're here to warn you," confirmed OCD.

"Ignoring the fact that this is an infuriatingly perfect seating plan, why is my life in danger?"

"Stepmother." Windy swigged the remaining vinegar from the pickle jar. "She's planning to kill you."

Ella pulled the pantry door shut behind her.

"Right. Words of one syllable. I don't know why my life is now filled with weird stuff like dwarfs, but now you're here you can explain to me, why do you think Myra's going to kill me?"

"Myra?" said Windy.

"That's her name," said Ella.

"Or that's what she told you her name was," said OCD.

"Evil stepmothers can be tricksy beasts," said Windy. "Silent but deadly."

Windy gave her a crafty smile and Ella recoiled, gasping, as his flatulent stink reached her nose.

"There's plenty of evidence she means you harm, if you'd care to open your eyes," said OCD. "I believe she took you out for lunch last week?"

"Yes, but what does that mean?"

OCD consulted his Filofax.

"Do you have *any* idea how many people die during lunch in an average week?" he said. "Heart attacks, choking, cocktail stick accidents — oh, I can see you're not impressed." Ella fixed him with a stony stare. "Well what about these then?" OCD waved a sheaf of papers at her.

"What are those?" Ella asked.

"Your evil stepmother's plans for remodelling this house." OCD pointed to a pencil drawn diagram. "Apart from showing a shocking disregard for accuracy and scale, you'll notice that there is a new dressing room planned for the place your bedroom currently occupies."

Ella grabbed the paper and scanned it.

"Well, this clearly shows that Myra doesn't want me living here, but that doesn't mean she wants me *dead*."

OCD opened the door a crack and peered out.

"Looks like your dad's about to go. You'll want to say goodbye. One last time."

"One last time?"

OCD nodded sagely. Windy farted loudly for emphasis and Ella wrinkled her nose as she edged out.

"Stay here. I've still got questions for you two. You, Gusty-pants —"

"Windy."

"Whatever. Find a way of communicating that doesn't involve gas. Farts are not punctuation."

Windy looked crestfallen and gave a sad bottom toot.

"Does he do that instead of actually speaking?" Ella asked OCD.

"Oh he does. With relish," said OCD.

"He should be ashamed, not enjoying it."

"No, I mean he's eaten the relish. You can make it out in those fruity top notes."

Ella tried to put dwarfs from her mind as she waved her father off and hurried upstairs to get showered and changed. She was due at Myra's hen do and doomsaying dwarfs or no doomsaying dwarfs, Ella hated to let people down.

She opened her wardrobe and a hand shot out from between the hangers, holding out a pair of trousers.

"Reckon you'll want these. Practical but still fun. See they've got a shimmer of Lurex."

"I thought I told you to stay in the pantry!"

"The smell's pretty bad down there." OCD, emerged

sheepishly from the wardrobe. "Windy's found the pickled eggs."

"Where's my dress?" Ella flicked through the rack. "I bought a new dress for tonight. I hate dresses so the only time I buy one I bloody well expect to wear it."

"You can't run for your life in a dress if someone's after you! That's why I've picked you out another outfit. Layers, trousers, that sort of thing."

"You hid my dress?" yelled Ella. "Smaller than me or not, you're going to feel the toe of my —"

"Flat shoes?" said OCD. He offered up some practical footwear, and made a hasty exit.

Ella eventually gave up hunting for her dress and pulled on the outfit that OCD had suggested. If this was all in her mind, she'd done a convincing job of forgetting where that new dress was. Could the human subconscious do such a thing? She had no doubt that it was possible.

As a child, she'd possessed an imagination that defied adult logic. Her father had never understood her flights of fancy. Maybe it was Roy's mentioning of family but she found herself recalling one of her few memories of her mum's mum, Granny Rose.

Ella's memory of her was faded and faint, but she was certain that Granny had always taken her childish ramblings seriously. She recalled one time when she had told her Granny about a fairy that she'd met in the garden (which garden or whose, Ella wasn't sure) and Granny had stopped peeling the potatoes or coring apples or whatever it was she had been doing and crouched down.

"How does tha know it's a fairy?" Granny had asked her.

"It's a pretty little lady with wings," Ella had replied.

"I see," Granny had said, stubbed out her cigarette, went to the cleaning cupboard and got out a bucket and a bottle of bleach and then went out into the garden to carry out some sort of exorcism featuring lots of hot soapy water and swearing.

2

The first part of the hen party fun was to be beauty treatments in a boutique spa located in one of the affluent small towns near to Solihull. The taxi dropped Ella in front of a building on the high street that looked more like a chic champagne bar than a spa. When she went inside, she discovered that it did indeed feature a champagne bar, where Petunia and Lily were poring over a menu of shiatsu and tsubo therapy treatments with Myra. The three of them wore floral cocktail dresses and high heels. Petunia and Lily still had vestiges of the chemical burns they had inflicted on their own faces earlier. Myra wore the cat-that-got-the-double-cream look of a very happy fifty-something living it up like a woman half her age.

Ella felt the weight of their judgement as they all looked up and took in her sensible, possible-murder-fleeing outfit.

"Evening everyone," she said.

"Ah, here she is," said Myra. "Little Miss 'it's what's inside the cake that counts'."

"What are you wearing?" asked Lily.

"Clothes," said Ella. "I did say."

She decided not to mention that this particular outfit had been picked out for her by a dwarf who was probably now in the middle of sorting out her sock drawer.

"So pleased you've come to join us," said Myra, patting a stool to the side of her. "Petunia and Lily were just telling me about some of these treatments. We all want to look and feel our best for the big day, don't we?"

Myra, sipped her neon coloured cocktail and indicated to an attendant that she should bring one for Ella.

"They've got the latest Scan2Beauty machine here," said Lily. "This is one of the first places in the country to get one, I can't wait to try it."

"And that would be?" said Ella.

"Well, the first part is the scanner," said Petunia. "You put your face in, and it scans it. Then it shows a three-dimensional model of your face on the screen while it runs through its libraries. It's programmed with lots of science —"

"Science, huh?" said Ella.

"Yes, about how faces are supposed to look, and celebrity faces and things."

"I want to be Kiera Knightly!" said Lily, jigging with excitement, "or Eva Green!"

"How faces are supposed to look?" said Ella, not liking the sound of that.

"Don't worry, dear," said Myra. "Even your face has some earthy charm to it. My looks have always been compared to Raquel Welch or a young Julie Christie."

"I tried to read one of her books once," said Lily. "I think the butler did it."

"Once it's analysed your face, and you've answered its questions, it recommends the best possible makeup for you," said Petunia. "Even better, you put your face back in and it applies the makeup for you, with an airbrush."

"Remarkable," said Myra. "I simply cannot wait."

ELLA HAD HER NAILS BUFFED, which was forty minutes of her life she spent marvelling at the human capacity for building industries around unnecessary services. It seemed that so many things could be done to her nails, many of which were miniature works of art. Why were people happy to pay for art that they would destroy in a matter of days, when artists were struggling to find work? Would Picasso be working in a nail bar if he started out today?

Lily and Petunia had undergone some of the more unpleasant sounding treatments, and both now sported circular welts across their arms from the Ventosa hot cup which really didn't look all that therapeutic. Myra had opted for a full body massage, although she rejected the first two masseuses on the grounds that they were female, insisting that she needed a masculine energy if she were to get the most out of the experience.

"That was most exhilarating," she said when she emerged. "I'm a firm believer in enhancing one's touch sensitivity at every opportunity. I want to give Gavin a night to remember on our wedding night."

Ella wasn't all that keen to hear Myra's plans for pleasuring her father, and was glad when a woman wearing a white tunic led them through to the Scan2Beauty treatment room.

"Good evening ladies, I'm Mindy and I will be setting up the Scan2Beauty machine for you to use. Now, you've all read the literature and signed the disclaimer?"

They nodded as Mindy handed a packet of wipes around.

"It will be best if you remove your makeup, so that the machine can get a better reading," she said.

Ella took a wipe and whisked it across her face. Myra, Petunia and Lily each grabbed a handful and started to scrub away at what appeared to be quite a significant covering. Mindy found them another packet and asked Ella to step forward to be first at the machine.

"I'll run through the first one with you and then leave you to it," she said. "It's really very simple, the machine will guide you. Right Ella, put your face here and press this green button to start things off."

Ella framed her face inside the moulded oval face rest and found that it wasn't as uncomfortable as it looked. She pressed the button.

"Scan commencing," a robotic female voice informed her. There was a whining sound as something moved in the base of the machine.

"Please maintain your position for twenty seconds," said the voice, and then counted down as Ella was aware of a small light flickering below her face.

"Processing results," said the voice. "When prompted, please speak into the microphone to your left and the voice recognition unit will analyse your answers."

Ella saw the microphone as Mindy pointed it out.

"Facial analysis complete. Your score is nine point five out of ten. The horizontal symmetry of your face is almost ideal, the ratio of your face length to face width is almost ideal. There is a slight imbalance between your mouth width and nose width. The celebrity that you most resemble is Audrey Hepburn. Would you like me to correct any imbalances when I apply your makeup?"

"Yes!" yelled Lily, before Ella had a chance to reply. She was mildly annoyed, but then she'd signed up for this.

She put her face back on the rest when asked and the machine told her when to blink and breath for a few minutes, then told her that she could raise her head and look in the mirror.

She looked up and was surprised to see that she really liked the effect. She touched her face. The machine had tinkered with the line of her lips, but the effect was subtle.

"Wow, Ella, you look really amazing," said Petunia.

"We're all going to look amazing!" said Myra. "Now who's going next? I think we can manage this, thank you, Mindy."

Mindy left while Lily settled into position in front of the machine. She winked at Petunia and scrabbled in her bag for a piece of paper.

"We found some information on an online forum," she explained. "You can override the normal settings and customise your look." She addressed the machine with the microphone. "Machine test sequence five-five-fifty."

"Engineer access granted," said the machine. "Test mode engaged. All functions accessible through voice commands. Scan commencing."

Lily was silent throughout the scan and then the machine announced the results.

"Facial analysis complete. Your score is six point one out of ten. The horizontal symmetry of your face is imbalanced, the ratio of your face length to face width is imbalanced. Would you like me to correct any imbalances when I apply your makeup?"

"Override coverage," said Lily, reading from the paper.

"Set coverage level," said the machine.

"Maximum," said Lily. "Override celebrity target."

"Name celebrity," said the machine.

"Eva Green."

"Retrieving facial images," said the machine. "Please return your face to the rest."

A few minutes later, the machine announced that she could raise her head.

"Test complete. Coverage maximum, celebrity image Steve McQueen."

Ella wasn't sure whether she was the only one who heard the

machine correctly, as Petunia and Myra were busily making cooing noises as they examined Lily's face. Ella marvelled at the way that she really did resemble an incredibly over made up Steve McQueen. Pantomime dames would have balked at the look, but Lily grinned proudly at them all and handed Petunia the piece of paper as she took her turn in the seat. Lily went to fetch more cocktails.

Petunia set the machine into test mode and scanned her face. Ella thought that she was pouting throughout, although it was hard to see properly.

"Facial analysis complete. Your score is six point nine out of ten. The horizontal symmetry of your face is imbalanced, the ratio of your face length to face width is imbalanced. Would you like me to correct any imbalances when I apply your makeup?"

"Override coverage," said Petunia.

"Set coverage level."

"Maximum. Override celebrity target."

"Name celebrity."

"Liv Tyler."

Ella suppressed a grin as she realised what must surely happen next. She managed to emit a gentle cough at the crucial moment as the machine spoke up again.

"Test complete. Coverage maximum, celebrity image Steve Tyler."

Petunia beamed at them all as Lily came back in with the cocktails. The face of the Aerosmith frontman was etched upon hers, complete with an authentic set of wrinkles.

"Cocktails, lovely!" said Ella brightly, keen to draw attention away from Petunia who was peering into a mirror with a confused look on her face. "Now it's your turn Myra."

"I think I might let the machine work with its default settings." Myra settled into place and started the scan. "You girls have got the skin tone to experiment, I prefer a classic look."

"Facial analysis complete. Your score is eight point four out of ten. The horizontal symmetry of your face is almost ideal, the ratio of your face length to face width is imbalanced. There is a large imbalance between your mouth width and nose width. The celebrity that you most resemble is Julie Christie."

"Told you!" yelled Myra victoriously from within the machine.

"Would you like me to correct any imbalances when I apply your makeup?" said the machine.

"Yes," said Myra.

The machine started to apply her makeup. Petunia was poring over her phone, and showing something to Lily.

"Look, you can browse all of the different settings and celebrities. Shall we try it?"

"You're supposed to do it at the start," said Lily.

"It's a smart machine, it will figure it out," said Petunia, and then she leaned over the microphone. "Override browse."

"Overriding brows," said the machine, and one of the small hissing noises that accompanied the air brush got noticeably louder.

"What did you do?" shouted Myra, turning her head.

The hissing stopped and Myra lifted away from the machine. It had clearly given her eyebrows everything it had. Because she moved her head while it was doing so, the machine had continued the eyebrow across the top of her nose. She now sported a luxurious monobrow which gave her the look of a slightly perplexed hawk. Myra gazed into a mirror and seemed to be weighing up whether she liked it or not.

"Bring me that cocktail menu," she said. "If I can't fix my face then I need to fix everybody else's eyesight."

Ella laughed in an effort to convince herself that Myra was joking.

"Oh, as an eight point four, I think I can withstand a little make-up malfunction," said Myra. "What was yours, dear? Five point five?"

"Five point five," Ella agreed.

Myra's gaze stayed on her a little too long.

MIRRORS NIGHTCLUB, despite its low lighting and thumping tunes, couldn't avoid feeling like a parochial dancehall in the dying days of the dance-round-your-handbag nightclubs. True to its name, the walls were almost entirely lined with mirrors. This was perhaps meant to give the little club an enhanced sense of space but, in truth, made it feel like a cross between the set for a bad 80s sci-fi film and a stage on the Crystal Maze.

Myra danced provocatively with a group of attentive younger men. At some point she'd scrubbed out the middle of her monobrow, so she was left with the expression of an angry goblin, but these men were either attracted to goblins or too drunk to care.

Ella occupied a booth, trying to conduct a conversation with Lily and Petunia. It wasn't easy, given the loud music. And they were all now feeling the effects of several mojitos. And conducting a conversation with Lily and Petunia was difficult at the best of times.

"So, which one do you fancy?" said Petunia.

"What?" said Ella.

Lilly waggled her hand towards the blokes on the dance floor, her long painted nails flashing like blades.

"Oh," said Ella and looked at them. She couldn't focus on them properly and not just because of the mojitos. "I don't know. That one?"

"Which one?"

"Honestly?" she said. "I'm not that into men at the minute."

Petunia and Lily shared a knowing look.

"What?" said Ella.

"Flat sensible shoes," said the others in unison.

Ella slapped the nearest of them on the shoulder.

"No, I'm not into women either. Look, I like men it's just there are more important things in life. Taking care of dad. The business. A healthy bank balance."

"Shopping," said Lily.

"Clothes," said Petunia.

"Hair."

"Nails."

"Makeup."

"Girly nights out."

"Girly nights in."

"*X Factor* on the telly, a box of chocolate truffles and new products to try out," said Petunia.

"Bliss," agreed Lily.

"Right," said Ella. "So which of your products sell best at the garden centre? Will the customers there try new things?"

"Oh no," said Lily. "They know what they like and they stick to it. Our biggest seller is lavender hand cream, or anything that looks like a fancy gift for ladies."

"We always ask them to try different things though," said Petunia, but some of them don't even know what a décolletage is, never mind that they might want to put cream on it."

"Customers can be so difficult," nodded Ella, "and it doesn't help when dwarfs come and mess things up for you."

"Surely you mean persons of reduced stature?" said Lily. "I don't think we're supposed to call them dwarfs."

"Yeah, dwarfs of reduced stature. With coloured hats and beards," said Ella.

"Oh you mean Disney dwarfs," said Lily. "I think it's probably all right to call *those* ones dwarfs."

"Why would they be messing things up?" said Petunia, confused.

"Have you not seen them?" said Ella with a drunkenly cavalier manner. "They're all over the bloody place. In my office, in the water features, hiding in my pantry or my bedroom."

"You have Bashful, Grumpy and Dopey in your bedroom?" giggled Lily.

"Actually, that's the last three men I had in my bedroom," said Petunia.

"No," insisted Ella. "These ones have got even more stupid names. I've met Windy, OCD, Shitfaced and Psycho."

"Ella! Those names are much too rude, and there's only four of them," said Petunia. "There's meant to be seven."

"Well I've only met four so far but I bet the other three are lying in wait somewhere. They'll pop out on me when I least expect it, in the loos or something."

Out on the dance floor, Myra ran her hand down a pretty boy's face in tipsy farewell, staggered back over to the table and sat down with an 'oof' of exhaustion.

"Oh, the spirit is willing but the old ticker is a bit knackered. I need a drink."

"Glass of water?" said Petunia.

"I'll disinherit you if you dare. I want a Sex on the Beach."

"Then I'll have a Slow Comfortable Screw Against the Wall," said Petunia, getting up with her purse.

"I've always fancied having a man take me roughly in a back alley," said Lily.

"We're still talking cocktails, right?" said Myra.

"Cocktail?" said Lily.

"Help me carry the drinks," said Petunia and dragged her away.

Myra fanned her face. "I'm having the best night, Ella."

"Can I remind you that you are marrying my dad in eleven days' time?"

Myra laughed and looked back at the young men on the dance floor.

"What? Them? I'm just having a bit of fun. Your dad knows exactly what he's getting into. Nothing wrong with flirting with the cutest guy at the school dance." She smiled. "Of course, back then, Gavin Hannaford was the cutest guy at the school dance."

"Not sure I want to know," said Ella.

"Nothing to tell back then," said Myra. "Gavin was like a brother to me. I found it very frustrating. But I was friends with your mum, Natalie, too. Natalie Thorn she was back then."

"Did you ever meet my mother's family?" asked Ella.

"I met her parents. Her dad only briefly. And that was all before you were born. But then I did go with Natalie once to Rushy Glen."

"You did? I barely remember my grandma."

"Oh, this was in the seventies. Your Granny Rose was something of an acquired taste, if I'm honest. One of those Great British eccentrics."

Ella frowned. "I remember her being lovely."

"I'm sure she was. But I was nearly an adult when I met her. Children see things differently to adults, don't they?"

Myra's gaze drifted away. Ella turned to follow it. Myra was staring into one of the many mirrors that lined the venue. Myra's eyes flicked from her own reflection to Ella's and back again.

"The magic of childhood gives way to the dull day-to-day of adulthood. Charm and glamour fade. That sweet and kooky woman reveals herself to be as lost and bitter as the rest of us."

"Myra?"

"As we grow up," said Myra wearily. "We start to see things as they really are."

Ella could find nothing to say for a time.

Maybe I should go and seek out my Granny sometime," she said eventually. "Where is this Rushy Glen exactly?"

Myra creased her thickly made-up brow, a move that almost made Ella shriek with horror.

"Do you know, I'm not at all sure," she said. "I was never any good at geography."

Petunia and Lily wove across the dance floor.

"We are here!" declared Petunia.

Myra waved impatiently for her drink.

"Here, Sex with a Tucson Barman. It's great."

"Better than being taken in a back alley?" said Myra with a wry smile.

"We got you a Pink Lady, Ella."

Ella nodded in thanks. "Think I need to freshen up a bit before I plunge into more drinks."

"We're going to get a fishbowl next."

"God help me." Ella propelled herself upwards and over to the toilets.

She wasn't impressed with the loos, given the lateness of the hour and the inebriation of nearly everyone in the club, but at least they were dwarf-free. However, as she washed her hands, she heard a tiny noise that sounded exactly like a small body slipping under a cubicle partition. She ducked down rapidly and spotted a small booted foot clambering up onto the toilet seat. She lunged for it and hauled the attached dwarf back where she could see him.

"Another one!" she said. "What are you doing accosting women into public toilets?"

"Accosting? I was hiding until you tugged me off and got my purple hat all moist."

"Ugh." She let him go in disgust.

"You've got a strong grip," said the dwarf, massaging life back into his little leg. "I like a girl with a strong grip."

"Enough."

"S'true. I've not got anything against chicks with a bit of muscle — not as often as I'd like."

"Okay, now that's just inappropriate."

The dwarf bowed low. "At your service," he said.

"So there's five of you."

"I don't suppose anyone's in the slightest bit interested," came a voice from the ceiling, "but there *is* another dwarf you know."

Ella raised her eyebrows and looked at Inappropriate. "Don't tell me. This one's called Passive Aggressive?"

Inappropriate nodded.

"Talking about me behind my back?" called the voice from the ceiling.

"I'm just telling her that you're a twat," said Inappropriate.

A black-capped and beady-eyed dwarf dropped from the ceiling, planted its hands on its hips and stared at a point halfway up the wall, avoiding anyone's direct gaze.

"Oh well, fine. Try to make me look bad," he sniffed.

"Are the others here too?" Ella looked around at the cubicles.

"That's right," said Passive Aggressive, "because we're not the important ones. All too used to being overlooked, I am, so just carry on."

"So, are they here or not?"

"I mean, it's not as if I add anything, do I? It's not as if I'm the one working silently away in the background while certain other dwarfs take all the glory? Ooh, no. Unk!"

Passive Aggressive slumped to the floor as Psycho leapt down from the ceiling and coldcocked him with the haft of his little dwarfish axe.

"Whinging little shite," said Psycho and then addressed Ella. "Told you before, bab. You're in a lot of trouble. Well it's all about to kick off in there. That old bag's been talking to some blokes she's organised. It's their job to drug you and take you away in a van."

"No, no way," laughed Ella. "You're mistaken. Those men? The one's Myra's been dancing with who are young enough to be her sons? She loves that sort of attention."

Psycho huffed in exasperation while Passive Aggressive murmured and stirred.

"I grabbed something out of the tall one's bag," said Windy. "Does it smell like chloroform?" he asked with a questioning parp.

Windy offered up a small white jar, and OCD took a tentative sniff. He keeled over backwards without a word, landing on the grumbling Passive Aggressive.

"Right you lot, that settles it," said Psycho. "Get that silly sod back up to the ceiling to sleep it off and let's get Ella out of here before the same happens to her."

"I'm quite capable of getting myself out of here," said Ella, "even if I am a little bit tipsy."

"A little bit tipsy?" Inappropriate huffed. "I thought women drivers were bad enough. You can't even walk. I saw you fall over a line on the floor on your way in here."

"S'nothing." Shitfaced staggered forward. "I can fall over the line on the floor before it's even there."

"I'm sober enough to see there's only six of you," said Ella. "Shouldn't there be seven?"

"Yeah, well he's busy." Psycho turned to his companions. "Shitfaced, with OCD out of it, you'll have to help with her legs."

"What about my legs?" Ella tried to focus on them.

"Inappropriate, Passive Aggressive, you take her top half. Windy, I think it's best you take her feet."

"No one's taking my feet anywhere!" said Ella.

"Can it, Cinders."

"Meanwhile," said Psycho, "I will supervise and clear a path for our exit."

"Ooh, who died and made you King of the Dwarfs?" said Passive Aggressive.

Psycho slapped him. "Shut it, whinger!"

"Or what?"

"Or they won't find your bones till Christmas."

"Wait. Wait," said Ella. "How's this supposed to w—"

Psycho ran at her and head-butted her in the stomach. She toppled back and was instantly lifted by small, strong arms that carried her away at a fast pace. Ella was too alarmed to react as she was transported across the room and out through the door.

"Windy!" shouted Inappropriate. "Keep your end up! It's drooping!"

When Ella realised that she was being carried out of an open window and tipped head first over the edge, she managed to gather enough breath to protest, but her scream was lost in the wind as the dwarfs leapt from ledge to gutter to drainpipe as they made their way toward the ground. In her panic, she thought she saw two bluebirds, flying just overhead and pointing directions with their wings.

The last but one thought Ella had before she passed out from a mixture of alcohol and dwarf-induced travel sickness was that birds, (real, non-cartoon birds anyway) did not point with their wings. The very last thought she had was that she hoped Lily and Petunia wouldn't hurt themselves, as she heard them shrieking from the bathroom window that Ella had invented a fun new Hen Night game, and that they wanted a go too.

3

Ella rolled deeper into her lumpy bed and clutched the bedsheets to her neck. She wasn't yet sure if her hangover was just going to come on stage, perform a little nauseating dry-mouthed pirouette and depart, or if it was going to treat her to an all-day brain-pounding revue with technicolour special effects. She decided not to ask herself. The fact that she felt she was rocking like a ship at sea did not bode well.

At a distance — was it her radio? — she heard voices. Male voices. All of them were familiar but she couldn't quite place them.

"I know it's not our usual bastard play but I say we go for the Glass Slipper Gambit."

"Are you sure? I mean you need lions and flying monkeys and a tornado."

"I can do one of those." A third voice, with a little grunt, unleashed a whining parp like a runaway party balloon.

"Oh, *really* impressive," snarked a fourth.

An appalling smell began an assault on Ella's nostrils.

"*Glass* Slipper Gambit, you big twat," said the first voice.

"Actually," said a new voice, "that's a mistranslation from the original. It was originally a fur slipper. And, frankly, a glass slipper is a health and safety nightmare."

"But much less messy if you're going to drink out of it."

"Why would you drink out of a woman's shoe?"

"I've drunk out of a shoe," said a drunken voice. "Actually it was a barrel."

"So, not a shoe then?"

"Someone was standing in it," argued the drunkard.

"But the Glass Slipper Gambit isn't our speciality."

"But all the bloody pieces are in place. We've got a ball in ten days. Our brother Disco is working his way through the royals. We've got a PC lined up."

"Who?"

"That inbred fucking toff with the shotgun and too many teeth."

"Really? He's hardly charming."

"But it's okay because our princess is, to use the correct scientific terminology, 'on the shelf' and will probably fall into the arms of any man who'll have her."

Ella groaned as it all came back to her. She opened her eyes. It hurt.

It was morning, not much past dawn by the quality of the light, and she could see the reason her world was rocking. She was on a train, specifically a slightly shabby commuter carriage with hard plastic and foam seats and an above average level of graffiti. Her 'bedsheet' was a red paramedic blanket stamped with the words 'West Midlands Ambulance Service'.

She sat up.

The dwarfs were huddled in argument at the far end of the otherwise empty carriage. None were looking her way. Ella was a practical soul with little time for nonsense and make believe and other fancies. A day job among hammers and nails and load-bearing walls had left her with a firm grasp of what was real and what was important. Nonetheless, Ella found herself facing up to the fact that these dwarfs were real; she doubted her delusional psychoses were organised enough to buy train tickets and rustle up blankets.

"Can't we just deal with her *our* way?" said Windy, with a plaintive pump. "You know, the old Glass Coffin routine."

"I do prefer routine," said OCD.

"Yeah, let's drag her back to our digs and get her cracking on the housework," said Inappropriate. "Women like that. Chores are their heroin."

"Like you know what chores are," said Passive Aggressive.

The train was slowing for the next station. Ella recognised nothing of the landscape outside. Farmland, pylons, scattered woodland; it could have been any piece of rural England, ten miles from home or two hundred. Wherever it was, she wanted out.

The train decelerated further. The station sign for Little Wangford came into view.

Little Wangford! Mrs Jubert with the dodgy rendering! Ella wasn't one for dropping in on clients unannounced but any port in a storm...

"She can help me with my drinking problem," said Shitfaced.

There was a sudden silence among the dwarfs.

"I can't get the lids off sometimes," explained Shitfaced.

"No, you turd-brained cocknuggets!" yelled Psycho. "We're not taking her home! We're not going to wait for the evil witch to come after her with a poisoned apple. And the glass coffin's already being used, isn't it."

The dwarfs were still engrossed in their conversation. Ella waited for the open door light to come on and then slipped from her seat, blanket still wrapped around her, and pressed the open door button.

"We're doing the Glass Slipper Gambit," said Psycho. "We just need some mice and lizards and a pumpkin and then get old Bossy-boots to pay a visit. Hey!"

He leapt up onto his seat and pointed as Ella slipped out the door.

"This isn't our stop!" said Shitfaced.

"Get her, you knobs!" yelled Psycho.

Windy gave a war-like bugle parp and they charged. However, in their hurry, half the dwarfs tripped over the other half and before any of them came within five feet of the door, it closed.

Ella stood and watched Psycho's incandescent face as it yelled muffled insults at her through the window. Inappropriate provided some helpful interpretive hand gestures.

She hugged the blanket tighter as the train pulled out of Little Wangford. It might be June and the sun bright but the air was cold and sparkling dew clung to the grass at the platform edge. It was a rural station with metal railings between the platform and the tiny car park, but no sign of any other people. Ella's hangover headache was still just a dim thing at the edges of her mind which either meant she still drunk from the night before and it was going to hit her with a vengeance soon enough or it wasn't going to amount to much and a good walk would blast it away.

Ella tied two corners of the blanket around her neck to make a cloak of it and walked along the platform, past the unmanned ticket office and onto the hedge-lined single track road that led down to the village.

As she walked she considered her resources. She did not have her purse, so no money, no cards. However, she did have her mobile phone; a phone that had accumulated two dozen text messages in the night, mostly from Petunia and Myra wondering where the hell she was. There was one from her dad, letting her know that he had arrived safely at Thornbeard House once more and would probably be staying with Mr Dainty for two or three days at most. There was also one from Roy, asking if she had time in her busy schedule to join him for a day at the Cornbury Park Game Fair on the thirteenth. There was also a text from Tilly Chapel, the supplier of the ecologically-sourced exterior render, replying to Ella's query from yesterday.

Ella tried to make a call to her dad but there was no signal to be found. A call to Myra proved equally fruitless.

Instead, she wrote a single text to each person: to Myra and Petunia that she was fine and apologised for fleeing the festivities; to her dad that she was in Little Wangford and going to visit Mrs Jubert; to Roy that the thirteenth, two days' time, was short notice, and weren't game fairs for the Barbour jacket / wellies / shotgun and golden retriever types she generally disapproved of?; to Tilly Chapel the broad details of Mrs Jubert's complaint which she was going to investigate this morning. She left her phone to its own devices to send them when it found a signal.

Ella almost missed the turning for Mrs Jubert's cottage. She recalled that Mrs Jubert lived down Spinney Lane which ran off from the main road not far from the tiny village green. What she did not recall was that Spinney Lane was little more than a dirt path, overshadowed by low, shady trees and threatened by bramble on all sides. Even the sign for Spinney Lane was overgrown with bindweed and encrusted with lichen which rendered it all but unreadable. She had driven this way only a fortnight before and couldn't picture her car making its way up such a narrow track.

But, she told herself, "There can't be two Spinney Lanes," and began to walk up it.

The canopy of broad, dark leaves instantly cut out the sunlight. Shafts of morning light shot through here and there, picking up this tree trunk, that patch of pebbly path.

Ella rehearsed her pitch.

"Morning, Mrs Jubert. Yes, it is early but when I heard that you were less than happy with our work on your cottage, I jumped on the first train here to inspect the... ooh, yes, I can see what you mean. We've never had that happen before." Ella ducked to avoid a particularly low-hanging branch. "Now... My goodness, do you know what I've just done, Mrs Jubert? I left my purse on the train; cash, train tickets, the lot. I am a fool. Could I possibly use your phone to call a taxi? You're driving over to Solihull this afternoon? Well, as long as I'm not imposing. A cup of tea while I wait would be absolutely de—"

Ella stopped.

"—lightful," she said and looked round.

The narrow track was now definitely nothing more than a path. The route ahead, hardened earth intermittently crossed with questing tree roots, was still clearly visible but there was no way a car could make it up here. It wasn't even wide enough for two people to walk side by side.

She looked back. There had been no turnings. Odd.

Had it become overgrown in the time since she had since been here? Midsummer was fast approaching. England was a riot of greenery. The landscape did transform rapidly. She considered it for less than a second. No, of course this hadn't all sprung up in the past two weeks.

"Bloody odd," she said softly.

Bloody odd, like dwarf-odd, like bluebirds-with-messages-odd. She scanned the trees for weird birds bearing cautionary messages. As she turned, something cracked under her foot. It felt like a seed or a nut. It wasn't a nut, not quite.

Ella picked up the yellow peanut M&M. There was another one, green, six feet ahead. There was a red one a little further on.

A notion stirred in Ella's foggy mind and it didn't involve careless hikers or bags of sweets with holes in the bottom.

"Breadcrumbs," she said.

There was a noise of agreement from the undergrowth to one side. Ella looked and where she was quite sure there hadn't been a wolf before there was a wolf now. Her mind skated over the notion that it might be a dog without even touching it. This thing, grey-furred, long-snouted, orange-eyed and taller than any hound she had ever met, was a wolf.

Ella froze.

"Hello, little girl," the wolf said.

The wolf had petrified Ella but the *talking* wolf had tipped her over into frantic terror. She punched the wolf straight on the nose.

"Ow, goddamn son of a bitch!" the wolf yelled, recoiling. "What d'you do that for?"

Ella tore a near-dead branch from the nearest tree and hefted it like a baseball bat.

The wolf rapidly blinked away tears of pain. "Right on the hooter," he said unhappily.

"You surprised me," said Ella, shifting nervously from foot to foot.

"*I* surprised *you*?" said the wolf. "I said hello. You hit me."

"You called me little girl."

"You are little."

"I'm thirty-five."

"But you are a girl."

"I'm thirty-five! And, just so you know, 'Hello, little girl' is pretty much the creepiest thing you can say. Even to little girls."

"Jeez," said the wolf. "You try to be civil to folk and you get a mouthful of abuse."

"What do you want?" Ella was trying to be brave but she felt like jelly. She really wanted to be home, lying on the sofa with a bucket of tea, a packet of chocolate hobnobs and a fistful of painkillers. Definitely no wolf.

The wolf gave Ella a look. "You want to do the conversation *now*?" he asked incredulously.

"What?" she said.

"Well, I was going to say, 'Hello, little girl'"

"Which is creepy."

"Noted, princess. And then I was going to ask, 'Where are you going in your pretty red hood and a basket full of —'. Where's your basket?"

"I don't have a basket."

"What do you have?"

"Are you mugging me?"

"What?"

"You're not having my phone," said Ella.

"What would a wolf do with a phone?" He waved a paw at her. "No thumbs."

"It's voice activated." She looked at the wolf's nonplussed expression. "M&M?" she offered.

"You trying to poison me now?"

"The chocolate. Sorry." She threw the M&M down. "I was following the trail."

"To grandma's house?"

"I'm going to visit a client."

"Grandma?"

"What? No."

"I know a short cut," said the wolf. "Through the wood."

"Good for you," said Ella peering at the unappealing, crowded mass of trees, slick with green moss.

"I could show you."

"No thanks."

"Is it because you're afraid to take a walk on the wild side, sister?"

"No, it's because you're a talking wolf."

"That's offensive," said the wolf.

"I'm sure you'll survive."

"I bet I'll get there before you."

"Where?"

"Grandma's house."

"I'm not —." She stopped. "Sure. Let's see who gets to 'grandma's house' first."

"A race," said the wolf and smiled. Ella was sure wolves didn't possess the muscles for smiling but he smiled nonetheless, a roguish lopsided smile. "And if I beat you there..."

"You can have my phone," said Ella.

"Thumbs," said the wolf, turned tail and loped off.

Ella watched him go and continued to scan the woods as she continued up the track. She held tight to her makeshift club.

The increasingly rough path and trail of M&Ms led on for another half mile up to the front door of Mrs Jubert's cottage. Or, at least, to the place where Mrs Jubert's cottage had definitely been and to a building that might have once been Mrs Jubert's cottage, although it was hard to tell.

Ayleen Jubert, a former harp teacher and academic expert on medieval musical instruments, had retired to Little Wangford and sought Ella's help with refurbishing her new home according to her carbon-neutral sensibilities. The cottage that Ella had worked on and visited as recently as two weeks ago had been a plain, almost brutalist, renovation in reclaimed timber, natural building materials and, in the absence of sufficient sunlight for solar panels, two small wind turbines on tall poles.

The cottage before her now, whilst being essentially the same structure, was a work of chaos. The ramshackle roof was covered in glistening caramel-coloured tiles. The windows were ill-fitting frosted Georgian panes held in with a ridiculous excess of white putty. The door, the window sills and the rest of the dark wood sagged and bowed as though it were melting. And the walls... that fine sandy render she had sourced and even helped apply was now a cracked, clay-like mass and, indeed, had peeled away in fat doughy slabs here and there.

Ella clenched her club tightly. She wasn't merely shocked; she was furious.

"Time and energy I've put in," she muttered as she stomped to the door. "Not easy to get hold of either." She rapped sharply on the door. It was sticky to the touch. "If I find out this was bloody dwarfs, I'm going to throttle them."

A pink blob of a face appeared at a frosted window.

"Is it the wag man?" called a muffled child's voice. "Or the cops?"

"It's a woman," replied another child's voice.

The letterbox flipped open. A pair of eyes peeped out.

"Piss off," said the pair of eyes and the letterbox snapped shut.

There was further muffled talking, the sound of giggling and then silence.

"What the...?" said Ella, huffed a couple of times to show the world that she was not best pleased and then knocked even louder on the door. The door cracked under her knuckles and finger-sized splinters of dark chocolate came away.

A chocolate door. And those windows were spun sugar. The putty was fondant icing.

Ella was unimpressed, not primarily by the confectionery building materials but the shoddy workmanship on display.

"Open up!" she yelled.

"We're not in!" yelled back one of the children.

Ella looked around. "There's never a wolf to huff and puff when you need one," she said. "Right!" she shouted. "You asked for it!"

The children's response was laughter.

"Gonna open a can of Jackie Chan on you," muttered Ella.

She took a step back and kicked the door squarely in the

centre. The door buckled but remained in place. A second kick smashed it from its hinges.

"Stranger danger!" yelled a voice from the kitchen.

Ella strode in. The smell of sugary treats was overwhelming. She kicked aside a marshmallow footstool, pushed past a giant rich tea biscuit coffee table, and stormed through the strawberry lace bead curtain into the kitchen. Two filthy pre-teens with food-smeared faces glared at her, poised in the act of trying to light the enormous wall-filling aga.

"Assault! Assault!" shouted the girl and pointed at Ella.

"I haven't touched you," said Ella.

"But you looked at her!" the boy accused.

"Yeah, with your eyes," agreed the girl.

"What are you doing in here?" said Ella.

"You can't ask us that," said the girl.

"That's invasion of privacy," said the boy. "We have rights."

"I'm just asking a question," said Ella.

"Yeah, that's how Hitler started," said the girl.

"By asking questions?" said Ella.

"Are you saying I'm wrong?" said the girl.

"That's bullying, that is," added the boy.

"I haven't even begun to bully you yet." Ella thumped the giant rich tea biscuit table for emphasis.

"You threatening me?" said the boy.

"I could suffer post-traumatic stress because of you," said the girl.

"Flashbacks."

"Whiplash."

"I could be on the news because of you."

"Shut up," said Ella.

"That's swearing, that is," said the girl.

"What? 'Shut up'?"

"It's abuse. You can't tell us what to do. It's a free country."

"Is it?"

"We got rights," said the boy.

"The United Nations says so," said the girl.

"European Court of Human Rights," said the boy. "They could send you to prison for telling us to shut up."

"I've got low self-esteem. Which is medical."

"We've got conditions."

"So if you're horrible to us, it's like racism."

"It's discrimination."

"We should call the cops on you," said the girl.

"Good idea!" said Ella loudly. "Either of you got a phone?"

That shut them up for a moment.

"I'm looking for Mrs Jubert," said Ella.

"Who?"

"The woman who lives here."

The children simply stared at her. The boy licked a crumb of cake from his lip.

"Where is she?" said Ella.

The pair of them looked worriedly at each other.

"I take the fifth," said girl.

"This is Britain, you twerp."

"You can't talk to me like —"

A chocolate teapot smashed on the floor where Ella had thrown it. The smell of chocolate made her lick her lips, somewhat reducing the drama of the moment. "I'm losing my patience."

The boy began to sniff repeatedly, tears welling up in his eyes.

"You did that to him," said the girl. "It's like you hit him. With words. Abuser."

A shelf of glassware made from boiled sweets exploded beneath Ella's club. "Tell me!" Ella growled.

"It was her idea!" squealed the boy, pointing at the girl. "She told me to do it!"

"I did not!" cried the girl. "You were the first one to push her!"

"She shouted at us!"

"It was self-defence!"

"She wanted to cook *us* and eat *us*!"

Ella's eyes went to the vast cooking range. "Oh, hell!"

She pushed the children aside and pulled open the largest door. It's rare in life that one gets to find an old lady, folded up like a circus contortionist and stuffed into an oven.

"Mrs Jubert!"

"I don't like this," trembled a tiny, squashed voice from within.

Ella hooked her hand into the rag-covered folds and tried to ease the older woman out. She was wedged tightly and it was slow work.

"I can't believe you did this," she hissed at the children.

"You can't blame us," argued the girl.

"No one told us we couldn't do it," added the boy.

"We just copy things we see on TV, products of our environment."

A foot and a leg popped out of the oven.

"Where are your family?"

"Not telling," said the boy.

"Data protection," said the girl.

"We'll refuse to go back."

"Yeah. Serve them right for turning off the wifi at night."

The second leg came free and Ella was able to slide Mrs Jubert out. The older woman gasped painfully as she came free and Ella brought her up to her feet.

"Monsters!" she groaned as she squinted at the irritating youngsters.

"You hit us!" shouted the girl.

"You were eating my walls!"

"You tried to cook us!"

Mrs Jubert gave Ella a guilty look. "Perhaps," she said and then said to the children, "But you should respect your elders."

"Children are the future," said the boy.

"Yeah," said the girl, "and thanks for screwing up the planet before we even got our hands on it. I bet global warming was your idea, wasn't it?"

"Give it a rest," said Ella and helped Mrs Jubert over to a toffee dining chair.

Mrs Jubert's clothes, which she had initially taken to be sooty and torn from her oven ordeal, were a ragged mass of skirts, shawls and cloaks, all black. The only things the outfit was missing was a pointy black hat and a broomstick.

Ella stepped back.

"Mrs Jubert. You stay there, rest up. Don't go anywhere and don't try to eat any children."

"Abuser!" sneered the girl.

"And you two!" snapped Ella. "Shut your traps and wait there while I phone the police or social services or... or whatever."

She took out her phone and prayed that she had some sort of signal. The little icon flickered between one bar and none.

"With me," she said to the children and waved for them to follow her outside. She stepped over the smashed chocolate door and into the wild garden.

One bar. One bar of signal.

As Ella began to dial 999, the screen switched to an incoming call from Tilly Chapel, the builder's merchant, and with a careless tap of her finger she answered it. Ella silently cursed herself and put the phone to her ear.

"Hello, Tilly."

"Hi Ella. Replying to your text reply to my text reply. Good to finally speak."

"Thanks for calling back. Sorry, it's probably a moot point now. Things have... um, moved on. There are other issues here."

"I'm concerned that someone has a problem with one of our products. And I'm not just concerned about our reputation."

"I don't think that's at stake. No, the client —"

"Is the client's grievance genuine? You know how funny some of these old biddies can get."

Ella thought about Mrs Jubert, one-time harpist, now a grubby and mad-eyed witch.

"I do think Mrs Jubert's been through a lot lately."

"But the render. Tell me."

Ella looked at the cracked and fragmenting layers on the exterior wall.

"It's definitely coming away," she said and dug her fingers in the golden-brown layers. A light slab, the size of a dinner plate, broke off effortlessly in her hand. She smelled faint wafts of ginger and treacle.

"That's just no good," said Tilly.

"I don't think your product's to blame. There are... additives."

Tilly huffed audibly. "What have they added?"

Ella brought the gingerbread to her mouth. "Flour, treacle..."

She opened her mouth to take a bite. Out of nowhere, a green-hatted dwarf leapt up and smacked the gingerbread from her hand.

"No!" scolded OCD, landing at her feet.

"What?" gasped Ella.

"You were going to eat it!"

"So?"

"Dwarfs!" yelled the boy, although in joy or fear Ella couldn't tell.

Diminutive beard-wearers closed in on the cottage at speed from all sides.

"I thought I'd lost you," said Ella, disappointed.

"And who's bloody fault is that, bab?" spat Psycho, red-faced, as he ran up to her.

"Trust a woman to get lost," added Inappropriate.

"What are they?" squealed the girl.

"We're the party crew!" yelled Shitfaced jubilantly from the spot at which he had fallen over in the vegetable garden.

"We're here to save you," said OCD. "From yourself."

"Secure the bastard area," Psycho ordered the others. "Shitfaced, you're lookout on the roof. Passive Aggressive, check inside."

"That's right," said the black-hatted dwarf. "Send me in alone. I'm expendable."

Psycho growled. "Fuck's sake. Inappropriate! Put that down and help him. I don't care if it is an amusingly shaped vegetable, you juvenile cockwomble!"

OCD shook a wad of gingerbread in Ella's face. "Did you not consider the dangers of this stuff?"

"Dangers?"

"One, this gingerbread has been stood outside for — well, I'll need my field kit to determine specifics — but there's clearly opportunity for dirt and bacteria to accumulate."

"Our bodies can cope with a little dirt."

OCD looked horrified. "And, two," he squeaked indignantly, "what about an allergic reaction to ginger?"

"I'm not allergic to ginger. Is anyone allergic to ginger?"

"Three! Molasses."

"What?"

"The treacle. Do you know how many people are killed each year by treacle?"

"Uh, no. No one does. No one would want to know that. It's a pointless fact. Zero?"

OCD gave her a hard look.

"1919. Twenty-one people were killed and over a hundred and fifty were injured when a vat of molasses burst and swept through the streets of Boston, Massachusetts."

"Not a common accident, though."

"Like a shark, treacle is waiting for you to turn your back."

Ella made a dismissive "pff!"

"You're playing with fire, missy. When you're up to your eyeballs in molasses, don't come running to me." OCD opened his Filofax. "A thorough site inspection is called for here. Wouldn't be surprised if this whole place was a death-trap."

Ella became aware of a strange rhythmic noise round the side of the building, a metronomic 'nom, parp, nom, parp, nom, parp.' She peered round to see Windy working his way along the lower wall chomping and farting his way through foot after foot of construction-grade gingerbread.

"He thinks it's okay to eat," she said, but OCD had gone, wandering off with an extendable tape measure and a critical eye.

Ella realised that her phone was still on and Tilly was on the line.

"So sorry, Tilly," she said. "Something, some *things*, have just turned up."

"Is everything all right there?" asked Tilly.

"Yes, well no, but I can sort it out. But I do need to get off the line to call the police."

"The police?"

"It's nothing critical. Two prepubescent delinquents have been making a nuisance of themselves."

And, at that moment, Ella realised that the children were nowhere to be seen.

"Where have they...?"

"They ran off into the woods," said Shitfaced from above.

The yellow-hatted dwarf hung from a caramel-covered gable end, waggling his feet.

"Any chance of a hand?" he slurred. "I can't get up."

Ella rolled her eyes.

There was a thump and a clatter from within the house and

Ella immediately feared what the dwarfs might do upon finding a 'witch.' She ran inside, narrowly avoiding Windy as he munched his way along the front wall.

There was no one in the living room or kitchen but there were the shattered remains of a toffee dining chair on the floor.

"Mrs Jubert!"

Ella searched the rest of the house. There was no one in the bathroom, no one lurking behind the jellybean shower curtain. She opened the bedroom door. It was dark within, the window shutters closed. She flicked the glacé cherry light switch, on, off, on. Nothing.

Something dark shifted in the lumpy bed.

"Mrs Jubert?"

The something in the darkness cleared its throat.

"Who is that?" said Ella.

"It is I, your grandma," said a manly voice in a strained falsetto.

Ella closed her eyes and sighed heavily.

"Really?"

"Yes, my dear, and have you brought me a cake and a small pot of butter from your mother?"

Ella threw up her arms in exasperation. "Yeah," she said. "Why not?"

"Then put the cake and the little pot of butter on the stool and come get into bed with me, little girl."

"Excuse me, what did I tell you about calling me a 'little girl'?"

"You said it was creepy," said the wolf and then coughed. "I mean, I wouldn't know, we've never met before."

"I've never met my grandma before?" said Ella archly.

"I mean," said the wolf quickly, "we've never met *and* discussed such things."

"Nice recovery," said Ella. "So, what now?"

"Slip your things off and get into bed."

"Er... no."

"Please?"

"No. Can't we just do the 'Oh, grandma, what big teeth you have!' thing?"

The wolf shifted position making the tiny bed creak. "Arms."

"What?"

"You start with arms. Oh, what big arms..."

"Really? Not eyes. Or ears."

"I don't mind," said the wolf. "It's just, you don't just cut straight to the teeth bit, sweetheart. That's, like, the punchline. And you've got to build up the repetition. Arms, legs, ears, eyes and *then* teeth."

"Whatever. Oh, grandma, what big arms you have."

"All the better to hug you with, my dear," said the wolf.

A ripple of something passed through the room. It wasn't physical. It wasn't tangible. It was as ephemeral as a sigh, as fleeting as a breath of air. It was a shudder of pleasure up the spine of the world.

"What was that?" demanded Ella.

"It's good," said the wolf. "Keep it going."

"Oh, grandma, what big —. No, wait. Stop. What the hell was that?"

"Seriously. Don't stop."

"It went right through me like..."

"It felt good, yeah?" said the wolf.

"It did," said Ella warily. "It felt... right."

"Exactly," said the wolf. "Go with it, sister. Don't lose the moment."

Ella was caught on the balance of moment, torn between two deeply primal feelings. She felt the joy of the rhythm and rightness of the game they were playing, the roles that she and the wolf were acting out. At the same time, she felt a drowning person's fear, a sordid horror at how easy it would be to give in and play along.

She looked at the wolf and felt the pull of the words. "No."

The wolf stirred in the dark. "No?"

"No. And I hope I don't have to explain the meaning of the word 'no' to you, Mr Wolf."

There was movement that might have been a shrug.

"Nope," said the wolf, "I guess I'm just going to have to cut straight to the teeth bit."

He leapt at her, white fangs visible in the gloom.

Ella yelled and leapt back, slamming the door as she exited. The wolf hit the door with an 'oof' and a howl. As Ella stumbled away, she heard the wolf hit the door a second and far more effective time. Chunks of dark chocolate embedded themselves in the nougat plaster and skimmed far across the Tic-Tac parquet flooring.

"Wolf!" she yelled at the four dwarfs in the kitchen.

"No animals in the food preparation area!" exclaimed OCD.

Windy trumpeted in fear as the wolf smashed through a barley sugar doorjamb and into the kitchen, a lacy bonnet slipping from his head.

"Every dwarf for himself!" yelled Inappropriate.

Ella grabbed the largest piece of toffee chair leg on the floor and spun around to defend herself.

The wolf, an unnaturally large beast when she had first met him, appeared even larger now. Rounder, full-bodied, as though he had just swallowed an entire...

"Oh, now I'm really angry," she said.

The wolf leapt, jaws wide. Ella swung. They crashed to the

floor together and rolled. Ella sprang up again automatically, dazed, and looked for her lost weapon. It was clenched tightly in the wolf's bared fangs.

Ella crouched for a split second and grabbed another chair leg, although this one was barely more than a stump.

"You'd better spit up Mrs Jubert right now!" she said.

"Nng ead ugh furf!" growled the wolf around a mouthful of toffee.

"What?" said Ella.

The wolf blinked, went momentarily cross-eyed as he stared at his own snout and then grunted.

"Nng fedd nng ull ead ugh furf."

He coughed, shook the drool from his jaws and grunted again with effort. His jaws remained firmly closed on the toffee mass.

"Got something stuck in your dentures, grandma?" said Ella.

"Gud dumm," swore the wolf and bowed his head sheepishly.

He laid on the floor, braced his front paws against the ends of the chair leg and pushed, to no avail.

"Let's kill it!" yelled Inappropriate, already rooting through the kitchen drawers for a knife.

"No one's killing anyone!" said Ella firmly. "We're going to get Mr Wolf's jaws open somehow and... I assume you swallowed Mrs Jubert whole?" she asked the wolf. "I believe it's traditional in these... cases."

He nodded dumbly.

"Then you're going to spit her up," she said.

"We're also two dwarfs down," said OCD.

Ella looked at the wolf. He gave a 'maybe' shrug.

"Right," she said. "We need to prise those jaws apart."

"We could melt the toffee with boiling water," suggested OCD.

The wolf gave him an alarmed look.

"We could go get a woodcutter," said Inappropriate.

"Why?" said Ella.

"They know what to do."

"They know how to cut wood," Ella conceded.

"I'm just saying," said Inappropriate, "it's a practical problem. We need a bloke."

"Get a man?" said Ella. "That's your solution?"

Windy parped in the affirmative.

"Ridiculous," said Ella.

She made a quick search of the house and came back with a pair of fireside tongs. She knelt down beside the wolf and searched for a gap in his teeth in which to insert them. The wolf looked at Ella nervously.

"Be a brave boy," she told him and wedged the tongs in sharply.

She flexed the tongs and the wolf grunted in pain but his jaw remained closed.

"Id hurrs," he complained.

"Big baby."

She strained at the arms of the tongs. The wolf whined, "Muh deef! Muh deef!"

Ella feared that the toffee was going to prove stronger than her but then Inappropriate helpfully commented, "You see, this is why we needed a man" and the resultant anger gave Ella the required muscle power to wrench the wolf's mouth open.

The wolf yelled in pain. The toffee leg was still stuck to his upper teeth (with at least a couple of lower teeth embedded in it) and it hung there like a ridiculous handlebar moustache.

"Yuh weally hurd me," said the wolf around the toffee.

"You swallowed an old lady!" Ella countered and viciously smashed the toffee from his upper jaw, one side then the other.

"Mother Hubbard!" swore the wolf.

"Enough of that," said Ella firmly. "Mrs Jubert. Now!"

The wolf licked the new gaps in his teeth and eyed Ella's tongs bitterly.

"I'm the Big Bad Wolf..." he said, warningly.

"You're fat. I'll give you that," said Ella. "Vomit her up now."

"Sister, I can't hurl on command."

"Wolves, *canis lupus*, like most mammals, have a gag reflex," said OCD.

Inappropriate took hold of the wolf's front teeth and held his mouth open.

"Maybe I could reach for them," he said. "Coo-ee! Old crone! Psycho! Can you hear me?"

The wolf tried to say something but it was indecipherable with two dwarfs tucked in his mouth. Ella had the tongs handy in case the wolf decided to swallow them too.

"You could try massaging the uvula," said OCD.

"I can never find the uvula," said Inappropriate.

"Leave this one to me," said Windy, strode forward and proudly presented his buttocks to the wolf's mouth. "I've got some quality gingerbread a-brewing inside me."

Inappropriate stepped back, still holding the wolf's mouth open, and Windy let loose with a powerful, flappy fart. The wolf recoiled, retching.

"Go with it!" said Windy. "Let the medicine do its work."

The wolf heaved two shuddering hurls and then up came a dwarf.

"Psycho!" Shitfaced, delighted, hugged the bile-drenched dwarf.

"That was fucking horrible," declared Psycho.

The wolf heaved again and disgorged a heavy electrical fuse, a taxidermy badger, an empty jar, a car licence plate, a large egg and then, jaws distending impossibly, a black cloaked and very confused old lady.

"I thought I was dead," she murmured as Ella helped her up.

"Not quite," said Ella.

"I wasn't impressed," said Mrs Jubert. "I thought I ought to complain but I didn't want to make a fuss."

Ella guided her to a chair, then took the knotted blanket-cloak off her own back and put it around Mrs Jubert's shoulders.

"Hang on," said the wolf with a concerned look on his face. "One last..."

He retched and spat out a second dwarf who hissed and kicked as he landed on the floor.

"That's right!" grouched Passive Aggressive. "Leave me 'til last, why don't you!"

OCD catalogued the contents of the wolf's stomach in his Filofax.

"One Solomon jar. One infernal fuse. One licence plate: Louisiana, Sportsman's Paradise. One duck egg containing the hidden heart of Koschei the Deathless."

"Where did all this stuff come from?" said Ella.

"I get around," said the wolf. "I'm a wolf with a mysterious past."

"Bad diet, more like."

Ella became conscious of her phone buzzing and automatically answered it.

"Hello?"

"Ella?"

"Myra!" said Ella, moderately surprising herself by being glad to hear from her future stepmother.

The dwarfs reacting with scathing frowns and worried looks at the mention of her name. Even OCD paused in the middle of packing all of the wolf's stomach junk into a little sack.

"Where on earth are you?" said Myra.

"Hard to say," said Ella and looked at the woman who was clearly Ayleen Jubert but definitely not the Ayleen Jubert Ella knew. "I've come out to see a client."

"But where did you vanish to?"

"Vanish. Well, I..."

"You and I were having a nice chat in the night club and then I was going to introduce you to some eligible young men I'd met."

"Sorry. I don't need any eligible young men in my life right now."

"And then you vanished."

"Yes, I know. Sorry. Things have been a little crazy."

Crazy, Ella thought, was a scandalous understatement.

"And I see the seating plan is *still* not ticked off on the shared to-do list," said Myra.

"I've been, um, off-grid but I do have a seating plan."

She reached into her back pocket and removed the neatly folded seating plan OCD had given her in the pantry the day before.

"It's really quite good," she said.

She turned the paper round and saw for the first time that the reverse was covered in various scribblings (if one could call OCD's precise penmanship scribbling). One small section caught her eye.

POTENTIAL PCS

R. Avenant — classic PC, distant royalty.

Mr D — wealthy with aristocratic lineage, Bloody Chamber Gambit? Red Rose Gambit? Mr D = perfect beast. Good "persuasion" potential - hold GH until needed

???? — Could we engineer a Handsome Jack / Woodcutter scenario?

"WHAT THE HELL...?" said Ella.

"Is there a problem?" said Myra.

"No," said Ella, without conviction.

"Look," said Myra, "whatever happened last night, I think it's important you come home."

"I'm kind of in the middle of nowhere," said Ella.

"Then I'll send someone to get you."

"There's no need to send someone to get me," Ella assured her.

The dwarfs gasped in alarm (apart from Windy who parped in alarm).

"The huntsman!" hissed Inappropriate.

"You put that phone down now, bab," said Psycho.

"Is someone there with you?" said Myra. "Do you need help?"

"Psychiatric maybe," Ella said to herself.

Before she could react, Psycho used the wall as a launch pad, leapt up and smacked the phone from Ella's hand. It span across the floor towards the door.

"Christ's sake, Psycho!" she snapped.

Ella picked up her phone and tapped the blank screen. She tried to turn it on and, when it didn't, peeled the back off and experimented with removing and replacing the battery. Nothing.

"Bugger," she said softly.

"Broken?" said the wolf who had padded silently up beside her.

"The battery might have gone flat," she said.

The wolf sat down and scratched his ear with a hind leg.

"To be honest, sweetheart, I'm surprised it lasted this long," he said. "It's hardly in-keeping with the... the, um, aesthetic." He jerked his snout up at the gingerbread cottage behind them.

Ella nodded. "Wolf?" she said.

"Uh-huh?" he said.

"If I asked you to tell me what the hell's going on here, would you give me a straight answer?"

"As straight as I know," said the wolf.

"Fine. What the hell's going on?"

The wolf licked his fangs. There was still toffee clinging to them. "It's leaking out," he said.

"Leaking?"

"Yup. You know when you catch a rabbit and you crush it between your jaws. All the blood and snot and rabbit goo comes out. Some comes out where you bit it but it also comes out its mouth, its nose, its eyes and —"

"Stop," said Ella. "This rabbit chomping analogy. I'm not really feeling it."

The wolf sighed and tossed his head.

"Okay, sister. It's like the rain. Are you okay with rain? Is that a palatable enough metaphor for you?"

"Yes, thank you."

"The rain comes down and it trickles down the hillside. And the streams become rivers and it all goes rushing towards the sea."

"Uh-huh."

"It's like that." The wolf as he rootled in his mouth, trying to get toffee out of his teeth.

"What is?"

"This," said the wolf. "There are certain places and times and people that it happens to. Just like winter storms and flood valleys and even if someone builds a dam and tries to hold it back, it finds another way."

"What does?"

"Look, I was happier with the rabbit metaphor, to be honest," said the wolf.

"I don't even know what you're talking about yet," said Ella.

"Happy endings," said Shitfaced from up high.

Ella had forgotten she had left the dwarf there. The yellow-hatted drunkard sat on the roof.

"Happy endings," agreed the wolf.

"Happy endings?" said Ella. "As in Thai-massage-with-a-happy-ending?"

"I don't even know what that means and I don't want to," said the wolf. "All this, the cottage, the witch, the gnomes — "

"Dwarfs," said Shitfaced.

"Whatever," said the wolf. "All this — even me — is nature's way of trying to give you the happy ending you deserve."

"Did I ask for one?"

The wolf huffed. "Most people would give their eye teeth for a happy ending. But they don't get the chance. You, princess, you're special."

"Me?"

The wolf nodded.

"You're like... a sewer."

"Gee, thanks."

"All right, like a drainage ditch."

"Not much better."

"Dyke?"

"Stop it."

"Point is, it's got to come out through *you*."

"But why? Why me?" said Ella.

"Why does the stream trickle this way, not that? Why does the raindrop on the leaf roll left, not right? Who can tell the water where to flow? Who can say when the storms will come, when the rivers will run dry?"

"Wow, man," said Shitfaced. "That was poetry."

"It's not an answer," said Ella.

The wolf shrugged.

"All I know is you can't fight it. Even if you do, like that madwoman at Rushy Glen, you can't put it off for ever. And I bet you she wishes she'd got herself a knight in shining armour and a castle of gold instead of a busted-up hovel and sciatica. I know I would."

"Wait. What did you say?" said Ella.

"I said, I'd rather have a castle of gold than some busted up hovel."

"Before that. You said Rushy Glen."

"I did," said the wolf.

"You know where it is?"

"Not exactly."

"But it's my grandma's house."

"Oh," said the wolf, surprised. "In that case, yes. I know where your grandma's house is. I know where everyone's grandma's house is," he said, confidently.

"No, you're not allowed there," said Shitfaced.

"Why not?" said Ella.

"You've got to come with us. We've got to keep you safe until it's time for you to go to the ball."

"I'm not going to a ball. I'm going to Rushy Glen." She turned to the wolf. "And you're taking me."

"No, he can't!" Shitfaced began to shout. "Lads! Lads! She's running away!"

"Quick, let's go," Ella prompted the wolf.

"What's in it for me?" said the wolf.

Ella was momentarily stumped. "You could do it to make up for trying to kill me?" she suggested.

"That's between me and my conscience," countered the wolf.

Ella dug in her trouser pocket. There were two of the biscuits she kept for Buster lodged in the bottom.

"Dog biscuits?"

"Do I look like Scooby-Doo?"

Five dwarfs came running out of the house.

"What's the bastard problem?" demanded Psycho.

"She's going to run away with the wolf!" squeaked Shitfaced, leaping down from the roof.

"That's not part of the plan!" said OCD. "She has to come with us."

"I'm going nowhere with you," spat Ella.

"You see," said Inappropriate, "this is the kind of thing that happens when you let women out of the kitchen."

Psycho unhitched his tiny axe from his belt.

"Enough bloody talk. Kill the beast. Grab the lass. No more dicking about."

Ella backed away. The wolf's nose nudged her armpit.

"Get on my back," he said.

"Really?"

"Would you rather I fought them? I can take the little axeman but that leaves the drunkard and the one planning a gas attack."

Windy was indeed approaching, pumping threateningly as he came. Shitfaced was coming up alongside him, swinging his fists like a windmill.

Ella grabbed the wolf's shaggy neck and swung herself up onto his back.

"So quick to get a hairy beast between her thighs," noted Inappropriate.

The wolf turned tail and ran, Ella clinging in fear to his back. None of the dwarfs got within ten feet of them. Psycho gave a roar of fury. Ella heard rather than saw his axe spin close past them and embed itself in a tree trunk. She ducked the spray of flying bark and buried her face in the wolf's musty fur.

THEIR INITIAL FLIGHT from the dwarfs lasted no more than five minutes but Ella was sure they had raced further than she could have covered in an hour by herself. It ended when the wolf burst into a mossy clearing, slowed and, without warning, pitched Ella onto the ground.

Ella grunted, rolled to her feet and stretched her aching legs.

"I've ridden ponies that were thinner than you," she told the wolf. "Shorter too."

"Dog biscuits," demanded the wolf.

Ella blinked, dug them out and tossed them into his mouth. The wolf swallowed them without a single chew.

"Well, it was nice knowing you," he turned to go off into the woods.

"What?" said Ella. "You were going to take me to my Granny's house."

"No, I wasn't," said the wolf. "We both needed to get out of there. I took you with me. You paid me in dog biscuits that tasted like dust."

"You can't leave me!"

"I could eat you," said the wolf, levelly.

He turned to go again.

"The happy ending..." Ella called.

"What about it?"

"When I get my happy ending, what happens to the Big Bad Wolf?"

"These days? If it's the Red Cap version, it's traditional for a woodcutter to slice me up. The one with the pigs and the houses, I would expect to be boiled alive. The one with the seven little goats, I have my guts filled with rocks and then I drown in a well."

"I'm sensing a theme," said Ella.

"It used to be better in the old days," said the wolf. "I'd just gobble down the girls or old women and that'd be that. Huh. In the *proper old* days, I'd swallow the sun and usher in an age of darkness but none of us are as young as we used to be."

Ella perched on a rotting tree stump.

"So, it seems to me that a 'happy ending' doesn't do you any favours?"

"Well, sure, but you can't fight it."

"Not being a coward, are you?" said Ella.

"No..."

"Afraid to take a walk on the wild side, Mr Wolf?"

The wolf treated her to one of his lopsided grins. "You can't win."

"I'm quite persistent," she treated him to smile of her own.

The wolf held her gaze for a long second.

"Okay," he said.

"Okay?"

"I will take you to see the madwoman at Rushy Glen and you'll see where fighting a happy ending gets you."

"Oh, it's a bet, is it?"

"Exactly."

THEY WALKED SIDE BY SIDE, following the sun for much of the morning. The woods were as dense as before. Paths that barely saw sunlight wove between tall trees. They passed no people, no buildings and didn't even see an electricity pylon.

"Wolves do get a bad rap in stories, don't they?" Ella, reflected.

"Oh, yeah," said the wolf. "It's always about eating children or livestock and causing terror. People never stop to think about the positive community work we do. The charity work. The performing arts."

She looked at him askance.

"I mean, you might be a ravenous carnivore," she said, "but you're always to the go-to bad guy in stories. You don't see the same thing happening with bears or big cats."

"You don't get many of them in these parts though."

"And you do wolves?" said Ella. "They must have been extinct in the United Kingdom for what? Three hundred, four hundred years?"

"I am here, you know."

"I had noticed."

They forded a small river and climbed a steep earthy embankment.

"This is all a bit of a mess, isn't it?" said Ella.

"Well, it's a forest," said the wolf. "They tend not to get the cleaners in very often."

"I wasn't talking about the woods," said Ella. "Although that's another thing. I know the woods around Little Wangford. They're like half a mile across at the most. We must have covered at least eight miles so far."

"Well, we're in the Deep Dark Forest now," said the wolf.

"And where's that?"

"Here," said the wolf as though it were obvious. "So, what is a bit of a mess?"

Ella ticked her worries off on her fingers.

"Six dwarfs turn up at my home. There's some less than polite talk about an evil stepmother and ugly stepsisters. And a ball. I've been to a gingerbread cottage and met a cut-price Hansel and Gretel. And you, you came preloaded with dialogue straight out of Red Riding Hood."

"Right," said the wolf, understanding.

"Which story am I supposed to be acting out here?"

"Well, sister, if I may hark back to my earlier analogy, despite it not being as visceral and as pleasing as the dead rabbit metaphor. You're asking drops of water which river they're from. There's this narrative pressure building up. It wants to come through. It *needs* to come through. It's the right thing. When you played along, back in the cottage, you felt it working through you."

"I did."

"Every time you try to block it, it switches paths. It tries to find another way. The actual format doesn't matter, sweetheart. The outcome is going to be the same. The stepmother dies. You're reconciled with your father and reunited with your mother. You marry your Prince Charming or your handsome jack and live happily ever after."

Ella nodded thoughtfully. "My mum's dead."

"Right," said the wolf and walked on.

Something small and wet hit the ground ahead with a soft

splat. A second something caught her shoulder a glancing blow, leaving an unpleasant black and white stain.

Grimacing, Ella looked up. A pair of bluebirds swooped and spiralled overhead. One of them let go of the small roll it was carrying. Ella found it in the leaf mulch ahead. It was a scrap of paper torn from a pad on which was scrawled the one word:

Bich

She automatically looked for something to throw and immediately gave up.

"How long to Rushy Glen?" she called to the wolf.

"Not long," he replied.

"How long to Rushy Glen?" Ella asked, as the sun disappeared below the horizon and the world was lit only by the dying ember glow of red clouds to the west.

"Not long," said the wolf. "You keep asking."

"Probably because your definition of 'not long' is very different to mine."

"It's not long," said the wolf.

Ella sighed and tried to wiggle her toes inside her shoes but they felt as if they had welded together into a slab of swollen soreness. "Compared to how long is it until the heat death of the universe, maybe."

"You moan too much," said the wolf. "I didn't sign up for moaning."

"We've been walking all day," said Ella reasonably. "I'm tired, I'm hungry and it's getting cold."

"I found you those berries," countered the wolf.

"Five berries."

"I've had two crap dog biscuits today. You don't hear me complaining."

"Yeah, but you had an old lady for breakfast."

"*Had.*"

"Are we going to get there tonight?" said Ella.

The wolf looked at the sky.

"Probably not."

"Right, so...?"

"So, we'll camp for the night in that cave."

"What cave?"

Ella looked and there was a cave where she hadn't noticed one before, a large and roughly circular tunnel into a low sandstone cliff.

They stopped at the mouth of the cave. It was at least ten feet high and deep enough that its end was lost in darkness.

"Are there bears in this forest?" she asked, hoping, naturally, that the answer would be no.

"Maybe."

"Dragons?"

"Are you scared, princess?" mocked the wolf.

"Just a perfectly healthy fear of death."

The wolf sighed and then addressed the cave.

"Hello! Any bears or dragons in there?"

His voice echoed back to them. He looked at Ella. "See?"

And then a deep, rumbling, Dolby-Stereo-sound-at-the-multiplex voice replied, "No."

"Ah," said the wolf and then asked, "Who is in there?"

"Me," came the considered reply.

"Good," said the wolf. "And are you dangerous?"

There was a thoughtful silence, then: "Yes."

"Let's go," said Ella.

"Wait," said the wolf and then called into the cave again. "Will you harm us?"

The silence was longer this time.

"You are welcome to spend the night in my cave," said the voice. "I will not harm you or allow harm to come to you whilst you are in my cave. On this I swear."

The wolf grinned. "Seems fair enough."

Ella put a hand on his shaggy shoulder. "What? You're going to take his word for it?"

"He swore."

"I know people who swear all the time. Doesn't mean I trust them."

"Then trust me," said the wolf and padded into the cave.

Ella looked back at the encroaching night. "I've got a bad feeling about this," she said, and followed him in.

The cave was warm but there was no fire, no light. In less than a dozen footsteps, Ella was in complete darkness. She stumbled and put her hands out and felt something hairy and warm. She recoiled a moment and then recognised the wolf.

"Everything okay?" she whispered.

"Oh, yeah," whispered the wolf in an unconvincing voice.

"You stopped."

"Mmm-hmmm."

"What are you doing?" she asked.

"Looking at our host."

Ella blinked rapidly and stared into the darkness but could see nothing but black.

"Sit," said the massively resonant voice of their host. If the sea could speak or if bees could buzz in a multi-part harmony that sounded like speech then it would sound like that. The voice came from in front and *above* them. "Sleep," it said.

"Our host..." said Ella.

"Yes?" said the wolf.

"Is he... jolly and friendly looking?"

The wolf paused. "Would you sleep better if I said yes?"

"Probably."

"Then he's very jolly and real friendly looking, yes."

"Sleep, little ones," said their host.

"Where?" said Ella.

"Here," said the wolf. "Close to me."

The wolf lay down and Ella sat beside him. In time, she leaned on him, resting against his thick musty hide. Soon enough her breathing fell into rhythm with the rise and fall of his great chest and, she eventually realised, the faint but pervasive sub-bass rumble of their host's breathing.

As sleep came to her, something wet brushed the tip of her nose. It was the wolf's tongue. His breath smelled of toffee.

ELLA DREAMED OF GRANNY ROSE.

Ella dreamed a memory that she was unaware she still had.

Ella (how old she was, she couldn't tell, but it couldn't have been more than seven) was helping her Granny with the housework, polishing the brass and pewter ornaments in the glass-fronted sideboard in the living room. Ella loved the mellow sheen that she could achieve with lots of rubbing, and smiled at her reflection in some of the larger pieces. She set aside the tankard Granddad Doug (who had died ten days before Ella's birth) had been given for captaining the darts team and pulled out an item she hadn't come across before. It resembled a covered gravy jug with a large ear-shaped handle. It was particularly dirty.

Ella grabbed the handle, dabbed her cloth in the Brasso and began to rub the side, when she was abruptly enveloped in a cloud of smoke and not the smoke of Granny's cigarettes which permeated the place.

Her coughs were loud and Granny was there in a flash (Ella

certainly remembered a flash, which was odd). Granny Rose smacked the object from her hand as though Ella had done a very, very stupid thing and then dragged her out into the garden. Ella stood on the lawn, sniffling to herself, wondering what she had done wrong, what rule she had broken. Meanwhile, Granny Rose hoovered inside the front room, clattering around as though she was doing battle.

Ella put her ear to the dining room window and listened in.

"No, I don't want nowt," her Granny growled. "We're all perfectly happy as we are, thank thee very much."

There was much more hoovering and banging about and even some grunts and groans like the men on the Saturday lunchtime wrestling and some final, bizarre words from Granny: "I don't care how cramped it is in there, you bugger. Get in!"

They had jam sponge and custard for tea and nothing further was said of the matter.

5

She was woken by the wolf moving beneath her, his chest jerking as though with hiccups. She groaned as she opened her eyes.

"Quiet," the wolf whispered softly in her ear.

There was daylight at the cave entrance. Down here in the depths of the cave, Ella could make out the shape of the sandstone cavern they had slept in. Off to the side was a large dry pile of sack-like rags that might have been their host's bed. Beside that there was a neat stack of dry, white kindling. There was no actual sign of their host.

"We're going to leave very, very quietly," whispered the wolf.

Ella nodded and licked her dry teeth, not awake enough to question him. She stood on stiff legs. Her foot touched a loose round stone and it rolled away from her. It wasn't a stone; not with those eye sockets. She looked at the stack of white kindling. It wasn't kindling; not with those wrist joints and ankles.

She glared at the wolf.

"You said to trust you!" she hissed at him.

"I was wrong!" the wolf hissed back.

"You said he looked jolly and friendly!"

"I lied!"

Ella looked daggers at the wolf and tapped her feet. The wolf wrinkled his nose. "He's an ogre."

"An ogre," said Ella.

"An ogre."

"You can come out now," called their host pleasantly from outside.

Ella sighed with a curious blend of terror and irritation and, with the wolf, walked towards the cave entrance.

It was a beautifully sunny morning, yellow sunlight cutting through the treetops and burning away the last of the mist that clung to the grass. This was of no consolation at all to Ella but it was nonetheless true. On the patch of earth in front of the cave, a fire had been lit and a giant iron pot placed on top of it. The ogre was throwing grasses and wild radishes into the bubbling pot.

"Good morning." The ogre adjusted his enormous spectacles to see them better.

The ogre looked... well, the ogre looked like an ill-advised cross-breeding experiment between a professional wrestler and a baked potato. He stood fifteen feet high, his eyes as large as watermelons, his fingers as thick as tree branches, his frog-like mouth big enough to swallow a sofa.

"Do come out," urged the ogre.

Ella made to step forward but the wolf held her back with a nudge of his head.

"That's a fine smelling breakfast you're cooking," said the wolf.

"Thank you."

"A vegetarian breakfast perhaps."

"No," said the ogre and smiled.

"You said you wouldn't harm us," said Ella.

"While we were in the cave," said the wolf dourly.

Ella shuffled back, more firmly into the mouth of the cave.

"We could run for it," she whispered to the wolf.

The ogre's laugh was like distant explosions. Suddenly, the ogre wasn't there anymore, replaced by a powerful and sinewy lion. And then the lion was gone, to be replaced by a huge, hulking white-furred bear. And then the bear was transformed back into the gnarly ogre.

"You could," said the ogre.

"I have heard that you can transform yourself into any animal," said the wolf.

"T'is true. T'is true," said the ogre.

"Obviously, big animals are easy but I bet you can't squeeze yourself down into something really, really small."

"Like a rat?" said the ogre.

"Like a rat," said the wolf.

The ogre peered at them over the top of his spectacles.

"Do you think I am so stupid that I would fall for that trick and let you gobble me up?"

"Maybe," said the wolf hopefully.

"We'll just stay in here," said Ella defiantly.

"And starve?" said the ogre.

"Better than being eaten."

The ogre rumbled in his throat and stared into his pot. "A compromise then."

"Not eating us?" suggested the wolf.

"A challenge," said the ogre. "I will ask three riddles and, if you can tell me the answers to all three then —"

"No," said Ella.

"No?"

"I'm useless at riddles. Can't stand any of that Dungeon and Dragons bullshit. I want a challenge that we actually stand a chance of winning."

"Such as? A test of strength? A running race?"

"Name that smell?" suggested the wolf.

"Karaoke," said Ella.

"What's a karaoke?" said the ogre.

"A singing contest," said the wolf.

"And what are the rules?" The ogre gave the pot a stir.

"We each sing a song and the best one wins. You win, you can eat us. We win, you let us go."

"And we can eat you," said the wolf.

"Do we want to?" said Ella.

"I'm hungry."

"What song do we sing?" asked the ogre.

"We each pick one for the other person."

"But it must be a song we know."

"Agreed. And if you stop halfway through the song then it's an automatic failure."

"And that person's life is forfeit. But it is forbidden to distract one another."

"Fair enough," said Ella. "And distraction includes?"

"Pulling faces, throwing insults, making noises, talking, touching, tickling, biting, spitting, poking, grabbing, punching or kicking," said the ogre.

"So, we can't touch the other person while they're singing?"

"No," said the ogre, "but no running off while you're singing either. You must stay and complete your song."

"Whatever," said Ella.

"I agree," said the ogre, brushed the last of the grasses from his hands and turned to face them. "You will sing first."

"Very well," said Ella. "Name your tune."

"*Go No More A-Rushing*," said the ogre.

"Sorry. Not heard of that one," said Ella.

"Very well. Then *Old Maid in the Garret*."

"Sorry."

"*Rosetta and Her Gay Ploughboy*?"

"Definitely not."

"*Bohemian Rhapsody?*"

"No. Wait! Yes. What?"

"You know it?" said the ogre.

"And *you* know it?" said Ella. "'*Is this the real life? Is this just Battersea?*' That one?"

"It's a classic," said the wolf.

"Then sing it," said the ogre.

Ella hesitated. She had no backing track. She closed her eyes, pictured the music video for the Queen song and began. The trick, she knew, was not to start too high otherwise she'd be squawking by the time she got to '*Look up to the skies and see.*'

When she got to '*Mama, oo-oo-oo,*' the wolf joined in as a backing singer with a restrained '*Any way the winds blows.*' And then, when she reached the '*little silhouetto of a man*', the wolf came in with some hearty '*Scaramouche*'s. Finding confidence in their solid teamwork, they bounced '*Galileo*'s back and forth and tried to outdo each other in declaring exactly for whom Beelzebub had put a devil aside.

As they wound down to the emotional climax, Ella could see the wolf truly getting into it and imagined that, if not for the lack of arms and functioning digits, he'd be playing air guitar. Small mercies, she thought.

She let the last note die gently and looked at the wolf.

"Nailed it," he said bluntly.

"A passable effort," said the ogre.

"Harsh," said Ella. "Your turn."

The ogre cleared his throat and hummed an arpeggio. "Name your song," he said.

Ella grinned. "*One Million Green Bottles.*"

The ogre was unimpressed. "That's not a song."

"It is."

"But it's not a famous song."

"Isn't it?" said Ella. "Do you know how the song *One Million Green Bottles* would begin?"

"Well, yes," the ogre conceded.

"And how it ends?"

"Yes."

"And what would go in the middle?"

"But it would take forever to sing."

"Not my problem."

The ogre sneered at her.

"But I will still sing it better than your pedestrian effort."

"That's fighting talk," said Ella.

"You'd better stop stalling and start singing," advised the wolf.

The ogre gave them one final glare, took the deepest breath and sang.

"One million green bottles, hanging on a wall..."

His diction and intonation were perfect. He made the nursery rhyme tune actually sound good.

"And if one green bottle should accidentally fall, there'd be nine hundred and ninety-nine thousand, nine hundred and ninety-nine green bottles hanging on the wall."

Ella tapped the wolf on the shoulder and jerked her head to indicate they should go. As they moved away the ogre, still singing, turned angrily towards them.

"You must stay and complete your song," Ella reminded him, "or you lose."

The ogre, still singing, gestured furiously at their departure.

"The rules never said the listener had to stay where they were," Ella argued.

"Stay and sing or move and lose," said the wolf. "And then your life will be forfeit."

The ogre sang a vindictive and threat-laden verse but nonetheless kept on singing.

"He will finish it, you know," said the wolf as they re-entered the forest.

"I think we've bought ourselves enough time," said Ella.

"Maybe."

Ella looked at the path ahead and put a hand to her rumbling stomach. "How long is it to Rushy Glen?"

"Not long," said the wolf.

"You've said that before," said Ella.

'Not long' turned out to be all of the morning and most of the afternoon. More than a dozen times, Ella told herself, "If Rushy Glen isn't over *that* rise" or "through *those* trees" or "across *that* stream" she would abandon the wolf and strike out by herself, hopefully in the direction of the nearest pub or coffee shop. She was partway through thinking what she would do if Rushy Glen wasn't on the other side of *these* brambles when she burst through and saw that Rushy Glen was indeed there, squatting in the middle of a thickly overgrown wildflower meadow.

"Told you," said the wolf. "Didn't take us long at all."

She would have punched the wolf but she was too travel-soiled, ragged, hungry, nettle-stung, fly-bitten and just too damned exhausted to raise the energy.

Ella knew her fair share of country cottages. She'd renovated a few, stayed in others and scoffed at the architectural folly of several more. Rushy Glen occupied safe middle territory. It wasn't the impractical stone barn in the wood fantasy of a wealthy big city commuter. It wasn't a functional, weatherproof box like Ayleen Jubert's cottage (and it certainly wasn't the confectionery nightmare Ayleen Jubert's cottage had turned into). Rushy Glen was simply a modest inter-war brick and mortar house that happened to be in the middle of nowhere. An unpainted picket fence that was being slowly consumed by the meadow ran around the borders of the property. Within, Ella could see the runner bean frames of a vegetable plot, an evil looking goat tethered to a stake, a covered well and a structure that could easily have been a hen house or a garage, considering it appeared to contain both a dusty old car and a small flock of chickens.

"Do you think she'd mind if I ate the goat?" said the wolf, licking his lips.

"I think she might," said Ella.

She was reading a sign posted fifteen feet from the gate. It read: *Go away. We don't want any.*

"What about, say, one leg?"

"You're not taking one of the goat's legs."

"Of course," said the wolf, "I'll just get chicken-to-go."

There was another sign further on: *Trespassers will be shot and I don't know first aid.*

"I don't think Granny Rose likes visitors," said Ella.

"It's like I said. Fighting your happily ever after will make you mad."

Ella waved his nonsense away. "I'm sure she'll be delighted to see me."

There was a third and final sign on the gate itself. It simply read: *You were warned.*

Ella put her hand on the gate.

"If she shoots you and buries you in the wood, I will dig you up," said the wolf.

"Why?"

"I am *that* hungry," said the wolf.

Ella gave him a withering look, opened the gate and immediately fell into a covered wolf pit on the other side. The impact with wet earth knocked breath and sense out of her and it took a good few seconds to colourfully express her surprise and distress. The ground beneath her was several inches deep in a soup of rainwater, mud and roots. She rolled over and looked up at the wolf looking down from eight feet above her.

"Don't you say a sodding word," she growled through gritted teeth.

"Not saying a thing," said the wolf.

Ella sat up and clutched her aching ribs. The wolf watched.

"Well, don't just stand there. Help me out."

"How?"

"I don't know! Fetch a ladder or something."

"Fetch a...? Once again, princess, I will point out my lack of opposable thumbs."

"Just do it!"

The wolf disappeared. Ella stood slowly and painfully. Her foot caught under something stiff in the mud. As she freed it, a bleached white leg bone with a tiny pixie boot on the end momentarily surfaced and then sank again.

"Wolf!" she yelled.

A shadow passed over her and she wisely sidestepped as a long plank slid down into the hole and came to a rest at a steep angle. The wolf peered over the side. Ella considered the slope of the wet plank.

"This isn't a ladder," she said.

"I got splinters in my mouth for you, sister."

There was a sudden explosive bang, a yelp from the wolf and he vanished from sight.

"Wolf!"

Ella grabbed the plank and attempted to climb it, hands gripped tightly, feet shuffling inch by inch up the slick surface. Halfway up, she realised that someone was standing over her with a double-barrel shotgun pointed directly at Ella's head.

"Can tha not read t' signs?" said the old woman fiercely.

The old woman wore a much-mended cardigan, a grubby laminate apron and a hairstyle that could be most charitably described as natural. Ella didn't recognise her, not fully, but there were traces here and there — the angle of the nose, the set of the brow, the shape of her scowl — that begged to be remembered. It had to be twenty years or more since Ella had actually seen her.

"What are you anyroad?" demanded Granny Rose. "Too big for a pixie. Too mucky for a dryad."

Ella could see right down the barrel of the gun. She could also feel her grip beginning to give on the plank. She didn't want to think what would happen if she slipped and startled her grandma.

"Granny Rose, it's me. Ella."

Rose gave her a powerful squint.

"Ella?"

"Your granddaughter."

"I know who Ella is," said Rose as though her mental faculties were being called into question. She lowered the shotgun. "What's tha doing in a flaming hole in t'ground?"

"Trying to get out."

Rose was unimpressed. She put the gun aside, took hold of Ella's wrist and with surprising strength for a seventy-something hoisted Ella out and onto solid ground.

"Tha'll have to help me cover it up again," Rose told her, brushing leaf mould off Ella's shoulders.

"Do you need a pit trap in front of your house?" Ella asked.

"For unwanted visitors, aye. Especially, them as can't read." Rose brushed a smudge of muck from Ella's cheek and then, her crusty manner cracking, hugged her tightly. "It *is* thee."

Ella, feeling tears prick her eyes, returned the embrace. The woman smelled of cigarette ash and disinfectant, the smells from her childhood she had almost forgotten.

"I've missed you, Granny," she said.

Rose broke the embrace gently.

"I'm getting thee all creased up."

Ella laughed and regarded her ruined clothes.

"These are beyond creased, Granny."

"And whose fault is that, going gallivanting hither and yon? It's been near on thirty years. I thought t'world had forgotten me. How'd tha find me?"

"The wolf showed me." Ella suddenly looked round. "Where is he? Did you shoot him?"

"Who? Zeke?" said Rose. "No. I just scared him off. He should know better than to come sniffing round up here."

"You know that wolf?"

"Aye. Of old. He's all right really, long as he stays the right side of my fence. Not having him coming in t'house, trying to gobble up pigs or dress like a bleeding jessie in my best nightgown. Come on, love, let's have you inside and out of them rags. Look like they're held together with nowt but muck and wishful thinking."

Ella followed Rose to the back door of the cottage. She remembered — remembered remembering — that Granny Rose was of that generation that didn't use the front doors of their houses except for weddings, funerals and visiting royalty.

Rose spun on the doorstep, fiddling with something on her sleeve.

"First things first," she said and stabbed Ella in the arm with a safety pin.

"Ow!" said Ella loudly.

Rose ignored her cry and inspected her eyes closely, like an amateur optician.

"That hurt," said Ella.

"Did it burn with t'fires of hell?" asked Rose.

"No. It stung. I'm bleeding."

Rose looked at the bead of blood that had formed on Ella's arm and dabbed it suspiciously.

"And what does tha make of this?" said Rose, taking out a small gold cross she wore on a chain.

"It's pretty?" said Ella with a shrug.

"And this?" Rose dipped into her pocket and then blew a pinch of salt into Ella's face.

"I... really don't know," said Ella.

"Hmmm," said the old woman thoughtfully. "Well tha's not a changeling, pixie or one of the land of fairy."

"No, I'm not," agreed Ella, still a bit miffed.

"Is tha carrying any gifts made to thee by fairy folk?"

"I don't think so."

"Be sure. Has tha had any fairy-bread or fairy-wine?"

"Definitely not."

"Are these tha clothes?"

"Um. Yes."

"And did tha pack tha pockets thesen?"

Ella inspected her pockets. She was still wearing the 'practical but fun' outfit OCD had forced upon her two days ago, plus the red ambulance blanket turned cloak she had taken from the train. She dug out the contents of her pockets.

"What's them?" said Rose.

"Nothing," said Ella and threw the M&Ms on the ground.

"And that?"

"A seating plan."

"And that?"

"It's my phone."

"Phone? Wonders will never cease."

She poked in a miserly fashion at Ella's loose change.

"Right. Indoors. No use standing on ceremony."

The kitchen at Rushy Glen was large, functional and probably hadn't been changed (although it had been meticulously kept) since the middle of the last century.

"What was all that pocket business about?" said Ella.

"Can't be too careful," said Rose, flipping open the lid of a huge twin-tub washing machine. "I've been in hiding since eighty-nine."

"Hiding? From who?"

Rose poured a handful of washing powder into the tub.

"From Carabosse, of course."

"Carabosse?"

"Aye. Carabosse. Now strip off them rags and straight into the tub with them." She suddenly looked at Ella. "Tha doesn't know who Carabosse is?"

"No."

Rose put the box of powder down. "I thought..." She sighed heavily, the lines on her sun-worn face deepening. "I thought that, with tha being here, with Zeke an' all, that tha knew."

"Knew what?"

Rose was silent for a second then said, "I reckon I've got some of tha mum's clothes that might fit thee."

ELLA SPENT a good half hour in the bathroom, scouring, scrubbing and rinsing until she came out with pink skin and hair like dry straw. Across the hall was the guest bedroom, containing a single bed, a corner table holding an old cathode ray tube TV, and a wall of sturdy shelving. Rose had laid out some clothing suggestions from the piles, boxes and stacks on the bedroom shelving. Ella picked a mustard crew-neck, embroidered jeans and, for lack of other options, a pair of pink jelly shoes. It was curiously touching to know that these had been her mum's clothes, although that feeling was dampened by the discovery that her mum had been a somewhat slimmer fit.

Ella went downstairs. The twin-tub rattled noisily, pumping steam into the air. Rose had set out the table with a pot of tea, bread and butter and cheese.

"I didn't know if tha had had tha lunch."

"No," said Ella. "Not lunch." Or anything at all for the last two days, she thought.

"Help thasen."

With as much decorum as she could muster (which wasn't

much), Ella sat down and stuffed her face. Granny Rose poured pitch black tea, took out a thin packet of Park Drive cigarettes and lit up.

"See tha mum's clothes don't quite fit thee," said Rose.

Ella, whose mouth was chocked full with a mush of bread, cheese and hot tea was unable to reply. She gurgled and swallowed hard.

"Ah, she was allus skin and bones," said Rose blithely. "Nice to see a Thorn girl not afraid to eat her fill."

"Um," said Ella.

"Don't mind me, love," said Rose. "Eat up. I'll have my fag and then we'll take a look at t'garden and I'll tell thee about Carabosse."

"What is that?"

"She." Rose inhaled deeply on her cigarette. "She's tha fairy godmother."

THEIR WALK around the garden was a tour of odd jobs and tasks that probably made up much of Granny Rose's daily routine. The first job was throwing a pot of food scraps to the goat.

"Got Nanny here and about two dozen hens in t'shed," said Rose. "I has only one rule with t'animals."

"What's that?"

"The moment any of them starts talking, that bugger's going in t'pot. That's rule number three."

"Number three?"

"Of the rules. I've got them all writ down somewhere. Got to have rules on account of Carabosse." She picked up a bucket of chicken feed and then stopped. "It were my fault."

"What was?" said Ella.

"All of it. I released her." She carried the bucket up to the henhouse-cum-garage and threw handfuls down. Chickens came running out from underneath the boxy old car. "When I were a kid. We lived in a rotten back-to-back in Cottingley."

"Cottingley?" said Ella.

"Bradford, love. S'where I grew up. My folks, my brother and me. There weren't much of a yard. Big enough for a washing line and an outhouse and not much more."

"And did you have to work down t'pit for twelve hours to earn one farthing?"

"Cheeky bugger. This was the fifties. We still had rationing from after the war. Meat rationing. Sugar too. Only one kind of cheese."

"War is hell."

"And this was before they'd got started on building council houses. Yes, we lived in a back-to-back. Two up, one down and we had to do our business in the garden. Anyroad, we played in t'yard when we weren't playing out in t'street. I was probably nine. Tha Great Uncle Jack would have been ten. He was sat on the step reading his Dan Dare and I was digging in t'ground with a stick." Rose mimed the actions as she spoke and pretended to hold something aloft. "I found a jar. A pickling jar, I suppose. Someone had painted summat on t'glass but I couldn't read it. And it had a fairy inside it."

"A fairy?"

"A fairy."

"Any particular kind of fairy?" said Ella.

Rose shrugged and held her thumb and forefinger, five inches apart.

"It were a fairy, love. Yay high. Wispy clothes. Little wings like a thingamajig... a butterfly. A fairy."

Chickens done, Rose took the empty bucket to the well. She drew up the rope and filled one bucket from the other. A mallet hung from a string beside the well.

"So this fairy in a jar," said Ella. "It had been buried alive?"

"I don't know if alive and dead are things that apply to fairies. But she looked pleased as punch that I'd dug her up."

"So you let her out."

"Of course, I did. I was a nine-year-old girl and I'd found mesen an honest-to-God fairy. Off popped t'lid and the fairy flew out and in a tiny, high-pitched Pinky and Perky voice said to me" — Rose put on a squeaky voice that sounded more Donald Duck than either Pinky or Perky — "'Thank you for freeing me. In repayment, I will grant you your heart's desire.'"

"She granted you a wish then."

"Well, no. She just said that and flew off. Of course, we ran to tell mother but she just thought we were making it up. Jack and I tried to convince her and we only stopped when our father came home and gave us a clip round the ear for talking twaddle."

Rose saw Ella looking at the mallet.

"For bopping any frog prince, mermaid or troll stupid enough to come crawling out," she explained. "Anyroads, father gave us a clip round the ear and that were it. Least for a few years. My father got a building job down this way, through a feller who was his commanding officer in the war, so we moved here. Rushy Glen was tha great grandparents' house. It was a palace to us. And mebbe I forgot about that fairy. Couldn't rightly say. That were Carabosse, not that I knew that then."

Rose led Ella down towards the vegetable patch. "You can help me inspect the beans," she said as she poured water out on the vegetables.

"What am I looking for?" said Ella and then immediately saw that one of the runner beans was glowing with a regal and golden light.

"Pop it in here," said Rose. "Don't let it fall on t'floor or we'll have bloody giant beanstalks everywhere."

Ella dropped the magic bean into the empty bucket.

"This is a lovely garden," said Ella.

"I loved this place as a girl. We — tha Great Uncle Jack and me — went to the local school. Moreton-in-Marsh Secondary Modern. Can't say I enjoyed it. All us girls learning typing like we were going to land plummy secretarial jobs in the city. Weren't much use if tha lived in t'wood. Even less use when a bear comes knocking at t'door."

"Did you just say 'bear'?"

"Aye."

Happy with the beans, Rose led her further round the house to where a climbing rose had entwined itself around a rotting trellis.

"Here," she said, and passed Ella a pair of secateurs. "I hate bloody roses."

With a pair of shears, Granny Rose snipped the head off one of the red roses. The stem recoiled like a snake and waved its thorns threateningly.

"What kind of rose is this?" said Ella.

"Don't know its actual name, but I'm pretty sure it ends in 'magicum'."

Ella lunged forward like a fencer and cut down a thick stalk. The dying stem writhed on the ground.

"You mentioned a bear," she said.

"I was fifteen. It were raining that night, coming down in stair-rods. Father would've been at t'pub. My mother was babysitting for some family a few miles over. Can't remember where Jack was, but I were alone in the house. There was a knock at t'door and there stood a bear. Big teeth. Huge paws."

Ella nodded. "Well, I can imagine you were a little lost for words."

"Not huge *pause*," said Rose irascibly. "Huge *paws*, as in — Oh, I see."

Ella was smiling. "You were telling me that a bear came to your door, Granny. It's a bit unbelievable."

"Don't mean it didn't happen though. He knocked at t'door. I looked him up and down. He was dripping head to toe. And he asked if he could come in and warm up by the fire. Naturally, I was bloody terrified but I had my manners an' all so I let him in, all stinking like a damp dog, and he sat in front of the fire. Steam came off his fur in clouds. We talked. I don't remember what about. And I gave him some tinned spam which he wolfed down. And then he was gone leaving a damp patch on the hearth rug and me having to explain to my parents where the spam for tomorrow's tea had gone."

"Fairies in jars. Bears. I'm not seeing a link here, Granny."

"Give me time," said Rose.

"I mean, some people might argue that there never was a bear."

Rose paused in her vigorous rose-slaying.

"Is tha saying I'm lying, girl?"

"Maybe it wasn't a bear. Maybe it was someone else."

Rose nodded in slow understanding.

"Oh, tha think it might be one of them repressed memory jobbies? Some sinister bloke who I've confabulated into a bear to protect my fragile mind?" She cut away a trio of rose heads with a vicious one-two-three. "No, we were too busy in them days for such nonsense. It were a bear."

"Okay," said Ella.

Rose picked up a pump-action spray and doused the remains of the rose plant with weed killer.

"It *is* okay, girl," she gathered up the chopped pieces of rose plant and threw them in her bucket. "Now listen. Couple of days later, I were walking through the wood and I met a dwarf who was chopping wood and who had — Lord knows how — got his beard stuck in t'cleft of the log he was chopping." She eyed Ella suspiciously. "Tha's all right with dwarfs? Tha's not going to tell me it was my imagination?"

"No," said Ella. "Me and dwarfs, we have a history."

"Well, this little bugger were swearing fit to burst. He just kept tugging and hurting hissen and swearing some more. I offered to help. He were so intent on his beard, I don't know if he even knew I were there. I stepped in and, with the little knife I carried, I cut his beard and set him loose. Well," said Rose with a theatrically exasperated sigh, "tha'd have thought I'd cut off his goolies way he reacted. Swore like a trooper, he did. Ruined his fine beard, I had, apparently. Not a word of thanks out of him."

Crossing back over to the henhouse/garage, Rose dumped the rose cuttings and the magic beans in a brazier.

"Over t'next few days," she said as she doused the lot with lighter fluid, "I met that dwarf again and again. I found him dangling from a tree branch and pulled him down. I found him stuck in a fast-flowing stream and hauled him out. It weren't 'til afterwards that I saw t'pattern of things. These weren't chance meetings. This were a... What would tha call it? A *set-up*. Each time, I'd rescue him. Each time, the ungrateful bugger'd shake his little red hat in my face and swear at me."

"Red hat?"

"Aye."

Rose lit the brazier and the whole lot quickly caught light.

"Psycho, I've met him," said Ella.

The magical rubbish burned with a pungent blue smoke and what sounded like the faintest of screams.

"He's a git, is what he is," said Rose. "Final time we met he were down t'bottom of a steep bank. All gravel and loose earth and roots. He were trying desperately to climb up, on account of t'bear that wanted to kill him."

"The bear you met earlier."

"Exactly, love."

"I can see where this is going."

"Then tha's smarter than I were at fifteen. Come on."

They returned to the henhouse and Rose rooted around in the

straw and on the back seat of the car for eggs. The car badge
identified the vehicle as a Zastava Podvarak. It had all the elegance
and aerodynamics of a motorised fridge.

"So," said Rose as she scrabbled around. "I grabbed a branch
and lowered it to that rum bugger of a dwarf and helped him up
out of reach of the bear. Was he grateful?"

"No, he wasn't."

"Correct," she said, emerging with a bucket full of eggs. "That
dwarf had a right go at me, about how I'd been too slow and how he'd
nearly died. In t'meantime, the bear had found his own way up the
bank. He comes snarling towards us. We were trapped. That dwarf,
he starts pleading with t'bear and tells him he should eat me, instead,
on account of me having a bit more meat on my bones, which wasn't
summat to be ashamed of in them days neither. Course, bear paid his
snivelling no mind and, with a swipe of his claw, knocked him dead."

"You're sure he was dead?"

"As I say, I'm not sure if dead and alive apply to these folk. I
took him for dead and so did t'bear and, as the bear turned to me
he was at once transformed into a young man."

"A handsome prince."

"I don't' know about prince. And I don't know about
handsome. But he were a young man and completely in the nuddy
an' all. I were fair gobsmacked. Turns out he had been cursed by
t'dwarf, summat to do with buried treasure. I don't clearly recall.
Any roads, he was mighty... grateful I'd helped him. Never
underestimate the value of a grateful young man, particularly one
in the nude."

"Granny!"

"What? You think we didn't have sex in them days? We didn't
have televisions then and didn't have none of tha YouTube or
t'internet. We had to make our own entertainment."

"And then what happened?" Ella asked.

Rose shrugged. "Well, I married him, o' course. Time for another brew, I reckon."

Ella followed her back to the kitchen in stunned silence.

"That bear was Granddad Doug?" she said eventually.

Rose nodded. She filled the kettle from the tap, placed it on the wood-burning stove and then, considering the bucket of eggs, said, "Yorkshire pudding for tea I shouldn't wonder."

Ella stared in stunned thought a little longer.

"I'm one quarter bear?"

"I don't know about that. This is magic stuff we're talking about."

"I do seem to spend half my time shaving and waxing."

"I'm not sure it works like that..."

"And I *really* like salmon."

Rose opened the twin tub and began arranging Ella's sodden clothes on the clothes horse in front of the stove. That done, Rose lifted the boiling kettle off the stove and made a fresh pot of tea with tea bags. She glanced up and saw Ella's look of surprise at such a 'modern' concession.

"Won't give time of day to loose tea," she said. "I don't want crowns and stars and other mystical portents appearing at t'bottom of my cup."

"I can see that might be off-putting," said Ella.

Rose put a cuppa in front of Ella and set about mixing eggs, flour and milk to make batter.

"Doug and I were married the year after we met," she said, "and your mum was born not long after that."

"Married at sixteen? Wasn't that a bit young?"

"Times were different then, love. No one minded if tha were married at sixteen."

"To a bear."

"I met in t'wood. Aye. I didn't question it. I was happy. And mebbe then I had an inkling that this was the fairy's doing. This was my heart's desire."

"A husband and a child."

"I know what tha's thinking."

"I didn't say anything, Granny."

"But you're thinking it loud enough to hear. Bugger women's lib. Just because my dreams might be small, they were still mine. Oh, would you look at that."

Rose showed Ella an egg she had just cracked. Curled up inside the shell was a tiny little girl with skin as pale as albumen and a flower-petal dress the colour of yolk. The little creature yawned, awoke and looked up at Rose with large, innocent eyes.

"I am Eggselina," it spoke. "Are you my mummy?"

Rose opened the kitchen window and threw the thing out as hard and fast as she could.

"Waste of a bloody good egg," she said, returning to her mixing bowl. "Now, what was I saying? Oh, aye. Doug and I moved up to Warwickshire. He got a job in woodland management which, far as I could tell, was being a lumberjack without actually cutting down trees. We went up there when your mum, Natalie, was a new-born. We were very happy."

Ella smiled and felt a curious emotion, the realisation that this woman knew her mum far better and more intimately than she ever would.

"Tha knows tha mum and dad were school sweethearts," said Rose.

"I do."

"That was her contrary nature."

"Contrary to what?"

"What with the fairy trying to set her up with every magical suitor between here and Scotland. You see, the fairy wasn't just set on giving me my happily ever after. She wanted one for my daughter too. We'd have gentleman callers at all hours. Frog princes. Seventh sons of seventh sons. And wolves, aye. She had to beat them off with a stick. We even came back down here for a bit to get away from them one summer, not long after my own folks died — me and tha granddad, tha mum, young Gavin and some mardy little miss of a friend."

"Myra."

"That were her. I wouldn't say that girl was a wrong 'un but if you gave her the world on a plate, she'd complain you'd used her best china."

"I know what you mean."

"Oh, you've met her, have you?"

"Um," said Ella. "She's marrying dad. In nine days' time."

"Dad? Your dad? Gavin?"

"Yes. My dad. I would have sent you an invite but you've been kind of hard to find."

Rose's face was suddenly ashen. She nearly dropped the bowl of batter, caught it and put it down on the side before she could drop it again.

"No. She can't," she whispered. "He can't."

Ella took hold of Rose's upper arm to support the old woman.

"It's not that bad," she said. "She is a bit forthright and little bit... totalitarian, but —"

"No, you don't understand," said Rose. "He can't marry her."

"Why not?"

There were tears in Rose's eyes.

"Tha mum's not dead, love. She's not dead."

Ella's first thought was that her Granny was speaking metaphorically, saying that those we love never truly die. But she rejected that thought in less than a second; the profound sadness in Rose's eyes was evidence of a deeper and more concrete truth. Ella's second thought was that her Granny was delusional, demented, mad. This was a woman who had just declared that her late husband had previously been a bear. Yes, that was it. Granny

Rose had masked it well but she was clearly suffering mental problems in her old age...

Ella stopped herself.

"What do you mean?" she said.

"Tha mum had to allow everyone to move on."

"My mum suffered from undiagnosed hypoglycaemia, fell into a diabetic coma and died," said Ella, her voice rising and her tone hardening as she spoke. "She died over thirty years ago. Don't tell me she is alive. That's a wicked and terrible thing to say!"

"But it's true," said Rose softly.

6

The guest bedroom again.

Rose bent down and, with an arthritic groan, pulled a large cardboard filing box with reinforced metal corners from under the lowest shelf in the alcove on the right-hand side of the chimney breast.

"Tha'll have to lift it onto t'bed," Rose told her. "It's tha mum's things, might be summat in there."

It was heavier than Ella had expected and it bounced heavily on the bed.

"I'll leave tha with it," said Rose.

Ella looked at her.

"It's fine," Rose reassured her. "I've got to sort tha washing and I suppose tha'll be staying the night?"

The sky beyond the half-drawn curtains was turning a darker blue. Ella nodded and Rose left her. Ella opened the curtains more fully to let the last of the light in. She glanced out over the garden and to the woods beyond, hoping for a sign of the wolf. He might have been a wolf, might even have tried to eat her, but she wanted to know he was unharmed. She couldn't see anything in the darkening forest. Up above, two distant birds chased each other round.

She returned to the bed and lifted the lid off the box. It contained a cross section of her mother's life. Small pieces of jewellery that ranged from gold chains to fluorescent plastic earrings tangled with a fountain pen and a wristwatch as she lifted them out. There were a handful of video cassettes, but no obvious way to play them. There was a pair of large photograph albums that creaked dryly as Ella lifted them out, and something wrapped in newspaper.

This was how a box of memories should be, thought Ella: big, bulky, weighty with importance. If she ever had to put together something similar for any of her descendants, it would just contain the memory card from her phone and a link to her social media feed.

She inspected the photo albums first. Flakes of dried glue fell as she opened the first. She smiled. These were pictures she hadn't seen before. Rose as a twenty-something mum with a prepubescent Natalie. Here, a few years down the line, Natalie as a tall, leggy but shapeless teenager. She turned the page and laughed.

Under a written heading of *Rushy Glen, 1974*, a picture of three teenagers slouched against a wall. Natalie was all sunburn and freckles, her eyes almost invisible under a heavy fringe. Gavin — "looking slim, dad!" said Ella — was wearing a goofy grin and a pair of shiny shorts that were so high and tight, nothing was left to the imagination. And Myra, the cause of Ella's laughter, was a striking, almost imperious figure, with a ridiculously frizzy perm that wouldn't have looked out of place on an international footballer or a German porn star.

A flick through the pages was an accelerated trawl through time. Natalie's freckles and that impractically long hair were swiftly replaced with a sensible bun and squidgy bundle of flesh and blankets that Ella guessed was herself as a baby. Gavin, often appearing half in shot, was already starting to fill in around the waist. Did work and fatherhood automatically make one fat?

A photograph of Natalie, knitting something shapeless and white. Another, of Natalie with a pram, possibly empty, possibly occupied, outside Nailcote Antiques, where Gavin had worked before setting up by himself. Here, a photo of Granny Rose at Ella's christening. Ella grunted in surprise. She had always thought of Granny Rose as an old woman, had always remembered her as such, but here she was, holding the baby Ella and she didn't look a day over forty, barely five years older than Ella was now.

Ella scratched at a mark on the photo. A yellow streak of light wound round Rose's head and past baby Ella. It was like the trailing flare of a handheld sparkler but no one in the picture appeared to pay it any mind.

Ella considered the video cassettes. Was there a way that she could play these things? There were very few electronics in Granny's house. An ancient television sat in the corner of the room, but it had no video player that Ella could see. She went back to the shelf and pulled things out. Finding nothing, she went to the shelves on the other side of the chimney breast and eventually found an old video camcorder, a lump of black plastic the size of a breeze block (and which weighed about the same) with a smashed lens. She put one of the cassettes into the camcorder (it took four attempts to get it in the right way up and the right way round) and then realised it had no screen of its own. Some fiddling with some accompanying cables and the tiny television set proved generally fruitless until, by the twiddle of a particular aerial cable or the flick of a critical switch, she couldn't be sure which, something came to life and Ella heard her mum's voice for the first time in thirty years.

"Hang on! Hang on!"

Ella scooted back from the screen.

The camera viewpoint swung around a tiny kitchen. It was being carried but not aimed at anything.

"Mummy!" shouted a child's voice.

"Hang on!" replied Natalie firmly.

Out the back door, down the short grassy garden, underneath the washing line. A young Ella — three? Four years old? — stood by the borders, pointing with muddy fingers.

"Where is it?" said Natalie.

Ella shook her pointing finger and glared as though her mummy was an idiot. Natalie crouched with the camera. The image was blurred for a few seconds before Natalie found the focus.

"Is a fairy," said Ella.

"No," said Natalie patiently. "That's a beetle."

The fat black insect on the leaf, still but for its waving antennae.

"Fairy?" said Ella.

Natalie laughed.

"No, Ella-Bella. It's a beetle."

"Bee-tul."

"Yes."

Ella felt her cheeks tighten with emotion. She couldn't remember her mum's voice and hearing it now, sounding so very much like her own...

"Squash it?" said little Ella.

"No," said Natalie. "We only squash fairies, goblins and sprites."

"Sprites!"

"And what do we do if it's a fairy?"

"Don't let fairies come and play. Tell an adult right away."

"And if it's Carabosse?"

"Run!" yelled little Ella and, with a playful scream, dashed off down the garden.

The recording ended and the screen turned to static.

Ella took out the photo albums to look for another tape. A

flurry of faded Polaroid prints fell out. Most of them appeared to have been taken at Christmas. Young Ella appeared in some of them, looking perhaps a few months younger than she did in the Betamax video. Ella tried to put them in some sort of order. Toddler Ella next to a large red Christmas present. The present now unwrapped to reveal, bizarrely, a wooden spinning wheel as tall as the bemused Ella. Natalie, in a grey and frosty garden, smashing the device apart. Mother and daughter posed together in the lounge in front of a roaring fire composed almost entirely of spinning wheel. In the picture, Natalie wore a grin so fierce and defiant, she might as well have had the word 'Fuck you' stitched into her Christmas jumper.

Ella set them aside and pulled out the next video tape. It only took two attempts to get this one in the machine.

It took Ella a few seconds to recognise the setting as the back room of Nailcote Antiques. The camera was a steady tripod shot of the mouldering book stacks and a chair that had been placed before it. Natalie came round and sat at the chair to address the camera directly.

"This is for you. I don't know how long we're going to have to keep fighting this thing or who will be doing the fighting."

Natalie held up her left hand to show the big plaster across the flesh between thumb and forefinger. She looked irritable and tired, her face lined.

Ella's mum had died — Ella had been *told* she'd died — at the age of twenty-six. This video couldn't have been made much before that.

"Fairies," said Natalie. "Fay. Fee. Fates. The names all mean the same thing. They're the ones who control what happens. Go back further and it's all bloody Latin for 'that which has been spoken.' It's the power of words."

Natalie looked at the thick book on the table in front of her. It was bound in green cloth with gold emboss.

"We can't kill Carabosse. But we can trap her." She opened the book. "There's a story in the One Thousand and One Nights about a fisherman who finds a genie in a bottle. Yeah, like the genie of the lamp. It's been imprisoned there by King Solomon. Apparently, in myth and legend, that was his thing."

Natalie pointed to something on the page not visible at that camera angle.

"There are a lot of similarities between fairies and genies, or djinn. They're like angels but they're not angels. They're like devils but they're not devils. We just need to find the right bottle to stuff this wicked fairy godmother into."

She looked directly at the camera again.

"I've done the research and added to my mum's list of rules for handling these creatures. If... If I don't succeed, maybe they'll help you succeed in my stead."

A voice called off-camera, from a distance. It was Gavin.

"Nat, are you talking to someone in there?"

Natalie stood and turned the recording off as she made the opening sounds of a denial.

Ella ejected the videotape and inserted the next. This video was another straight-to-camera piece by Natalie. If nothing else, Ella had the basis of a fine found footage horror movie: *Natalie Hannaford: Fairy Hunter.*

Natalie was in a shed. The camera was angled down to get a wide workbench in the shot.

Natalie had a large jar in one hand and what looked like a partially melted toy action figure in the other. The melty Action Man kicked and struggled against her hold.

"Okay," said Natalie in tones that clearly indicated this was not the first take. "Here we have your common or garden boggle."

The boggle snarled and spat.

"I caught this one at a local farm where it was entertaining itself by making the newborn lambs lame."

The boggle snickered.

"And here," said Natalie, "we have a Robinson's Jam jar which I have inscribed with what Professor Makepeace Alexander assures me is a fair replica of the Seal of Solomon. And now..."

Natalie opened the jam jar one handed and attempted to stuff the slimy goblinoid inside. It resisted and, as she adjusted her grip, it bit deeply into the fleshy part of her left hand. Natalie gave a high-pitched grunt of pain but did not let go. She thrust the creature in, though there was barely room, and forced the lid on top.

Blood poured from her hand and, as she wrapped the wound with an oily rag, the boggle rattled and flexed and cursed inside its prison. With its growing exertions, a sickly green glow surrounded the creature. But it did not break free.

"It works," said Natalie. She regarded the glowing jar of angry boggle and then her ineffectively bandaged hand. "If you've given me rabies," she told the boggle. "I'm throwing you down a well."

She stood clumsily and turned the camera off.

Ella gave a start at a sudden rapping at the window. Two bluebirds hovered in front of the glass. Each clutched the sleeve of black-hatted dwarf who was doing his best to cling to the generally smooth and hold-free window.

"What are you doing here?" said Ella.

"Oh, that's a fine hello," said Passive Aggressive. "Not a 'how do you do' or a 'can I possibly help you inside?' Oh, no, not from Little Miss Egocentric."

At the edge of the forest, Ella could see purple, green, brown, red and yellow hats bobbing through the tall grass.

"Go away!" Ella hissed through the glass.

"Oh, I suppose you don't want rescuing?" said the dwarf sarcastically.

"From what?"

"From that witch downstairs."

"That's my grandma!"

"She *says* she's your grandma."

Ella growled in frustration.

"You're idiots. The lot of you."

"Says the woman trapped inside the witch's house."

The bluebirds trilled in agreement.

Ella closed the curtains.

"Oh, so you're not going to open the window?" snapped the dwarf. "How rude!"

Ella ran for the stairs. "Granny! Granny!"

Rose appeared at the foot of the stairs, oven tin in hand. "I was just doing t'gravy."

"You've got visitors," said Ella.

"What kind?"

"Dwarfs."

Rose's mouth set into a firm line. "The little buggers can try."

In the kitchen, Rose set the gravy aside, tssked at the fact that the Yorkshires were nearly done but would have to wait and then offered a shotgun to Ella.

"God, no."

"Right. Then tha's on broom duty."

Ella looked at the broom Rose thrust into her hand.

"For whacking the little gits. Now, where are they?"

"Five of them coming from the wood. The other was dropped on the roof by these two bluebirds that keep —" Ella stopped as the flue leading off the stove started to clank and thump.

"I'd wager t'other one thought to come down t'chimney," said Rose. The thumping intensified. "Which is all fine and dandy in books but, in real life..."

A muffled howl emanated from the metal flue pipe.

"That's not going to end well," said Rose with a devilish smile.

"I'm stuck!" shrieked the stifled voice of Passive Aggressive. "Don't all rush at once to help me!"

Grandmother and granddaughter got outside in time to see

the dwarfs reach the picket fence. Rose unhurriedly broke open the shotgun, removed the one spent cartridge and replaced it with a fresh one from her pocket.

"I covered the pit again while tha was doing tha ablutions," said Rose as Inappropriate bounded through the gate and disappeared into the hole.

Psycho gave a Braveheart yell as he ran, swerved to avoid the gate and vaulted over the fence. He landed on a concealed bear trap. Spring-loaded jaws snapped up and grabbed him by the thighs.

"Aaagh! You evil old cow!" he screamed.

"Oh, that *is* the dwarf I met!" said Rose, pleasantly surprised. "I'd recognise that swearing anywhere."

Beyond the gate, OCD held out his arms to stop the other dwarfs rushing in.

"Stop," he told them. "It's too dangerous."

Windy parped worryingly.

"You think she's set more traps?"

"It's not that," said OCD. "Gardens are *dangerous* places. Did you know, over six thousand people are put in hospital each year in lawnmower accidents? Over five thousand injured by flowerpots."

"I got attacked by flowerpots once," burbled Shitfaced.

"Attacked?" said OCD.

"Okay," Shitfaced admitted. "I might have started it but I swear one of them was looking at my pint."

OCD got down on his hands and knees and peered down into the pit.

"Are you all right down there?"

"Sure," said Inappropriate. "S'not the first time I've gone down in an old lady's garden."

"Enough talking!" grunted Psycho as he struggled against the trap. "Get in there!"

Rose stepped forward and raised the shotgun to her shoulder.

"I don't think tha's going anywhere but back the way tha came."

At that the two bluebirds swooped down, twittering, claws at the ready, at Granny Rose. Ella instinctively swung at them with the broom but only succeeded in throwing Rose's aim wide.

"Attack!" screamed Psycho. "Attack now!"

With one member stuck up a chimney, another stuck down a hole and another still wriggling out of a bear trap, the dwarfs attacked as a not entirely threatening band of three. Windy got his foot stuck in a hidden snare and went down with a bugling bum-pop of distress. OCD ran down the path, ensuring he noted any trip hazards and making sure didn't tread on any cracks in the paving. Only Shitfaced, arms windmilling like an after-hours pub car park fighting champion, presented a credible threat.

Ella caught the dwarf in the chest with her broom, swung him up and round and, entirely by accident, flung him in through the open kitchen window. Rose pointed her shotgun at the two still mobile dwarfs. OCD burbled something about shotgun injuries being mostly self-inflicted but ran for the bushes when Rose put her finger to the trigger.

There was the sound of smashing crockery from within the kitchen.

"Why'd tha let him inside?" Rose snapped at Ella.

"I didn't *let* him in, Granny," but she was already talking to Rose's back.

In the kitchen, Shitfaced had magically located a bottle of booze and was jigging along the counter, kicking bowls and cups aside.

"That's my best cooking sherry!" Rose exclaimed. "That's only for trifles and medicinal purposes!"

The thumping from the stove had changed in tone now. The banging was not coming from the flue but, seemingly, from inside the oven itself. Ella thought she could hear faint and desperate squeals of "Hot coals! Hot coals!"

Rose swung her gun towards the destructive dancing dwarf, a futile threat given that the alcoholic fellow was moving very nearly drunk beyond caring.

"Hang on," said Ella, nipped forward and opened the lid of the twin tub washing machine and let the dwarf tap dance himself right in. She slammed the lid shut again.

"I'm blind!" peeped Shitfaced. "They said it'd be the drink that'd do it but I said, no, it would probably be the frantic mastu —"

"Now, hold it there, you conniving cows!" growled Psycho from the doorway.

He had freed himself from the bear trap but his tunic was ripped and his trousers missing. Gathered menacingly behind him were Windy, OCD and Inappropriate.

"You need to come with us, bab," Psycho said to Ella. "She means you no good."

"You said that about Myra."

"Her too," said Psycho. "Bitches and witches the lot of them."

Ella jerked a thumb at her grandma.

"She says my mum's still alive."

Psycho frowned. "Was that the Glass Coffin Gambit?" he whispered tersely to his companions.

"The Spinning Wheel Gambit," OCD corrected him.

"You knew?" said Ella, furious.

"Don't you get fucking riled with me, bab," countered Psycho. "We're just doing our bastard jobs. Now are you coming with us or are we taking you down?"

"Don't you dare come near her!" spat Rose, taking aim.

"Don't need to," said Windy, clenching.

With the whine of an insect behind glass, Windy let loose with a tightly controlled and seemingly endless fart.

"Filthy little bugger," said Rose and then gagged as the expanding cloud of flatulence reached them.

Dwarfs stuffed their noses and mouths with their beards or their hats. Ella coughed at the stink which toured a colourful but disgusting path from human digestion, through rich farmyard stench and beyond into an uncharted, reeking realm of noxious smells. Ella clutched her throat and realised she couldn't breathe. They would either have to flee or pass out.

"S'horrible," spluttered Rose hoarsely.

Then Ella had an idea. It probably wasn't a good idea but Windy's fart was starving her brain of oxygen and, in the heat of the moment, it seemed a brilliant idea.

"Get down, Granny," she instructed and then pulled the oven door open.

Ella whipped her still wet blanket-turned-cloak off the clothes horse and threw it over herself and Rose as Passive Aggressive leapt out howling, his trouser legs on fire.

Covered by the blanket, she didn't see what happened when the flaming dwarf met Windy's cloud of methane-laden guff but she heard it and felt it. With a sound like the world's biggest paper bag popping, a hot and unyielding blast threw them to the ground. Metal dented, glass shattered and a lone voice yelled, "Bastaaard!"

Ella had landed with her elbows locked and her body arched protectively over her grandma. Beneath the now steaming blanket, Ella said, "Are you okay?"

"Are *you*?" replied Granny Rose, which was good enough for Ella.

She threw the blanket aside and helped Rose to her feet. The kitchen had been devastated. The windows had been blown out. What crockery had survived Shitfaced's rampage had been pounded to dust. One of the kitchen tables had been turned to matchwood.

The table was badly charred. And the cosy on the teapot was burning merrily. Additionally, there were four unconscious dwarfs, variously dangling from pan hooks, curled up on the stove, wedged head first into cupboard doors and slumped in the sink. One dwarf lay in the centre of the room, clutching his behind.

"My arse," whimpered Windy. "You've ruined it."

He gave a toot of misery and immediately winced in agony.

Ella didn't know what to say; she hadn't meant to cause such damage.

"Granny..."

"Into the tub with them," said Rose briskly.

Ella opened up the twin tub.

"I can see the light!" slurred Shitfaced. "What was that noise? Sounded like the end of the world."

"It was Windy," said Ella.

"Ah, the trump of doom," said Shitfaced.

Rose scooped up and dropped the comatose dwarfs one by one into the tub. The last to go in was the weeping and repentant parper.

"Shouldn't there be seven of them?" said Rose.

"Apparently, there's only six."

"Disco's on a secret mission," mumbled Inappropriate.

Rose shut the lid and dragged over a cast iron shoe repairing last to hold the lid firmly in place.

"They'll need a long overnight soak," said Rose with no small amount of vindictiveness and turned the washing machine to its hottest setting.

"The Spinning Wheel Gambit," she said. "Surely, there was a funeral for mum."

"There was, but Carabosse had spirited her away by then."

"Where to? What happened?"

"Did tha not listen to the tapes?"

"Those little audio cassettes? There's no player upstairs. Have you still got one?"

Granny pulled a face. "Try the pantry. Top shelf."

Ella went into Granny's tiny pantry, which was really a darkened cupboard filled with storage jars and ancient kitchen gadgets. The top shelf appeared to be where Granny kept things that she didn't need very often. Ella inspected a tin containing cake decorating nozzles. Another held a dismantled mincer. Finally, she found the Dictaphone underneath a stack of recipe clippings and lifted it down in triumph.

"Got it! Might need some batteries though." She flipped open the battery cover. "It needs, wow, it needs four."

Granny raised an eyebrow. "There's some in that drawer there. Listen to the answer phone message. The conversation with Carabosse. Tea'll be a while longer now I reckon. I'll give thee a shout."

IN THE GUEST BEDROOM, Ella speculatively placed another video cassette in the camcorder. In the recording, the camera rested on the seat of a wooden picnic table, its gaze encompassing a pair of denim clad knees, the underside of the table and, a little way off, the swings and slides of a children's playground. Ella recognised the embroidered jeans in the picture as the ones she was wearing now. Apart from the distant and almost inaudible action in the playground, nothing happened. Ella guessed that, unless her mum was into making avant garde video art, there had been a slip of the finger on the record button.

Ella set the Dictaphone on her lap and pressed play.

"- a menial task, do not offer to take their place, not even for an instant. Rule number eighteen, do not accept food from a stranger. Rule number nineteen, never stray from the —"

She turned it off, not because she didn't want to hear but because, on the screen, the denim knees had just stood.

"You came," said Natalie.

"Regretting it by the moment," said an invisible woman.

The denim knees sat and were joined by the folds of a many-layered skirt.

"I don't approve of playgrounds," said the woman. "What's wrong with climbing trees and jumping off logs?"

"Playgrounds are safer."

The woman made a disgusted noise.

"Fun's not fun if it's safe. There's no reward without suffering."

"Ah," said Natalie.

"Ah?"

"I was wondering what you got up to on your days off but, no, I can see it now. A little kinky fun with whips and leather."

"Natalie Thorn! Don't be so vulgar!"

"It's Hannaford. I'm married."

"Not to the right man!"

There was a lengthy pause and then Natalie said, "Your name is Carabosse."

"Maybe. Names are like faces. It's practical to have more than one."

"We've been getting your 'gifts'"

"Gifts?"

"It's not going to work. Every time you send one to us, I'm just going to smash it up."

Carabosse laughed, a girlish titter.

"It's not me, dearie. It's the universe. Before her sixteenth birthday, she will find a spinning wheel and —"

"Is this because we didn't invite you to her christening?" said Natalie.

Carabosse tittered again.

"You have everything on its head. I'm the good one. I'm her fairy godmother, as I was yours. Oh, the princes I had lined up for you."

"Just what do you want?" demanded Natalie. "You want an apology? You want me?"

"I want what I've always wanted. Six little words."

"What?"

"'And they lived happily ever after.'"

"Then lay off with the magical curses!"

"It's just a little prick and a sleep. Most women have had to put up with worse to get their heart's desire. She won't age, Natalie. I can arrange for you and that bore of a husband to sleep too if you wish."

"So you can go out and find a bloody prince to wake her? She doesn't need that kind of help."

"Now, my dear, that's all very progressive but people do undervalue the success of arranged marriages —"

"We don't want your help!"

"Shush, dear. Godmother knows best."

There was a bang of glass being placed forcefully on the table top.

"What's this?" said Carabosse.

"Libertatibus perierat et ignaro —"

"How dare you!" spat Carabosse in a voice that was far deeper and far less constrained than before. "You think you can bind me like some garden sprite? In what? A bottle?"

There was a sharp pop and glass shards scattered down. A crack appeared across the camera lens and the recording stopped.

That was the last video cassette in the box and, judging by the crack in the lens, it was indeed the very last video recorded. Ella looked down at the Dictaphone and inserted a different cassette.

There was a second-long beep. It was an answer phone recording.

"Mum. Mum?" It was Natalie. She was outside somewhere. Distant but fast-moving traffic could be heard in the background. "Mum, it's me. I found it. The spinning wheel she intends to use. I'm at this pub, the White Hart, and she's got it at this place a few miles down the road. I'm going in there." Natalie paused and the sound deadened a second as

though she had her hand over the receiver. "I can't destroy it. She'll just make another one. She said that the magic will just keep going until a finger is pricked and the spell is cast. If someone's got to prick their finger, I'd rather it was me than Ella. She's going to be pissed off, mum. I need you to look after Gavin." Natalie sniffled. "Look after Ella for me."

Click.

SOMETIME AFTER NIGHTFALL, they ate a dinner of slightly burned but nonetheless delicious Yorkshire puddings (cooked in lard, of course), beef gravy and runner beans from the garden. Six unhappy someones thumped and gurgled in the washing machine.

"Do you know where my mum is?" said Ella.

Rose shook her head and spooned gravy into her mouth.

"I only know what's in that there box," she said.

"I have to warn dad."

"And what will tha say, love?"

Ella gazed at her beans — her tasty and reassuringly non-magical beans — and shrugged.

"I can't let them get married."

"No. Not least because that Myra lass was a right hoity-toity miss."

"My phone is dead. As a doornail. Do you...?"

Rose shook her head again. "Who'd phone me?" She put her spoon down. "T'woods are too dangerous at night. In t'morning, tha'll take my car and go find tha dad."

"Will you come with me?"

"No, love. It's been trouble enough keeping mesen safe here. I'll not be going out there again while Carabosse is free."

Ella reached over and squeezed her hand.

"I'll come back."

"Course tha will," said Rose. "I reckon tha owes me some fresh china and a new window an' all."

There was gooseberry and apple pie for pudding and then, as tiredness came over her like an avalanche, she said her goodnights and made her way upstairs. Tripping out of her clothes in the guest bedroom, Ella saw there was still one item in her mum's box of memories. It was the cylindrical bundle wrapped in yellowed newspaper. It was a jam jar and, inside it, glowering with livid fury and glowing with a vivid green light was a misshapen figure, all fatty folds, teeth and scabs.

"So that's what a boggle looks like," said Ella.

The boggle threw rude gestures at her.

"Zxxxkrt! Zhveee! Skrbble! Release! Jaaaql! Free!" it squeaked.

"You bit my mum," said Ella.

The boggle laughed and threw further rude gestures at her, some of them quite creative.

"Zaarb! Jkreeet! Kill! Squaxl-squaxl! Whore!"

Ella put the glowing jar on the bedside cabinet and used it as a nightlight as she climbed into bed and went to sleep listening to her mum's voice.

"- path. Rule number twenty, if you are given a rule, follow it. Rule number twenty-one, never trust a man with an axe. Rule number twenty-two, never trust gingerbread..."

7

T here is an old fairy tale regarding the nature of time and of infinity which ponders the length of time it would take a bird to grind down a mountain by sharpening its beak upon it. Ella woke in the morning to discover that it took two determined (possibly even demented) bluebirds a single night to peck and scrape their way through a bedroom window. Ella sat up as a large chink of glass fell down and the first bluebird pushed through.

"Oh, no you don't," she said and leapt up.

The bluebird flew straight for the bedroom door and Ella slammed it a millisecond after it had passed through.

"Intruders!" she yelled.

The other bluebird had now pushed through. She grabbed the nearest thing to hand, the Dictaphone, and swiped at it. The swift bird did a barrel roll to evade her, swooped along the bed head and tipped the boggle jar off the cabinet.

Ella roared in frustration as with a smash, a pop and a "Xlor! Jizzimus! Hurrah!" the boggle was free. The ankle-high sprite gave an evil chuckle and then bounced like a rubber ball from floor to ceiling and to the door. It swung on the handle, pulled the door open and, a second later, it and the bluebird were through.

"Granny!" shouted Ella, giving chase in her underwear.

Ella followed the twitters and thumps and the greasy smears the boggle left on the walls. She blundered through the kitchen door and found Rose fending off two birds and a slimy fairy with a frying pan.

"Modesty, Ella!" said Granny, seeing her state of undress.

"But..."

Rose gave Ella one of her patented *looks*. "But me no buts 'til tha's covered tha butt."

Ella grabbed her now dry clothes from the horse by the stove and, as she struggled into her trousers, Rose landed a direct hit on one of the bluebirds. With a satisfying and feather-splattered thunk the bird ricocheted off the fridge hard enough to bounce the door open.

However, Rose's victory was short-lived. The boggle had slipped under the heavy cast iron shoe last that was holding the twin-tub closed and was levering it away.

"Don't!" yelled Ella.

"Jaxl! Bot-bot! Knickers!" snorted the boggle and with astonishing strength, thrust the shoe last aside.

Rose leapt onto the twin-tub lid to hold it down as the angry occupants attempted to force their way out. The boggle, pleased with his wicked work, chortled. Ella scooped him up mid-chortle, threw him into the fridge and shut the door on him. She hurried to help her grandma but Rose waved her away and pointed to the hook by the back door.

"Take t'keys," she said. "And go! Warn tha dad."

Ella dithered for a second then complied. She grabbed the car keys off the hook, OCD's wedding seat plan off the side and, with the Dictaphone in her free hand and no shoes on her feet, ran out of the house. She ran round the borders, into the hen house and jumped into the driving seat of Granny Rose's Zastava Podvarak. She turned the ignition and was surprised to hear it catch first time. A couple of chickens on the back seat gave fright and flew out.

The car had three gears: 'И', 'б' and 'P'. Ella stuck it in 'И', hit the accelerator and, with straw spinning under the wheels, burst out onto the grassy track that passed for Granny Rose's driveway. The driveway led down to a pair of gates that were as rotten and overgrown as the fence. With a silent apology to her grandma for yet more damage, Ella kept the pedal down and rammed the gates. They flew apart, not so much smashed as mulched.

Ella looked in the rearview mirror as Rushy Glen receded from view. She spotted a blur of colour in the wing mirror. Specifically, it was a bobbing red hat, with Psycho the dwarf underneath it. The other dwarfs were behind Psycho. Six hats sped purposefully towards her, although it appeared Shitfaced had already fallen over.

Ella hurriedly tried to change up gear. Glancing over her shoulder, she saw Windy gain an extra turn of speed while Inappropriate, who was behind him, reeled with horror at the after-effects of his flatulent turbo boost. Windy had his hands on the car's bumper when Ella finally managed to push the gear stick into 'б' and accelerated ahead with a screech. Ella heard voices under the throaty roar of the car's engine.

"Don't forget, *Mirror-Signal-Manoeuvre!*" shouted OCD.

Windy held on to the bumper for as long as he was able, trumpeting in defiance as Ella sped off.

Ella accelerated to a bone-shaking thirty miles an hour and Windy fell away, the brown-topped bundle rolling and bouncing in the dust.

Only then did Ella allow herself a sigh of relief.

A hen jumped from the back of the car onto the head rest of the passenger seat.

"Well, I declare, madam," said the hen, "that was jolly dramatic, what."

Ella gave a little shriek.

"You can talk!"

"Indeed, I can. Indeed, I can. Of course, a clever hen knows better than to open her mouth in Mrs Thorn's company, what."

Ella nodded then wound down the window and heaved the chicken out.

"Rule number three," she recited. "If animals talk to you, don't reply."

Granny Rose's car was showroom-ready. Unfortunately, the showroom in question had been behind the iron curtain and devoted to the egalitarian creed that everyone deserved an equally shitty car. The bodywork had probably only survived this long because Grandma stored the car in her chicken shed. The ammonia stench of chicken manure fought a brave battle for Ella's attention, but it never really stood a chance against the mechanical terrors of the car itself.

There was a perfectly alarming hole in the floor, just ahead of Ella's feet. (Had a hungry fox burrowed in through the floor?) It was disconcerting to see the ground rushing beneath her as she turned off the dirt track and onto a narrow road paved with gravel. Ella could have ignored the hole and kept her eyes resolutely on the road ahead, but something was lodged under the pedal. (Perhaps the fox had a taste for talking chicken?) The clutch was stuck. Ella would need to pull up on the pedal to release it, which meant either taking her eyes off the road or groping blindly toward the finger-devouring blur she had been struggling to ignore. In time, she decided to give up on the clutch and change between the three unknowable gears without it. But the technique of listening to the engine revs to decide when to change gear was ruined by noise from the broken radio. It was stuck between stations, and Ella hadn't yet found a way to turn it either down or off.

"Police are investigating — *kxzzz!* — apparent disappearance of Princess Sofia of Holland — *kxzzz!* — family from their home in County Durham — *kxzzz!* — a family celebration. Eyewitnesses say — *kxzzz!* — were last seen on the dancefloor before —"

Ella bashed the radio with the palm of her hand until it stopped. The silence gave her a chance to compile a verbal list of her priorities.

"One. Tell dad something — the truth, something a bit like the truth — and stop the wedding."

She turned left onto an actual road, a narrow lane of genuine if poorly maintained tarmac. She pushed the tiny engine to its top speed, which seemed to be something around fifty miles an hour, but felt like so much more with the bone-jarring ride.

"Two," she said. "Find mum. Find her, revive her, rescue her. Whatever."

The road was edged with an endless car-high vista of green hedgerows but she passed signposts for villages with names like Little Burnley and Much Darkling. They meant nothing to her. Trekking across country with the wolf had been a disorientating experience, and she suspected that the normal spatial arrangement of the countryside had also been tampered with.

"Three," she said. "Find that fairy godmother of mine and kick her in the tinkerbells."

She slowed to approach a junction and thought she might be in luck. There were street lights and a tree-shaded sign. She leaned forward to read the sign, but was immediately distracted by a large shape rising up from behind the hedge. She had time to register that it was a bed sheet, and she had time to recognise the two birds carrying it. She even had time to decipher their misspelled message as the banner wrapped around her windscreen.

Yur grans a mad ol wich

Unfortunately, she had no time at all to apply the car's feeble brakes before it tilted blindly into a ditch and flipped onto its roof. An informative warning light brightened the dashboard as the car slid slowly to a stop. "Цар је наопачке."

Ella squeezed out of the window into the scratchy claws of the hedge. It took her a few more minutes to extract herself and stumble onto the road. She looked around for those birds, but all she could hear was a distant tweeting that sounded suspiciously like laughter.

"Bastards," she muttered. She took a long look at Granny's car. It was going nowhere. It seemed to be in one piece, but that piece was wedged firmly into the hedge at an irretrievable angle.

Ella's options were limited. Her first point of interest was the road sign on the main road. Cirencester, Stow-on-the-Wold.

The Cotswolds then, she thought. Not local, but not the ends of the earth either. Now without transport, she looked up and down the road. There was no sign of any other vehicles, although she was wary that if anyone stopped it would undoubtedly turn out to be a busload of elves or a troll driving a taxi.

She stepped back to the hedge and climbed on top of the car, balancing on the side of the window to get a good look over the top of the hedge.

For a dizzying moment, she had the impression that she was much higher up, looking down on a house of doll-like proportions. She wobbled with the sudden sense of vertigo, but swiftly reappraised what she was looking at when she realised the house was indeed a miniature, no more than two feet high. There were more of them, tiny houses stretching out towards the hedge borders of a well-manicured formal garden.

"A model village."

Oddly, there was something wonderfully mundane about a model village. Model villages were the kind of Sunday afternoon tourist attraction that drew bored families, retired couples and the holidaying middle classes. A model village meant there'd be a car park full of practical estate cars and a café/gift shop where one could buy overpriced scones and bafflingly pointless fridge magnets. A model village meant middle England at its most tedious and glorious best.

"Almost home," she said and climbed carefully down from the hedge.

She looked at the first house, the one that had initially caught her eye. It was a knee-high cottage with a real thatched roof. Ella couldn't resist reaching out to run her fingers over it, wondering which thatcher (she knew several) had received this strange commission. It was familiar in a distant way, and Ella wondered if she'd seen a picture.

She moved on, following a path that ran between a diminutive pub and a farm, and continued from that miniature rural idyll to a more fanciful landscape with low-lying hummocks that might have been designed for hobbits or teletubbies. A turreted castle with a moat soared above a valley that housed cosy-looking caves. The path crossed over the valley on a small footbridge, and Ella couldn't help peering over the side to check whether ogres or dragons could be seen in the caves.

"Hello dearie."

Ella looked up, startled to see a young woman beaming at her from a few feet away. How had this woman appeared so silently, especially since every movement that she made was accompanied by a rustling sound? She was dressed in a fifties ball gown made of yellow silk, supported by numerous layers of petticoats. Her waist was cinched in with a contrasting belt that made Ella wince just looking at it. Her hair was piled into an elegant chignon and her face was made up in the style that Lily and Petunia often called *department store assistant.* When they said it, they were normally mocking someone who was trying too hard, but Ella associated the look with someone who took a great deal of care with their appearance. The woman affected a look of casual insouciance, but then tilted her foot to admire the glossy red shoes she was wearing and made small swivelling movements of her skirts (purely, it seemed, for the satisfaction of hearing them swish).

"Welcome to our fantasy kingdom," she said.

Ella sighed. Could this woman possibly be a normal human passer-by who just happened to be dressed like a Disney princess? Maybe she was a model village employee? Or maybe an unabashed fashion dress aficionado?

"Lovely dress," said Ella.

"Nineteen fifty-three," said the woman.

"Got yourself a bargain there," said Ella approvingly. "Did you get it on eBay or second hand shop?"

"Second of June, nineteen fifty-three," replied the woman with smiling lips of perfect cherry red.

"Pardon?"

"It was the pinnacle of style. I get all my best things from there. Fashion flattered women in the best way possible. Surely you must agree?"

"Oh. Right."

Ella could see the odds of this being an ordinary person diminishing rapidly. She was still holding out for the possibility that the woman was a delusional Lucille Ball cosplayer.

The young woman made a very obvious appraisal of Ella's tattered garments and raised her eyebrows in a pointed manner.

"I think something like this would suit you very well, dearie."

Dearie?

Ella realised she had heard the woman's voice before, on a Betamax video tape.

"You're Carabosse," she said coldly.

"Oh well done, dear."

Ella turned round to look for something to use as a weapon. There was nothing behind her but a small-scale windmill. With a passionate strength, she wrenched the roof off, sails and all, and swung it round intending to clout the fairy in the face. But, Carabosse's hand was already raised and the impromptu weapon smashed harmlessly apart in mid-air as though the fairy stood behind bulletproof glass.

Carabosse gave Ella a look of gentle rebuke.

"Ella, dear. The sooner you embrace your destiny, the sooner we can make sure that you get that happy ending that we all want for you."

Ella threw a punch. It stopped a hand's breadth from Carabosse's nose. It didn't hit anything. It didn't hurt. It just stopped.

"What have you done with my mum, you cow?"

"Me? Nothing. Why? Have you been listening to the ramblings of mad old ladies?" She clapped her hands together, beaming. "Now, dear. Let's get our priorities sorted out. If you'll just let me fix your clothes and hair, we can sit down and have a delightful girly chat about your Prince Charming."

"I don't have a Prince Charming!"

There was instantly a hand of playing cards in Carabosse's hand.

"No, we have a choice of several, don't we?" She grinned. "Oh, it's like that on-line dating thing, isn't it, except you've got your very own fairy godmother to help you make the correct choice." She suddenly frowned, plucked out a card and threw it away. It vanished in a shower of golden sparkles. "Lovely lad but not quite right." She fanned out the cards. "Shall we pick one? One, two, three, four, five guaranteed tickets to your very own happily ever after."

"I don't want a happily ever after!"

"Who doesn't want to be happy? Your dear grandmother has been so deluded about that point. I blame her for your mother's troubles, I really do."

"Don't you dare," said Ella, stung by the casually cruel references to her family. "If you hadn't stuck your nose in, I'd have my family with me now, instead of them hiding out in limbo."

"And there you go," smiled Carabosse. "That's your grandmother talking. Mistaking my offer of wisdom, support and guidance for interfering control. No one gets anywhere without a little help these days. It's not about what you know; it's about who you know. And you, my lucky dear, know a fairy godmother who is happy to help."

"I don't need your help."

"No, you don't," Carabosse agreed. "Without your grandmother's malign influence and your poor confused mother to cloud the waters for you, I can see that you've grown into a strong and confident young woman. And that's lovely. You don't need my help but you'd benefit from it. Top athletes need a coach. The greatest actors need a director. Think what I can do for you!"

"I don't want whatever it is you can do for me. I want my family back."

"Ah, so you *do* want a happy ending," said Carabosse, bent right into Ella's face with a smirk. "You'll have your own family soon. Strong sons, beautiful daughters. That's the family you need to focus on now, my dear. You're not getting any younger, you know."

Ella roared with frustration, forcibly uprooted a model church and brought it crashing down over Carabosse's perfectly coiffed bonce. It crumbled like Legos and cascaded to the floor, not a single piece actually touching the smug fairy.

Looking down at the rubble of the church's steeple, Carabosse nudged the painted clock face with the toe of her glossy red pump. "Ah sweetie, none of us like to be reminded of that biological clock do we?" she smiled, patting her hair. "But — tick-tock — I have something I need you to see."

She pulled Ella's arm into a tight lock with her own. Ella, reeling from the uselessness of her attack, could only comply.

Carabosse held her close and spoke in a conspiratorial whisper. "Allow yourself to think of it for a moment, Ella. A future that's guaranteed to hold happiness for you. Love and fulfilment without ever having to worry about it."

"But I want to worry about it!"

"You want to worry?"

"Nobody's life should be that easy. The journey's there to be savoured, with its ups and its downs. The most important thing is that it should be *mine*, not someone else's idea of what my journey ought to be."

"I don't believe you mean that," said Carabosse stiffly.

"I do."

"Oh, I believe you believe you mean that. But you don't. Not really." Carabosse ran her fingertips along the crenelated top of a castle wall as they passed. "You want ups and downs but you mean the ups and downs of 'will there be cake for tea?' or 'will it rain on the bank holiday weekend?' You don't actually want any major upsets."

"I want life. As it comes," said Ella.

Carabosse put a hand to Ella's belly. Ella tried to wriggle away but the fairy had her tight.

"What if I were to say you have tumours?" said the fairy. "Festering. Growing."

Ella blinked.

"I have cancer?"

"I said 'if'. I'm a fairy, not an oncologist. What if I were to tell you that your firstborn will one day find a medicine bottle and, thinking they are sweets, eat every last pill? What if I were to tell you that someone you care for dearly frequently thinks about just 'ending it all'?"

"Is this true?" said Ella. "Any of it?"

Carabosse patted Ella's arm.

"What do you care? You just want life as it comes. Now, where's the thing I need to show you. It's just round... ah."

The path curved around a grassy hummock to reveal a model tower, shaped like a lighthouse. It was built of stone, with a charming gothic window at the top.

"In there, Ella," said Carabosse.

"In there?"

Carabosse pointed at the tiny window. "I think you'll find it very interesting, dear."

Ella stooped to peer into the window, but the bright sunlight made it impossible to see what was inside.

"A little closer," said Carabosse.

Ella cupped her hands to keep the light away, and put her face right up to the window. "I can't see any—"

Just for an instant she thought she saw a tiny figure: a woman with a confused expression and bits of hedge sticking out of her hair. The woman looked up at Ella and shouted. Ella stepped away in fright. She was about to yell at Carabosse, then somehow she stepped backwards across a rough wooden floor. The window was still in front of her only now she was looking out rather than looking in.

A huge face appeared at the window. It had a cherry red smile. Ella could see every pore on the nose and thready little veins in the eyeballs.

"You bitch, let me out of here!" yelled Ella.

"Tsk," said her fairy godmother in a voice as loud as worlds. "Do you really think I'm going to give in to your tantrums, my dear? I've waited a long time to see this through, and if you think I'm about to let you ruin it with your naive ideas about *your journey* then you need to pull yourself together. You'll remain here for the time being while I organise things properly for you."

"Organise? Organise what?"

"There's a ball to attend. There's the carriage. The horses. Your wicked stepmother will inevitably try to stop you..."

Ella rushed to the window but Carabosse was nowhere to be seen. She peered from side to side, but the view was restricted to the path that she'd walked up and the treeline on the other side. She looked down. It was a long way. When she'd been on the outside, it had been something like three feet; but from in here, it was a bone-shattering drop. She wondered, briefly what would happen if she jumped out. Would she revert to her proper size and find herself sitting on the ground, unharmed? Would she stay tiny, but find that a squadron of bluebirds swooped down and rescued her? Or would she simply plummet to an unhappy ending. Probably not worth the risk of finding out. Not yet.

Ella turned her attention to the inside of the tower. It was circular, with bare stone walls and a wooden floor. There was no sign of a handy staircase, or even a doorway that might lead to one, but that came as no surprise. She knew this story. The dwarfs would probably call this the Tower Gambit or the Hair Gambit.

There was no door. However, there was a deep and comfy-looking brass bed, a huge clawfoot bath and a surprisingly modern kitchenette. There was also a spinning wheel and an embroidery frame.

"Everything a medieval maiden could ask for," she muttered.

It crossed Ella's mind that she might benefit from a soak in a bath, while she was assessing her options. She turned on the taps and then, as she picked up a towel, she heard a distant cheeping.

"Oh no. We're having none of that. If you blue-faced little seed-gobblers think you're going to slide into *helping with chores* and *holding up towels*, you've left it too late. I'm sure I could use the help, but if I'm honest, I just don't like you."

She ran to the window and slammed it shut. The tweeting turned into a malevolent hiss as she did so. She returned to the bath, inspected the products lined up along the sides and rapidly dismissed them all. They had names like *Irresistible Allure* and *Come Hither, My Prince*. If she could find a simple bar of soap she'd be happy. If she could find a loofah in the shape of a blue bird to clean the sweaty bits between her toes, she'd be even happier.

Once she was cleaner, and marginally less frustrated, Ella investigated further. There was a wardrobe full of clothes, so she dug in eagerly, keen to change out of the outfit she'd been wearing for at least thirty-six hours. She flicked past some jewel coloured ball gowns with puff sleeves, totally impractical, but she found only more ball gowns, increasingly gaudy and outlandish. There were some slightly lighter-weight dresses, made from pale cottons, but they featured corset lacing and plunging necklines — just the sort of thing that might be called for in a pantomime production of *Milkmaids Like it with Cream on Top*. She searched the room for a pair of scissors with which to modify some of the clothing to suit her needs, but was unable to find anything sharp enough to cut fabric.

Ella stomped back to the bath and washed her own clothes in the tub, draped them over the side to dry and then went over to the bed, which looked incredibly comfortable. She tested the mattress and slipped between the sheets naked. She'd catch up on her sleep and sort out some clothes in the morning.

AT THE BUMBLES, the sprawling Avenant family house, Roy Avenant snoozed in his leather armchair, in front of a muted television. The Cornbury Game Fair had taken it out of him. It had been a smashing day and it was a shame Ella hadn't been able to attend. Nonetheless, he, 'Prince' Jasper and 'Whirlybird' Wilbur had made an absolute occasion of it. They had made a good showing in the clay pigeon competition, thrashed a Land Rover round the 4x4 off-road course, sampled the cultural delights of the beer tent and then done something absolutely hilarious and *not at all dangerous* in the falconry display area. (Roy's fuzzled brain was vague on the details.) Then, Wilbur had gone off for a chat with some members of the local constabulary so Roy and Jasper had returned to the beer tent where, over a pint or four of something hoppy, Jasper had tried to explain how his uncle, the Duke of Westmoreland, and all his family had vanished the night before in what Jasper described as a 'conga-related accident'. Befuddled by such nonsense, Roy had called it a day and somehow wound up back at home with every intention of rounding off the evening with a meat pie, a bottle of something apple-ish and a little sleep.

Roy snoozed on, with an empty bottle in his lap and Buster lying at his feet, while strange little voices chatted in the shadows.

"Now this plan can only work if we are careful to make sure of two things," a precise little voice was saying. "Number one. Roy, our Prince Charming, must not see us at any time. Number two, we need to follow my plan to the letter. Are you all clear on your roles?"

There were mumbles of assent and a discreet, farty toot.

"Can we not just whack him on the bonce and kidnap him like the others?" said a gruff Black Country voice. "It's a solid approach. Never fails."

"Of course not," said the precise one. "There's no point in Disco rounding up the other ones unless we leave this one alone. Now, equipment at the ready."

"Lads?" came a voice. "This crossbow?"

"What is it?" said the precise one.

"I'm struggling to get it up. Can one of you help me?"

"You want a job doing, you might as well do it yourself," sighed a whiny and impatient voice.

There was a twang and then a thunk from the wooden beam

above Roy's head. He woozily wondered what the voices and sounds were. Either the apple-ish drink had caused some remarkable dreams or the television surround sound was far better than he recalled.

"And hoist, ya bastards," said the gruff voice.

"Ooh," said a suggestive voice as it rose up from behind Roy. "Bit thin on top for a Prince Charming, this one."

Roy felt something brush his forehead.

"Glasses away," said the suggestive one. "Now, pull me off, boys."

"You're on dog tail duty, Shitfaced," said the precise one. "One, two, three, tug."

Buster gave a sudden bark.

Automatically, Roy sat up.

"All right, lad. I'll take you for a walk in a short while," he mumbled.

He blinked drunkenly at the TV screen.

Roy's living room was the sort of man cave that Avenants had enjoyed for hundreds of years, with a fireplace, a set of decanters and comfortable chairs. Roy had added a sixty-inch plasma television as a concession to the modern world. However, to his bleary eyes, the plasma screen looked more like a large rectangle of cardboard with a hole cut in it.

Roy fumbled for his glasses but they weren't on his forehead. He grumbled and shifted and prepared to go back to sleep.

"Attention!" barked an ugly little fellow on the TV. (Was he standing on an upturned flowerpot?) "We interrupt the scheduled programme to bring you a bastard newsflash. There has been a spate — *What the fuck's a spate?*"

"It's a lot," hissed the precise voice, "stay in character!"

"There have been a *lot* of mysterious disappearances of garden centre staff."

"What?" Roy leaned forward and squinted. "Crikey O'Reilly!"

"All right, keep your hair on," said the gruff one, turning back to his script. "People are advised not to panic as those staff who are missing are said to be safe and well. Expect further details in the newspaper tomorrow — *What's all this shite?*"

"He's been drinking, he can't go now!" said the precise one.

"He'll miss all the boring bits of the journey if he's half-cut."

"Fine!" The gruff one rolled his eyes and finished the script. "This concludes the newsflash and you will now be returned to your regular programme."

"What?" said Roy again and yawned.

"We've got a few hours before we need to edit his morning newspaper," he heard the precise voice say as it trailed off into the distance. "Let's go and get the paints out."

8

When sunlight slanted through the window to wake her, it also brought the scraping and tapping of blue birds. Ella resolved to employ one of those ball gowns as a makeshift curtain. She shifted position but her head felt heavy with sleep. Unusually heavy. She raised herself slowly and found that her hair was trapped under her shoulders. Her hair hadn't been shoulder length when she went to bed.

"What the hell...?"

She pulled the covers aside and found that her entire body was twisted and tangled up in her hair, which was at least eight feet long by the look of it.

"Oh great, I'm a Wookie."

She stumbled out of bed and tried to stand upright. It took a while, and every movement tugged on the hair, causing pain on her scalp. When she had recovered the use of her arms and legs she pushed hair from her face and shuffled over to the full-length mirror.

It was barely possible to tell that a human was at the core of the mess in front of her. She looked like something cleared out of the plug hole in a giant's bathroom and shaped into a pile to dry.

"Scratch that. I'm Cousin Itt."

The scraping at the window was accompanied by a gleeful chirping sound, but Ella, gripped with a truly horrible thought, ignored it. She wove a hand through her matted tresses, aiming for her groin. Had this appalling hair growth spread to other areas?

"Pubes normal," she breathed with relief. "Probably not a fairy tale thing to have a handsome suitor climbing up your minge."

The cheeping turned to angry squawks.

"What? Am I spoiling the magic by being rude? Is there a No Swearing rule for ladies? Well it's all wank, do you hear me? It's not just wank, it's bastard bollocking cunting wank with... with nipple custard."

The birds squawked even louder.

Turning, Ella tripped on her hair.

"Oh, this is impossible," she said. "Knob-gobbling impossible," she added for the benefit of the birds.

Ella took a few moments to try and work out a system with her hair. It pulled down on her head in every direction, causing a dull ache. She was unable to separate or manage any part of it, and she grunted with pain and frustration. A renewed tapping at the window made her look over. The birds held up one of their messages on a chip wrapper.

Yo shud be mor ladylike

She opened her mouth to unleash another round of Tourette's for Amateurs, but realised that they had dropped their sign and were holding some objects. One held a hairbrush, and the other held a comb and a pair of scissors. She shuffled over to the window and opened it to let them in.

"Against my better judgement, you understand?"

The birds set to work, picking up beakfuls of hair and teasing out the tangles with the comb and cutting through the more truculent knots. Ella stood in the centre of the room and let them get on with it, slightly unhappy with the smugness of their tweeting. After an hour and a half, they had it brushed and braided. They'd also fetched Ella a dress from the wardrobe that she put on, rolling her eyes.

"Is this Disney Princess or buxom Bavarian wench?" she asked them but they ignored her sarcasm.

Nonetheless, a dress was better than standing there naked. Her hair was still as heavy as a sack of potatoes pulling at her scalp, but at least she could move around, taking armfuls of it with her as she went. It was growing so quickly that the top couple of feet was now unbraided, but that was fine because it was coming straight off as soon as she got hold of those scissors. She looked at the bird who was holding them and held out her hand. It gave her a questioning look.

"Scissors," she said.

It flew back a little.

She stepped towards it, dragging her monster thatch with her.

"I just need to trim a bit more."

It settled down on top of the wardrobe and gave her a look.

"You don't want me to get split ends, do you?" she asked. "No prince wants that."

The bird looked at her, tweeted something unmistakeably insolent, and then dropped the scissors on the top of the wardrobe. It whistled to get the attention of its companion and then they flew up and out the window, but not before the one on the wardrobe aimed a kick at the scissors and sent them clattering down the back of the monstrous oak edifice. The birds looped the loop as they twittered at their combined cleverness.

Ella hauled her hair over to the wardrobe. "I'm going to have weightlifter's arms by the end of this," she said, and felt round the back. The gap behind the wardrobe was tiny. She gave the wardrobe an experimental shove. It didn't give by a single millimetre. It was solidly built and felt as though it might even be bolted to the floor.

"Bollocks."

She hurried to the window to shout abuse at the birds but the words died in her throat. The view outside the window had changed. Yesterday, she had been shrunk and stuffed inside a model tower. Now...

Now, she suspected, the apparent one-hundred-foot drop had become quite real. The path running through the model village was gone as were the green verges beyond. Now, the tower was planted in the centre of a wide forest. (Another bloody forest!) There were open fields and the suggestion of villages in the distance.

"Bollocks," she said again, softly.

Stymied, Ella spent several minutes coiling her braided hair around her waist so that she could move around. She ended up almost as wide as she was tall, but it relieved some of the pressure on her scalp having the weight supported, so she was able to waddle about with relative ease.

She needed something to eat — no point starving out of spite — so she went to the kitchenette to check out the food. There were several boxes lined up in a cupboard, but on closer inspection their contents were eerily similar. *Mix for gingerbread* sat next to *Make your own classic teatime treats (gingerbread)* and *Cookie mix (ginger flavoured)*. Ella frowned.

"Rule twenty-two. Never trust gingerbread."

However, it looked as though she'd be having gingerbread for breakfast or starving. Ella put the oven on, made up some of the mixture and carefully arranged separate islands of mixture on a baking tray. She examined it from every angle to be sure that no two blobs of mixture were touching or could possibly end up in any way person-shaped.

"You're not tricking me, gingerbitch."

Satisfied, she put the tray in the oven and went back to consider the wardrobe and the vital scissors that rested behind it. She paced out the width and depth of the wardrobe, the distance from the bed (the second-heaviest thing in the room) added them together and concluded that her plan might work. She was momentarily distracted by a tiny sound, which might almost have been the sound of dough re-arranging itself in the oven. She narrowed her eyes but refused to be distracted. Heavy things. She cast around the room looking for the heaviest things and began to pile them on the bed. The spinning wheel and embroidery frame went on top along with everything out of the kitchen cupboards. Plates and jugs crashed into each other as the pile grew bigger. There was a tapping at the window.

Yor making a mes

Ella grinned.

"Just doing a little interior decorating," she told them. "Don't worry. I'm an expert."

It filled Ella with a perverse pleasure to know that her actions caused the birds' disapproval. The oven pinged, announcing that the gingerbread should be ready. She waddled across to the oven, wishing that it had a glass door so that she might see what was in there.

"Never trust gingerbread."

She opened the door a crack and peered inside. Nothing moved, there was just the delicious smell of fresh baking. Her biscuits lay perfectly still on the tray and looked very tempting indeed. She opened the door fully and pulled out the tray with a cloth and placed it on the side.

"Surprise! Skeep-beep de bop-bop!"

A bizarre figure bent upwards from the tray. Ella's biscuits had melded into the most humanoid combination that they could manage, but given their beginnings as defiantly lumpy blobs of dough, the end result looked something like a space hopper orgy. It moved with surprising agility for something whose limbs were basically rocks.

"No breakfast for me then," said Ella.

"Ooh and I'm so very, *very* tasty! Ski-bi dibby dib!" said the gingerbread creature, strutting along the counter like a bag of oranges falling down the stairs. "I bet you'd love to chase me, wouldn't you?"

"A bit tied up at the moment," said Ella, but then a thought crossed her mind. "I could chase you in a few minutes if you give me a hand with something first."

"Well, all right. As long as it's not a trick. Boop-ah-doo! You wouldn't take advantage, would you?" It bobbed, a coy, questioning look somehow conveyed in its stance.

"No, of course not," said Ella. She felt a pang of something like parental responsibility for this odd, camp creature. "We'll sort a couple of things out and then you can run free."

"And you will chase me?"

"Yes."

Ella got to work while the gingerbread creature jigged in anticipation and performed improvised scat singing. She unwound her hair from her waist and threaded it between the legs of the bed. She trailed it along to the wardrobe and threw a large coil onto the top. With some adjustments from the side, she got it where she wanted it, which was along the top, wedged in the small gap between the wardrobe and the wall. She then trailed the rest of it back to the bed and joined up with the other end, so that she now had a huge loop of hair that she could use to pull the wardrobe at its highest point. She really didn't want to take the strain on her scalp, so she twisted the two ends around the leg of the bed and trod firmly on the join before heaving on the loop with all of her might. There was no movement whatsoever in the wardrobe. She heaved again. There was the smallest sound of settling or shifting. She heaved again and again, in an attempt to rock the thing, and almost imperceptibly it started to move, thumping heavily on the floor.

"Can we do chasing yet?" asked the gingerbread creature with more than a hint of petulance. "Sham-pa dabba dam-pa-dah!"

"Just give me a minute, will you?" grunted Ella. She was getting somewhere at last. The wardrobe thudded the floor and banged the wall as it rocked. Ella ignored the angry bird sounds coming from the window and dragged harder. The wardrobe toppled and slammed to the floor with such a monstrous crash that Ella feared briefly that it might cause a complete collapse.

Moments later she went to find the scissors amidst the plaster dust. She plucked them out in triumph and wasted no time in giving herself a drastic haircut. She grabbed a handful at her shoulder and just cut and snipped, cut and snipped. Her gargantuan hair fell to the ground with an audible thump.

"Right then, my little gingerbread friend?"

"Boop-a-la-la doop-doop?"

"Let's climb down this rope of hair and do some chasing, shall we?"

The gingerbread creature jiggled and swung various spherical appendages with joy.

"You know what would be more fun than climbing down, Shoop-a-doo?" it squeaked.

"What?"

"Getta load of this skiddle-iddle! You tie that end to something and follow my lead."

"Okay."

It grabbed the end of the hair-rope and bounced to the window.

"Open up!" it commanded.

Ella finished knotting the rope to the bed and opened the window, not sure what it would do next. She didn't expect to see the gingerbread creature hurl itself straight to the ground, where it bounced and wobbled away, still holding the rope. It made its way across to a tree and climbed up. Quite how it climbed up, Ella would have been hard pressed to say, but it looked as though it involved blind optimism combined with an ability to fling its centre of gravity into any available crevice. About twelve feet from the ground it stopped and tied the rope securely to a branch. It tested the tautness with a brief tug and yelled up to Ella. "Chase meeeeee! Um-pum de pam-pam!"

Ella grabbed a coat hanger from the wardrobe carnage and fashioned it into a two-handled boomerang shape. She sat on the windowsill, popped it over the top of the hair rope and jumped off, sliding down towards the tree on her new zip wire. It was a relatively gentle ride, but it was made all the more interesting by the birds performing angry fly-bys. Even more interesting was the question of how she was going to stop. She didn't need to give it that much thought as the tree intervened. With prehistoric animal instinct, she released the coat hanger, hugged the tree and rode its rough and painful bark the few short feet to the ground.

She landed with a loud 'oof' and a bruised nose.

She was in the midst of a forest, the high and doorless tower behind her. But it seemed she hadn't quite left the model village behind. It was as though the world, tugged between reality and fancy, had schizophrenically given up on the struggle and settled on a mish-mash. For here was a model watermill by a tiny brook. And here was a moss-covered model church. And here...

"Wait a minute!"

One house made her gasp with its familiarity. It was a facsimile of the house that she lived in with her father in Nether-cum-Studley. It was so real that she could almost see someone moving around inside. She squinted. Yes! She could see Myra in there. Specifically, Myra was in Ella's room, wheeling a rack of clothes across the floor, in front of a huge mirror.

"She's really done it!"

"Chase me! Shoop papa-doo!"

"She's made my room into a dressing room. Great."

"Come on, chase me now!" demanded the gingerbread man. "You promised."

"Just a moment," said Ella, looking across at the other buildings. There was a castle, a huge thing, partially smothered with aggressive thorny bushes that came down, level by level, to the banks of a pond. Ella had seen that place before in a book her dad had shown her: Thornbeard House, the home of Mr Dainty. If she looked hard enough, could she see her father there? Yes! He sat alone in a room and looked utterly miserable.

"Dad!"

Of course, he couldn't hear her. This was just a vision, a trick of the magic. If only she could reach out and tell him everything she now knew. Ella felt a pang of anxiety for him; he looked positively morose. Cataloguing Dainty's valuables was still clearly proving a major headache.

"You need to chase me now! Skiddly bop-bop!"

Ella had never heard such an angry and petulant 'skiddly bop-bop!'

"Come on then," she sighed.

"Wheeee!" The creature ran gleefully through the forest of model buildings and Ella gave chase, not really sure what she was supposed to be doing, but keen to repay her obligation in the fastest way possible.

She ran past a house where an elf leaned carelessly out of a window.

"Got any shoes you want making?" he said. "Good rates." He didn't really sound as if his heart was in it.

Ella was genuinely surprised at the speed of the gingerbread thing, who kept looking back at her and whooping with joy.

"Run, run, as fast as you can, you can't catch me, I'm the gingerbread man! Shabba!"

Ella abruptly stopped running. That feeling was passing through her again. The peculiar but pleasurable shudder of rightness that meant she was playing straight into Carabosse's hands.

"No more. That's enough chasing now," she called.

"Aww!" The creature slumped visibly and wandered off down a side street, kicking a pebble as it went. "Poopy doo!"

Ella heard familiar voices ahead. They were coming from a relatively normal sized house of mud-caked stone that appeared to have a tree growing through it. Shitfaced was sitting on the roof of the house singing *The Good Ship Venus.*

From inside, she heard OCD talking.

"All I'm saying is that with us all working together we could straighten this town right out, instil some much-needed order. The cottage needs to move four feet to the left and the windmill, when we rebuild it, could do with coming across by about eight feet. I've made a plan. It's going to tidy things right up."

"Does your bastard plan involve Windy giving it a pebble dash finish?" asked Psycho. "Because it's a distinct possibility now that he's discovered he can make it go round with the power of flatulence."

"I suppose it's too much to ask that we do what we're supposed to be doing," said Passive Aggressive. "Namely, looking out for the girl?"

"I'm looking out, aren't I?" yelled Inappropriate. "She's nowhere to be seen. Only girl in sight is wearing a pretty dress and we all know our girl must have legs like a gorilla — why else would she dress like a man all the time?"

Ella took that as her cue to make a very brisk exit.

She hurried away down a different path, taking turnings at random. Her focus was on running away; where to could wait until later. She was therefore surprised when she passed through an archway in a wall to find herself standing beside a road. A real road: with white painted lines and cats' eyes and everything and not at all like the tracks and byways she'd endured of late.

As she was wondering if she might be able to hitch hike home there was a blast of car horn and a Jaguar convertible screeched to a halt in from of her. She peered. It was Roy Avenant behind the wheel. She'd always thought that his car, with its open top and its leather seats, was both vulgar and ridiculous, but right now it looked like a wonderful mirage, shimmering in the Cotswolds sunlight.

"What on earth are you doing here?" she asked.

"You know, that's a funny story," he said, standing up to talk over the windscreen. "We've all been terribly worried about you, just disappearing like that."

"Who's we?"

"Well me, mostly," said Roy. "Lily and Petunia are on some sort of starvation diet to get into their bridesmaid dresses. I found them both passed out in the plant pot section yesterday, but then one of the reps came round with samples of pork scratchings and they descended like a pair of crazed harrier hawks. Wonder he didn't lose a hand. They went and hid afterwards in the Wendy houses, sobbing with the shame of it. I'll never understand those two. So yes, I tried to find you, I tried to call you. I tried everything. Then I was just watching telly and suddenly I knew that I needed to come and rescue you."

"Rescue me. I see," said Ella, not seeing at all. "Do I need rescuing?"

"You might," he suggested.

His boyish hopefulness made her smile.

"I think I'd quite like to rescue myself actually, Roy. But I am glad to see you and I would be very grateful for a lift home."

"No problem." He stretched over to open the car door for her.

"I must say, that's a very pretty dress you're wearing," he said as she struggled to get all her skirts inside.

Roy spun the car around in the road with unnecessary speed and powered northward.

"Have you got a phone with you?" Ella asked.

"What?" he shouted back over the roar of the wind.

"A phone! Mine's dead!"

"Sure."

Ella dialled her father's number. It was unobtainable. She rang his house instead, but that went to voicemail.

"Dad, it's Ella. Um, first thing, I'm all right. Don't know if you've been worrying. If you have then... don't. If you haven't then don't start. But the thing is..." She paused to marshal her thoughts but there was no making sense or order of what she need to say. "Thing is, I think that mum might still be alive. My mum. Natalie. Um, yes. Well, we need to check this out, so you might want to delay the wedding. Ring me when you get this."

Roy looked across at her as she ended the call. "Want to talk about it?" he asked.

"Not really. I'm not sure I really understand what's going on if I'm honest."

"It sounds unusual," said Roy diplomatically.

Ella sighed deeply and looked at the road ahead of them.

"So tell me how you knew where to come and find me?"

"It was in the paper," he said.

"In the paper, huh? Don't throw it away. I might want to see that."

Roy nodded and then pointed ahead. "Look. Someone's dumped a horrible old car in a hedgerow. How irresponsible."

"Terrible," Ella agreed.

. . .

ROY DROPPED Ella at the family home in Nether-cum-Studley. She was looking forward to a hot shower and being able to bolt the door against any fairy tale intrusions, but when she got inside, she found her future stepmother in the kitchen pacing the floor, a glass of fizz in one hand and the open bottle in the other.

"Is everything all right?" said Ella.

"Oh, well if it isn't Little Miss Wedding–Wrecker! What the hell are you wearing?"

"It's a dress."

"I can see that. Why are you wearing —" Myra stopped herself. "I heard your phone message. Have you actually gone insane?"

"No."

"Is this a prank?"

"No."

"Then, for pity's sake, what is going on?"

"Myra, I'm really sorry if you don't like the idea of postponing the wedding but —"

"But nothing!" Myra advanced across the floor, wagging her finger. "I don't know what's got into you."

"Nothing's got into me. It's just that some... new information has come to light."

"Are you perhaps jealous of the love and affection Gavin now lavishes on me?"

"I'm not jeal—"

"We have such passion!" Myra's voice cracked with emotion, and she sighed, her whole body deflating. "*Such* passion. I had treats lined up for him this week, this final week. Like an advent calendar with a special outfit or a, you know, *toy* behind every door, leading up to the main event."

"Riiight."

Myra's eyes closed. "Do you know how my body reacts when he touches me? Do you know how his caresses make me feel inside? When his hand slips between my —"

"Myra! Please! I understand that you miss him."

"But you want us to cancel the wedding?"

"Not cancel. Postpone."

Myra gave a sudden nod. "I understand."

"You do?"

Myra smiled. On the face of a woman so domineering and brittle, it was a disconcerting expression. She took down another glass from the cupboard and poured a glass of fizz.

"It's the seating plan, isn't it?" she said, offering the glass to Ella.

Ella took the glass. "Er... what?"

"You've not done it. You're ashamed. You're too proud to admit you need help. I understand. You can be honest with me. We're friends, aren't we? Cheers."

Myra raised her glass. Ella automatically did likewise but didn't drink. She looked at the glass. Visions of Myra talk to strange young men on the dance floor and the dwarfs' dire warnings flitted unhelpfully through her mind. The fizz of the yellow drink. Was that bubbles? Or was that a dissolving poison?

"I've got a seating plan," she said.

"It's not ticked off on the group to-do list," said Myra.

Ella rummaged around in her corseted cleavage and whipped out OCD's plan.

"Look! I've got the plan. Here." She smoothed it out on the kitchen table. "I've done it. See? I want you to be happy, I do."

Myra gave her a shrewd look. "Has he put you up to this?"

"Who?"

"Gavin. He is spending too much time with that crime lord in his castle. You would never think he's about to get married."

"Crime lord? Dainty?" asked Ella. "Dad's still at Thornbeard House?"

"Where else?"

"Yes," said Ella. "I thought I saw him there."

"You've seen him?"

"I saw a castle…" She shook her head. "I've not been able to get hold of him."

"Well, I'm glad to hear he's ignoring you as well. I was beginning to think that he'd just got cold feet about the wedding, but I'm sure he wouldn't ignore his precious daughter on purpose."

Ella tried to let Myra's vicious rant wash over her, but that last barb proved too much.

"Myra, I'm not trying to come between you. I know you're starting… planning to start a life together. And I know you'd much rather I wasn't here. I know you want my bedroom as a dressing room."

"Well yes, it's hardly appropriate for you to still be living with your father at your age. What do you want from life, hmmm? You know you live for other people at the moment, don't you? You should stand on your own two feet." Myra's expression softened slightly. "Listen, I know that probably sounds harsh, so I've sorted something out for you. How would you feel about moving in with Petunia? You girls have so much in common! I can tell you that Petunia's thrilled at the idea, she's talked non-stop about all the girly things you two could do together."

Ella's horror was so complete that she was unable to form words. The idea of being thrown out of her childhood home and sent to live with someone who signed a petition to protect coral because it was her favourite shade of lipstick was so completely abhorrent that she was struck dumb.

Myra mistook Ella's silence for submission. Myra patted her on the arm.

"I can understand that this isn't easy for you. Take comfort in the fact that we only want what's best for you. Drink up."

Ella twiddled her glass stem. "I'm not sure I'm in the mood for drink."

"Oh, but this is the good stuff, dear. Your dad wouldn't be half as discerning. But then he has had some last-minute nerves. Who wouldn't? Marriage is such a life-changing undertaking."

"It's just words and a piece of paper," said Ella.

Myra humphed. "In that case, he has nothing to worry about. He can't hide out at that crime lord's castle forever. He will come back soon enough."

Ella sighed. "Myra. Mr Dainty isn't a crime lord."

"Of course he is. You only need to hear his voice on the phone. He's some dodgy-dealing foreign type. I'm sure he's a perfect beast. How else does someone with an Eastern European accent end up owning a castle in England, eh? Mr Dainty, huh? Clearly a false name. Now, drink."

Something clicked in Ella's brain.

"Oh, crap."

She put the glass down, flipped the wedding plan over again and looked at OCD's scrawled note in the corner.

Mr D — wealthy with aristocratic lineage, Bloody Chamber Gambit? Red Rose Gambit? Mr D = perfect beast. Good "persuasion" potential - hold GH until needed

Mr D, a perfect beast. Hold GH until needed.

"Gavin Hannaford."

She now knew why her father wasn't answering calls. She also knew that it wasn't an option for her to lock the door against the fairy tale onslaught. She had to get out there and fight it to get her dad back. She grabbed a bag and flung some clothes into it, trotted downstairs and called over her shoulder as she went out to her car.

"I'm going out, Myra, and I'm taking the car."

"But your drink..."

"Can wait."

"And you're going out in that dress?"

"If I must," she said defiantly. "I'm off to Thornbeard House."

9

Ella flung her bag into the back of her own car — her clean, green, nearly carbon-neutral machine — and set off with more determination than planning towards Thornbeard House. She didn't have much of an idea where it was but her dad had said it was on the south Devon coast and that gave her at least three hours of motorway driving time to contemplate a fuller plan.

As she drove, she tried to audit her feelings, hoping to deduce whether this course of action was complying with Carabosse's fairy tale trickery or fighting it. Certainly, Ella's fairy godmother would have wanted Ella to be at her dad's wedding to either dance with her Prince Charming, or engage in a life or death tussle with her 'wicked' stepmother, both of which seemed good enough reason to stay away. However, it was clear that Thornbeard House was the potential backdrop to other narrative gambits. Maybe it didn't matter which way she ran; she would always be running towards her fate.

But surely, she thought, an obvious sign that she was on the path Carabosse had laid for would be the appearance of the dwarfs or the bluebirds to shepherd her towards her destiny. And the fact that the bluebirds did not appear at every critical junction on her journey was therefore somewhat heartening, although motorway speeds were probably too challenging for birds, even annoyingly chirpy Disneyfied bluebirds.

Nonetheless, she entertained herself en route by imagining what their tweetnav (which didn't take long to morph into twatnav) instructions would be.

"Turn left into the Red Rose Gambit because you're clearly too stupid to think for yourself," she squeaked. *"Carry straight on to the life of a simpering princess because you need a man to come and make your life complete."*

A short distance beyond Exeter, with no bluebirds to steer her, Ella was forced to pull in at a garage and seek help. She searched through the road atlases in the garage shop but, finding no evidence of Thornbeard House anywhere along the south coast, had to ask the attendant behind the counter. The attendant had clearly run out of fucks to give long, long ago — particularly when it came to lost women in ridiculous dresses.

"Do you know where it is?" she asked.

"What?" said the attendant, her eyes fixed firmly on the silent TV at the end of the counter.

"Thornbeard House," said Ella.

"Have you seen this?" the attendant nodded at the news channel. "The Prince of Wales, the Duke of Cornwall and the Duke of Rothsay have all disappeared in a mysterious dancing incident."

"All of three of them?"

"And their families."

"Fascinating. Now, can you help me?"

"Help you what?"

"Find Thornbeard House!"

The attendant finally shifted her attention to Ella.

"You off to a wedding or summat?" she said.

"Yes," Ella lied, swished her dress as evidence and then did her best impression of a distraught woman about to lose it big style. The attendant chose the course of least resistance and googled it on her phone.

"Never heard of it," said the attendant, "but this website says it's near Staunton Tracey," and then proceeded to give Ella directions.

Ella drove on, slowly now as she entered the narrow deep lanes of south Devon. She was forced to stop and ask for directions again at the White Hart pub in Staunton Tracey and then, with evening approaching, she continued south and, a mile later, found the driveway turning as described.

The drive took her over a bone shaking cattle grid then climbed steeply up a coastal track. On the one side, gorse bushes growing above the road scratched the side of her car, and on the other side the world dropped away down to a rocky shoreline. Ella hoped that she didn't meet another vehicle coming down, even a child's bicycle. The drive ended at a set of tall iron gates and she pulled up, wondering how to get someone's attention. She stepped out and went to the gate. It was locked although without padlock or chain on the gate. There was a small lodge house beyond the gate and she called out but had no answer.

The gates swung open, although there was nobody in sight. Ella returned to her car, drove through and, after following the winding thread of driveway for a considerable distance, past near-fallen trees and through muddy gullies, parked the car in front of Thornbeard House. She stared at the building in front of her. The word house was a misnomer. This was to most houses what a rainforest was to a bonsai tree. To the north side, tall mullioned windows gazed down on the terrace and sweeping lawn. To the south, turrets and towers staggered in crazy stepped and ivy-bound layers towards the cliffs and the sea.

Between the two halves of the house, , the front door, which she could have comfortably got the car through, stood open. A servant in a waistcoat and striped morning trousers bowed deeply.

"Good evening, Miss Hannaford," he intoned.

He had a faint accent, not quite Eurovision, not quite Bond villain. His mournful basset hound face perfectly suited his butler attire, but the livid pink scar bisecting his left cheek and that accent (not quite Eurovision, not quite Bond villain) instantly re-categorised him as something much more sinister. Henchman, back street knife-fighter, mercenary. Or maybe he's just had a really unfortunate encounter with an angry rodent, she told herself. No point jumping to conclusions.

"We've been expecting you," said the butler with the cheek scar.

"Have you?"

"For some time," said Cheeky. "May I suggest that you took a wrong turn at Bovey Leys and should have stayed on the B road a mile longer, miss."

"Um. I've come to see my father."

"Naturally, miss."

"He's still here, is he?"

"If you will allow me to show you to your room."

"I wasn't planning on staying..."

"You're expected at dinner with Mr Dainty in thirty minutes."

"Right," she said, perplexed.

Your father will be present, naturally."

"Naturally," said Ella.

Cheeky ushered her inside.

"My bag," she said.

"Will be brought up," he said smoothly.

He accompanied her up a grand wooden staircase, which featured huge carved beasts standing on each post: griffins, dragons and other heraldic-looking things. They continued along several panelled corridors. They passed portraits, animal heads and small tables holding old vases. Similar sets of objects repeated over and over again. Eventually they came to her room. There was a fire in the grate, a large sheepskin rug, a four-poster bed and enough floor space to accommodate a light aircraft. Ella put her hand to one of the scagliola pillars beside the fireplace. She might be an eco-builder but she knew her classical interior design. This was either one of the finest Georgian bedrooms she had ever seen or it was a criminally perfect recreation of one.

"And you were expecting me?" she said.

"Dinner will be served at nine sharp," said Cheeky. "I'm sure you will want to freshen up."

"My bag," said Ella but the door was closed and the butler was gone.

Ella saw that there was a sheer satin dress laid out on top of the bedspread for her. For her. She rolled her eyes.

"Christ," she growled. "Why does everyone want to *dress* me? Do I look like Malibu Barbie?"

She could choose between her current heavy ball gown with multiple petticoats and full whalebone corsetry or the homely attire of a working-class girl who opted for the ever-practical option of using all available fabric on a full swishing skirt leaving only tiny scraps (and some artfully threaded string) to cover her breasts.

"I'm supposed to get my tits out for Mr Dainty, huh?" said Ella. "Well bugger that."

There was a brief scuffling sound in the darkest corner of the room. Ella grabbed a poker from the fireplace and went over to check for dwarfs, bluebirds or other intruders.

"I will smite the living billy-o out any magical git thinking of offering me fashion advice," she warned the room at large.

But she was only talking to herself. There was a Regency table on which stood, oddly, a round painted teapot and a rococo mantel clock. Ella peered into the teapot, checking for tea pixies or whatever but there was nothing.

"Right. Clothes," muttered Ella. Another table was covered in a large white tablecloth, so she removed that and checked its size. It would do.

She climbed out of her ball gown, fought her way out of it like a Houdini wannabe, shook the tablecloth open and held it to her back, like a giant bath towel. She pulled it round her body under her arms. Then came the clever bit. She kept hold of the corners but swapped hands, crossing the tablecloth across her front, then tied the corners at the back of her head and formed a halterneck.

She admired her tablecloth dress in the full-length mirror and grinned as she adjusted it. It wasn't bad. It was certainly more modest than either alternative on offer. She'd watched Lily and Petunia trying to make sarong dresses often enough that she knew the routine. There was a time when they had a promotional video, running on a loop in the garden centre, that showed a dextrous woman demonstrating the many ways that one could wear the sarongs that were on sale. Ella never could decide what was more tiresome, seeing the same video a hundred times a day, or having to witness Lily and Petunia wrapping themselves up like mummies in their attempts to imitate it.

A few minutes before nine o'clock, there was a knock at the door. It was Cheeky the butler. He looked at her improvised dress but said nothing.

"Dinner?" she prompted. "With my dad?"

"This way, miss," he said and she followed him out of the room.

THE SCALE of the dining table made her gasp in shock and quickly check her surroundings to be sure that she was still a full-sized human.

"Good evening," came a voice from the distance. Ella looked to her right and could just about make out the end of the table, where a huge figure sat.

"Do make yourself comfortable," directed the figure.

Ella saw that the only available chair was in front of her, in the middle of the table. She looked left, to the other end of the table, and saw someone hunched in a chair. Was that her father? She walked towards him. A discreet cough behind her made her turn and she saw Cheeky indicate the vacant chair with a meaningful nod.

Ella gave him her most pleasant 'fuck you' smile and continued to the end of the table.

Her heart both leapt and sank at the sight of her father. Gavin Hannaford, the fifty-something bon viveur she knew, casually incompetent dad and weekend alcoholic, had been replaced with a tired red-faced little man. The look on his face was that of a rabbit caught in the headlights, a rabbit that had just seen its own daughter behind the wheel.

"Dad," she said, reaching out for him.

He half rose, stopped and then, frozen, clutched her outstretched hand.

"Oh, Ella love, what are you doing here?"

"I came to find you. I have so much to tell you."

"You can't be here!" he hissed, giving her hand a squeeze.

"But I just arrived."

"You have to go."

"Why?" she asked.

"They're about to serve the soup."

"What the..."

A servant stepped towards her. "We are about to serve the soup, miss," he said. He had the same exotic accent as Cheeky and had a hook for a hand.

"Manners are very important to Mr Dainty," said her dad.

Ella considered the hook-handed man and her situation. She decided to ignore the possibility that all of the household staff were battle-scarred henchmen and instead chose to believe that Mr Dainty made a special effort to employ individuals who had suffered life-altering injuries. 'Help for Heroes' sounded better than 'hired henchmen'.

It took a full thirty seconds to walk back to her seat. The table could easily have seated a couple of hundred people. She saw more servants carrying food — there was one with a metal plate screwed to his forehead, another with an eyepatch — and realised that the table was so long that it required a series of different doors to service different parts of the table.

As she sat down, a bowl of soup was placed before her.

Ella wondered what level of etiquette this situation demanded. She didn't want to start eating before her dining companions, particularly if her dad lived in fear of Dainty's manners, but she could hardly see them, let alone tell whether they were wielding cutlery. Perhaps there would be some sort of verbal cue. She waited.

"Excellent soup!" boomed the figure to her right.

Ella's soup was whisked away. She reached after it with a spoon but it was gone.

A main course was set before her, delicate slices of something that might have been turkey. Ella's picked up her cutlery, determined not to miss out on this course.

"Miss Hannaford," boomed Mr Dainty. "I wonder if you would be kind enough to pass me the salt?"

Ella looked and sure enough, the salt was set before her, and ludicrously, there was none by Mr Dainty. She got up from her chair and carried it to him, which took longer than seemed reasonable. The man was tucking fiercely into his meal, stuffing folds of meat into his mouth. Ella set the salt down on the table, but before she could move away his hand came down on top of hers, so she was pinned in place.

She looked at him properly as he smiled at her. He was just a man, she thought, surprised. And then she followed that thought with, *what did you think he would be?* He was a man of perfectly normal size and yet there was a strange 'hugeness' about him, as though she was viewing him through a magnifying lens. There was a roundness about him, that couldn't decide if it was muscle or fat and, though he was clean-shaven, there was a nascent bristliness about him as though he could probably command an imperious moustache or patrician beard to spring forth at will. He oozed importance, significance and power.

It was the way that he held himself, she decided, as if he was the only thing in the room that might be worth looking at.

"Interesting dress," he observed. He had the same unplaceable, middle-European accent as the other men. "But your figure deserves better, you should know this."

"Should I?"

"I am an expert on the dressing of women, Ella Hannaford. There are whorehouses in my home country that have doubled their margins since they took my advice. This is good, hah?"

Ella couldn't believe that she was supposed to respond to this, but Dainty looked at her expectantly.

"Is that your business then?" she asked eventually.

"What, fashion or whorehouses?"

"Yes," she said.

"No, I do not mix business and pleasure." Dainty laughed loudly as though he had made the greatest joke ever and released Ella's arm. His face morphed from convivial host to a threat-laden scowl.

"My business interests are many, but I build my empire by being extremely well-informed. I miss nothing, do you hear what I am saying?"

Ella nodded.

"You are like your father," Dainty continued.

"Am I?"

"He has also taken liberties with my possessions, and I want them back."

Ella stared down the table to the shadow that was her dad.

"Possessions? What possessions?" she said.

"Antiques. Valuable antiques have gone missing since your father started his cataloguing work."

"That's not my dad's fault."

Mr Dainty patted his lips with a napkin.

"I can see how he thinks that perhaps I have so many things that he might decide to take items for himself."

"What items?"

"It is what we call opportunism, yes? You would know about this also, I think?"

"Sorry?"

"My tablecloth, Miss Hannaford. I would like it back please."

"Oh that! I wasn't planning to keep it. I was only borrowing it."

"Only borrowing it," he echoed. "Ha! You hear that, Gavin?" he called out, grinning widely. "Only borrowing it! You should have tried that one!" He looked at Ella. "I would like it back now, please."

Ella stared at him. "The tablecloth?"

"Yes, the tablecloth."

"Are you a bully, Mr Dainty?" she asked.

He shrugged. "I have been called many things. I think that perhaps some people who find themselves in a difficult situation will call me that and worse. In both business and life, it is important to remain impervious to insults from the desperate."

"I am not desperate Mr Dainty, but I don't have my own clothes, so I will wear your tablecloth until I find an alternative. I do not intend to steal from you, any more than my father does, so I'd be grateful if you'd let us both leave now."

He roared with laughter and slapped the table.

"Hey, the little girl has a backbone! This is something I did not expect! You may keep the tablecloth. Consider it my gift to you. Your father must remain here though, he has much work still to do, and there is the matter of my missing antiques."

Ella couldn't imagine leaving her poor, defeated dad one day longer with this dreadful man.

"You know," she said, "I am also an expert in antiques."

"A woman expert?" said Mr Dainty. "There are only two areas of expertise in which women excel."

"I can easily pick up my father's work," she continued. "It's even possible that with a fresh pair of eyes I can locate the misplaced items."

"You will find my Wedgwood teapot?"

"I'll get straight onto it."

Mr Dainty gave her a long appraising look, as though she were some prize beast he was thinking of buying.

"You must realise," said Mr Dainty, "that I have the means to make you both..." He waggled his fingers, heavy with rings. "Disappear?"

"Okay," she said.

"I tolerate your presence as long as you are useful or interesting to me."

"Good, that's settled then," she said. "Dad, you might as well get going when you've finished your —"

Ella turned to see that servants were carrying all of the plates away from the table and that, at the far end of the table, servants lifting her dad from his chair.

"Dad!"

She ran down to the other end of the table and only caught up with them as Hook and Cheeky physically escorted her dad from the room.

"What's going on?" he said.

"You're going home," she said.

"But my work..."

"I will finish it."

"What?"

He resisted then as Hook and Cheeky, each with an arm under his, carried him out the front door and down to a waiting car.

"I have to tell you something," she said, but it was hard to do so when the two manhandling manservants would not slow. "It's about the wedding."

"Is Myra angry with me?"

"No. Well, yes, probably. The thing is, mum —"

"Aww," he smiled. "That's nice."

"What?"

A chauffeur opened the rear door.

"I had hoped that my two girls would get on. That, one day, you would think of Myra as not your mum but a sort of new kind-of-mum-type person."

"No," said Ella and then had to pause as the servants, swiftly, politely but firmly inserted Gavin Hannaford into the rear seat. "I'm talking about mum."

The door was shut.

"Jesus!" she spat. "I've trying to have a conversation here."

But the servants said nothing and the chauffeur got in the car and, as Cheeky gently prevented her grabbing the door handle, the car pulled away into the night.

Ella snatched her arm out of Cheeky's grip.

"I didn't even get to properly say goodbye."

Cheeky gestured for her to return to the house. "I will escort you to your room."

"But I've not even eaten yet."

"I will have something sent up."

"Forget it!" she snapped and stomped inside.

In her room, she wedged a velvet chair (which would have been classified as a throne in a normal domestic setting) under the door handle, checked the windows were locked and climbed in the bed, which turned out to be very comfortable. She folded the tablecloth securely beneath her pillow so it couldn't disappear in the night.

On the cusp of sleep, she heard a faint scratching sound somewhere in the room. She couldn't have said why but she thought it sounded like scampering china.

ELLA WOKE REFRESHED.

A table by the window had been set out with a monstrous breakfast of meat, eggs, cheeses and bread. Her bag rested on an ottoman at the foot of her bed. The tablecloth had gone from beneath her pillow. The chair was no longer by the door but in its original place in the corner.

"Creepy fuckers," she said matter-of-factly before getting up and demolishing the breakfast.

She then dressed. The contents of her bag hadn't been magically transformed into impractical feminine attire and she relished the pleasure of being able to wear jeans and a t-shirt once more.

Cheeky was waiting in the corridor outside.

"Good morning, miss."

"Let's see about that, shall we?" she replied.

"You will no doubt wish to make a start."

"Start?"

Cheeky led her down to the first floor and a room that might have once served as a study but which was currently occupied by boxes, piles of forms and loose notes and shelves of ornamental knick-knacks and oddments, some wrapped in crepe paper. There were also (artfully hidden and not so artfully hidden) a number of wine bottles dotted around the room.

"My dad's work, huh?"

"I shall send lunch up at one," Cheeky told her.

"I'm not expected to sit at table with the lord of the manor?" she said.

"Mr Dainty is attending to business today. He will send for you if he needs you."

"Oh, will he?" said Ella but Cheeky was already walking away.

Ella settled in for the morning, sifting through the paperwork that her father had left behind. She had worked alongside him often enough to know the bare bones of the business (even if her assertion that she was an antiques expert was far from true). Her dad's catalogue work seemed thorough and organised, but there were piles of other things that defied categorisation.

"We'll work it out," she told herself.

She was on her own in this crumbling Gormenghast, and she had to survive long enough to form a plan and get out of here.

"One," she said. "Finish dad's work so I can get out of here. Or escape. Run away."

She looked out the window, across the lawns and onto the scrubby gorse bushes that stretched off into the distance. Escaping — with the sea on one side, wilderness on the other and a bunch of dangerous looking serving staff on the prowl — might prove difficult.

She returned to her dad's notes. The next item looked like a poem, with lots of crossings-out and alterations.

THERE'S no-one quite like Myra, she makes my life so sweet
When she puts on her kinky boots it makes me feel complete
There's no-one quite like Myra, with all her chains and whips

I like to go down on my knees and kiss her ruby lips

"Euw!" Ella turned the paper over quickly. "Two. Stop the wedding," she said emphatically.

She quickly sorted her father's detritus into four piles, namely work papers that made sense, work papers that didn't make sense, erotic poetry and bottles of wine.

"Three. Find Mum," she said. "And four. Find that bloody fairy and stick her wand where the sun don't shine."

A curious gurgling noise came from the corner of the room. It sounded like laughter being expressed through a china nozzle. Ella went across to look, but it was a very crowded corner. Her father had clearly been researching some of Mr Dainty's possessions, as there were several tables pushed against the wall, crowded with household goods, tasteless ornaments and reference books. She scrutinised each one in turn, looking for signs of life. She paused over a rococo clock, all gilded leaves and swirls.

"Weren't you in my bedroom last night?" she said.

Its face, somehow, seemed to be inexplicably looking at her. She mentally dared it to move but it did nothing. She put the clock down when she saw the teapot.

It was an ugly globular thing painted with brown swirls, as though it was wearing a badly knitted jumper. In a white oval on its side was a painting of Thornbeard House.

"You were definitely in my room," she said.

She picked it up, wondering if it might have *Wedgwood* helpfully marked on its bottom, but it wriggled out of her grasp before she could tilt it.

"Awright treacle, don't let's get too familiar eh?" It scuttled across the floor on its stubby tripod legs and hopped onto the desk, sending Gavin's paperwork in all directions. "Hows about a nice cuppa, hm?"

"Tea? No. Thank you," said Ella.

"What? Fink you mean yes, dontcha? If it's good enough fer the Great Earl of China, it's good enough fer you, darlin'."

"Great Earl of China?"

"Yeah. Pretty sure that was 'is name. You know 'im. Big tea drinker."

Ella was torn. If Granny Rose had been there, she would surely have wasted no time in bringing a heavy poker into play and silencing this teapot in the most final way possible. Ella had chosen to walk into this situation though, and wondered if she might learn something.

"I'll have a cup in a bit," she said. "Now, I bet you know your way round this castle really well, don't you?"

"Yer looking for the best tea drinkin' locations?"

"Um."

"Oh yes, I know all about them. There's a drawin' room as gets the sun in the mornin', lovely it is. Nice roof terrace a few floors up if the rain stays off. Fer evenin' sophistication, yer might want the velvet room, wiv its decanters to slip a little nightcap in —"

"Good, let's go and see those places," said Ella. "You can take me on a tour and I'll decide where to have a cup of tea."

"Right you are!" The teapot bustled over to the skirting board and pushed it, revealing a tiny door which led to a tiny staircase. "This way!"

"Whoa! I can't get through there!" said Ella.

"Yer what? You one o' them difficult types as likes to go the *long* way round?"

"Yes, that's me," said Ella.

The teapot wasn't equipped with a face, but Ella could tell it was rolling its eyes at her.

"C'mon then, doors it is."

They walked down the corridor. Ella was starting to realise that all of the corridors in the castle looked roughly the same.

They were badly lit and uncarpeted, with ridiculous tiny tables dotted at frequent intervals, so that even more antiques and nick-nacks could be accommodated.

The teapot walked happily ahead of her, whistling through its spout. It paused at one of the tables which held a set of highly glazed ceramics, including another teapot. With a swift flick of its tripod, the teapot upended the table, and sent the contents crashing to the floor. Ella looked at the shards of broken pottery.

"What did you do that for? Do you hate other teapots or something?" she asked.

"Gotta weed out the weak opposition, aintcha?" it replied and sauntered on.

They came to a staircase. Ella peered over the bannister, looking up and down. There were at least three floors lower down and maybe six higher up.

"I'm just going to have a look for my car," said Ella.

"Is it a brown one, with a sticker that says *This Car Runs on Compost*?"

"Yes!"

"I saw them towing that away. You're not getting out of here that easily."

They went up a flight of stairs to a floor where the ceilings were higher, and the rooms on a much larger scale. The teapot crossed to a doorway, and then without warning, sprang onto a nearby table and froze, with a brief hiss of warning to Ella.

Mr Dainty emerged from the doorway. "Aha, our young antiques expert is exploring the castle!" he said with a broad smile. "You have seen some of my valuable treasures already, yes?"

"I thought you were attending to business today. Elsewhere," said Ella.

"Maybe I am," said Mr Dainty. "Maybe I am doing that right now."

Ella nodded and peered through the doorway into a grand corridor lined with tall windows.

"You are lost," Mr Dainty stated. "My home is huge, yes."

"Yes, just getting my bearings. I see you have suits of armour. Fascinating."

Mr Dainty wheeled around and made an expansive gesture. "Oh yes, you must see. My armoury is fascinating. The suits of armour are for show, like a toy, yes? Come through here and see the more interesting items."

He led Ella into a room that held racks of firearms and swords on every wall. In a siege situation, Ella imagined you could crush an army just by dropping a ton of antique weaponry from a convenient vantage point.

"Here is a very primitive ancestor of a Gatling gun from my home country. I would very much like to fire it one day, but there is a high probability that it would explode in my face."

Ella regarded the unlikely looking weapon that was mounted upon a small table. It looked as though it was designed as a film prop, with a fat cluster of brass barrels and ornate patterns etched into the sides.

"So where is your home country?" she asked.

"Ach, it is a country that no longer exists, apart from in here." He thumped his chest. "And in here." He grabbed his crotch with solemn sincerity. "Here I will always carry the precious memory of those small things that define a nation. Our national dance for instance..." He hummed a brief atonal refrain. "*Dance, dance, for tomorrow our sons will die and you will walk no more.* It is very pretty song but a manly dance. It is very precious to me, you know?"

Ella nodded and moved amongst the exhibits. She moved quickly past some massive crossbows and some iron monstrosities bearing shackles that were clearly instruments of torture.

"Used for the birthing of babies in my former country," said Mr Dainty, running his hands over the framework.

Ella tried to picture how that might work but her mind shrank away from the image.

"Ah, now this is something that you should see." He stepped towards a corner, where a large pair of millstones were mounted horizontally, like a giant Victoria sponge cake. "Used for the disposal of enemies in times gone by. You will see the metal chute here, where you can load up the body, yes? You can put a person in head first or feet first, depending on how whimsical you are feeling." He laughed loudly at this. "Whimsical. I love this word. You know it?" He threw a huge lever, which made a large leather band quiver into life above their heads. It turned the upper wheel with a loud noise. "Powered by water from the stream outside. Efficient or what? The drain in the floor washes the remains into the same stream for simple disposal. You can raise and lower the grindstone to accommodate a crowd if you like." He slapped his thigh and roared with laughter. To Ella's relief he reversed the lever and the grindstone halted.

Ella was very nervous about approaching the awful machinery, but she stepped towards the drain in the floor. "The stains there look so fresh. Has it been...used?"

He paused for only a second.

"But of course! A building this size has a rodent problem."

"Big rats," she said quietly.

"Yes. And it is helpful to keep the machinery in good order."

"Nice. Well, you must be busy."

"Always."

"I'll just carry on taking a look round, shall I?"

"Very well," said Mr Dainty. "You may go anywhere you wish. There is one thing I must tell you first. Come with me."

He led her through the castle-like house.

"I'd like to know something," said Ella.

"For you, I will answer one question," he said.

"What have you done with my car?"

"Ah, it has been taken for a service at my expense. You will find I am a very generous host. I saw that one of the tyres was slightly worn and I take your safety very seriously."

They went up stairs, along corridors, down further stairs (which seemed quite unnecessary from a logical perspective), along numerous passages and came eventually to a room with a single window. Ella looked out and saw a dizzying drop down into the sea. Rough Atlantic waves pounded against the rocks on the shore.

"How high up are we?" she said.

Mr Dainty shrugged. "Here is the one place you are not permitted to go."

"Where?" Ella looked around the empty room.

"A secret doorway, built into the panelling," said Mr Dainty, indicating the wall. Ella couldn't see the doorway but she was prepared to believe that one was there.

"Why am I not permitted?" she asked.

"It is the south tower. Only I am allowed," he said.

"Okay," she said and then thought about. "So wait. You have pointed out a door that I wouldn't have found in a month of Sundays just to tell me that I mustn't go through it, is that correct?"

"Yes."

"Are you really *sure* you don't want me to go through it?"

"I am."

"You could have just not mentioned it, or locked it or something."

"It is indeed locked. However, because this is a matter of trust, I will tell you where the key is."

"Oh, I know this one," said Ella. "It's on a chain hung around your neck?"

"No."

"It's in your bedchamber, on a special hook?"

"No."

"It's at the bottom of a tank where you keep your pet piranhas?"

"No, Ella. It is on the keyring which is carried by my most faithful servant, Ernst. A safe place, as Ernst owes me his life."

"Ernst?" she said. "He's the one with the...?" She drew a line down her cheek.

"There is an interesting story that I might tell you one day," said Mr Dainty. "It involves a failed assassination attempt on the president of our homeland, a forty-day siege and a military coup. All hushed up, as with so many things from that unfortunate time. Very few details were leaked from our country, to protect the royal family, you see."

"You had a president *and* a royal family?"

"Hmm," said Mr Dainty with a dismissive wave of his hand. "An outsider would never understand the complex politics, the divide between North and South, the fluctuating nature of our economy. Some it has killed. Others it has made very, very wealthy."

Ella nodded, acknowledging that comprehension was indeed well beyond her powers.

"But I can see that you have much work to be doing."

"I do," she agreed.

He ushered Ella back to the study by a decidedly different route to the one by which that had come. As they went, he spoke more (and clarified less) regarding the wars and cultural divisions that had made, shaped and destroyed his country.

Nowhere along the route back or in the study did Ella spot a rare teapot with a penchant for mindless vandalism.

Lunch arrived at one on a silver platter, by which time Ella was engrossed in the paper trail her dad had created. Besides the cataloguing and evaluations, there were some attempts to map the layout of Thornbeard house, but rather than providing a cross reference for the location of the antiques it was more like a set of crazed TripAdvisor reviews.

NORTHERN BALLROOM. *Chandeliers are unpredictable.*
Don't leave breakables on the second floor, things get thrown downstairs.
Ebony room – teapot spotted!

IF THERE WERE errant teapots and other ambulatory furnishings then it was no surprise that Gavin Hannaford had failed to keep track of the household valuables and thereby aroused Mr Dainty's anger. However, she realised, Gavin's haphazard mapping did provide a rudimentary plan of the house. She cleared a table and began laying the notes and sketches out. If there was a way to escape easily and unnoticed then she would eagerly take advantage of it.

The lunch tray was removed and, some hours later, an evening meal was also brought to the study and, when Cheeky (also known as Ernst) had stealthily cleared that away, the sun was setting on her second night in Thornbeard House and Ella had a passable plan of the building about her. It was an insane, asymmetrical hodgepodge of a house. It was a maze. But, of course it was.

A labyrinthine castle. An imposing and dangerous foreign gentleman. Forbidden rooms. Talking ornaments. This was one fairy tale she had walked straight into without any help from her fairy godmother.

Tired and sore-eyed, Ella managed to find her way back to her own rooms. She stuck the velvet chair under the door handle again, not because she thought it made a difference but because she thought it a statement worth making. She undressed, climbed under the covers and turned on her mum's Dictaphone. She had listened to the tape in its entirety already but there was something comforting in the sound of her mum's voice.

"Rule eight, do not enter buildings or gardens that do not belong to you or you are forbidden to enter —"

"Like the forbidden south tower, you mean," Ella said, snuggling down.

"— breaking and entering is a crime. Rule nine, do not take anything that does not belong to you; theft is a crime also. Rule ten, many things do not want to be stolen and will try to stop you."

"That's right." The teapot jumped onto the bed beside her. "Anyone tries to 'alf-inch me and I'll give 'em such a scalding."

Ella huffed and sat up.

"I thought I'd left you downstairs," she said.

"An' leave you in your hour of need?" said the teapot.

"Hour of need?"

"You awake and unable to sleep. You know what you need?"

"Tea?"

The teapot gave a jolly jiggle.

"Be nice to 'ave a night cap, dontcha reckon? Cup of tea before you settle down? Hmmm?"

Ella rolled over with a groan and pulled the pillow over her head.

10

P oorly behaved furniture even invaded her dreams. In her sleep, she heard scuffling from the skirting board. And in her drifting mind, she heard snippets of conversation.

...order some furniture please, charge it to my credit card

...any kind of table. Anything you've got with four legs and a bit of love in its heart.

Ella woke to a Westminster chime which sounded unnervingly close. She opened her eyes and saw the rococo mantel clock on her pillow, looking pleased with itself. She wriggled to a sitting position and saw that the teapot was on the other side.

"'e don't say a lot, but 'e's got a beautiful singing voice, ain't 'e? Now, 'ow d'ya like yer cuppa?"

Ella looked to the breakfast that had been set out on the window table. The silver teapot had been knocked onto the floor and pounded flat.

She gave the Wedgwood teapot a reproachful look. "What's with the violence towards other teapots?"

"It's economics, ain't it?" declared the teapot.

"What do you mean?"

"Supply and demand, treacle. I'm valuable 'cos I'm rare. The fewer teapots there are, the more I'm worth, yeah?"

"I'm not sure it's that simple."

"Course it is. If I was the only teapot in the 'ole wide world then I'd be priceless and everyone would come to me for their cups of tea. Speaking of which..." The teapot jiggled its spout.

Would a Regency teapot be able to magically make fresh tea, or had it been stewing for a hundred years or more? It had to be worth a go, it wasn't every day that she got the offer of tea in bed.

"Milk, no sugar please," she said.

She wasn't sure how the cup and saucer came to be in her lap, but she sat still as the teapot wasted no time in pouring steaming liquid into it.

"And do you want to be the only teapot in the whole wide world?" she asked.

"You've gotta 'ave dreams, aintcha?"

She took a sip. "This is good."

"Only good?" said the teapot, crestfallen.

"I meant very good. Excellent in fact."

"That's awright then. So what are our plans for today then?" it enquired.

"*Our* plans? I don't know about you, but I've got some antiques to catalogue."

"Yeah right. Cos everyone that comes here tells the truth. You'll be looking fer treasure or the answer to a mystery, surely?"

"Maybe. But right now I have work to do."

"'ow's about I take you dahn the dungeon, eh?"

"What's down there?" asked Ella.

"Nuffin' really, but everyone always wants to see the dungeon."

"I have no desire to see Mr Dainty's dungeon," she said. "He still probably uses it."

Ella looked across at her bags and saw that her purse sat, unclasped, on the top.

"Has someone been in my purse?" she said.

The teapot said nothing.

LATER THAT MORNING, among the more comprehensible files her dad had left behind in the study, Ella discovered a detailed index of books in Mr Dainty's collection. There were hundreds of items, many of which she knew to be extraordinarily valuable: *An Olde Thrift newly revived* by R.C., *English Homes* by Tipping, *Birds of Britain* by J.J. Audubon. She scanned down the list, looking for anything that caught her interest. She wondered if there might be material about Thornbeard House, but couldn't find anything. As she slid her finger down the entries, she hesitated. Something tugged at her memory. She looked up the list to see what had made her pause. There. *Solomon Re-examined* by Makepeace Alexander.

"There's a library here," Ella said to the teapot.

"Course there is," said the teapot as it rummaged through a box looking for undamaged crockery to assault.

"Can you take me there?" she asked.

"Not the dungeon?" said the teapot.

"What is it with you and the dungeon?"

"I'm just saying..."

"Maybe later."

"Right-o. Library, a fortifying cuppa tea to keep us goin' then the dungeon."

The library turned out to be another celebration of antiques. Ella scanned the books on the shelves, and nearly everything appeared to be at least a hundred years old. The reference books in the workroom must be Gavin's own. The library contained accounts of battles, catalogues of flowers, books of household management and animal husbandry.

She looked at her father's notes and went quickly to the shelf that related to the Makepeace Alexander book. The system was a good one, and it took her only moments to establish that the book wasn't there. In fact there was a line in the dust that indicated it had been removed. Ella sighed in resignation.

"Aw, someone sounds like they're in need of a lovely cuppa!" said the tea pot. "Am I right?"

"I was hoping to find a book."

"Is it a book about tea?"

"No. It's about Solomon. King Solomon, I supposed. It's something my mum mentioned. And OCD too, actually. Something to do with a jar."

"Jar!" spat the teapot venomously. "Teapot wannabee you mean!"

Solomon Re-examined might have been missing but there were a number of volumes on fairies and fairy tales in the library. There were first editions of Lang's *Red, Blue* and *Green Fairy Books,* an incredibly old binding of the works of the Brothers Grimm and a nice imprint of WB Yeats' *Irish Fairy and Folk Tales* among others.

"A bit of bedtime reading," said Ella, gathering them into a pile.

"It's not bedtime yet," said the teapot. "It's off to the dungeon."

"Really?"

"After a nice cuppa tea!"

The teapot really did make excellent tea.

AFTER A REFRESHING BREW, Ella followed the hyperactive teapot down a staircase towards the dungeons. The very bottom of the staircase was bare stone, decorated in the traditional shades of sludge green and grey. It was extremely chilly. The dungeon smelled of mildew and was bare except for a set of four cells, which were all locked. Ella peered into them and failed to see anything. There was nothing down here.

"Everyone wants to see the dungeons, huh," she said.

"Wanta look inside one of the cells?" said the teapot.

"Is there anything to see?" said Ella.

"There's a table in that one."

Ella wobbled and gripped the wall for support.

"A table?" she said sarcastically. "I might just wet myself with excitement."

"It's a nice table," said the teapot. "Keys're on the rack up there."

There was indeed a rack on the wall at the bottom of the stairs which held large iron keys. She fetched the keys and tried each one in turn. Moments later she had the door open. She took the key out of the lock (she wasn't taking any chances) and stepped inside.

The short table was short, made of polished walnut with a veneer inlay and probably not worth a great deal. There was a narrow crescent window in the cell wall. Ella stood on tiptoes and looked out. She could see only sky.

The teapot burbled happily behind her. Something grasped her leg and she cried out with shock. She looked down and was startled to see that the small table was humping her leg like a randy beagle.

"Not one of your better ideas, Oscar mate," yelled the teapot, smacking the table with its tripod leg. "Soz about that, he's excited to be free, see."

The table released her leg and ran out of the cell door. It failed to stop in time and slammed into the opposite wall, gave a yelp and then scuttled around the corner out of sight.

"Friend of yours?" said Ella.

"Partner in crime," said the teapot. "We're like Batman and wossisname."

"Oh, yes?"

"I'm 'elping 'im in 'is personal quest for justice." There was a clattering sound from the stairs. "And 'es really good at breaking stuff."

The teapot gave an excited whoop and scuttled off after his table friend. Ella followed the sound of things breaking.

At one o'clock sharp, Cheeky was at the study door with a plate of sandwiches for Ella.

Ella put her finger on the page she was reading.

"Hey — Ernst, isn't it? — did you know that the fairies of European folklore are pretty much the same as the djinn in Arabian tales? Wish-granters who are controlled or who control others with words."

"Is that so, miss?"

"They're not part of this world but they're not one of God's creatures. They're just... *other*, part of a secondary world."

"Fascinating, miss. Mr Dainty would like you to join him for dinner this evening."

"Oh, okay."

"And he has provided some alternative clothing, which you will find in your room."

"Ah."

ELLA WAS PLEASANTLY surprised to discover that the clothes Mr Dainty had provided for her were of a style and fit she would have gladly chosen herself, albeit of a much higher quality. It was as though he had instructed his stealthy serving staff to neatly ransack her bag of clothes and made purchases accordingly. It was creepy, chauvinistic, domineering and controlling but it was nice nonetheless to climb into trousers and a jumper.

When Cheeky returned to take her to dinner, he led her to a different dining room, with a much more reasonably sized table. In the corner a record player played mournful string quartet music, its tones gliding up and down as though the record player couldn't decide what speed it should be played it.

Mr Dainty beamed at Ella as she entered.

"How delightful to see you. The clothes are pleasing to you, yes?"

"They're very nice, thank you."

"And your accommodation is most splendid, yes?"

"Very nice too," she said. "Actually, I wonder if I could make use of a telephone."

"A telephone?"

"Just to call my dad and let him know how well you are treating me. He is getting married in five days and I'm sure he'd like to hear from me."

Mr Dainty stroked his chin.

"Sadly, there are no telephones in the house. It is a very old building. And I am most afraid that there is no signal for cell phones out here."

"That is a shame," said Ella, displeased.

Mr Dainty indicated for Ella to sit.

"But I tell you what. I will ask one of my men to make a call to your father when they are next in town. They will pass on any messages you have."

Ella sat. Mr Dainty poured a glass of wine for her.

"This is an excellent red, from a vineyard that I own. I am an expert in all matters of food and drink. Try the *gritnicu*."

Ella politely picked at the starter in front of her. Spirals of something pink and rubbery sat on a bed of dark leaves. She tried one of the spirals and chewed it with increasing thoughtfulness.

"Pickled fat?" she asked.

Mr Dainty nodded encouragingly. "From the ram's belly. Food

is something that is taken very seriously in my home country. How would you like to taste a dish that has been famous in my family for at least twelve generations, hmmm?"

"Yes, that sounds very nice," said Ella.

"Hah! Very nice!" yelled Mr Dainty, thumping the table. "*Very nice.* The English gift for understatement. How I would love to hear you say that something is *fucking glorious*. You have the words in your language, but you are afraid to use them, yes?"

Ella gazed at him steadily. "We have plenty of words, it's true. It means that everyone can choose the ones that they like the best."

Mr Dainty thumped the table again. Ella noticed that no tableware was placed anywhere near his thumping hand.

"I love this girl! She knows her own mind. Let's get married, what do you say?"

Ella laughed, and then stopped as Mr Dainty's face registered no amusement.

"I'm sorry, but I can't marry you," she said.

"Why not?" he asked. "I'm great catch. I am rich and extremely cultured. You only have to see how many antiques I have, yes? You will want for nothing. Give me one good reason why you shouldn't marry me."

"I'm already engaged to another man," said Ella, in a desperate attempt to close the conversation down.

"Hah! I know this to be a lie," roared Mr Dainty. "You think I entertain house guests without knowing all about them? I know you are good friends with some guy who owns a garden centre, but seriously? He is not the man for you. Now, I have made my offer, and it simply remains to convince you that it is in your best interest. I will do this, believe me. I am man of passion. I know love."

He stood and crossed to the record player.

"This music," he said of the meanderingly dour string quartet.

"My man, Ernst, is playing the violin. And my chauffeur, Plev, is playing the cello."

"Is that so?"

"They were members of the People's Committee's National Orchestra. I saved them from the noose, yes, when the generals sent their tanks into the capital. We escaped through the sewers, myself, two men and two sheep."

"Sheep?" said Ella.

"My people revere the sheep. I love the sheep. The descendants of those two rescued sheep live now in my barn. They are queens among sheep and we are honoured to eat them on special occasions." He clicked his fingers and servants cleared the starters away. "You will try the *schleppie* and you too will love sheep as I do. Sheep-angels are so popular that an animated cartoon *Ovcá* was made in the nineteen eighties. It remains one of my country's most famous exports."

He lifted the needle on the record player and reverently placed another vinyl long player on the turntable. The record crackled and then, a reedy voice sang. Mr Dainty joined in, softly.

"*Dashuria ljubav, onaj me crvenim obrazima kuqe rukama punih plot.*" He quickly translated. "My love, the one with the red cheeks and hands full of yarn. I will take you to my barn and marry you. But your hands are so cold. *Një ću pranje gjatë ovce, bërë dati pitati, atit za ovce do ćemo.* Too long you have been doing your father's washing. I will ask dear Ovcá, sheep of my heart, to give his wool to me."

There was a tear now in Mr Dainty's eye and a catch in his voice as he translated.

"We will weave gloves of love with his yarn. Oh, Ovcá, Ovcá. Your wool warms my love's hands and my heart. *Vjenčanja ruke Ovcá. Mi dashurisë.* We will feast on your eyes at our wedding banquet. Ovcá, we love you."

There was a tearful sniff behind her and Ella turned to see Eyepatch and Hook dabbing at their eyes.

Cheeky came in with their dinners and placed them before the two diners with the solemnity of a priest at communion.

"Eat your *schleppie*," Mr Dainty told her. "Cherish the meat our sheep-angels have given us. Feel, in the marriage of potato and onion, the greatness of a country now lost. Taste the passion and know that I am capable of great acts of love."

Ella stuck her fork in the potato topping.

"This is shepherd's pie, isn't it?" she said.

ELLA WENT BACK to her room after Mr Dainty had made multiple promises to woo her in a way that would show her why English men were second rate lovers. As she walked along corridors, she again heard the distant sound of destruction and wondered if Mr Dainty would be quite so keen if he knew she had unleashed a very naughty table from his dungeon. Back in her room, she considered the situation and wedged the velvet chair under the door handle to keep the disruption at arm's length while she slept. As an afterthought, she unwedged the door, carried the rococo mantel clock outside to the corridor and went back inside to renew her barricade.

She woke in the morning to the clock chiming next to her head, and the chirpy tones of the teapot.

"Rise and shine! Time for a nice cuppa!"

There was the rumble of an engine outside, as of a lorry. Ella opened her window and leaned out slightly so that she could see the courtyard at the landward side of the house. There was indeed a huge lorry there, and a man closing the rear door, having just unloaded a great many tables onto the ground.

"Wait!" called Ella.

She ran from the room, sprinted down the corridors and took

the stairs two at a time, crashing through the door just in time to see the rear end of the truck disappearing through the courtyard gate.

"Now that's annoying."

She turned to the furniture that crowded the courtyard. There were mostly tables and chairs, smaller pieces piled on top of large ones. Sideboards and troughs for plants were in the minority, but were some of the most eye-wateringly horrible things that Ella had ever laid eyes on, all cracked vinyl, peeling laminate and rusty iron. A couple of aged tea trolleys completed the picture.

"These aren't antiques," said Ella. "I can't imagine Mr Dainty wanting stuff like this."

The teapot was close behind.

"Right, let's 'ave a bit of order! Oscar! These are your people."

Oscar the table bounded forward and moved amongst the newly arrived furniture. Ella couldn't hear any noise, but had the feeling that Oscar was murmuring small comments, and somehow appraising his new recruits. Moments later, there was movement. Hard to spot at first, but not only was the furniture starting to move, but it was organising itself. It moved position according to Oscar's instruction. Some of the pieces were immediately light on their feet, while others were a little bit slower to come to terms with their new abilities. One of the tea trolleys had a squeaky wheel that made a piercing *eep-eep* as it wove through the crowd.

"Has he just taught all this furniture how to move?" whispered Ella.

"Nah, it already knew, deep down. He just reminded it. He's telling it *how* to move. Lining it all up."

Sure enough, there were now orderly ranks of furniture, arranged by size. A nudge from Oscar and the small pieces at the front started to make their way up the steps into the castle, followed by the rest.

"What's going on?" Ella asked the teapot.

"I told you, treacle. Oscar's 'elping me weed out the competition. An' I'm 'elpin' in 'is quest for vengeance."

"By...?"

"Recruitin' a table army so 'e can get revenge on the one who killed 'is parents."

"Parents? How can a table have parents?"

But the teapot had vanished.

"Ella, good morning!" called Mr Dainty, across the courtyard. "Did I hear you talking to someone?"

"No, just myself," said Ella.

"I have been hearing many unusual noises," said Mr Dainty, "some of them sounded somewhat like *breakages* of vases and urns and wotnot. I like that word, 'wotnot'. Very English. I trust that you haven't damaged any of my precious possessions?"

"No," said Ella truthfully. "I've been very careful."

"That is good, very good. Feel free to put my vases to use, should you find yourself in possession of any flowers."

"Thank you," said Ella.

"But what are you doing out here? Exploring?"

"A little," she said.

"Perhaps, you thought to see my queens."

"Your...? Oh, the sheep."

Mr Dainty nodded deeply. "I piqued your interest, yes. Tell me, Ella, do you ride?"

"Sheep? No."

He bellowed with laughter.

"You are funny as well as clever, Ella. Rare qualities in a woman. Come with me."

A low door in the side of the courtyard led through narrow corridors that must have once been part of servants' quarters and out into a stable yard where tall, silky-coated horses looked at them over stable doors. A servant with ragged scars across his hairline paused in the sweeping of dung and straw and nodded servilely at Mr Dainty. Ella noted the pistol holstered beneath his tweed jacket. The place was like a retirement home for battle worn villains.

"Where are my queens, Uric?" asked Mr Dainty.

"In the upper field," Scarhead replied.

"Good." He looked at Ella. "Then we ride."

Ella had ridden before but that had only been a weekend's pony trekking in the Brecon Beacons. Controlling one of Mr Dainty's mares required more strength and skill than Ella had ever utilised before. She soon gave up on exerting her will over the beast and just settled for staying in the saddle and letting it follow Mr Dainty's even bigger mount.

They rode out along the coastline, up to where the wind-blasted fields of grass and gorse rose to a high promontory. Mr Dainty halted his horse at the prow of the promontory and, to Ella's relief, her horse stopped too.

Mr Dainty sat high in his saddle and made a great show of taking deep breaths of the sea air.

"It is good, isn't it?" he said.

"Oh, yes," Ella agreed.

"A man could be a good man in a place like this." He pointed into the fold of the land ahead. "See. See there."

Ella squinted and saw a dark thin man-blob and a dozen fluffy white sheep-blobs.

"They are perhaps the only good things in my life," said Mr Dainty. "White. Pure. Like the skin of children."

Ella's eyes were drawn to movement even further away among distant bushes. She couldn't be certain at all but an eerily insistent part of her brain told her that the object slipping furtively from gorse bush to gorse bush was a long grey wolf-blob.

"Are you a good person, Ella?" said Mr Dainty.

"Hmmm?" She pulled her attention away from the wolf-blob. "I try to be."

"But are you?" he asked.

"I suppose so."

He nodded.

"I am not a good person," he said. "I am a bad man. A beast."

"Oh, Mr Dainty, I'm sure that's not true."

"I am a beast but not a liar. I have a wicked soul and I do harm to others. You are my last hope, I think. And I will die if you reject me. I have been married before."

"Back in the old country?" said Ella.

He shrugged.

"Perhaps. I will seek your hand in marriage and, if you accept, there will be such feasting." He wheeled his horse about and looked at Thornbeard House. "You will be mistress of my house and want for nothing in all your life."

From this distance, Thornbeard House looked even more amorphous and organic, merging from land into sea, not belonging to either. At the seaward edge, the spikey gorse bushes seemed to rise up and take hold of the castle, as though they were the only thing that stopped the building falling into the waves. Poking out from this mass of stone and thorns, like a righteous finger, was the south tower. A light sparkled in the topmost window.

"And if I don't accept?" said Ella.

"It is an ancient house full of rooms where things — even the most precious things — can be lost forever." Mr Dainty's voice was not threatening; it was filled with sad resignation. "I am not a good person, Ella."

11

B ack at the stable yard, Ella silently handed the reins to Scarhead and, before Dainty had a chance to speak to her, went inside the house. She made her way quickly back to her room with every intention of barricading the door and then either punching some walls, planning a reckless escape plan or having a bit of a cathartic cry. She wasn't yet sure which.

Flowers were arrayed on every surface. There were cellophane-wrapped arrangements and buckets of single blooms. There were even some potted plants and some gaudy tufts of greenery poking out of a china teddy bear. It looked very much as if an entire florist's shop had been transplanted to her room.

This is what passed for a romantic gesture by Mr Dainty, she thought bitterly.

"Feel free to put my vases to use, should you find yourself in possession of any flowers," he had said.

"Oh, yes. I'm going to use them all right," she said, picked up a vase of flowers and hurled it against the wall.

"Yeah!" yelled the teapot and bounced on the bed.

Ella picked up another and dashed it onto the ground.

"Smash 'is face in!" yelled the teapot.

"I thought you only hated other teapots," said Ella.

"Death to all receptacles!" it said.

On the night stand, the tea cups trembled querulously.

"Of a certain size!" the teapot amended rapidly.

It scuttled rapidly over to the window (for a piece of pottery, it had quite a bit of bounce), nudged the catch and threw the windows wide.

"Go long!"

Ella did just that. Vase followed urn followed bucket followed pot followed stupid china teddy bear out into the evening. This last one produced a distant "Ow!" and Ella feared she had just murdered a magically animated ornament.

She went to the window and then took a rapid step back as the wolf hooked his claws over the sill and launched himself inside. He skidded across the floorboards, claws scrabbling for purchase. Ella heard a slamming sound from the skirting board and knew that the teapot had made a hasty exit.

Ella immediately went down on her knees beside him.

"Did I hit you?"

"Clearly, hurting wolves is a family hobby. But I'll take ballistic floristry over your granny's shotgun any day."

"She said she didn't shoot you."

"Nicked my ear," he said and angled his head to show her the tiniest indent in his ear. "But I'll live."

She scratched him on the top of his head.

"What are you doing here?"

"Came to see how you're getting on with the whole being in charge of your own destiny thing."

"But how did you find me?"

"I had a very informative lunch yesterday, although gingerbread does repeat on me."

"You ate my gingerbread man?"

"He enjoyed it. Those guys are all masochists. 'Chase me. Chase me.' Seriously, he kept up a running commentary while I was eating him." The wolf looked around. "Nice digs, sister. I have to say that it's a surprise to see you here. Your granny's managed years and years of ducking out of Carabosse's reach. You didn't even last a week."

Ella glared at him. "I came here under my own steam, so I could find my dad. I know what I'm getting into, thank you very much."

The wolf sniffed at the sheepskin rug, intrigued.

"What *are* you getting into exactly? Your dad's not here anymore."

"Let's say that I need to find a sensible way to leave this place, that's a given. In the meantime I am *fact finding* at the same time as avoiding being ensnared by the Red Rose Gambit."

"Red Rose Gambit?" mumbled the wolf as he chewed experimentally on the edge of the rug. "This place." He sniffed. "This is the Bloody Chamber Gambit."

"Bloody Chamber?"

"The name 'Bluebeard' mean anything to you, sister? Trust me, it's far worse."

"I don't think so," said Ella, who had been reading up on her fairy tales in the past few days. "I'm here because my father offended his host. That's the Red Rose Gambit."

"This host being a dark and mysterious foreigner?" asked the wolf.

"Well, yes."

"In fact, he's not just from a foreign country. He's a walking cliché of the dodgy foreigner. Bloody Chamber Gambit."

"But the house is full of magical furniture. Red Rose."

"And treasure," countered the wolf. "Lots and lots of treasure which he has presumably promised to you if you marry him. Bloody Chamber."

"He even described himself as a beast," argued Ella.

"And he's threatened you with violence if you betray him."

"But if I leave him, he will die. At least he said so. That's the Red Rose story."

"Fair enough," said the wolf. "And so he's not explicitly said, 'You are forbidden to enter so-and-so room and oh, by the way, here's the key'?"

"Well, there is the south tower," said Ella.

"Ha!" laughed the wolf. "So it's forbidden."

"It's so forbidden that the way there is practically lit up with neon signs. Maybe it is filled with the dismembered corpses of Mr Dainty's previous wives."

The wolf nodded sagely. "So, we need to go there."

"What? No we don't."

"Haven't you been paying attention? The roles are there to be played out. You can pretend you're going to avoid the south tower all you like, but you and I both know you'll end up there. Don't know why you don't just get it over with."

Ella shook her head.

"So what's he like then, the Dainty guy who owns this place? Woodsman type? Got an axe?"

"An axe," mused Ella. "I think an axe is possibly the only weapon I haven't seen in here, although he might have some in the armoury. Oh, and there are these servants who look as though they would be happier garrotting house guests than sweeping floors."

The wolf nodded. "Henchmen. I'd expect no less, no point messing with a classic. So why does this place have so much furniture?"

He finally gave up on the sheepskin rug.

"I'm starving," he said. "Haven't eaten in days."

"You just told me you ate a gingerbread man."

"I mean real food," said the wolf. "Meat."

"I could probably get a slice of something when Cheeky comes up with my dinner."

"A slice?" said the wolf. "I'm using to guzzling down pigs and swallowing goats whole."

"Then you might have to go and actually hunt for your dinner," she retorted. "Like a wolf."

"You know, princess, that's no way to treat a dear friend who's just dropped by," said the wolf and leapt up onto the window sill to leave. "Let me know when you're planning on visiting that forbidden tower."

"Do I need you to protect me?" said Ella.

"No, sister. I just enjoy a dismembered corpse as much as the next wolf."

THE WOLF LOITERED around the house for the next day or more and, like the teapot and the army of tables under Oscar's command, managed to avoid being spotted by Mr Dainty or any of his servants. Ella continued her father's work and, removing certain delinquent furnishings from the equation, realised that there was not much to be done. Mr Dainty had brought certain items with him when he acquired the place some ten years ago and bought more since, often at more than market price. However, most of the fixtures and fittings had belonged to the house for some decades and, once Ella had located the hand-written inventory taken by the previous owner, it was mostly a matter of ticking off what was still in situ and what had been removed by means magical or mundane.

She managed to get the teapot to assist in the stock-taking. As long as the items in question were not teapots or other viciously despised teapot-analogues then the energetic china pot was happy to go off, enumerate and report back.

While the teapot was away on such an errand, counting the

gilt-framed Romantic paintings in the north galleries, Ella found an entry in the older house records that gave her pause for thought. She went to the window. Oscar and his ragtag band of tables were doing drill formations on the rear lawns with Oscar capering around in front of them like a crazed general or maybe a hyperkinetic majorette.

"Eighteen!" declared the teapot, springing back into the room. "But that paintin' of the cart stuck in the river is rubbish and I wouldn't bother countin' that."

"Thank you," said Ella. "Would you come and look at this for me?"

The teapot vaulted onto the window ledge and turned its spout to the marching tables outside.

"Beautiful, ain't it? All them different tables, arranged around their glorious little leader. It's like that, wossname, the Lion King. Except, you know, with tables."

Ella put a finger on the inventory.

"Three nesting tables in the Sheraton style (walnut with inlay)," she read.

"Yep," said the teapot.

"What happened to the other two? Oscar's parents."

"I told you. They were murdered, weren't they?"

"Broken?"

"That's furniturist talk that is. Tables are people too, you know."

"I'm fairly sure they're tables. How did they die?"

"We don't know. They went missing, years an' years ago."

"So how do you know they were murdered?"

Without a word, the teapot disappeared into the skirting board and emerged again, moments later, nudging a broken table leg before it.

"We found Tony's leg on the beach up the coast," said the teapot. "Snapped clean off."

"I'm so sorry," said Ella.

There was a loud and inhuman roar somewhere within the house that drove Ella automatically to her feet.

"What on earth...?"

She hurried out along the corridor. There was shouting now, only a smattering of it in English. It was Mr Dainty and he was furious. Ella came to the top of the grand staircase. Dainty stood in the hall below, a rifle in his hand, bellowing instructions to his servants, several of whom were either armed or in the process of arming themselves. His wild, roving eyes caught sight of Ella.

"Are we being attacked?" she asked.

He approached her, up the stairs, gun in hand, wild and uncontained emotion on his face. His breath came in ragged gasps as though he were about to burst.

"My queen," he said. "All that is good and pure in my life."

Ella, confused, put a questioning hand to her chest.

"My sheep," he said. "A monster, a beast, has killed and taken one."

"Oh," she said and then, foolishly, "I thought something terrible had happened."

Mr Dainty closed the distance between them in an instant. He looked huger and more terrible than ever.

"This, this is a stain on my land, on my heart. One of my queens is dead. It is a sign."

"A sign?"

Ella suspected that he didn't mean that it was sign he needed stronger fences or more watchful shepherds or anything so ordinary.

"A darkness has come to Thornbeard, Ella. I can feel it," he said. A tear glistened in his eye.

Mr Dainty withdrew a handful of .303 rounds from his pocket and began feeding them into the rifle magazine.

"I had planned a ball for us this evening," he said. "There was to be fine food and wine, there was to be dancing and music. Ernst and Plev have been practising."

"That does sound lovely," Ella said diplomatically. "It would be nice as a sort of farewell thing. It is my dad's wedding tomorrow and I really must —"

"There will be a wedding," said Mr Dainty simply.

Ella groaned inwardly. "We've discussed this before, Mr Dainty."

Mr Dainty slapped the magazine into the rifle.

"There is a darkness here, Ella Hannaford. A stain on my heart. I cannot bear it much longer. I will go out and kill the beast that has offended me." He shouldered the rifle. "And then you and I will conclude our business."

He turned on his heel and marched down the stairs, bellowing orders at his men.

THE MOMENT the hunting party had left the house, Ella was back in her rooms and throwing her belongings into her bag.

"Tea up!" called the teapot, sauntering across the carpet.

"I'm leaving," said Ella.

The teapot paused, momentarily downcast.

"But packing's thirsty work, ain't it?"

Ella held out her hand for a cup. "A quick one."

"Nah, you can't rush quality tea."

Ella looked the teapot directly in the spout.

"The owner of this house is a psychotic loony. My mate, the wolf, has just eaten his favourite sheep. Said psychotic loony has gone out with a small army to kill the wolf, not that he'll be stupid enough to stay within ten miles of this place, and when the psycho returns, I'm either going to have to marry him or find myself dead, dismembered and stuffed in his forbidden closet. I am leaving before they get back."

"Oh. Well, I'm gonna miss you," said the teapot and jumped affectionately into her lap. "We 'ad good times, din't we?"

"I'm sure we did," said Ella. "You've certainly been the most upbeat and chipper person in this dour place."

"Chipped?" said the teapot. "I ain't got no chips."

Ella gripped the teapot suddenly.

"Oi!" said the teapot. "I know you're leaving but there's no need to get so physical."

"Staunton House," she said.

"What of it?"

Ella traced her finger over the painted script below the image of Thornbeard House on the side of the teapot.

"This place is Thornbeard House," she said.

"Is now," said the teapot. "Wasn't always."

"But it was when Mr Dainty bought it a few years back. Who changed it?"

The teapot struggled out of her grip.

"Let's get you that cuppa lovely tea before we get to all the questions."

A tea cup was magically in Ella's hand.

"The place changed name after it went to sleep," said the teapot. "What was that? Thirty something years ago."

"It went to sleep?"

"Sure it did. One day it was Staunton House and then that woman turned up. No patience at all, just like you. Tea's a drink to be savoured, not gulped. Sit still while I'm pouring, will yer? She loved a cuppa, didn't she? She told me that mine was the best she'd tasted. Lovely woman."

"What woman? And who changed the name?"

"No one. It just changed."

"That makes no sense."

"I did wonder about that. Is it called Thornbeard House cos there's like a beard of thorns growing over all of the south tower?

Seems obvious but then the word beard also means to sort of challenge or confront, dun't it? So is this a place where you've got to confront the thorns *or* is that someone called Thorn was confronted 'ere? Language is a funny thing. Oi, you're gonna spill it."

"I'm an idiot," she said.

"Only an idiot wastes good tea," agreed the teapot.

"This isn't the Red Rose Gambit or the Bloody Chamber Gambit. This is the Spinning Wheel Gambit."

"Yeah," said the teapot. "She did say she had an appointment wiv a spinning wheel. Most unfortunate business that. Now, take hold of your cup."

Ella took the cup and saucer and willed her hand to remain steady. "And is she still here?"

"Course she is! What did you think was in the south tower?"

"Oh, God. I feel faint."

"You know what's good for that, dontcha?" said the teapot. "Now drink up before you go dashin' off."

Ella slurped her tea as quickly as she could, while the teapot tutted with disapproval, then she made her way downstairs, her feet racing as fast as her thoughts.

She found Cheeky in the kitchen, rolling out pastry on the table. He raised his eyebrows at Ella.

"Miss."

"Ah, hello, Ernst" she said.

"Yes. How may I help you, Miss Hannaford?

"Well," said Ella. "The thing is, I need you to show me the way to the south tower."

He stopped rolling pastry and frowned. "Miss Hannaford, the south tower is strictly forbidden. Mr Dainty is very clear on this matter."

"Yes, he was. I definitely received and understood *that* message. Unfortunately I have forgotten the way there."

"And this is a problem?"

"Well yes, of course it's a problem," said Ella. "If I can't remember where it is, I might accidentally go there. Do you see my dilemma?"

Cheeky brushed flour from his hands. "So you wish to be reminded of the way so that you can avoid it?" he said slowly.

"Yes please."

He looked at her levelly for a long time and then said, "Come this way if you please, Miss Hannaford."

Ella dawdled as she followed Cheeky (she couldn't think of him as Ernst and feared it was only a matter of time before she called him Cheeky out loud). She had the man with the key and they were off to the forbidden south tower but that was as far as her current plan went. She hoped that if she played for time a brilliant stratagem would spring to mind.

"You have known Mr Dainty for a long time?" she said.

"Indeed, miss."

"He mentioned that the two of you were involved in an assassination attempt on your country's president?"

Cheeky gave her a sideways look but said nothing. They were passing through a dining room, and Ella thought she heard movement from one of the walls ahead.

A tiny voice was just audible.

"'e's bigger than I thought, 'e's bloomin' stuck! You push an' I'll pull."

Ella straightened and tried to gauge exactly where the voice was coming from. A dumb waiter plinked open halfway up the wall directly ahead of them.

What she really wasn't sure of was why a horribly deformed sheep's head was leering at them from the opening. Cheeky saw it and immediately made a complicated ritualistic signing across the front of his body.

"*Ovcá?*" he whispered.

He approached the sheep with tentative steps.

"*Ovcá, mi dhënë grije rukavice tij ruke svojom ne srce,*" said Cheeky, going down on two knees before his sheepy goddess.

And then, like a cork from a champagne bottle, the wolf, complete with the sheep carcase that he clearly wasn't ready to give up burst from the dumb waiter. The teapot and Oscar the orphaned table tumbled after him but Cheeky was oblivious to this as the wolf had knocked him clean off his feet and cracked his head on the edge of a sideboard.

"Right princess, where's this henchman you need help with?" asked the wolf.

"You're sitting on him," Ella said.

The teapot looked down and regarded the unconscious Cheeky. "Think we've got the situation under control here."

Ella unclipped the fat bunch of keys on Cheeky's belt.

"So we're off to this forbidden tower," said the wolf, as he took a bloody gobbet of flesh from the sheep's innards.

"My mum's there," said Ella and hurried onward.

The wolf abandoned his woolly prize to catch up with her. Oscar was maintaining pace, with the teapot riding the little table like a bareback circus rider.

"It's a good job then," said the wolf, "that I created that wonderful diversion to get the lord of the manor and his armed gorillas out of the castle."

Ella gave him a withering look.

"Don't pretend you were thinking with anything other than your stomach."

The south tower was a short distance away and the teapot corrected Ella when she made her one and only wrong turn.

"We just need to find the door," said Ella, tapping the wooden panelling.

She tapped, felt and peered at every panel, looking for a keyhole, but she couldn't see where the door was.

"Cuppa might be nice at this point," said the teapot. "You've been on yer feet for a good while now."

"I just need to get in there, then I'll have some tea," said Ella.

"Oh. Right you are," said the teapot, and disappeared into the skirting board. Moments later a door swung open towards them, and the teapot looked extremely pleased with itself as it stood in the opening. "Tea first!"

Ella regarded the keys and sighed. She took the tea and necked it in record time, then she hurried through the door and up the spiral staircase.

"Well, this is far from natural," she said as she squeezed through creepers and brambles that crowded the tower.

"Lots of old buildings are covered in ivy and stuff," said the wolf.

"Not on the *inside*."

The stairs came to a stop at a stout wooden door. Ella looked at the teapot in case it was going to circumvent this door too. The teapot gave an improbable pottery shrug so Ella cycled through the keys to find one that fit. Her hands were shaking.

The door unlocked with a loud thunk and swung open of its own accord. The room within was circular with a conical ceiling. The arrow-slit windows were crazed with cobwebs and mildew.

Ella was drawn to the raised stone dais in the centre of the room. A large patterned rug lay across it and, on top of that, a glass coffin. An actual coffin made of glass, held together with iron brackets and window lead. The glass coffin was, in sharp contrast to the rest of the room, pristine.

Ella looked down through the lid at the young woman sleeping inside. Ella felt a void of feeling open up inside her. It was as powerful as any positive emotion. She recognised the twenty-something woman from old photos and more recent videos. She knew who this woman was and yet...

"She's younger than me."

"That's the power of the spell that is," said the teapot.

Natalie Hannaford's chest rose and fell almost imperceptibly. The skin of her face and her crossed hands was as pale as dried bone.

"She was twenty-six years old," said Ella. "Barely an adult, really. Frozen."

"It's just cruel," said the wolf.

Ella nodded.

"Putting the meat behind the glass," he said. "Tantalising."

"That's my mum!"

"I know," said the wolf. "I'm just saying she looks tasty."

"That's still my mum!"

"What? It's a compliment."

Ella had no idea what to do next. She tried gently rapping on the glass.

"Mum. It's me, Ella." Nothing happened. She knocked again, louder. "Wake up!"

Again, no response. Ella ran her fingers around the lid but could find no handle, clasp, hinge or seam.

Her investigation was interrupted by a wooden clattering. Oscar had made an exciting discovery on the far side of the dais. Two tables — two familiar looking tables — stood beneath a window. They creaked and slowly came to life, struggling as though emerging from a deep, drugged sleep.

"Tony!" shouted the teapot. "Persephone!"

The largest table stumbled and tripped on its three legs and Oscar quickly inserted himself under the legless corner to offer Tony some support. There was a green cloth-bound book resting on Persephone. With a nod of thanks to the table, Ella picked it up. It was, she knew before she even saw the gold embossed title, a copy of *Solomon Re-examined*.

"Oh! I see!" said the teapot as though it had just concluded a lengthy conversation with the tables. "So, you were trapped in here when the girl pricked her finger? And because you couldn't get out the tiny windows you broke your own leg off and threw it out as a cry for help, like a message in a bottle?"

Ella flicked through the book, looking from the pages to her mum and then back again.

"We thought you'd been murdered. Trapezicide," the teapot told the furniture. "Oscar here swore to avenge your deaths. He's built himself an army an' everythin'. You'd be dead proud."

"So," said Ella, "my mum already had a copy of this book before she came here but it's also the same copy that's missing from the library. That doesn't make sense." She put her hands on the coffin. "And this is clearly the Glass Coffin Gambit. That's Snow White, right? But the Spinning Wheel Gambit is something completely different. I mean, is she meant to be dead like Snow White or asleep like Sleeping Beauty."

"You still don't get it, do you?" said the wolf.

"Get what?"

"This happy ending you're so keen on avoiding. It *doesn't care*. I told you it was like rainwater running off the hillside. When you tell Lord Euro-Villain you don't want to marry him, you block the happy ending off. It's like putting a dam in its way. But the water's still coming. It works its way round, princess. Your carriage breaks down, then you'll get a magic pumpkin carriage. Your dad dies and leaves you penniless, then your boot-wearing moggy will find you a new one. You prick your finger or eat poisoned apple, then a bloody prince will pop up out of nowhere and kiss it all better. It doesn't matter that it doesn't make sense. The world will bend and break and mash every possible story together until you get what you deserve."

"To hell with that," said Ella.

The edge of the rug fluttered briefly as though blown in a breeze.

"We're getting out of here." She put her hands on the coffin.

"The Glass Coffin Gambit probably needs love's true kiss or something but does that mean I have to take the coffin and everything? Surely I could smash it open or something?"

"What if it's the coffin that's keepin' her alive?" said the teapot.

"What?" said the wolf.

"You know, like Sigourney wossname in that Alien film."

"I'm at the highest point of a castle that's filled with stairs," said Ella. "My car's gone missing and I've got to get her and me far from here before Mr Dainty notices." Ella tried to lift one end of the glass coffin and was able to shift it by about an inch before she had to put it down again with a grunt. "Well one thing's for sure, I'm not putting it under my arm and carrying it out."

There was a small cough, and Ella turned to look at the teapot.

"What are you looking so smug about?"

The teapot stepped aside with a brief *ta-da*. The three nesting tables had arranged themselves into a line in front of the dais.

"They can carry it?"

"And we have a bajillion tables waiting to help downstairs."

Ella took one corner of the rug the coffin rested on and the wolf took another in his jaws and, together, they slid the carpet and coffin off the dais and onto the tables. The nesting tables were, by their very nature, different heights and Tony struggled on only three legs but the tables coped and, with much banging and rejigging, were able to get the coffin down to the lower floors and the secret door.

Tables were already waiting for them there, lined up to make a giant wooden centipede. With a buck of their table tops, Tony, Persephone and Oscar heaved the rug and coffin on the next table. It in turn, kicked up its rear legs and propelled the coffin further forward along the table-top conveyor belt.

"Hop on!" said the teapot, jumping onto the coffin.

"What?" said Ella.

"You're out of time!"

Ella jogged to catch up with the accelerating coffin, grabbed the leading edge and flung her legs astride the glass box. The wolf ran to keep pace with some difficulty. With the Makepeace Alexander book still clutched under her arm, Ella gripped the edge of the coffin with her free hand, slippery as it was. She just about managed to stay on as they landed on another table, and another, and another. Down the stairs they slid on a series of tables, Oscar bounding around and directing their progress, making sure that the furniture lined up to receive them. The tables pitched themselves at an angle on corners to keep them on course. On stairs the coffin and carpet fairly flew but on the flat corridors their progress was only slowed, not halted, as the taller tables made way for lower tables, chairs and stools, always making sure that the coffin would keep moving.

Several more flights of stairs fell away beneath them on the gut wrenching ride, and Ella dared to hope that maybe today *wasn't* the day when she would be killed by being crushed beneath her mother's coffin.

"Traitor!"

Mr Dainty was ahead, advancing up the grand staircase with rifle in hand and animalistic fury on his face.

Interesting, thought Ella, that the man was more concerned with notions of personal betrayal than with a giant table/coffin toboggan. It wasn't every day that one encountered such things.

He raised the rifle. The table beneath Ella bucked reflexively and other tables ran to position themselves as the coffin swung round and away along the long north-south corridor. There was gunfire and a puff of exploding plaster that was quickly far behind them.

There was a doorway and open sky ahead and — she could plainly see — not enough tables to carry them much further.

"Maybe we ought to stop," she said.

"It'll be fine!" shouted the teapot beside her, its lid rattling.

"Er... no," she said.

The leading edge of scrambling tables, the ragged end of the slide before them, ploughed through the doorway and onto a wide balcony. Beyond, there was only the night and sea.

"Stop!" yelled Ella. "For fuck's sake!"

As the tables banked and tried to divert the glass coffin, some force from below flung rug, coffin, teapot and Ella up into the air and over the cliff edge. They pitched forward and down, towards the rocks and the surf far below.

12

I n the vast kitchen of The Bumbles, Roy built himself a tower stack sandwich of cold meat cuts, deli relishes and a token leaf of iceberg lettuce. Every third slice of meat was casually tossed to Buster the dog who made sure that not a one reached the ground.

Buster back-flipped to catch a slice of glazed venison.

"Show-off," said Roy.

"If I may continue," said his father's secretary, holding a handful of messages.

"Sorry," said Roy, waving a mayo-streaked knife at him. "Do go on."

The secretary read. "The chairs are already out and the tables are arriving at seven a.m. The woman from The Wild Bunch —"

"The Wild Bunch?"

"The florist. She wants to set up at seven a.m. also but I've held her back until eight. The balloon unicorn will be assembled in the marquee as soon as the staging area has been wrapped in silk, at seven forty-five. And there has been a telephone message from Mr Liddell-Grainger."

"Wilbur? Is it about his court date?"

"No. He says he'll pick you up from the Hannaford's house in..." The secretary consulted the clock. "Twenty minutes."

Roy put the final slice of bread on top of his massive sandwich.

"Pick me up?"

"In his helicopter."

"Helicopter?"

The secretary looked at the piece of paper and read. "'Got your message. Always happy to help a damsel in distress.'"

Roy licked a smidge of tomato relish from the edge of his thumb.

"Did he sound drunk?" he asked.

"I wouldn't know," said the secretary. "What does he sound like when he's sober?"

Ella felt wet sand on her face and sat up suddenly.

Had she been unconscious? Had she blacked out? She could remember only the fall from the balcony, the rush of the air and then...

She put her hand to her head. No pain, no bump. She looked up. The light of day was almost gone and she could only see how far she had fallen by the height of the lights in the house far above.

"No way should I have survived that," she said. "Not that I'm complaining," she told the world at large.

She was sitting on the woven rug which itself was draped across the edge of a rock and a sliver of sandy beach with one edge trailing in a rock pool. Waves broke against more prominent rocks a few yards further out from the cliff. Glass shards were sprinkled around her like so much razor-sharp confetti.

"Oh, no!"

The wreck of the glass coffin was off to one side and Natalie Hannaford lay, limbs splayed, in the midst of it.

Ella scrambled wetly over to her mum and took her face in her hands. Natalie's skin was cool but not cold. Ella frantically felt for a pulse at the young woman's wrist and had to check once, calm herself and check again to be certain that, yes, she was still alive.

There was shouting above. Ella looked up. There were the silhouettes of men on the cliff top. Cautiously, the silhouettes began climbing down the cliff face.

"Okay," said Ella (who recognised that things were patently *not* okay). "Tiny beach, middle of the night. Cliff on one side, sea on the other. A comatose mother, no way out and less than twenty-four hours to stop my dad committing bigamy. Have I missed anything?"

Ella had been talking to herself but the fact that there was no response made her look around with concern.

"Teapot?"

And then Ella saw the broken shards on a nearby rock. Not glass, but china, the shattered remains of the lid from a rare Wedgwood teapot.

"Oh, crap," she said.

In the rock pool, the carpet rippled.

WHEN ROY ARRIVED at Gavin Hannaford's house in Nether-cum-Studley, the back door was open and raised voices could be heard from upstairs. He entered the kitchen and called out a hello but, getting no response, proceeded upstairs.

"No daughter of mine — or her idiot friend — is wearing a veil to my wedding!" said a firm and implacable voice.

"Mrs Hannaford?" called Roy. "I mean, Ms Whuppie?"

"We can't go looking like this!" said a despondent, near tearful voice.

"Petunia?" said Roy.

"Everyone knows that mango is good for the skin," said a third voice: Lily.

"Agreed," said Myra stridently. "However, one cannot simply slap it all over and then sit out in the garden for the afternoon and expect to be unmolested by flying insects."

Roy reached the top of the stairs.

"You'll just have to put on some foundation and make the best of it," said Myra.

Roy knocked on the door. "Ladies?"

"Who is that?" demanded Myra.

"Roy. Roy Avenant."

Lily shrieked. "You can't see us the night before the wedding."

"Isn't that just the bride and the groom?" he said.

Myra flung the door open.

"Don't talk to me about the groom!" she snorted. "Ridiculous man!"

Myra Whuppie had, quite understandably, decided against a white wedding dress. However, it appeared that Myra nonetheless wished to make a statement with her wedding ensemble. Roy was no expert on couture but even he could see that Myra's dress was a statement of power: borrowing a leaf from the late Margaret Thatcher's book, a smidgeon of the look of Chancellor Angela Merkel and even a flourish perhaps taken from some wild barbarian queen, Myra gave the appearance of a woman not only ready to conquer the world but also ready to assume command of an intergalactic empire.

"What a beautiful dress," said Roy automatically.

Myra humphed.

"Not happy?" he said.

"Oh, I'm fine!" she snapped. "It's not me who decided to ruin the big day by letting flying ants have a party on their faces."

Roy looked past Myra to Petunia and Lily. If Myra was a

galactic empress, then these two were clearly her imperial guard (assuming the imperial guard was happy with peach fabrics and puff sleeves). Both looked thoroughly sorry for themselves, with faces as red and shiny as a prize Edam.

"I think they've laid eggs in my brain," said Lily miserably.

"It will no doubt increase her IQ when they hatch," said Myra. "Now, if you're looking for Ella, I can't help you. Haven't seen her since she went off to that Dainty character's place. She's just like her father. Causing all manner of ructions and then running away from any responsibility. Here. Try some of this."

This last was to Petunia as Myra passed her a tube of concealer. Petunia squeezed out a glob of it and smeared it over Lily's face.

"What ructions?" said Roy.

"Oh, the rumours she's been spreading. It's all attention-seeking behaviour, you know."

"Attention-seeking," agreed Petunia.

"Is this about Ella's mum still being alive?"

Myra shushed him loudly and mashed his lips shut with her fingers.

"None of that here," she whispered angrily. "Gavin's in the next room, sleeping off a bottle of Merlot and I'll not have him hearing such vicious lies."

"You haven't told him?"

"Of course not! Lies! All lies."

"Mum," said Petunia. "You can still see the bites. They poke through."

Myra regarded the now flesh-coloured but otherwise perfectly evident eruptions on Lily's face.

"You'll need to fill in the gaps," said Myra. "Build it up in layers. Slap it on with a trowel if you have to." She returned her attention to Roy. "I loved Natalie," she said. "Truly I did. And if I could do anything to bring her back, Mr Avenant, I would. I really would." She gave him a tired but earnest look. "But she's dead and the man I love has had enough heartache for one lifetime."

"Of course," said Roy.

"Now, I've got some facial reconstruction to do on these two which I think is going to require both olyfilla and a high-powered hairdryer to complete. So, is there anything I can help you with before you go?"

"Ah, yes. I got a message earlier about —"

Roy was cut off by the roar of a helicopter engine and the appearance of a piercing spotlight over the back garden of the house.

"My friend, Wilbur," Roy explained. "Ex-RAF pilot. Said he was coming here to pick me up in his private chopper."

"Private chopper?" said Lily, excited.

"RAF pilot?" said Petunia.

"Is he single?" asked Lily.

"Intermittently," said Roy.

ELLA TRIED to gather the shards of pottery together but there were so few of them. Perhaps the rest had rebounded and scattered into the sea. Lost and gone. She did find the copy of *Solomon Re-examined*, damp and sandy but otherwise whole, and picked that up.

"Ella," called Mr Dainty invisibly from above. "What are you doing?"

"Good question," she said.

"You went into the south tower, Ella. Now, I thought I made myself very clear on this matter, but it seems that you chose to defy me. I am afraid that I am no longer prepared to tolerate your presence in my home."

"That's good then because I was just leaving," said Ella, with more bravado than she felt. "God knows how," she muttered to herself.

As though blown or wave-tossed, the rug rolled over, flopping across the beach towards Ella.

Suddenly, arms reached round and grabbed Ella from behind. She yelled.

"I have her!" shouted Cheeky in her ear. "I have her, sir!"

"Goddamn ninja butler!" she growled.

The carpet fluttered into the air briefly before drifting down again like an autumn leaf.

"What the...?" said Cheeky.

Ella seized on the distraction; she braced her feet against the rock directly in front of her and pushed back against Cheeky with all her might. They fell apart on the sand. Ella rolled away and to her feet. Cheeky was up too, a knife in his hand and a wadding of dressing where he'd clonked his head earlier.

"If it's any consolation, miss," said Cheeky. "You would have been my favourite Mrs Dainty."

A shadow fell out of the darkness, landed on Cheeky and powered him into the cliff face where his head bounced off a rock and knocked him unconscious for the second time in an evening.

"Sorry, princess," said the wolf. "I know you normally like to rescue yourself from these kinds of situations."

"Er, no," she said. "Actually, I could do with a bit of rescuing right now."

There was the sound of shifting feet on the rocks above. She suspected there were a good number of armed men arranged not far above her.

"Ella?" called Mr Dainty. "Are you aware of the game Marco Polo?"

"Er, yes," she said.

A shot rang out and there was a tiny wet thud in the sand next to Ella.

"Bastard!" she snarled.

The carpet rose up into the air for several seconds.

"Okay, what's going on with this thing?" she said.

"Do you want this?" said the wolf.

"Want what?" she said and then saw him sniffing vigorously about the form of her comatose mother. "Don't you bloody touch my mum, wolf!"

The carpet rose again. Ella looked at it.

"Shit," she said, experimentally. The carpet rose a little higher.

"Knob." The carpet rose further still.

"Wolf," she said. "Help get my mum onto this thing."

"What's the plan?" he said.

Another shot rang out, this time ricocheting off a rock.

"We're getting the buggering fuck out of here," she said and the magic carpet shuddered, like a revving engine.

ROY LOOKED DOWN at the dark, light-speckled landscape rolling away beneath them.

Wilbur Liddell-Grainger was a fine chap, had been a damned fine air force officer for fifteen years and seemed, at this precise moment, to be as lucidly sober as Roy had ever known him to be. Nonetheless, Roy wasn't entirely sure of the wisdom of letting the man whisk him away into the night, because Wilbur had apparently received a note — purportedly from Roy himself — pleading for help.

"What did this note say again?" said Roy.

Wilbur dug into his flight jacket, giving the Eurocopter a little wobble that made Lily and Petunia giggle in the back seats. Yes, acceding to the women's pleas to come on a "jolly ride" had not been a wise decision either. So far, they had spent the entire journey, misshapen faces melting like failed waxworks of the Elephant Man, with their flight headsets on, channelling the spirit of every Vietnam War movie ever. After fifteen minutes of "I love the smell of napalm in the morning", a startling rendition of *Ride of the Valkyries* and numerous exclamations of "You weren't there, man!" they had run out of inspiration. Petunia was currently wearing her headphones on one ear only and spinning turntables in the nightclub of her imagination. Lily on the other hand had gone into mental free fall and was simultaneously dancing to Petunia's imaginary beats whilst shooting down enemy aircraft and declaring there to be "Zulus! Thousands of 'em!"

Wilbur passed a crumpled note to Roy. Roy read it.

"'I need your bastard help'?"

"Sounded urgent," agreed Wilbur. "And after you fixed me up with a top barrister, I owed you one. Do you know, they want to charge me with molesting a bird of prey?"

"And do I usually sign my letters as 'Prince Charming'?" asked Roy.

"I think you're charming," said Petunia and put a hand on Roy's shoulder. When she removed it, it left a flesh-coloured palm print on his jacket.

"And he is four-hundred-and-something-th in line to the throne," said Wilbur.

The woman cooed.

"Practically royalty," said Lily.

"Not royal enough to get an invite to today's garden party at Buck Pal though," said Roy. He tapped the numbers scrawled on the note. "And where exactly are these co-ordinates?"

Wilbur pointed to the GPS navcom instruments.

"Somewhere in the Bristol Channel."

"We're going to the seaside?" said Petunia and clapped her hands excitedly.

Lily gave a little shriek.

"What is it?" said Roy.

"A bit of my forehead fell off. Someone help me look for it."

                              .   .   .

"DOUCHE CANOE!"

"Bum bailey!"

"Wank puffin!"

"Flap dragon!"

"Big dog's cock!"

The wolf gave Ella a look.

Ella gave him a look back.

"That's probably enough fuel for now," she said.

She looked down at her mother's head resting in her lap and brushed a strand of hair away from the young woman's face.

The wolf padded to the lead edge of the flying carpet and sniffed the night air.

"Do we know where we're going?" he said.

"North," said Ella, pointing out the Pole Star in the clear night sky. "We've got to hit the M4 or the M5 or something and then we follow the motorway home."

The carpet trembled as they rose to pass over some trees.

"Knobgoblin," said the wolf and the carpet accelerated.

"Is this the wrong time to ask why there's a magic carpet powered by swear words?"

"I'm not sure it's specifically swear words," said the wolf. "Exclamations and oaths are powerful words. Whey-faced bunhole!"

They had discovered early on in their flight that though the carpet took sustenance from swear words, it only accepted any particular utterance once. They had run through the traditional selection of 'tits', 'dicks', 'arses' and 'fucks' some time ago. Ella hoped that the wolf had a bottomless supply of curses because none of them powered it for long and Ella had discovered she knew far fewer swears than she had realised.

While the wolf sniffed out their path and fuelled the carpet with intermittent 'Strumpets!' and 'Puffy clackholes!' Ella sat with her mum and tried to bridge the thirty year gap of lost history between them.

"So," she said to the sleeping woman, "you remember your old friend, Myra? Dad's been seeing a lot of her lately. They're getting married tomorrow."

"Knobstench!"

"He didn't know what had happened to you. None of us did. Except Granny Rose. She's still alive and hiding out in the woods."

"Bellend!"

"Anyway, the wedding's tomorrow. Two o'clock. They're holding the ceremony and the reception at the Avenants' country house. I don't know if you ever knew the Avenants. Roy, the son, he owns the garden centre where I work."

"Muppet!"

"I'm an eco-builder." Ella decided eco-builder needed translation for a woman who went to sleep mid-Thatcher. "I help build and renovate properties using reclaimed or renewable resources. There has been a lot more concern about the environment and climate change since, you know, your day. Did people know about global warming back then?"

"Damp flange!"

"I guess a lot has changed," said Ella thoughtfully. "We've got the internet now. That's quite good. And satnav. And, um, Nando's."

"Fucknuggets!"

"Anyway, Dad and Myra are getting married tomorrow. She seems to make him happy, not sure how but love is strange. He does love her. I've read the poetry to prove it. And I do think that deep down — deep, deep down — she loves him too."

"Shitty whore!"

"But he has to know," said Ella. "We have to get you to him and wake you up and then sort out what we're going to do about you and dad and that sodding fairy."

Ella suddenly remembered that she had Makepeace Alexander's *Solomon Re-examined* and opened it. There were a dozen pages of black and white photographs on shiny paper in the centre of the book. She almost immediately came upon a picture of a familiar-looking jar.

Solomon jar (English variant), private collection, read the caption. *A much sought-after item, believed to have been used in the capture of ifrits and fabled malignants (see pages 201-224). The author has been allowed to photograph this but is not permitted to reveal its whereabouts.*

It looked exactly like the one that OCD had tucked tidily away into his sack after it was disgorged from the wolf's stomach.

"That's a convenient coincidence," she said to herself.

"Satan's jizz!"

"Maybe we need to find the dwarfs," she mused quietly.

"Shitgibbon!" said the wolf.

Ella closed the book. Maybe there was a way out of this whole fairy godmother problem...

"Damn!" said the wolf. "Shit. Bollocks."

"Everything okay up there?" said Ella.

"Cockwomble. Snecklifter. Dong. Dugs. Yes, we have a problem. Two problems. Twatwaffle."

"Are we going down?" said Ella, peering over the side.

"You noticed. Huggermugger fanny fart." The carpet wobbled slightly. "I think I might have run out of swear words."

"Wankspurt," said Ella. "Balls."

"You used both of those miles back."

She tried to make out the ground beneath them but it was flat and dark.

"Where are we?"

"And that's problem number two."

Light shifted on the surface below.

"Are we over water?" she said.

"I think it's the sea," said the wolf. "Shit. Crap. Ka-ka. Do-do. Turd."

Ella thought. They had been in Devon. It was a wide county, stretching from parts of the Cornish peninsula to... to... Hampshire? Dorset? She shook her head at her poor geography. But, yes, it was conceivable, probable even, that going north might take them directly over the Bristol Channel.

"We're over the sea," she said. "Minge." She pointed ahead to some tiny orange and white lights. "That's Wales."

"And we're never going to get there if we don't think of some fresh swear words."

There's a buoy over there I think," said Ella. "Let's see if we can't at least get to that."

They were less than ten feet above the sea now.

"But we've run out of words," said the wolf.

"Come on, be methodical. A. Arse."

"Ass."

"Arsehole."

"Asshole."

"Um. B."

"Bastard. Bitch."

"Bugger. Balls. Boobs."

"Butt."

"Butthole. Buttplug."

The carpet gave a tremble of fresh energy.

"Come on, buttplug!" yelled Ella.

"I MEAN you were there at the Cornbury Game Fair," said Wilbur.

"I was, to be honest, quite drunk," said Roy.

"But, as you no doubt remember, that falconry hottie had that kestrel on her arm and said that it enjoys nothing more than gobbling down a bit of meat."

"Ah, I remember," said Roy, wishing he hadn't. "And then you..."

"Undid my flies, slipped out my Monarch of the Glen and said, 'I've got a bit of meat for you right here.'"

"And then what happened?" said Petunia, shocked.

"She let the kestrel go," said Roy.

"Oh, you poor thing," said Lily, clutching at Wilbur supportively and giving him a flesh-coloured shoulder stain to match Roy's. "What did you do?"

"I fought it off. Naturally," said Wilbur.

"How brave."

Roy felt it important to point out that there was nothing brave about a man having to defend himself because he'd waggled his penis in a kestrel's face but loyalty to his friend made him hold his tongue.

"I picked up the nearest thing to hand and wacked the kestrel right between the eyes," said Wilbur. "It flapped away and the falconry girl recaptured it."

"And they want to charge you with what?" said Petunia.

"Molesting a bird of prey."

"But surely that was all just self-defence."

"Quite," said Wilbur.

"Tell them what you hit the kestrel with," said Roy.

"A barn owl," said Wilbur.

"Ah," said Petunia.

"That was quick thinking," said Lily. "Resourceful."

"Thank you, dear," said Wilbur. "I hope I have that kind of positive thinking on my defence team."

"We'd both love to be lawyers," said Lily. "We did look into it."

"Did you?" said Roy.

"We watched *Legally Blonde* three times back to back," said Petunia.

"I'm not sure that counts as —"

"Objection!" said Lily.

"Overruled!" said Petunia.

"You can't handle the truth!" said Lily.

Wilbur tapped the navcom display.

"Coming up on your co-ordinates."

"Not *my* co-ordinates," said Roy and peered out into the dark. The world was a black cloth dotted with distant street lights, the very distant but distinct lights of the works in Port Talbot and the blinking lights of ships heading down the Bristol Channel towards the Atlantic.

"There," said Wilbur.

"Where?" said Roy.

"Where that buoy is."

The helicopter descended.

"Are we allowed to do this?" asked Roy. "Do we need to submit a flight plan or watch out for boats or something?"

"God, yes," said Wilbur cheerfully. "This kind of thing is entirely illegal. Last time I did something like this, I had my pilot's licence revoked."

"For how long?" said Roy.

"What do you mean?"

"I mean when did you get your pilot's licence back?"

"Back?" said Wilbur. "Not sure I follow." He pointed ahead. "What's that to the side of the buoy? A dinghy?"

"I don't think so," said Roy. "But there's definitely two people on it. And is that a dog?"

"They don't look particularly happy."

One person on the raft below — whatever it was, it was as flimsy as a bedsheet — was trying to hold onto both raft and buoy and thus keep the second person afloat (who was either dead or unconscious).

"Ella!" shouted Petunia.

"That's not Ella... Oh, my God, it is!" exclaimed Roy. "Take us down! This thing doesn't have a winch, does it?"

"Correct, old chap," said Wilbur as he descended further. "Civilian aircraft."

"But is there some rope?" said Roy.

The women in the back searched around fruitlessly. Petunia got her headphone cables tangled up and, as the cable tightened, her phones pinged off and whacked Lily in the face (and splattered most of Lily's face against the door).

"Ow!" said Lily. "I've got it!"

"Got what?" said Roy.

"An idea."

ELLA'S BODY sang with pain. The iron strut of the floating device cut into her hand and every rippling wave yanked the buoy and the tendons of her arm. Her other hand clutched at her mum's shoulder. The magic carpet sat several inches below the surface providing minimal support. Either some residual magic or trapped air was keeping it vaguely afloat but, when that was gone and the carpet sank, Ella didn't hold out much hope of keeping anyone afloat. The wolf had abandoned the carpet and now did a miserable and desperate doggy paddle beside Ella.

The helicopter's spot light swung back and forth across them, the rotors throwing up unpleasantly unhelpful spray.

"I don't like drowning," said the wolf. "I mean it's not a boiling pot of water in the third pig's house and it's not like those bloody kids have sewed rocks into my belly but, damn it, drowning's drowning."

"Ella!" shouted a voice from above.

Ella looked up. "Roy?" she called back.

In the kaleidoscope of spotlight, flashing buoy beacon and sea spray, Ella could just about make out Roy Avenant climbing down onto the helicopter runner, using some sort of thin wire as a supporting rope.

"Catch this!" he lobbed something at Ella.

A pair of huge headphones bounced off the side of the buoy and plopped in front of Ella. Ella didn't have a free hand to grab them or the trailing length of audio cord that ran up to the helicopter.

"This can't support us!" she yelled.

"It's the best plan we've got!" Roy yelled back.

"Then think of a better one!" she yelled in return.

She looked at the wolf. "We're going to drown."

"I'm coming to you!" yelled Roy.

"That is not a better plan!" Ella replied.

The current tugged at the carpet, pulling Ella's arms further apart. She coughed in pain. Her muscles were shot, her shoulders on the verge of popping from their joints. It was only the stubborn tenacity of her hold on both buoy and mother that kept her there. Her hands were both numb with cold and burning in protest. She doubted she could let go if she wanted. She'd just cling on until a jerking wave sheered her fingers clean off or her grip on her mum failed.

Feet still on the runner and leaning heavily on his makeshift line of audio cable, Roy swung himself out.

"Try to take my hand!" he called.

"Don't be stupid, you ridiculous oaf!" shouted Ella. He was still a good six feet above them.

The carpet gave a small boost.

"I think I could reach him," said the wolf.

"What? Leap up and bite off his hand?"

"Worth a shot."

Roy wiped seawater from his face. "Did that dog just...?"

Petunia leaned out of the rear door.

"What's she doing here?" shouted Ella.

"Just grab his bloody hand, Ella!" shouted Petunia.

"This isn't safe! Get her away from here!"

"I'm not leaving my big sis!"

Roy turned on the runner to say something to Petunia at which point his foot slipped and he tipped head over heels and fell forward.

"Roy!"

Roy's leg caught on something — the audio cable rope thing — and he swung upside down in a low arc that brought him, for a moment, within inches of Ella.

"Crikey O'Reilly!" he warbled in panic.

The carpet rose a little.

Roy swung back, arms flailing. "Lumme!" he cried.

The carpet resurfaced. The wolf hooked his paws onto the damp rug.

Roy came back again. This time, with an audible clunk, he made an unfortunate connection with the top of the buoy.

"Gordon Bennett!" he roared.

The wolf barely made it onto the carpet before it cleared the surface. Ella flung herself away from the buoy and onto the carpet beside her mum.

Roy, clutching an apparently injured shoulder, and on his fourth or fifth backswing, bounced off the ascending carpet.

"Blimey!"

The carpet rose with fresh vigour.

"Poshtosh! Minced oaths!" said Ella.

"What?" said wolf.

"Gadzooks!" she exclaimed by way of explanation and the carpet set off, continuing its course northwards across the channel. "Zounds!"

The wolf twitched his ears in understanding. "Strewth! Holy mackerel!"

Ella looked back. It was impossible to make things out clearly but Roy was still there, hanging from the helicopter. A launch boat was making its way from the English shore towards the helicopter and the dangling country gentleman.

Ella shivered. The wolf shook himself off and laid down next to Ella's mum. Natalie Hannaford's cheek was cool to the touch but she was still breathing.

"By Jove!" said Ella.

"Tarnation!" said the wolf in agreement.

The carpet sped on towards the Welsh coast.

IN THE SMALL hours of the night, in a field just outside Burnham-on-Sea, Roy was faced with an irritable officer of the Civil Aviation Authority, a near incandescent captain of the lifeboat institute, a world-weary sergeant of the Somerset police force and little explanation for what had just happened.

"We were very concerned for my friend," he said for the eleventh time.

"My sister," said Petunia.

"Step-sister," said Lily.

"Soon to be step-sister," said Petunia.

"And what happened to these two?" said the police sergeant, waving his notepad at Petunia as she tried to reattach a slab of her cheek that had come off.

"Nothing," said Roy.

"Mangoes," said Lily.

"So," said the Civil Aviation officer, "you received a distress signal from your step-sister —"

"Friend."

"— and you asked Mr Liddell-Grainger here to use his

helicopter to rescue her."

"Well, no, he just turned up."

"Because I got the message," said Wilbur.

"From this Ella Hannaford."

"No, from him," said Wilbur, pointing at Roy.

"Not from me," said Roy. "It said it was from me but it was from someone else."

"Miss Hannaford?"

"No. Someone else. We don't know who."

"And then you took it upon yourselves to fly down here to rescue her," said the sergeant.

"Why in the blue blazes didn't you just call the lifeboat service?" said the lifeboat captain.

"We thought it might be a hoax," said Roy.

"Did we?" said Petunia.

"And was it?" said the sergeant.

"No," said Roy. "They were there all right. Ella and another woman and a dog."

"A dog?"

"A big dog."

"I thought it was a wolf," said Lily.

The sergeant stared at her. "What would a wolf be doing in the Bristol Channel?"

"This," said Lily and did a doggy paddle with her hands and stuck her tongue out of the side of her mouth.

"And where are they now?" said the sergeant.

"Oh, they flew off on their magic carpet," said Wilbur.

The sergeant blinked and looked at Roy for confirmation.

"I didn't see anything," he said. "I banged myself against the buoy." He clutched his shoulder and then his head. "I think I might have concussion."

"Concussion, eh?" He gestured at the other three with his notepad. "And what's their excuse?"

13

"Jumping Jehoshaphat!"

"Had that one."

"Suffering succotash!"

"And that."

"Son of a gun!"

The carpet gave a rev of energy but its slow descent did not halt.

"Head for that forest over there," said the wolf.

"What forest?" said Ella.

Daylight was a couple of hours away. It was midsummer's day, the day of her dad's wedding, but, for now, the world was a shifting mass of blacks and very dark greys.

"*That* forest there," said the wolf. "You really can't see it?"

"Hey, night-vision, I don't knock wolves for being colour blind."

The wolf huffed loudly.

"Down there. Left a bit. That's it. Left a bit more."

Wet and shivering from her dip in the sea, Ella squeezed a fraction more juice out of the carpet with an inspired 'Cheese and crackers!' before they brushed, snapped and bumped their way down through the tree canopy onto the ground.

And now it was truly pitch black. Ella crawled forward, feeling her way along her mum's body to the wolf.

"Where are we?" she whispered. "And why am I whispering?"

"Cos you're not stupid, princess. If I was blind and landed in the Deep Dark Forest at night, I'd keep quiet too."

"So where are we exactly?" she said.

"The Deep Dark Forest," said the wolf.

Ella shook her head. "We were in the Deep Dark Forest when we were near Granny Rose's house. This is Wales. The Brecon Beacons or something. Miles away. At least a hundred miles."

The wolf's hot breath on her cheeks told her that he had turned his head to her.

"It's all one forest, sweetheart. I thought you'd got your head around this. This is how your world works now. Dwarfs, castles, forests. It's archetypes all the way."

"Yeah, right. But I don't see why ninety percent of these stories I end up in have to feature a Deep bloody Dark Forest."

"It's symbolic, isn't it? I reckon that fellow, Freud, would be able to tell you what it signifies. All this dark wild overgrowth, full of secrets and adult mystery."

"All right. I get it. No need to beat around the bush."

"Well, exactly."

"You're saying that this forest extends across swathes of British countryside that, up until a few days ago, were cultivated field and towns and roads."

"No, not that. I'm saying —"

"Shush!"

Ella tried to put a hand over the wolf's mouth in the dark but missed slightly and stuck a finger up his nose which shut him up nonetheless. She thought she had heard something and now, in the silence, she heard it again, clearly but some distance away. A powerful but morose voice, exhausted but still able to carry a tune.

"— five hundred and thirteen green bottles hanging on the wall. And if one green bottle should accidentally fall, there'd be eight hundred and twenty-eight thousand, five hundred and twelve green bottles hanging on the wall."

Ella recognised the voice instantly.

"But he can't be here," she said. "His cave was miles from here."

"This is what I was trying to tell you," said the wolf. "It's one forest. It's not here. It's not there. It just is."

Ella stood and stared into the black. There was an orange flicker of fire light, tiny but definitely present.

"Does that mean that Rushy Glen is as near to here as it was the last time we met him?"

The wolf licked his nose.

"Your grandma's house is eight and a half miles north east of here."

"You're sure?"

"Hey, sister, I know how to get to grandma's house, short cuts and everything. Eight and a half mile thattaway."

An idea had formed in Ella's mind. Her subconscious mind had already made a decision but her conscious mind need a little persuasion.

"We need to stop that wedding," she said. "And we're going to die of hypothermia if we stay out in the forest."

"True," agreed the wolf.

"And I don't suppose you could carry the pair of us to Rushy Glen...?"

"I'm a wolf, not a mule."

"You're a big wolf."

"Not a mule."

"So we've got no choice."

"No choice but what?" said the wolf.

"Stay here a minute and take care of my mum."

"What? Why? Wait. No. That's a really bad idea."

"Have you got a better one?" she said as she made her way towards the tiny fire.

"Well, give me a moment to think," said the wolf but she was set on her path now.

Ella trod with care, feeling slick roots underfoot and pulling against the grasses and brambles that tried to ensnare her. The singing, miserable and monotonous, grew louder as she neared.

The ogre watched her approach but did not get up. The hulking rough-skinned creature crouched beside his pitiful fire and continued his song.

"Eight hundred and twenty-eight thousand, five hundred and nine green bottles hanging on the wall."

"Morning," said Ella and gave him a little wave.

The ogre looked at her and sang. What other choice did he have? In the space of a week, he was not yet a fifth of the way through his song but if he stopped or moved then his life would be forfeit and fairy tale creatures clearly took their oaths seriously.

"Can I join you?" she said.

The ogre, resigned and unhostile, gestured for her to sit. The wood on the fire was thin and burned quickly. By the light it threw, Ella could see that the ogre had plucked and denuded the trees, bushes and grasses within monstrous arm's reach of the spot in which he was trapped. Ella sat close to the fire and her soaked clothes soon began to steam.

"How are you doing?"

The ogre gave her a look and sang a verse that, though superficially about the possibility of green bottles falling from a wall, had an implicit subtext regarding the misery one might feel if compelled to sit in one spot and constantly sing a song about green bottles.

"I could release you from your oath," she said, "if you promise not to harm us."

The ogre peered at her suspiciously through his thick spectacles and made a question of the fall of the eight hundred and twenty-eight thousand, five hundred and sixth green bottle.

"And if you do me a favour," said Ella.

The ogre tilted his head, listening. The ogre made the universal signal for "please, do go on" by rolling his hands. He wasn't ready to commit just yet.

"All I need," said Ella, "is some hired muscle for a day or so. Reckon you could help with that?"

The ogre nodded slowly, still cynical.

"If you help us with a few brute force tasks, then at sunset tomorrow you'll have no further obligation to me. We go our separate ways. How's that?"

He spread his hands: explain.

"Mostly transport," said Ella. "We — that's the wolf and me and my mum who's in a magical sleep — need to get to my grandma's house. Rushy Glen? We ran out of swears for our magic carpet."

The ogre nodded as though this was a perfectly normal and not at all mad sentence.

"And then we might need your help stopping a wedding. No violence required. At least I shouldn't think so. Deal?"

THE WOLF DID NOT ENJOY BEING CARRIED by an ogre but their progress through the murky forest was rapid. The ogre seemed to loosen up as he went, clearly enjoying the chance to move around at last although he appeared to be fighting a battle with his lips which seemed trapped in a muscle memory loop and wanted to keep on singing.

They arrived at Rushy Glen just as the sun made a coquettish appearance through the trees. Ella nearly lost the flying carpet as a volley of inventive abuse greeted them.

"Tha's never brought an ogre along here? Tha's got cloth between tha ears, honest t'God!"

"Hi Granny," called down Ella from her lofty position on the ogre's shoulder.

Granny Rose's shotgun waved an emotional figure of eight. It seemed entirely unsure whether to shoot an ogre, a wolf or a member of her own family.

"The ogre's working for me, Granny," said Ella. "He swore."

"Aye, fairy tale things are creatures of their word," agreed Rose, sceptical nonetheless.

"He won't mind waiting outside for a bit if you don't want him to come in."

"Come in? I were debating whether t'marmalise the bugger. Tha can come into the garden, creature, but no further. Well away from the goat, mind!"

The ogre gave her a look. "Madam, I am an ogre, not a troll."

"Oh, so's tha don't eat goat then?" Rose asked pleasantly.

"I do."

"But tha thought I reckoned all ogres and trolls was the same, eh? I'm not one of those racialists. My husband were a bear, tha know."

"Indeed, madam," said the ogre and gingerly stepped over the white picket fence, carefully avoiding the various traps and pits, and sat down on a patch of bare earth.

And Zeke an' all," said Rose with a reproachful waggle of the gun. "Should have learned tha lesson the last time."

The wolf said nothing but leapt nimbly down and placed the ogre between Rose and himself.

Rose came over as the ogre carefully placed Ella and Natalie onto the ground.

"Who's that there with thee?" Rose's hand fluttered to her

mouth as she recognised her lost daughter. "Well I'll be...no! It surely can't be?"

"It's mum, yes," said Ella.

"No." Rose touched Natalie's cheek, prodding it as though it might be a waxwork model, an illusion. "But she's the same... Hasn't aged a day..."

Ella watched an intense conflict take place on Rose's face, between the tsunami of emotions that the reappearance of her daughter had stirred and the granite-faced façade that her Yorkshire genes and old-school stiff upper lip had built over the years. A weakness flickered in her eyes and a trembling set in around her lips and then decades of repression, self-denial and tea-fuelled British grit pushed aside those mere *feelings* and reasserted control of Fortress Rose.

"Well, there's no good to be had from sitting around like a pair of soppy wazarks. Let's get her inside, eh?"

The two of them lifted Natalie through the door and onto the kitchen table. Rose examined her from head to foot, feeling for a pulse and brushing hair away from her face. She also, Ella noticed, surreptitiously poked her with a pin, blew salt in her face and made the sign of the cross on Natalie's forehead.

"It *is* mum," said Ella.

"Oh, aye?" said Rose. "We'll see. Reckon I'll need to get a flannel on this one, freshen her up a bit." She regarded Ella for a moment. "Why's tha all wet?"

"We came down in the sea. A couple of times, actually."

"What were tha doing in t'sea?" said Rose, who clearly didn't approve of such fripperies.

"It's a long story."

"I bet it is."

"I think I'll go and get changed if that's all right, Granny?"

The old woman nodded brusquely and turned back to her task.

Ella climbed the stairs, realising just how cold and exhausted she was. In the guest bedroom she had slept in only a few nights before, she stripped off her soaking clothes and began to tremble with the accumulated cold and weariness. Telling herself that she would just warm up for a moment, she slipped beneath the cover of the single bed. In a few moments, the trembling subsided and Ella started to feel warmth stealing back through her body. She decided to stay for another five minutes before going back downstairs.

ELLA WAS WOKEN by the crow of Granny's cockerel.

Light seeped into the room — the golden light of mid-morning — and she realised that she'd been asleep for hours. She slipped out of bed. Her clothes remained in a sodden heap on the floor. She went to the cupboard to find more of her mother's clothes. She chose a pair of leggings and a sweater with a bizarre frieze of ski-jumpers arrayed across the chest. She went downstairs after finding a pair of flip flops to wear.

Granny Rose dozed in the chair next to the table. The wolf was curled up in front of the stove, which was a surprise. Had Granny softened and let him in?

On the table, Ella's mum had been stripped of her wet clothes and Rose had laid a bedsheet over her. Otherwise, she looked much the same, pale as death (although perhaps a little redder in the cheeks where Granny had applied some vigorous flannel action).

Ella decided not to wake any of them. A little peace was to be treasured. She slipped outside to collect eggs for breakfast. She went round to the henhouse that was no longer also a garage; at some point, she would have to tell Rose that she had parked the car in a hedge somewhere.

The ogre sat in a flower bed, head tilted to the sky.

"Are you all right?" she asked, cautiously.

The ogre gulped heavily. He turned his head to Ella with a sigh. "I have shown great patience, but no birds have landed in my mouth at all."

"Why would they do that?" asked Ella.

"Because I put all of the seed from the bird feeder in here," he said, pointing to his mouth. "It must follow that I should be irresistible to wildlife."

Ella left him to his efforts as he uprooted a whole sunflower plant and patted the soil ball into place in his mouth, turning his face hopefully back towards the birds.

There was a new rose tangling its way across the entrance to the henhouse, so Ella fetched the secateurs to deal with it. She spent five minutes reducing the thorny invader to a brazier full of pieces, and took a turn round the garden to see what else might need attention. She found a glowing bean on the bean pole and plucked it off the plant, popping it in her leggings pocket to add to the brazier. When she approached the well there was a handsome young man sitting on the low brick wall. His hairless chest glistened with beads of water and his eyes smouldered in the way that Ella had only ever seen before on the male models that did the Christmas perfume ads. She didn't even need to check to know that his lower half was formed of a fish's tail, which he flipped lazily.

"Morning," she said.

He didn't speak, simply stared at her with a well-practised boy band smoulder.

"Can I just say," she said, "in my entire adult life, excluding crotch-rubbing lechers and drunkards, I could count the number of blokes who've shown an interest in me on one hand." She did a quick head count. "One hand and a pinky. But in the past week, the forces of magic and goodness have tried to thrust at least two men on me. Repeatedly and often. So, you, my good merman, rather than being a welcome diversion — with your pecs and six pack and v-muscle thingy — are just another bloke I genuinely and respectfully have bog all interest in. Understand?"

The merman continued to stare mutely at Ella with a fake intensity that only grated on her nerves.

"Do you understand?" she said. "No? Sorry. I don't speak fish."

She looked around. Granny's mallet hung by the well but was a bit small for the task in hand so she went back to the henhouse and found a sturdy length of timber. The hunky merman, rather than take a hint, sat waiting for her on the lip of the well.

Ella hefted her club but didn't strike.

"You see," she said, "here's the thing. I know they didn't have dating websites and Tinder back in the dark ages but I'm guessing that it was pretty much a case of one king going to another — or one peasant going to another for that matter — and saying 'I reckon my son should marry your daughter' and the two kids having a look at each other and going 'yeah, you'll do' and bish bash bosh, they were married."

The merman's gaze of passionate adoration didn't waver. It was like talking to a sexually available brick wall.

"This fairy tale crap," said Ella. "Whether you believe in arranged marriages or love marriages, both are infinitely preferable to this nonsense. In what universe does it make sense for a guy to marry a girl because she's dropped her glass slipper or been poisoned by an apple or traded in by her kidnapped dad? You might as well just match people up by lottery."

The merman gave her the slightest sensuous pout and jiggled his pecs playfully.

"Oh, and don't get me started on true love's kiss," she said. "If anyone is fool enough to think you can tell if you're going to love someone because of their kiss then they should be legally barred from ever getting married. It's about... a shared outlook. And whether he makes you laugh. Whether you feel comfortable around him. It's about seeing yourself being with them in five years, ten years, fifty. True love's kiss? Bollocks, more like."

The merman's smouldering gaze intensified. It was starting to look more like a look of constipation than anything else.

"And true love's kiss was only introduced in the later tales," she told him. Fish boy was a good listener; she had to admit that much. "I read about it in one of Dainty's books. The seventeenth century collectors of tales tidied up all the rude and disgusting bits. In the old *old* tales, the wolf isn't the only one who eats granny's flesh, the ugly stepsisters end up as blind, lame cripples and, in Sleeping Beauty, the prince doesn't kiss her awake. Oh, no, he gets a bit of rape action in first. He..."

Ella stopped, struck by a thought.

"Oh, God."

She ran back to the house, remembered why she was carrying a length of wood, ran back to the well and then, with a mutter of "Sorry handsome, back where you came from," walloped the merman sideways back into the well and ran to the house once more.

"What's the rush?" said the ogre, around a fresh mouthful of bird seed.

"I think I can wake mum!" she said as she skidded past and in the back door.

Her clattering entrance was enough to wake Granny Rose who snorted, woke and instantly declared, "I wasn't sleeping."

The wolf opened his eyes, licked his chops but otherwise persisted in his impression of a shaggy fireside rug.

"I've got an idea," said Ella.

"Well, don't brag about it," said Rose. "Share it and we'll be t'judge."

Ella lifted up her mum's hand and inspected her fingertips.

"It's the Spinning Wheel Gambit."

"Aye?"

Ella squinted and examined them more closely. It was odd, she thought, that her mum's nails and hair hadn't grown during her long sleep. She truly had been put on ice.

"She pricked her finger on the spindle of a spinning wheel and fell asleep."

"I know t'story."

"Although it's the prince's kiss that wakes her in modern versions, in one of the old versions, written by some Italian guy, the prince not only kisses her but forces himself on her while she's asleep."

"Filthy bugger," said Rose.

"Giambattista Basile," said the wolf.

"What?"

"The Italian guy." He looked at them. "What? Can't I be a top predator *and* well-read?"

Ella switched to her mum's other hand and resumed her inspection of fingertips.

"Anyway, Sleeping Beauty becomes pregnant and gives birth to twins. Without waking up. The twins crawl up her body, looking for something to feed on. Because they're hungry, right?"

"Filthy," said Rose.

Ella could see a fleck of light brown underneath Natalie's index finger nail. She picked at it with her own fingernail.

"And one of them," she continued, "latched onto her finger and attempted to suckle. And sucked out the splinter. And with that..."

Ella gave up on picking at it, put Natalie's finger in her own mouth and sucked.

Natalie sat bolt upright and thrust out her arms, an action that caused her to automatically punch Ella in the face. Ella staggered back and rebounded off the wolf (who did not appreciate being treated as a cushion).

Natalie Hannaford stared at her wet and now splinter-free fingertip, blinking eyes that she hadn't used in thirty years.

"So, you finally worked it out then?" she croaked drily.

The sound of her own mum's voice brought a lump to Ella's throat. There were already tears in her eyes though mostly the result of a thump in the face.

"Mum."

Natalie looked down at her, sprawled on the kitchen floor.

Ella had thought of this moment many times, yes, in the past twenty-four hours of course but also before that, thinking of what would it be like to meet her mum again, to stand before her (or sprawl before her, as it turned out) and say, 'Here I am, mum. Here I am.' In her imagination, she had prepared herself for the outpouring of emotion, the questions, her mum's pride in what her little girl had become...

To be honest, she hadn't expected her mum's gaze to be so... not critical as such, but coolly analytical. It took her in from messy sea-washed hair, down to grubby feet. It made Ella wish she'd made more of an effort.

"Those are my clothes," said Natalie.

"Um," said Ella.

"They don't fit you," said Natalie.

Natalie gathered the bedsheet around her chest, swung her legs off the table and came down to Ella's level, hands outstretched. The expected hug, the first touch of reconnection, didn't come. Natalie, instead, placed her thumbs either side of Ella's nose and gave it a tweak.

"Ow," said Ella.

"It's not broken," her mum informed her.

"Okay," said Ella.

Natalie stood, turned to her own mother and gave her the greeting that Ella apparently didn't deserve. She took Rose's face in her hands and kissed the woman tenderly on the cheek.

"I'm sorry I was away so long, mum."

Rose said nothing, simply shook her head.

"And since when did you allow wicked wolves in the house?"

"He sneaked in while I was asleep," said Rose.

"I like grandma's house," said the wolf. "What can I say?"

Natalie turned. "Ella."

"Yes?" said Ella, knowing that this was now the moment, now that her mum had overcome the shock, now that she was ready to rekindle a long lost relationship.

"Put the kettle on," said Natalie. "I'm parched. And we've got a wedding to get to, haven't we?"

14

R oy's phone buzzed.

After spending the wee hours placating the police, Civil Aviation Authority and RNLI with personal details, promises of good behaviour and a large donation to the local lifeboat fund, he had returned to The Bumbles and slept for a grand total of forty-seven minutes before the first of the wedding organisers appeared and demanded answers to questions that apparently only he could answer.

He now sat in the marquee on the lawn, which was to serve for both the civil ceremony and the post-reception disco that day. Roy was not asleep but drifting off into a quiet thought-free space. In front of him, a team of earnest young men were enrobing a set of stage blocks in billowing silk fabric. It took four of them to hold the fabric clear of the ground, one of them to apply pins in hidden folds, and another to stand at a distance and advise them that they really needed to undo it all and allow a more *graceful* drape.

It was a surreal and genteel sight — the flowing silks, young working class types putting heart and soul into their job, the air filled with inane chatter. Roy could quite happily have sat there forever but now his phone was buzzing and he was forced to wake up properly.

Roy pulled out his phone. He saw that Buster was ready to chew some of the dangling ends of silk so he called him to heel and walked out of the tent and round to the driveway.

It was Wilbur calling.

"I hate you," Roy told his good friend.

"Have you heard?" said Wilbur.

Roy yawned. He thought he'd be out of the way out here, but he saw another lorry pulling up and knew that more wedding-related paraphernalia was being delivered. Roy sank down on a staddle stone.

"Heard what? If it's about your court appearance, I really don't care right now."

"No," said Wilbur. "Not that. It's about Jasper and your dad, and lots of other people too when you come right down to it."

"Have you been on the pop?" said Roy, watching the huge lorry reverse up the drive.

"Not since breakfast, no. Listen, I was a bit worried about Jasper. He didn't show up for the Fennington shoot."

"Don't care. Tired."

"So, I rang up Binky. Best pals. Binky fagged for Jasper at Eton."

"I know Binky. Life Guards. Stupid helmets."

"That's him. He told me that MI5 have declared some sort of critical something-or-other. Seems as though a whole load of folks have gone missing."

"So, MI5 are worried about Jasper?" Roy said, struggling to grasp Wilbur's point.

"Jasper and whole load of others as well. He was at Her Maj's garden party at the palace yesterday and there was an incident."

"What sort of incident?"

"Binky wasn't sure of the details, but he says the place is in uproar."

"I've not heard about any of this."

"They're keeping it hush-hush. They're looking at all the minor royals now, making sure they're safe. I thought of your dad when he said that."

Roy laughed. "Dad's not a minor royal!"

"Well, you're four-hundred-and-something-th in line to the throne."

"And he's four-hundred-and-something-th minus one," said Roy. "I think you need to be a little bit further up the pecking order to be called that."

"Well you should keep an eye out, just the same."

"For what?"

"Anything odd."

At that point, a seven foot balloon unicorn appeared from behind the enormous lorry.

"Oh, I will," said Roy. "I'm sure Jasper's just out on a bender somewhere. He'll turn up in a couple of days with a hangover and another nasty rash."

The man with the inflatable unicorn couldn't see that he was making a bee line for the holly tree that stood at the head of the path.

"Christ! I need to go, Wilbur. Chin up old sausage. Oi! Oi, you!"

THREE WOMEN SAT at the kitchen table in Rushy Glen, a pot of tea and a rack of toast between them. Rose was smoking a Park Drive reflectively. Natalie, now dressed in yet more of her old clothes (that, yes, did fit her slim figure far better than they would Ella's more 21st century body shape), had gulped down the first cup of tea, devoured three rounds of toast and sat nursing her second cup. She'd been nursing it for half an hour, not saying a word until she looked at Ella and said, "You're staring at me."

Ella didn't know how to respond to that.

"Aye, well this has all come as a surprise to us all," said Rose.

"You think I'm your mum, Ella," said Natalie.

"You are my mum," said Ella.

The twenty-something sniffed and sipped her tea.

"Which is worse?" she said. "To lose a parent or lose a child?"

"I wouldn't know," said Ella.

Natalie shook her head.

"I'm back and... and you've got me back exactly as I was. Want to pick things up where we left off? Me, I come back and I've lost so much. I had a little girl."

"I am that little girl," said Ella, hearing the petulant tone in her voice and wondering if she was regressing back to her teenage self to make up for lost time.

"Not so little," said Natalie. "I had this tiny dot of a girl, who loved chasing insects and singing made up rhymes and wanted to become a vet when she grew up. What is an eco-builder anyway?"

Ella frowned.

"You heard me when you were asleep?"

"It wasn't a true sleep. I heard everything. I had... how long?"

"Thirty years," said Ella.

"...thirty years to think and reflect." Her brow furrowed. "Thirty years and you haven't got married, got kids of your own?"

"Whoa," said Ella. "You're out of my life for thirty years and the first thing you want to know is why I've not had kids. Back off, lady."

"You don't want to leave it too late."

"She's picky, that's what." Rose tapped out cigarette ash into her saucer.

"It's my life and I'll live it as I like," said Ella.

"Do you not like men?" said Natalie.

"I... what?"

"Lasses these days," said Rose. "Think they can leave it as long as they like and then get that VHF treatment."

"I will or will not have babies if I want to. It's my bloody womb."

"And I respect that," said Natalie.

"Really? Because it sounds like I'm getting parenting advice from someone who is actually ten years younger than me."

"And I'd already had you by that age."

"Is that the problem?" said Ella.

"What?" said Natalie.

"You took a bullet for me. And are you now disappointed that I didn't become the woman you wanted me to be? You want to plan my life for me?"

"I didn't say that."

Ella pushed back her chair violently and stood.

"You didn't have to!"

Natalie threw her hands up in exasperation. Ella glowered.

Rose burst out laughing. Granny Rose wasn't one readily known for producing gales of laughter. Ella and Natalie stared at her.

"What?" said Natalie.

Rose pointed at Ella. "She's just like thee."

"What?"

"Just like thee," chortled the old woman. "Bloody wilful, that's what."

Ella looked at the young woman and tried to remember what she herself was like in her twenties. Natalie looked back, probably wondering if Ella was a reflection of who she'd be in another decade.

"We only get it from you, mum," said Natalie.

"I think not," said Rose. "Everyone knows I'm the very epitome of tolerance and forgiveness."

"Oh, in that case, Granny," said Ella, "I should tell you I crashed your car."

Rose's cup came down hard on the table. "Tha's a bloody menace, girl. If tha weren't full grown, tha'd feel t'back of my hand."

Ella caught Natalie's expression and they both laughed.

"Oh, yes," agreed Natalie. "Tolerance and forgiveness."

As Roy helped to get the unicorn past the holly tree without incident, the shutter went up on the lorry with a loud clatter. A tiny man with a beard stood on the tailgate, hands on his hips. Sequins covered his pointed hat, his wide-shouldered jacket and his flared trousers. Roy was momentarily stunned by the sight of the man who then jumped down with an exaggerated flourish. It wasn't possible to discern his facial features, as he was wearing a pair of sunglasses that were roughly as wide as he was tall, in spite of his glittering stacked boots.

"Er, hello," said Roy. "Would you be with the entertainment?"

"Not *with* the entertainment, brother," said the small man, thrusting his fist to the sky and his pelvis towards Roy's kneecap, "I *am* the entertainment."

"All by yourself."

"Better believe it, chief. You can call me Disco. Now, I've got sound equipment in here that'd make a roadie weep and think he'd gone to heaven and we've got —" He did a pelvic thrust and consulted his watch. "— only two hours to set up before the magic begins."

"Well, quite," said Roy.

"I'd normally have my six brothers to help me but they're on an errand."

"Six...?"

"So, I'm gonna need you to rustle up some muscle and help me get set up."

"If you so say."

"I do, posh boy."

Bemused, Roy led the little man up towards the marquee and wondered where he'd last seen that gang of earnest young men.

ROSE WAS LOADING the twin tub with her daughter's and granddaughter's sodden clothes.

"And this hasn't been running right an' all," she said critically. "Not since tha stuffed it with six dwarfs."

By the tone, Natalie knew that the cost of a new twin tub washer had been added to an itemised list that would soon be presented to Ella. Natalie remembered the time when, as a child, she had put her elbow through her mum's glass-fronted sideboard while looking at the ornaments. Her mum had pinned the glazier's bill to the kitchen wall and forced Natalie to pay it off out of docked pocket money. Some people never changed.

Ella had changed, had become a stranger to Natalie's eyes, and Natalie knew she'd not made the best first impression on this woman who had once been her little daughter. Natalie put a fresh cuppa in front of Ella, following that truest of British traditions, of trying to mend bridges and fix family crises with tea.

"Thanks."

Natalie tried to catch a glimpse of her own little girl in this older woman. It wasn't easy. Ella looked more like Natalie's mum than her daughter. It was, she supposed, nice to see Ella blossom into adulthood but, even though Ella was only in her thirties, there were already lines at the corners of her eyes, a tiredness that oh-so-slightly hinted at the old age to come and Natalie couldn't bear that. If Ella looked old to Natalie's eyes, what must Gavin look like now?

"Do you have a photo of him?" said Natalie.

Ella frowned.

"Your dad," said Natalie.

"Oh. Sorry. No. I had some on my phone but that died several days ago."

"Photos on a phone?"

Ella's mouth froze in a contorted expression as she formulated a no doubt detailed explanation of how telephones could contain photographs. Before Ella could hit her with some Star Trek mumbo-jumbo, Natalie asked, "Is he happy?"

"Yes."

"Really?"

Ella shrugged. "I think so," she said, and then, "He misses you."

Natalie felt both sadness and satisfaction on hearing that. "He can't know I'm alive."

"What?" said Ella. "But he has to. He's going to get married!"

"And having me turn up would ruin the wedding."

"Aye," agreed Rose. "The old wife turning up would put a right crimp on tha wedding day."

"But you *said*," said Ella.

"Said what?" said Natalie. "I said we had a wedding to get to. Not to stop."

"But... but..."

The wolf, still laid out by the stove, gave a lazy snort of laughter. "I like the way she thinks."

"What?" said Ella.

"She's talking about revenge, princess," he said.

"Justice," said Natalie.

Ella stared from one to the other. She still didn't get it.

"We're going to the wedding," said Natalie.

"Carabosse will be there," said Rose. "She'll want thee to meet tha Prince Charming."

And then the penny dropped. "No sodding way," said Ella. "I've just spent the past week trying to avoid my 'happy ending.'"

"And now we need you to play along to draw Carabosse out," said Natalie.

"This is not why I woke you up!"

"Oh, who's planning whose life for them now?"

"You'll let dad commit bigamy? And what will you do if Carabosse shows anyway, eh?"

"Give her both barrels," said Rose.

"Won't work, grandma," said the wolf.

"Worth a try though," said the old woman, gamely.

Natalie pointed at the thick green book on the kitchen counter. "You found Makepeace Alexander's book, Ella. You know there are ways of trapping fairies. If only we could lay out hands on a genuine Solomon jar."

"Ah," said the wolf, "Funny you should mention that."

Ella gave a huff of irritation at the wolf.

"You know where there is one?" said Natalie.

"The dwarfs have one," said Ella.

The twin tub produced a series of unhealthy sounding clunks and pumped thick clouds of steam up against the window. A thought belatedly occurred to Natalie.

"Six dwarfs?" she said to Rose. "Surely, there's meant to be seven."

ROY PUT a hand on Buster's collar.

"It's all right old chap," he whispered. "I know he looks as if his clothes were designed by a committee of sugar crazed toddlers, but that's not a good enough reason to bite him, I'm afraid."

Buster clearly disagreed and bared his teeth at the tiny entertainer who was ordering various people to carry amplifiers, run cables across the floor and get their funk on, whatever that was all about.

"You!" yelled the bearded terror as he saw Roy looking. "I need you to help me with a sound check. Stand there."

Roy obliged.

Disco flicked some switches and a deep bass line came through the speakers. It was so deep that it was almost beneath hearing and could only be felt through the vibrations it sent through his body. It was as soft as a sigh, as intangible as a breath of air. It was a shudder of pleasure up the spine of the world.

Roy gave a thumbs-up to the DJ.

"No, there's more," boomed a hugely amplified version of Disco's voice. "I need you to help me find the groove."

Roy nodded and looked around, as if he might spot the missing groove.

"Move like me," came the impossibly loud voice, over that thumping rhythmic sound that got right inside Roy's head. Roy stared as Disco made small but somehow suggestive gyrations with his hips. They were tiny movements, accompanied by a slightly raised eyebrow. Roy decided that such minimalist dancing was well within his capability, so he mirrored the movement. Disco smiled to show his approval, and then slightly increased the sway of his hips. Roy felt that he must follow suit, although a part of his brain questioned, quite reasonably, what this might have to do with a sound check. The question faded as the swaying increased again.

"You feelin' it?" asked Disco, his voice so loud and low that Roy felt it in his kidneys. Is that where the groove was to be found? By way of experimentation Roy increased the sway a little more and Disco smiled at him.

"Oh yeah, you feelin' it, brother. You got the groove and you'll do what Disco knows is right for ya. You gotta just trust the groove, ma brother. Disco won't let you down."

Roy carried on feeling the groove. Disco's words washed over him, along with the music, and it was all part of the beautiful thing called the groove.

"...cleared the way to the throne for you, brother. All four hundred and something been shown the door by Groovemaster Disco. You gonna take your fine lady as a wife and be the new royals. The House of Avenant, ruling the country. Sounds like a fairy tale, don't it? Oh yeah."

Roy nodded. He was in the groove.

ELLA POSITIONED herself at the side of the single lane road at the far end of Granny Rose's drive. There wasn't a lot of passing traffic but that probably wasn't the point. She cleared her throat and did her best to project her voice loudly and clearly. "I seem to be in need of rescue. I must get to the wedding which is miles away!"

"Tha needs to say *ball*!" Granny Rose hissed from her hiding place in the ditch.

"It might not work otherwise," agreed the wolf, crouched beside her.

"Why would *ball* work when everybody wants her to get married?" countered Natalie. "It's a wedding. There isn't even a ball planned. Is there?"

"No, the old stringy lady is right," said the ogre, who was doing a surprisingly good job at pretending to be a gnarly oak tree. "Everyone knows the fairy godmother helps poor Cinders get to a ball."

"Oh gracious me!" howled Ella, putting a hand theatrically to her brow, figuring she might as well go for broke. "I'm going to be late for the wedding, which, by the way, I very much hope is accompanied by a ball. How I wish I could get there!"

"Not bad," said Rose. "Mention the clothes as well."

"Oh but what am I thinking?" Ella bellowed. "I simply can't go like this. If a handsome prince sees me in these rags he won't even notice me!"

"That was my favourite jumper back in the day!" said Natalie.

"Shush," said Ella.

"Someone's coming," said the ogre.

A clatter of small boots on the road was accompanied by the unmistakeable sound of someone trying to fart a military march.

"Once more to the bastard rescue!" yelled Psycho as the dwarfs rounded the corner. Ella noticed that there were only five of them. She was about to ask who was missing when OCD stepped forward with an electronic tablet.

"Glass Slipper Gambit checklist."

"The what?" said Ella.

"I've chosen you a dress with a one hour delivery off Amazon. I've gone for a fit and flare silhouette despite the issue with your hips."

"What's wrong with my hips?"

"Nothing's *wrong* with them," snarked Passive Aggressive. "Perfectly decent for a child-bearing hausfrau."

"What's next?" said OCD. "Glass slippers! Oh my. This one's a toughie. I decided that the Disney ones probably wouldn't fit you, more's the pity."

"I like to glue mirrors on mine, so I can look up girls' skirts," said Inappropriate.

OCD ignored the comment and flicked through some images to show Ella. "A non-purist might have gone for some of these crystal covered Jimmy Choos, but frankly I think they've strayed too far from the theme. I've gone with solid acrylic heels from a specialist supplier. It's the closest thing to glass, you'll never notice the difference."

"They sound perfect," said Ella, struggling to fake any kind of enthusiasm for shoes that were likely to make her feet bleed.

"The final item on the list is transport," said OCD. "Should be here any minute."

"Oh. No pumpkin then?" asked Ella.

"Do you know how hard it is to get hold of a pumpkin in June, Ella? The pumpkin industry is geared around Halloween. No, we've had to go for something else in the same sort of colour scheme. Don't worry, you'll love it. I think this is it now."

Ella heard the sound of something with a large engine coming along the road. She looked towards the sound and a huge orange cement mixer came around the bend, swerving erratically. She saw in horror that a yellow-hatted dwarf was driving.

"Is that Shitfaced? Seriously, you let the drunken one drive a cement mixer? What's the matter with you?" she yelled at OCD. Shitfaced saw them all waiting, waved at them and then steered directly at them.

"It's simple statistics," shouted OCD as they all ran for cover.

The cement mixer narrowly missed a gnarly old oak (that might have taken a small sidestep at the last moment) and came to a juddering halt, the giant drum on its rear revolving slowly.

Ella waved the resultant cloud of dust away. "It's amazing that he didn't hit anyone."

Shitfaced opened the cab door and smacked Passive Aggressive in the face.

"Amazing," agreed Shitfaced as Passive Aggressive rolled around, clutching his nose.

"Right. Everyone in," said OCD.

"Oh right, I'll just take one for the team, shall I?" wailed Passive Aggressive. "No one going to check on me, no?"

"Um," said Ella. "Do I need to ask? Why a cement mixer?"

"Statistics," said OCD. "There are three thousand people killed or seriously injured every year in this country from drunk driving, yeah?"

"Ri-ight?"

"But the figures for people killed or injured by cement mixers in a drunk driving incident are statistically insignificant. See how it's the safe choice?"

"I guess I'm statistically insignificant," groaned Passive Aggressive.

"It's orange. It's round. It's as fucking near to a pumpkin as you're going to get, bab," said Psycho. "Get in."

With a final glance to the section of ditch where her mum and grandma were hiding, she climbed into the cab with the dwarfs. Once they were squeezed in, Shitfaced cranked it into gear and Windy tooted the wedding march. Ella wished she was next to the window so that she could open it.

"Finally! On our way to your bastard wedding now." Psycho nudged the steering wheel to avoid an oncoming police car, while Shitfaced drained the last from a plastic flagon of scrumpy.

"Nobody's actually proposed to me," said Ella. "It's my dad's wedding we're actually —"

"We've not come this far to let details like that get in our way. OCD, you got proposal on your checklist?"

"Have I ever missed anything off a list?" OCD challenged. "I've even got a list completion list for double-checking."

"You're very organised," said Ella, her mind switching to something she very much wanted to bring up. "I saw how you even catalogued the things that the big bad wolf vomited up."

OCD gave a gruff nod of professional pride. "A place for everything."

"And you still have it all?"

OCD pulled up his sack and rummaged around inside. "Checked and accounted for."

"Because if you want to get me a wedding present, I very much liked that jar," Ella said casually.

"Jars are the last thing you'll be needing tonight," leered Inappropriate. "Got kinky undies on your list, OCD mate?"

"As a matter of fact," said OCD, rustling in his sack, "I cleaned up some out of your private collection, Inappropriate. Thought it would save us some time. Lacy, crotchless, latex. Do you have a preference, Ella?"

Ella tried to convey the horror she felt but her words had to overcome the urge to retch in disgust.

"I'll handle my own underwear," she said. "And I certainly don't want underwear that's been anywhere near this grubby little man."

"I can order fresh undergarments," said OCD.

"Wedding present! Fresh undies! My arse!" shouted Psycho. "After all we've done for you, you've got a bastard nerve. We've had you rescued from that tower. We've had you rescued from the sea!"

Ella bit down on the obvious retort that she'd actually rescued herself on both occasions.

"Your Prince Charming's all ready and waiting for you, thanks to us," said Psycho, "and all you can think about is presents!"

A horn blared. The police car was heading straight at them. Psycho lunged across Shitfaced to steer them back on track, bouncing off the kerb as he overcorrected.

"That's torn it," said Ella. "They're bound to turn around and pull us over now."

"Nah," said Psycho. "They've got bigger things to worry about."

"Bigger than a stolen cement mixer driven by a drunken dwarf?"

"Oh, yes, bab. Big big things are afoot," he said, darkly.

15

Out on The Bumbles' lawns, Roy bumped and ground to the irresistible groove that the funky bearded chap had planted within him. Buster barked and worried at Roy's shoes but Roy just incorporated the dog into his dance.

He wasn't sure exactly how long he'd been dancing but it appeared that the furniture and decorations had been set out and, yes, here were the first of the wedding guests, coming up the path and collecting a glass of Bucks Fizz from the waiting staff. This was, of course, Gavin and Myra's wedding. Their guests were mostly unknown to him and Roy, merely host and friend to the daughter of the groom, didn't have a specific role at the wedding but he felt the irresistible urge to share his groove with them and funked and strutted his way across the grass.

"Hey," he called to an elderly couple as they arrived. "Bride or *groo-oove*?"

"I beg your pardon?" said the woman.

"Dance with me," said Roy and took her hands in his.

The woman gave him an irritable and confused look.

"I say, are you actually an usher?" said the old man, casting Roy's hands off his wife.

"Me? No. I'm..." Roy looked down at himself. He was wearing a morning suit with a gold cravat. "I'm getting married!" he declared in joyous surprise. "How could I forget?"

"I don't think this is your wedding," the woman said but Roy wasn't listening.

"Come on, Buster," he called as he dashed off. "We need to find Ella."

THERE WERE some positives to travelling by ogre, Natalie reflected queasily.

It was certainly fast. They had covered the forty-odd miles between the Cotswolds and Warwickshire in less than an hour. And the ogre, through stealth and some small magic, had avoided being spotted by regular people. He'd kept to fields, forests and canal paths for much of the journey. He'd leapt the River Avon in a single bound and even managed to sneak across the M40 motorway without anyone noticing.

However, there were negatives too. With Natalie held in the bowl of one hand (clutching the still damp copy of *Solomon Re-examined*) and Rose in the bowl of the other (clutching the still damp rolled up carpet), there was much swinging around and jolting. Speed and stamina the ogre might have had but he was certainly lacking in the suspension department.

"Slow down," Natalie called to the ogre as they crossed a field.

"Oh, crikey, yes," said Rose. "My innards are in turmoil, I tell thee."

The ogre slowed to a walk. Natalie pointed at a sign for Diggers and Dreams garden centre beyond the nearest hedge.

"We're almost there. You can put us down."

The ogre gently placed them on the ground. Rose staggered a

few steps before finding her feet. She leaned heavily on the shotgun and took several cleansing breaths as the colour returned to her cheeks. The wolf, who had been loping along in pursuit of the ogre all the way (and had gone under several times swimming the Avon and had nearly been flattened sprinting across the M40) caught up with them, panting heavily.

"Did we" — *gasp* — "beat Cinders and the" — *pant* — "dwarfs?"

"Don't know," said Natalie. "We need to get to the car park and find Ella and hope she was able to get the jar."

"Come on!" Rose, shotgun in hand, led the way towards the hedge. She paused before pressing through. "Ogre?"

"Yes?" he said.

"Tha can't come into t'car park, looking like a great lolloping ogre."

"Can't we disguise him?" said Natalie.

"What as? A Ford Fiesta?"

"Maybe you were thinking of putting a dress on him and saying he's a really ugly aunt," said the wolf.

"Now, Zeke, tha's got this far on account of my good nature," said Rose, "but we all know I'd shoot thee as soon as look at thee."

"But then, Granny, I wouldn't be able to point out that the ogre here is a shapeshifter."

"Is he?" said Rose.

"Are you?" said Natalie.

The ogre smiled and then had abruptly vanished, replaced by a low and long crocodile with a head full of sharp teeth.

"Bloomin' Nora," said Rose.

"Impressive, but not much use," said Natalie. "I can't see a crocodile sneaking surreptitiously into a wedding."

"Unless it's as a handbag and matching belt," said Rose.

"Maybe you need to transform into something smaller," suggested the wolf.

The crocodile eyed him suspiciously.

WITH A VIOLENT BOOTLEGGER turn that mowed down a bush, decapitated a row of garden gnomes and caused a wedding guest to faint, Shitfaced swung the cement mixer into a space in the garden centre car park. The vehicle swayed on its suspension and then, thankfully, it was still. Ella yanked the handbrake on with a powerful finality.

"See?" said Inappropriate. "Chicks love a man who can drive. She's all hot under the collar and can't wait to get her hands on your equipment."

"You're a bloody menace," she told Shitfaced.

"A sexy menace?" slurred Shitfaced.

There was a rap at the door. Windy opened it.

"One-hour delivery special," said a man in a peaked cap.

The man passed two parcels into the cab, one wide and flat, the other clearly shoe boxy. Ella looked at the first line of the address: *The bastard cement mixer in the bastard car park.*

Windy gave the man a bum-toot of thanks and closed the door.

"Time to get bloody changed then," said Psycho.

Ella looked at them all.

"Not in front of you lot, I'm not."

"It's nothing we haven't seen before," said Passive Aggressive.

"Well, you haven't seen mine before."

Inappropriate pulled a face of mild disagreement.

"Well, wireless webcams are so cheap these days," he said, "it would have been foolish not to."

"Ugh!" she spat and battled her way past three dwarfs to the door of the truck. "You know, for what's supposed to be my special day, you're not making it very special!"

Windy deflated like a whoopy cushion as she knelt on him and pushed open the door. She swung down to the ground and snatched the two parcels from OCD.

"We're sorry," said OCD. "I'm sure you're going to look radiant. Here." He rummaged in his sack once more and tossed the Solomon jar down to Ella. "Go on, have that. Happy wedding day."

Ella examined the jar, felt the weight of it in her hand. It seemed so ordinary. Just a dusty old jar with a snuggly fitting moulded glass lid. There were the faintest of marks around the rim that could have been ancient and powerful runes or merely accidental scratches. It looked as it should be holding boiled sweets or bath salts, not all-powerful fairies. Ella offered up a silent prayer that this was the right jar. If it wasn't, their plan had been reduced from one hope to no hope.

"I'm going to get changed in the garden centre toilets," she told the dwarfs. "No one is to follow me. Especially you, you bloody perv."

"She means you," Inappropriate told Windy as Ella slammed the door.

There were public toilets next to the café area. Ella scanned the sky, expecting to see a pair of annoyingly twee and helpful bluebirds coming down to assist her. And there they were, weaving joyful and celebratory spirals in the air. What Ella did not expect to see was a badger by the side of the path. Badgers were shy, nocturnal creatures and wisely stayed as far away from humans as they possibly could. Also, badgers were rarely spotted standing on their hind legs, desperately trying to convey a message through the medium of charades.

Rose, Natalie and the wolf were sitting on the far side of the hedge, when the badger-shaped ogre and Ella burst through. This was made all the harder for Ella by the huge white dress and petticoats she wore. The ogre popped back into his regular shape.

"Just in case you were thinking of eating me," he said to the wolf.

"What? And catch TB?"

With a grunt and zero care for her dress, Ella broke free of the hedge and tossed a jar into Natalie's hands.

"Good work!" Natalie grinned. "This is it?"

"I'm fairly sure," said Ella. "Can't stop. I've got to let the bluebirds do my hair. Not sure I can take much more of this Cinderella stuff."

"Tha dress looks lovely," said Rose.

"Beautiful," said the wolf.

"Like a snowman," said the ogre.

"It's very traditional looking and there's nowt wrong with that," said Rose. "Saw one like that when I was but a kid." She looked at Ella's shoes. "But tha's never wearing them on tha feet, is tha?"

Natalie looked down at Ella's feet and saw that they were pressed into transparent shoes that not only contorted and squashed her feet in the most brutal way but also seemed to magnify the redness and the chafing. It was like looking at a pair of well tenderised steaks stuffed into goldfish bowls.

"Apparently I am," said Ella. "Listen, the house is up that way. You can go along and pretend to be guests for the moment." Ella paused for a moment. "Granny, you might want to ditch the apron and the gun to, you know, blend in. Now, are you happy with the plan?"

"It was my plan," said Natalie.

"*Our* plan," said Ella. "The moment Carabosse makes a show, you nab her."

"Yes, yes," said Natalie. "As I said, *my* plan."

Ella squeezed back through the hedge again, hobbling only slightly in the agonising shoes.

Natalie and Rose gave Ella a few minutes' head start then gave the wolf and ogre instructions to keep a low profile, and snuck through the hedge themselves. Wedding guests were arriving in considerable numbers, exiting the car park for the short walk up to the posh house on the hill.

"Reckon I'll have to do more than lose t'apron to blend in here," observed Rose drily, slipping it off nonetheless and wrapping it around the shotgun to conceal it. "What on earth does tha suppose that is?"

She nodded at a large metallic tower that was being lifted from a van by a pair of men in kitchen whites. Natalie craned round to read the text on the side of the van.

"It's from *Cherry's Chocolate Fountains.*"

"What's one of them then?"

"I don't know, mum. I'm the one who's out of their proper time here."

"Well, it sounds downright decadent whatever it is," said. "Must be an American thing."

"You think everything 'decadent' is an American thing."

"Bet it cost a small fortune though," said Rose. "Stains'll be a devil to get out, mark my words."

They walked along towards the house that lay behind the garden centre. The path was indicated by flower-covered walkways and balloon arches

"Can you hear that?" said the wolf.

"Hear what?" said Natalie.

"That beat. That rhythm."

Natalie stopped and listened. She couldn't hear anything but she could feel something, like dance music for whales, thudding and subsonic.

"I like it," she said although she was unable to articulate why.

"It's awfully familiar," said the wolf. "It reminds me of huffing and puffing at straw houses, of what happens when I knock at grandma's door."

"Well, I can't hear nowt," said Rose, "and I'll shoot thee if tha gets any weird ideas."

"I'm just saying," said the wolf. "It makes me want to... I'll be with you in a moment."

The wolf nipped off. Natalie sighed; there was no time for this. She gestured to Rose and they continued up the path, beneath countless balloon arches.

"Someone's spent hours blowing these up. There's hundreds," she said.

"They taste funny too," came a squeaky high voice from behind.

Rose turned and raised a threatening fist. "Zeke, what did I tell thee about tha bloomin' drag act?"

Natalie recognised the clothes the wolf had squeezed himself into.

"Those are mine!"

"Ella left them behind," squeaked the wolf, adjusting the balloons he'd stuffed down his top. "She didn't need them. And I just felt that this was, you know, right."

Stop talking like a little girl!"

"I can't! The balloons are making me do it!" squeaked the wolf.

Natalie gave a balloon boob an experimental prod but decided that she had higher priorities.

"Tha Gavin's surely not spent all this money on his getting married to that hoity-toity Myra girl?" said Rose.

"He's not my Gavin anymore though, is he?" said Natalie. "But I've got to admit. This is amazing. It looks like a film set or a coronation or something."

"Blummin' heck," said Rose.

"What?" said Natalie.

"I knew I'd seen that dress afore, that one tha Ella is wearing."

"And?"

"It's the queen's!"

Natalie stared at her old mum. True, to Natalie's eyes, Rose had skip-jumped thirty years in age but she didn't think the old woman had lost her marbles just yet.

"It belongs to the queen?"

"It's same as t'queen's wedding dress. I saw it in t'Telegraph and Argus when I were a lass."

"So?" said Natalie. "It's a nice dress."

"No," said Rose grimly. "It means summat. That flamin' fairy godmother. She's always up to summat."

"Do it again," said OCD. "Again."

Ella muttered darkly under her breath and tried to modify her hobble into something more dainty as she walked from one end of the corridor to the other.

"She's not gliding. We might need to get a trolley or something!" OCD yelled.

The dwarfs had taken her into a side corridor in The Bumbles to add those supposedly important finishing touches. However, it was clear that OCD wasn't happy with the basic material he had to work with.

Only Shitfaced, Windy and the bluebirds remained with OCD, the others having scuttled off on God knows what errands. The bluebirds attempted to help by carrying Ella's wedding train for her. Shitfaced attempted to help by modelling a ladylike walk which, as far as she could tell, involved mincing about a bit, tripping over one's own feet, bouncing off the wall and then picking a fight with a mirror.

Ella was further distracted by the almost inaudible but omnipresent dance beat that was coming from somewhere. It had a catchy, almost sensual rhythm but what distracted Ella most of all was how much it put her in mind of the thrilling sensation she had felt every time she had played along with the fairy tale stories she found herself in.

"Was that your best effort?" said OCD.

The rhythm had carried her from one end of the corridor to the other without her realising.

"It was good enough, wasn't it?" she said.

"It'll have to do," said OCD sourly.

"Gee, thanks."

"It's not my fault someone didn't pay enough attention during her deportment lessons. This way."

Windy and Shitfaced held the doors for Ella and she did her best to appear at least a little regal as she walked through into the orangery.

The tables had been laid out for the wedding breakfast (according to OCD's fascistically precise plan, she noted) and the room was empty but for a solitary dancer. This was odd for a number of reasons, foremost of which was that the dance beat was barely audible in here. Nonetheless, he appeared to be lost in music, thrusting his arms and swaying from side to side with his eyes closed in rapture.

"Roy?" she ventured.

His eyes snapped open and he gazed up and down at Ella. She was horribly aware of the fact that she was in full bridal regalia. In normal circumstances, such attire would strike fear into the heart of an unattached man, but these were far from normal circumstances.

"Oh, my angel! My vision!" he gasped in wonder.

"Um, hello."

He rushed towards her with the unselfconscious and child-like movements of a drunk but Ella was quite certain alcohol had played no part in this.

"You all right, Roy?" she asked.

"Marvellous!" he said, wide-eyed. "You look so perfect, Ella."

"That's very... kind of you."

"I need to ask you a question," he said.

"Oh, I bet you do," she said and forced a smile.

"You do know that I love you, don't you?"

"Um. Was that the question?"

"No, silly. Will you make me the happiest man alive and help me find the groove?"

"The groove?"

He dropped to one knee, hips still rolling to a silent rhythm.

"Marry me, Ella!"

This was part of the plan, Ella told herself. This was what she had discussed with her grandma and her twenty-something mum. This was all just a charade. He was under some magical influence and she was playing along. It wasn't real, and yet...

Roy was before her right now and he was asking her to marry him. And she found herself wondering, what objection did she have to being married to this man, apart from the fact that she was a stubborn spinster who didn't like being told what to do? They were friends, good friends even. He understood her, cared about her. He made her laugh. They were comfortable around each other. And he was attractive enough (he was going to be as bald as a coot within five years but that just gave him a human edge).

Did they have a shared outlook? Well, that was tougher. He was of that breed that lived in a world beyond that of mere mortals, where the right school and the right tie ensured you a job for a life as a merchant banker or Tory politician, where the year was divided into shooting, skiing and sailing, where you could probably commit armed robbery and get away with a slapped wrist from a high court judge. She... Well, Ella definitely didn't live in that world. But was that insurmountable?

Ella shook herself. She wasn't being asked to marry Roy. Roy was not currently himself and there was only one answer she could give at this moment.

"Yes, Roy, I'd be delighted," she said.

"You will?" Her enchanted fiancé was so happy, she feared he might explode.

"Of course," she said. "Come on, we need to tell my father." She gave a girlish giggle for the benefit of OCD who trotted behind, brandishing his list.

THREE CIRCUMSPECT BUT nonetheless suspicious figures circled the wedding party on the lawn. They were, in perhaps decreasing order of suspiciousness, the young woman in casual attire from the nineteen eighties, the older, slightly mad-haired woman with the shotgun-shaped bundle under her arm and an extraordinarily hairy woman who didn't seem to be at all comfortable with the notion of walking upright.

"Not seen Carabosse yet," said Natalie.

"Nor Ella."

"You don't think she's whisked them away and married them already?"

"No, love. That shameless cow will want an audience. She'll want Ella to be centre of attention."

"I do love a good wedding," commented the wolf.

He was currently devouring a large silver platter of canapes. Little salmon cracker things and folds of cured meat disappeared into his huge mouth at an impressive rate.

"Where d'you get them?" said Natalie.

"One of the servant people," he said. "I asked her if I could have one, grinned at her pleasant-like and she gave me the whole tray."

He paused to down a jug of Bucks Fizz before continuing on the canapes. Natalie stared.

"What?" he said. "I'm famished. Keeping an eye out for your little princess is hungry work."

"What exactly are you doing here?" said Natalie. "I mean, at all."

"It's a bet," said the wolf. "With Ella. With myself. She thinks you can fight a happy ending."

"And you don't?"

The wolf shrugged and licked the empty platter clean.

"I think life is like a plate of little snacks. It's not exactly fulfilling but what can you do but grab what you can and don't complain when someone comes to take it away from you?"

The wolf nodded towards a man ambling across the lawn towards them. He looked like he shared the wolf's philosophy of enjoying the small pleasures in life and perhaps was, by his bumbling steps, enjoying them a little too much.

"Oh, my God!" hissed Natalie. "It's Gavin."

Gavin gave them a good natured but slightly confused smile.

"He recognises you," said Rose.

Natalie shook her head.

"No. No, he can't quite place me." A sudden panic seized her. "He can't meet me. He can't."

"Well, it might give him a bit of a shock once he realises it's thee," agreed Rose.

"And it will ruin the wedding and our chance of getting Carabosse."

Natalie looked about them. There was no place they could duck into or hide. Their options were either to face him or run away guiltily.

"I could rip his leg off," suggested the wolf. "As a distraction."

"That might also jeopardise the wedding," said Natalie.

"Well I was only... Oh, what's this?"

Ella was dashing across the lawn to intercept Gavin, dragging her wedding train and a besuited fellow behind her.

"Dad! Dad!"

Gavin turned, his attention caught.

"Quick, let's make an exit," said Natalie and steered Rose towards the marquee.

"Pursued by wolf," said the wolf.

ELLA GUESSED she would find her dad glad-handing the guests and ensuring that everyone (including himself) was well lubricated with drink. And here he was, weaving across the lawn, a glass of wine in his hand.

"Ella!" he beamed. "Darling!"

She hugged him tightly. It felt like she hadn't seen him in ages. And now here was her old dad, back in his old haunts again, in his rightful place. And he returned her hug just as tightly, this gently pickled man who smelled of fine wine and all that was good in life.

"Oh, it's such a relief to see you!" he said.

"Ditto," she said.

"I didn't know if you were still at Thornbeard House. Mr Dainty is a hard taskmaster."

"No, I am done there," she said firmly.

"Job complete?"

"Absolutely."

"You even found his missing Wedgwood teapot?"

That gave Ella pause for thought. A picture of shattered pottery shards on a rock appeared in her mind's eye.

"Found it, lost it again," she said flatly.

"Shame. And Dainty was okay with that?"

She laughed coldly. "Does it matter? I'm here now."

"In time for the wedding."

"I wouldn't have missed it for the world," said Ella.

"You've certainly dressed up," said Gavin, standing back to admire Ella's dress. "I bet Myra will be thrilled to see that you've taken the wedding theme so much to heart."

"Listen Dad, there's a good reason why I'm dressed like this. Roy and I are... Roy."

Roy, who was standing to the side, shimmying his shoulders, snapped to attention.

"Yes, dear."

"We're getting married," said Ella.

Her father's face went through a variety of expressions. Ella saw delight and confusion jostling for final position.

"Well that sounds lovely, sweetheart, but surely you remember that Myra and I are getting married today?"

"A double wedding, dad."

"Oh, yes?"

"It'll be so special, don't you think?"

Gavin nodded slowly, digesting the idea. "Yes. That does sound nice. I wonder what Myra will—"

A howl of rage rang out from the marquee's entrance.

"Oh. My. God. You've finally gone too far, girl!"

"Yes, I wonder what Myra will make of it," said Gavin timidly.

NATALIE LIFTED a flap of tent wall and ushered Rose and the wolf into the back of marquee.

"Right, let's just lie low in here and wait for... Blimey!"

The interior of the marquee was stunning. Decorated silks hung down the walls, vibrant with exotic birds. Small trees in planters were spaced at intervals, heavily jewelled model birds nestled in their branches. Across the canvas ceiling, vines carried more birds and brightly coloured lanterns. At one end, a huge disco and sound stage had been set up. It was from this that the subsonic and obscenely pleasurable beat was emanating. A sequinned head bobbed around the turntables but paid them no mind. At the other end of the marquee, beyond a hundred or more white garden chairs was a glossy arbour, an ideal platform for any couple ready to take their vows.

"This must be where they're doing the ceremony," said the wolf.

"Is this a tent or a church?" said Natalie.

"Tart's boudoir, more like," said Rose with a sniff.

The wolf chomped a jewelled bird off one of the trees, but pulled a face. "A wolf could starve around here, seriously."

They walked past rows of chairs to the other end and the wedding arbour. A huge cake was displayed on a table nearby. Natalie pointed out the four tiny figurines on top of the cake.

"Looks like we're on for a double wedding," she said.

"Attention to detail," nodded Rose. "She wants everything perfect, that blummin' fairy. Let's make sure we're well placed to mess things up for her."

Rose hefted the shotgun in her hands and indicated the table that supported the cake. A cloth hung to the floor, making a useful space, just about the right size to hide two women and a huge wolf.

ANGRY MYRA WAS a sight to behold and a sight Ella had witnessed before. Angry Myra in a leopard print wedding dress was something remarkable and new.

"I've put up with enough of your antics!" she growled as she strode over. "You've been disappearing here there and everywhere, keeping your father from preparing for his wedding."

"Things have kind of cropped up," said Ella gently.

"You've spread horrible vicious lies about your..." She glanced at the mostly oblivious Gavin. "... about your you-know-who not being you-know-what in a spiteful effort to disrupt our plans and now this."

"This?"

"Who turns up to a wedding wearing a bridal gown? Only someone who seriously wants to piss off the bride!"

Ella heard a small officious voice protesting that the groom should not see the bride before the wedding, but she tried not to let it distract her. "Actually Myra—"

"Don't actually Myra me. You go and get changed this instant!" Myra's face was turning an unappealing shade of beetroot and Ella could hear an obsessive-compulsive dwarf somewhere complaining that the photographs would be ruined.

"Darling," said Gavin, swiftly downing the wine that remained in his glass, "there's to be a double wedding."

"What?"

"Ella and Roy will tie the knot at the same time as us. Isn't that going to be lovely?" He balked at the look of fury on the face of his intended. "Isn't it?"

Myra's face clouded with fresh indignation. "You mean that she's so determined to steal my thunder on my wedding day that she's going to join us at the bloody altar? Can't you see that this is just attention seeking of the highest order, Gavin?"

"No, love. Ella will marry Roy and then come and live here with him at The Bumbles."

"You mean...?

Roy took hold of Ella. "*Mi casa es su casa, mi amor.*"

"See?" said Ella.

"*Hace calor aqui, o eres tu?*"

"Yes, enough of that," said Ella.

Myra's hostility visibly softened.

"Well," she said haughtily. "I must say it would be nice for us to have the house to ourselves, Gavin. Have you sorted out the paperwork then, Ella? Got a licence and so on?"

"A licence, yes, we're going to need one of those," Ella said loudly. She knew that any wedding-blocking problems would be magically removed, but she was pretty sure that no licence existed, unless the dwarfs were creating one right now.

NATALIE AND ROSE were positioned under the cake table, but it really wasn't as roomy as it might have been with a huge wolf breathing foetid breath over their shoulders as they tried to peek out between the table covering. Natalie put her hand in something sticky. "Is this icing? Have you been at the cake?" she asked.

"Not where anyone will see, no," replied the wolf, licking his lips.

Through her gap in the tablecloth, Natalie watched the guests entering and taking their seats. Up on the stage, the tiny DJ was keeping the subliminal beat going.

"That's Disco," said Rose.

"The music?"

"The dwarf."

Natalie's eyes narrowed as she considered the seventh dwarf. He was standing on the stage, like a cross between Elton John and a Christmas tree decoration.

"T'others said he was on a secret mission," said Rose.

"What secret mission?" said Natalie.

"Does it matter?"

"It does if we can't enchant Carabosse back into this jar."

"Well, then we'll have to go with Plan B."

"Which is?"

Rose unwrapped the shotgun and took a handful of shot cartridges out of her pocket. "Put a bowling ball-sized dent in any fairy tale creature as 'as the gall to show up."

The wolf behind them went very still in an apparent attempt to look less like a fairy tale creature and more like part of the table.

. . .

ELLA TURNED at the sound of muffled cursing. A strange figure wobbled towards them across the lawn. It bore a superficial resemblance to a man wearing a suit, but it was all too obvious to Ella's eyes that it was a stack of three dwarfs standing on each others' shoulders wearing stolen clothes. Psycho's red hat was pushed into the top pocket of the suit, and surely that was Inappropriate who was waggling his finger out of the trousers' fly opening.

"Don't suppose I get a speaking part this time," came a small whining voice from the centre of the stack, "not that anyone ever listens to me anyway."

"Bastard rumbling stomach," said the tall uneven stranger, thumping his mid-section forcefully with his tiny arm. "I'm the registrar for this double wedding."

"Where's the real registrar?" Ella asked.

"What do you mean?" said Gavin.

"Nothing. Clearly."

"Shall we get this bastard ceremony over with?" said the registrar.

"Guests are still arriving. They'll want to enjoy a relaxing drink first," said Gavin, picking up another glass to illustrate his point.

"I'm *not* sure we have a marriage licence for this second, impromptu wedding," said Myra. "There must be paperwork needed to—"

"All taken care of," shouted the registrar, who took the glass that Gavin offered. Was Ella the only one who noticed that another two glasses disappeared, taken by arms that squeezed out at the trousers' waistband?

"THERE'S THE GROOMS," said Rose as Gavin and Ella's would-be husband, Roy, entered the marquee.

"I can't believe he looks as old as he does," said Natalie softly.

"Tha Gavin? What did tha expect?"

"I didn't expect thirty years to hit him like a ton of bricks. God, mum, he looks like my dad."

"Love is supposed to be blind," said Rose.

Natalie made a deeply philosophical noise.

"Well, my love appears to be drunk rather than blind."

"I do believe he always enjoyed a drop of t'good stuff." Rose pointed. "Has tha seen yon pair of silly buggers?"

A pair of young bridesmaids were trying to touch up their makeup with small hand mirrors. It was clear that their makeup was peeling off their faces, so one of them delved into a handbag and came out with a reel of flesh-coloured sticking plaster. She ripped off a long piece and strapped it under her chin and up her cheeks. She dabbed it with a powder compact and nudged her companion who took the reel and started to tape up her own face.

"That'll be Myra's daughters," said the wolf.

"How do you know?" said Natalie.

"Ugly step-sisters. Stands to reason. All part of the tale."

"And is a weird vicar part of the tale an' all?" asked Rose.

Three figures stood in front of the arbour, waiting for the brides to arrive. Gavin had an even rosier glow to his cheeks than before, undoubtedly due to downing a few more glasses of wine. Roy, who looked harmless enough but who couldn't seem to keep his hips still stood to the side. Rose was right, the oddly shaped individual who stood with them was just... all wrong. His body wavered, and his ridiculously stumpy legs staggered to and fro constantly.

"It's the dwarfs," said Natalie. "Three of them on each other's shoulders."

Rose leaned forward. "Well, I'll be —"

She reached for the shotgun but Natalie stayed her hand. "We need to wait. We'll know when Ella needs our help. Hopefully the jar's our best weapon anyway."

Natalie's words were nearly drowned out by music blaring from the sound stage at an ear shattering volume. Myra had chosen *Ride of the Valkyries*, and she stalked imperiously into the marquee, every bit the Norse battle maiden, holding a large bridal bouquet as though it was a double-handed axe. The considerably more demure Ella was by her side. Now, whereas Ella was wearing something very traditional, Myra had plumped for a dress that combined the aesthetics of Cruella de Vil, the Third Reich and a buxom barmaid. It was a figure-skimming fishtail dress with a high collar and a plunging neckline. The entire dress was made from a leopard print lycra. Myra swung her hips provocatively as she walked, winking at Gavin as she approached.

The music was too loud to speak over, but Rose pointed at Myra's dress and rolled her eyes. Lily and Petunia followed Ella and Myra up the aisle, their mouths set and their eyes directly ahead in an effort to keep their makeup from falling off.

ELLA LOOKED up at Roy as she drew near to him. She was happy that walking very slowly was called for, as the shoes were causing her a *lot* of pain. She smiled, and he returned a soppy, glazed look. If Carabosse didn't make her move soon, Ella would have to actually marry him, which might make things awkward later on.

They all stood under the arbour that Myra had designed herself. (Ella had seen the sketches.) It was woven with flowers and their heavy scent made Ella's eyes twitch.

Or was it the pomander Lily and Petunia had given her that smelled so strange? It hung from Ella's wrist as a good luck charm, but she'd worried at one point that it might be on fire as it hissed slightly and emitted a visible puff of vapour. Lily had laughed and said that it was an invention they'd been working on for the shop, and was to keep everything fresh. Ella suspected that it was one of those air fresheners designed to squirt doses of scent in a little gift bag and planned to abandon it at the earliest opportunity.

The registrar didn't look any more convincing when he stood to preside over the weddings, and Ella marvelled at the way all of the wedding guests simply stood and smiled.

The registrar extracted a set of notes written on cards and held them out with his tiny arms.

"Right, you lot," he declared loudly. "We're gathered here today for a bastard wedding between two loving couples."

Ella kept her eyes forward, but she knew, she simply *knew*, that everyone was ignoring Psycho's sweary additions to the script because they were English and would assume that they had misheard.

"My name is Superintendent Registrar Tallman and the fire exits are to your— bollocks to that." He threw the card over his shoulder. "Right let's move on and talk about who's who. Keep up now, or you'll marry the wrong bastard person."

"Lovely isn't it?" said a voice behind Ella. It was the voice of the cat that had got the cream, oily and so very pleased with itself.

Ella froze, knowing that somehow Carabosse was standing directly behind her. She managed to turn her head enough to see out of the corner of her eye that there were now three bridesmaids standing behind her. Had nobody else noticed?

"This is all I've dreamed of for you Ella," Carabosse continued quietly while Psycho addressed the rest of the audience. I've worked very hard for this. You're about to realise exactly what I've managed to achieve."

"You've arranged a wedding. Hup-di-do. People do that every day."

"Not like this one, they don't, dearie. This is the perfect wedding."

Ella looked pointedly at her soon to be step-mother's wedding dress, the two bridesmaids who had mummified their own heads and the three-dwarf act that was the registrar and then at Carabosse.

"Perfect."

Your Prince Charming is the genuine article. He's royalty, Ella."

Ella snorted. "Four-hundred-and-something-th in line to the throne."

"Not for much longer," said Carabosse. "He's about to become king and you will become queen."

"But the others?"

"Aren't I the best fairy godmother? I am *very* good at my job."

"What did you *do*?" hissed Ella, as quietly as she could.

Carabosse laughed. "My small friend Disco has been extremely helpful. You'll have observed his talents when it comes to bending people to my will?"

Ella glanced sideways at Roy who was still bopping gently to an unseen rhythm, his eyes unfocussed. Yes, she understood what Disco could achieve.

"So those other inconvenient souls who stood in the way of your fairy tale happy ending have been collected up, Pied Pipered away by Disco to a single location."

"Where?"

"A mountain cave."

"*Where*?"

"It doesn't really matter. The cave did not exist until recently, and when I say the word, it will cease to exist. Solid rock will tidily replace those four hundred and something people and you will have everything that you ever wished for." Carabosse sighed with contentment and it took all of Ella's willpower not to spin round and thump her.

"But I didn't wish for this," said Ella.

"Pish-posh. What do you know? You are going to be married to a king and then you will be queen and live happily ever after."

"No one lives happily ever after."

"Leave it to me, dear," said Carabosse. "It will be a perfect moment in time, Ella. It's what I've worked so hard to achieve. Everyone will be happy."

"And then?"

"Then? Then the time will be right to put everyone to sleep so that it can never, ever be ruined."

Ella stared.

"When you say everyone..."

"Everyone," said Carabosse. "Everyone in the land."

"But you can't..."

"Oh, there will be loose ends, but I can sort those out, tidy them away."

"Has t'dwarf lost his ruddy mind?" Rose said, under the table. "Surely to goodness people've noticed every other word he says is a cuss word? And if that's not enough, that long thin balloon coming out of his flies is going to make people talk."

The wolf coughed. "You might want to take a look at the bridesmaids," he said.

Natalie stared at the bridesmaids. She couldn't quite put her finger on what was the matter.

"Try looking away. Use the corner of your eye," said the wolf.

Natalie stared at the two bridal couples. Myra glared suspiciously at the registrar as though she was not *entirely* certain that he was behaving badly. Gavin gazed happily at his bride. Roy was still unfocussed on anything but the inaudible groove. Ella looked extremely worried because — there!

Right behind Ella was another figure, somehow blended with the bridesmaids. Natalie gave a small low growl at the sight of her.

"I seen her an' all," whispered Rose. "Do we go now?"

"Let's wait for the I dos," said Natalie. "When she's most distracted."

The wobbly registrar tried to bat away the swelling balloon penis that swayed from his trousers but found that his arms were too short. He continued with the service.

"If anyone knows of any bastard lawful impediment —"

"Yes!" yelled Ella. "The wicked fairy Carabosse is manipulating us all and she's right here!"

"Or we go now," said Rose.

Natalie leapt out from under the table.

"Do it, mum!" yelled Ella. "Do it now!"

Gavin and Myra gaped in shock.

"Natalie?"

Natalie stood firm and held the open jar before her.

"*Libertatibus perierat et ignaro in ampulla ad imperium,*" she intoned.

Carabosse was now clearly visible to Natalie. She had become the focal point of the room. Everything else faded away.

"*Libertatibus perierat et ignaro in ampulla ad imperium.*"

Carabosse should have been quaking in fear at that point, her plan about to come unravelled and her form to be imprisoned in the jar once more but, instead, there was a playful and knowing smile on the fairy's lips. She raised a hand towards Natalie. Two bluebirds came from nowhere and swooped down at her face. Natalie ducked, curling her body protectively around the jar and her arm around her face.

ELLA SNATCHED Myra's bouquet and swatted at the birds with it, catching one with a satisfying backhand that send it thudding into the marquee wall.

"Is that really Natalie?" said Gavin, bewildered.

"Out the way, lass," instructed Rose.

She had the gun unwrapped and was taking aim at Carabosse.

"Mad old lady!" screeched Petunia.

"Let me take care of her boss!" yelled Psycho, and he wriggled out of the registrar's suit and jumped down.

"You! You haven't finished the ceremony!" yelled Myra.

The blast of the shotgun rang out throughout the tent, sending people into a panic, spilling chairs and expensive decorations everywhere. Carabosse crumpled up like a badly folded deckchair.

"Is that you, Natalie?" said Gavin.

Myra, who was a woman with some fixed priorities, windmilled her arms in frustration. "Would everyone stop trying to ruin my wedding! I know Ella's put you up to this... whatever this is."

Ella was watching Carabosse. The fairy godmother was still standing and now, slowly but surely, she was straightening, frowning down at the hole in the front of her dress. She swivelled to reveal that there was also a hole in the back of her dress, but her body was whole in between.

"Oh Rose," she said, with her head cocked coyly to one side. "Violence is unbecoming, don't you think?"

Psycho leapt at the shotgun in Rose's hand, dragging the barrel down. Rose's second shot blasted a minor crater in the ground. Ella swatted at the bluebird that was trying to peck Natalie's face. Myra was screeching at anyone she thought might be listening, including the now headless registrar. Psycho wrestled with Rose for control of the shotgun.

"You right horrible bugger," cried Rose.

"Bastard ungrateful child," Psycho retorted.

"Been on my case for donkey's and I'm sick to death of the ruddy sight of thee!"

The wolf bounded forward and bared his fangs.

Psycho gave a look of pure terror.

"Eat her! Eat her!" he yelped.

The big bad wolf opened his jaws wide and, with a chomp and gulp and a cry of "Not again!" Psycho was swallowed whole.

With a lucky swipe, Ella snatched the bluebird out of the air.

"How about second helpings?" she called to the wolf.

The wolf turned, Ella hurled the bundle of blue feathers and it was gone.

"Hmmm. Not all bad are you, Zeke?" Rose said.

"Not all," he said.

"The jar!" yelled Ella.

Natalie picked herself up and then held out an empty hand.

"I had it..."

Carabosse chuckled lightly. The jar was in her hand.

"We'll have no more of this nonsense Natalie. You're not part of this story, my dear."

"I do think that is Natalie, you know," said Gavin.

"Shut up," said Myra.

"It's time for Ella to have her happy ending," said Carabosse and dashed the jar against one of the marquee support poles. It came apart in a million snowflake fragments.

"Now, we need to get things back on track," said Carabosse.

"That's right," said Myra firmly, who clearly had no idea what was going on but was dead set on what she wanted.

"Disco, dear chap," said the fairy. "It's time for some music."

Ella put her fingers in her ears, suspecting what was coming next. She tried to signal to others that they should do the same, but it wasn't the easiest of messages to get across in the circumstances.

The sound system burst into life with a hypnotic thumping that made Roy break apart from the bridal party and raise his hands ecstatically, as his body swayed to the rhythm. Disco capered to his side and they led the dance. Those around them swiftly moved from mild embarrassment through fascination into a compulsion to join in. Even those guests who had been fleeing for the exit now found themselves bopping and gyrating to the beat.

A line formed, with Disco and Roy at the front, performing a wide-legged conga, pounding invisible drums as they went. They snaked around the room, gathering followers. Myra's solid mask of annoyance dropped from her face and she joined the dancing, dragging Gavin along behind her. Lily and Petunia squealed with delight and tottered out of time on their high heels.

Carabosse beamed with pleasure at the daughter, mother and grandmother who were the only ones unaffected by the spell.

"You can't fight a happy ending, girls," she said.

16

"**E**veryone will soon be in my control," said Carabosse, "and there will be no more interruptions."

A rapid burst of explosive gunfire by the marquee entrance argued otherwise. Disco faltered in his conga and the line behind him fell apart, wedding guests staring at each other and straightening their clothes in embarrassment.

Ella turned and was stunned to see Mr Dainty. He stood tall and carried the enormous and ancient Gatling-style gun from his private weapons collection. He wore bandoliers across his shoulders loaded with spare ammunition and added further to his action hero image with a rakishly angled beret and a cigar. He looked very pleased with himself indeed.

His black-clad henchmen — Cheeky, Hook, Eyepatch, Scarhead, the lot — flanked him, toting weaponry of their own.

"Ella!" cried Mr Dainty. "I order you not to marry this man. He is a feeble specimen and you will see that I am surely the better choice. Come to me now and I will make you mine."

"You tried to shoot me!" shouted Ella.

"What can I say? I'm a passionate man!"

"This will not do!" shouted Carabosse. "You had your chance and you blew it! Dwarfs!"

Passive Aggressive and Inappropriate wriggled free from the registrar's suit while OCD, Shitfaced and Windy dropped from the ceiling using leafy vines as ropes. Their weapons were limited to boots and offensive smells, but they launched into an attack on Mr Dainty and his sidekicks nonetheless. The henchmen replied with small arms fire and chaos erupted once more.

"Kill the groom!" Dainty shouted.

Scarhead knelt down and opened fire on the conga line with a submachinegun.

Ella threw herself at her pretend-fiancé and bore him to the ground, a task made slightly trickier by his persistent desire to dance.

Despite the unfolding bedlam, Disco was still making a concerted effort to continue his dance of bewitchment. He exaggerated the dance, throwing shapes that nobody could miss. The music was still playing on the loudspeakers, and a few of the guests fell back in line behind him. Lily and Petunia giggled together and started their own routine. Ella had seen it many times. They practised it in the garden centre when it was quiet, but it never seemed to get any better.

"And a *one*, two, three, four. *Step*, two, three, four!" yelled Lily. It looked as if the two of them were playing an invisible game of Twister in a wind tunnel. Ella had often wondered how they avoided brutalising each other with their flailing, but as an interesting side effect, the lack of rhythm (or perhaps it was the disagreeable spectacle) seemed to break Disco's spell. Several of the happy Conga dancers stopped to stare at the two girls and whispered to each other, trying to work out what had happened.

"FEEL THE RHYTHM WITH ME!" bellowed Disco, who jumped onto the table alongside the wedding cake. He used his hands as a conductor might, bending the crowd to his will.

Dainty's henchmen plus many of the wedding guests turned towards him and their expressions all changed to hollow-eyed euphoria as they linked arms to strut in time with Disco's instructions.

"Got to dance," mumbled Roy, underneath Ella.

"Stay down," she told him, and he seemed content to wriggle dazedly on the floor to the faltering beat.

"And a *one*, two, three, four. *Step*, two, three, four!" Lily and Petunia were concentrating hard, but still moved as if they were falling off roller skates in slow motion. Once again, their alternative and discordant beat cut straight across the steady hypnotic trance woven by Disco.

Ella saw Hook and Eyepatch, who had been mesmerised by Disco, shake themselves, look at their weapons, and remember who they were. There was a great deal of noise and shouting but the Euro-villains, who seemed to favour shooting in the air and shouting to actually harming anyone, were happy enough to cause panic and uproar.

She looked for the others. Myra and Gavin were still in the arbour. Myra, it was clear, was not going to budge one inch until someone married her. Dainty was battling with a determined Shitfaced who was fuelling his alcoholic rage with a pilfered bottle of Champagne. The wolf had his jaws firmly clenched around Hook's one good hand, which was understandably causing the one-armed thug a great deal of alarm.

Something hard slammed into Ella's temple, momentarily blinding her. She staggered, clutching her head.

"Didn't see that coming!" crowed Cheeky, gesticulating with the pistols he held.

"Fucking ninja butler!" she swore, looking at her hand to check for blood.

Cheeky had violent purple bruises on both sides of his head

from the repeated clonks he'd received before. The two bruises met in the middle over his angrily furrowed brow.

"You have upset my boss. Why do all of his wives choose to upset him?"

Out of nowhere, Rose swung her shotgun like a baseball bat and smacked Cheeky across the back of the head. He grunted in shock and turned, so Granny Rose adjusted her grip and jabbed the wooden gun stock into his face, knocking him down.

"She ain't his wife yet, lad." She gave Ella a terse look. "We need to do something afore someone gets hurt."

"I think that's already happened," said Ella.

Rose gave the unconscious Cheeky a dismissive glance. "I meant someone important. Tha needs to get tha boyfriend, tha mother and whoever tha can out of here."

Rose broke open the shotgun, expertly flipped out the spent cartridges and reloaded.

"And what will you do?" said Ella.

"Plan B," said Rose. She raised the shotgun to her shoulder and took aim at Carabosse. "Reckon that little missy can carry on having a tantrum if I blow her head off her shoulders?" she asked, letting off a couple of shots.

"You can't kill her," said Ella.

"No, but I can buy thee some time. Get to it."

NATALIE, on hands and knees, stared at the shattered remains of the Solomon Jar. It should have worked. It should have worked but they had rushed into this plan without thinking it through. And now they'd lost the jar. Natalie should at least have taken photographs of the jar before they tried to use it, maybe they could have deciphered those faint marks around the rim, maybe they could have fashioned new jars.

Maybe, maybe, maybe...

A series of loud pops overhead marked the demise of the balloon unicorn. Near to, Mr Dainty clubbed the drunken dwarf with the butt of his gun and waved his men forward. They were going for Gavin and Myra.

Natalie yelled a warning across to them but Myra wasn't listening. Remarkably, she had approached one of Dainty's henchmen — the one with a metal plate in his head — and was talking to him about his machine gun.

"I tried one of these at the Berlin arms expo," she was saying, "but the strap really needs to be modified for a comfortable working angle. Can I show you?"

The man released his weapon and handed it to Myra, who promptly whacked him with the stock. He crumpled to the floor. As Natalie made her way over to them, Myra pulled a cable tie from the man's top pocket and fastened his hands together.

"Idiot."

Gavin grinned at her. "You're magnificent, have I ever told you that?"

Natalie squeezed through a pair of hypnotised dancers to finally reach the betrothed fifty-somethings.

"That was very impressive, Myra."

Myra stared at her with unfettered dismay. "I don't know who you are."

"Reminds of that time at primary school when Linda Hepworth wouldn't give you your Bunty Annual back and you slammed it shut on her nose."

"But Natalie..." said Myra.

Natalie shrugged and then gave them a cheesy smile. "Surprised?"

"I need a drink," said Gavin.

"You certainly do not," said Myra.

"What we need is to get out of here," said Natalie.

A hand came down on Natalie's shoulder and nails dug sharply into her flesh.

"You should never have come," said Carabosse in her ear.

"Let her go!" shouted Rose, approaching with shotgun raised.

"I thought we'd established that violence did nothing," said the fairy, painfully dragging Natalie round into the line of fire. "No one is going anywhere until our Princess Ella gets her fairy tale wedding."

"That will not be happening," said Mr Dainty, approaching with Ella and Roy at gunpoint, "unless she is wedding me."

"Ella, I told thee to get away from here," said Rose.

"Evidently, we failed," said Ella.

"And that man there owes me a debt," said Dainty, waggling his enormous weapon at Gavin.

"I think you owe him payment for all that overtime he's done for you!" retorted Myra.

"He stole from me!"

"I can assure you I didn't, Mr Dainty, sir," said Gavin.

"That teapot never showed up!"

"Teapot?" said Carabosse. "What a small and petty man you are."

Dainty raised his gun threateningly. Carabosse moved Natalie once more as a human shield. Rose took a step forward and aimed. Myra stepped back into a defensive position, attempting to cover both Dainty and fairy with her submachinegun.

"I don't think this is going to end well," said Roy.

"Oi Oi!" sang out a loud voice. "Cavalry's 'ere!"

Ella looked round to the marquee entrance. Surely there was nobody left to make a dramatic entrance?

"Awright treacle!" shouted the teapot, riding on top of a magnificent sideboard steed.

"Teapot!" shouted Ella.

"My teapot?" said Dainty.

A mass of furniture surged into the marquee in battle formation. Tables, desks, trolleys, chairs, benches, credenzas, ottomans, night stands and stools rode into the melee of cheap Bond villains, embattled dwarfs, bewildered wedding guests (and one wolf). Eyepatch gave a wail of horror as a trestle table slammed down on him. Passive Aggressive leapt to attack a roll-top bureau which simply rolled open to swallow him and then closed again without breaking stride and anyone close enough might have heard a petulant little voice mutter "Typical" as the bureau galloped by.

"This is unacceptable!" yelled Carabosse, a split second before Oscar the nesting table bounded directly into her, directly followed by his 'parents' Tony and Persephone.

Mr Dainty had only a second to marvel at this peculiar sight before a giant Welsh dresser trampled him underfoot.

The teapot drew up his steed beside Ella.

"I thought you'd been smashed!" she said, delighted to see him.

"Just my lid, darlin', although I 'ad a proper dunking, right in the briney."

"I'm so sorry," she said. "Without a lid, you must be less valuable."

"Nah," said the teapot. "I reckon I'm like a curio now. You know, a talkin' point. So, we made it in the nick of time, eh?"

"You did and you were awesome," said Ella.

"She's talking to a teapot," said Gavin, just in case anyone else had failed to spot this.

"What's the dealio here?" said the teapot.

"No time for introductions, but basically take down anyone that looks as if..." — Ella counted off on her fingers. — "They work for Mr Dainty. They're um, a dwarf. Or, they're an evil, manipulative baggage."

Ella glanced at Myra.

"What?" snapped Myra.

"Oh right. There's only the one evil manipulative baggage that you need to worry about," said Ella. "That one there." She pointed at Carabosse who was fighting her way to her feet.

"Look sharp, lads!" shouted the teapot and with a spout-waggle waved his vanguard on. Carabosse sneered at the tables as they charged towards her, but they came in sufficient numbers to knock her to the floor.

The wolf vaulted a charging occasional table and landed before Ella, a hook hand dangling from his lower jaw. Ella didn't want to wonder where the rest of Hook was.

"Is now a good time to get the hell out of Dodge?" asked the wolf.

"A tactical retreat," agreed Natalie wearily as she massaged her injured shoulder.

Granny Rose led the way, through the wide gap the furniture army had left in the wake of its initial charge.

"Come on Gavin," commanded Myra.

A hand grabbed Ella's ankle. She gave a shout of surprise. Mr Dainty pulled himself up from the floor, his clutches working up from her ankle, to her knee and her arm.

"Come now Ella. I have tolerated enough of your foolish resistance."

"Steady on, mate," said Roy.

"You let go of my daughter this instant!" said Gavin in the sternest voice he could muster.

"Or what?" said Dainty. "You are a joke my little drunken friend. You are no more capable of resisting me than you are of resisting a glass of wine. Get out of my way."

"You'll need to go through me first," said Myra, as she walked round and trained the machine gun at Dainty. "I've seen enough jumped up wannabe dictators to know one when I see one. There's one thing you boys always forget."

"Oh? And what is that," said Dainty, an amused smile playing around his lips.

"That your Achilles heel is *actually* between your legs," said Myra, expertly kneeing him in the groin and using her free elbow to fell him completely as he sank to the floor.

"Now, let's move!" said Myra.

At the vanguard of the retreat, Rose was cutting a path to the exit. She brandished the shotgun, blasting some of the tables. They clearly fell into the category of magical things that she disapproved of.

Ella steered Roy in the right direction.

"I have to say, I find this all jolly confusing," he said.

"You've probably just had a bit too much to drink," she said.

"Really? Bit early in the day to have such a blinding hangover. Wedding go all right did it?" he asked Ella. "Can't seem to recall any details."

"I'll bring you up to speed as we go," said Ella.

Across the way, Ella saw the teapot trotting along the side tables, kicking champagne bottles onto the floor with cries of "Call yourself a bloody proper drink, eh?" Shitfaced was crawling along behind it, trying to save the bottles, or drink the contents as they fell.

"Although some of it isn't easy to explain," said Ella. She passed Roy the leg off a destroyed table. "Take this and hit any dwarfs you see with it."

Roy obliged by bopping the approaching Disco over the head.

"Uncool, brother," said Disco. "Join me. Find your personal *groooove.*"

Roy bopped him harder.

Together, Ella and Roy ran to catch up with Rose. Outside,

wedding guests fled in all directions, discarding high heels and good manners to hasten their escape. Ella pulled Roy along the path towards the garden centre. Balloon arches were pushed askew or ripped from their moorings by their passage.

"Where are we running to?" said Roy.

"From. We're running from," said Ella. "The further away we get from Carabosse, the harder it will be for her to marry us off."

"Marry who off?"

"You. Me. And that way you won't become king."

"Was there any danger of that happening?" asked Roy.

"Apparently."

"Oh," said Roy. "Can I ask another question?"

"Sure."

"Why is that badger waving at us?"

"Where?"

"There."

"Oh. Let's follow him."

"Is that wise?"

Following the badger-ish ogre, Ella hauled Roy through a hedge and into the garden centre car park where Rose stood over the wolf who was laid out on the ground, belly up, writhing in pain.

"What's wrong with your dog?" said Roy.

"Where's mum?" said Ella.

"And why is your dog wearing women's clothing?" said Roy.

"Thought Natalie were wi' thee," said Rose.

"She was with *you*."

"Poor boy appears to be in some pain," said Roy, crouching beside the wolf.

"He's et summat as disagreed wi' him, I reckon," said Rose.

"Buster once ate a whole bar of Fruit and Nut," said Roy sagely.

"I was more thinking o' that nasty red-hatted bugger that's in there." Rose pointed at the small fist shaped bumps distending the wolf's stomach as the dwarf battled to get out.

"Let me rub it for him," said Roy. "Buster gets bellyache all the time." He kneeled down and rubbed the wolf's belly, ignoring the thumping from within. "What's this?" He dug a lump out of the wolf's leggings pocket.

"How does rubbing help exactly?" asked Ella.

"Moves the gas around," said Roy," helps to move things along — whoa!"

The wolf gave a whoop of relief as his tail lifted, his whole body shuddered and Psycho the dwarf shot out in a filthy slurry.

"Blimey!" said Roy, wafting his hand.

"I know!" said the wolf in hearty agreement.

Psycho jumped up and hollered at the top of his voice. "Over here lads! Bastard wolf sharted me out!"

ROY REACHED for his table leg but Psycho stamped on his fingers. The ogre-badger snapped at him with his sharp, weasely teeth. Psycho recoiled and punched the badger on the snout and the ogre reflexively bounced back into his enormous natural form.

"Lawks a lordy!" exclaimed Roy, falling back in surprise.

Ella saw something fly from his fist, a small glowing something that he had found in the wolf's pocket, which of course was Ella's pocket, the leggings she had been wearing when doing the chores in Granny Rose's garden that morning.

"Magic bean!" yelled Ella in warning.

"Quick lads!" shouted Psycho. "They've got a troll. I bloody hates trolls!"

The bean touched the ground...

Ella had once been in a car accident when the airbag had been deployed. She had no recollection of the airbag emerging from whichever part of the car concealed it, only that at one moment it wasn't there, and then she had an airbag in her face and a bruised nose. In much the same way, there was now a beanstalk. With no sense or recollection of it actually growing, she was now clinging to a beanstalk, the width of a mature oak tree and the height of... Ella looked down.

The garden centre and The Bumbles already looked like a view from Google Earth and the beanstalk was still accelerating upwards.

"Crap," she muttered, and made sure that she grabbed a couple more of the leaves. They were incredibly coarse, the hairs like wire scratching her hands.

"Aye," came Rose's voice from somewhere just above Ella's head. The beanstalk seemed stable, but swayed in the rising wind and that did not feel good. "Was this all part of the plan?"

Above Rose, Roy clung to the beanstalk like a castaway to a barrel, holding the wolf beside him. Higher still was the ogre, apparently borne aloft on the stalk's spire.

"They're trying to escape!" yelled Psycho, tangled in tendrils up above.

Not far below, six angry little mountaineers climbed towards her.

"She's hoping to escape into the land of the giants," said OCD.

"I'm not. I'm really not," Ella muttered to herself.

At ground level, a disturbing quiet had settled over things. The wedding guests were either gone, in hiding or in such a dazed and awestruck state that they weren't going to be making much fuss anymore. It had suddenly turned darker too. The beanstalk that had sprung up in the car park — of course it was a beanstalk, thought Natalie — was so massive as to partially block out the sun but, more than that, it seemed to be racing upwards towards a layer of thickly gathering clouds. She didn't want to think what lay beyond those clouds.

Natalie had come down to the garden centre, hoping to find Rose and Ella (who she now suspected were far, far above her) but had found instead Gavin and Myra and the two bridesmaids, taking shelter inside the Diggers and Dreams building. In amongst a jolly display of garden hoses, rakes and other gardening paraphernalia, Myra had turned two wheelbarrows on their sides to make a little barricade. From somewhere far behind them came the continuous sound of crockery or some such being smashed. Myra aimed her pilfered weapon as Natalie approached.

"Friend," said Natalie, hands raised.

"What the hell's going on out there?" said Myra, not so much alarmed by the magical mayhem as annoyed.

Natalie gave her a blank and frankly exhausted look.

"Was that a rhetorical question or do you actually want to know?"

"The short version," said Myra.

"Okay." She took a deep breath. "A fairy godmother is hell-bent on making Ella happy and so is forcing her to marry Roy who is now next in line to the throne."

"Is he?"

"He is. She's got the seven dwarfs to help her but that's okay because we've got a wolf and an ogre. Incidentally to all this, Mr Dainty thinks Ella should marry him and that Gavin is responsible for the magical furniture moving around in his castle."

"I knew something strange was happening," said Gavin.

Myra hoiked a thumb over her shoulder towards the sound of smashing pottery.

"There's a teapot back there, systematically destroying all the plant pots."

"I think he's got receptacle envy or something," said Natalie.

"And you?" said Myra, a coldness in her voice.

"I don't have receptacle envy."

"No. Explain yourself."

"I pricked my finger on a spindle and I fell asleep for thirty years."

"Bollocks."

Natalie shrugged. "It's true."

Myra stood and her weapon was still loosely but undeniably aimed at Natalie.

"Stay there," she told Gavin, came round the barricade and approached Natalie. Natalie stood her ground and waited. Myra reached out and prodded Natalie's shoulder, as though to check she was real.

"We thought you were dead," she said softly.

"I know."

"I got you a huge funeral wreath."

"That's nice."

Myra looked back at Gavin.

"And we moved on."

"I'm glad."

"This was meant to be my special day... But..."

Myra threw her arms around Natalie and hugged her with spine-snapping ferocity.

"I missed you."

"Me too."

The bridesmaids whispered to each other.

"What's happening?" said one.

"Not sure," said the other. "I think she's a time-travelling robot sent back from the future."

"I did think it might be that."

"Gavin," said Myra. "Don't be such a cold fish. Get out here and hug your wife."

Gavin approached obediently. He flicked an indicative finger between Myra and himself. "This, this isn't what it looks like."

"What are you talking about, man?" said Myra. "She caught us getting married, not having a quick fumble in a stationery cupboard."

"I'm just saying," said Gavin.

"It's okay," said Natalie. She hugged him. He wasn't her Gavin. He was a remnant of her Gavin, like a distant cousin to the man she knew she had truly lost forever; but she hugged him all the same. "I'm very happy for you."

Gavin burst into tears.

"Soppy fool," said Myra.

Gavin dabbed his eyes with his sleeve.

"Sorry, dear," he said. He gave Natalie a panicked looked. "I, um, call her dear now. Is that... Is that okay?"

Myra huffed. "The man's insufferable. What's the plan?" she asked Natalie.

"Plan? We get out there. We find my mum and my daughter and we run for the hills."

"And where are they?"

Natalie pointed up.

17

There was a rumble of thunder and lightning flashed in the gathering clouds. Ella wiped the first raindrops from her face and looked again. It might have been her imagination but she thought she saw figures in the clouds, illuminated by the lightning flashes, vast humanoid figures as large as mountains. The ogre at the top of the beanstalk was already disappearing into the lower edges of the cloud world.

"Trapped between giants and dwarfs," shouted Rose above the growing gale.

"Oh, the symbolism," said Ella bitterly.

There was a holler of alarm from above. Psycho had hold of Roy and was using feet and fingers to prise the unhappy heir to the throne from the beanstalk.

"Wolf!" yelled Ella.

The wolf held out his paws, perhaps ready to explain that he was not well-suited to climbing leguminous vines. But it was too late already. Roy lost his grip and fell. The wolf snapped at him, Ella flung out a hand to him but he was already falling away from the stalk, falling far and fast.

A black folded shape shot past her, blasting the hair from her face as it passed. A bird. A huge bird. An eagle or some other raptor, as big as a man, diving after Roy.

"It's tha ogre friend," said Rose.

Ella watched them both, man and bird, falling until they were but dots, closing together but not quite touching. Ella peered, leaning out as far as she dared to watch them. She sniffed. There was a sudden stink in her nostrils: cabbagey, toilety, ripe...

She swung around, fist extended and punched Windy (who had been creeping up on her) clean off the beanstalk.

"Silent but deadly," she said.

The brown-hatter tumbled away and then with some industrial rectum-pumping began to control and direct his descent. Below, the others were closing in on her.

"Ideas?" Ella asked her grandma.

Rose regarded her shotgun. "I'm out of ammunition." She closed one eye and threw the gun downwards like a javelin. It struck Passive Aggressive in the chest and knocked him off the stalk.

"And now I'm out of ideas, love," said Rose.

Inappropriate's hand grabbed hold of Ella's ankle.

"Get off!" she shouted.

"Come on," he said. "I always look up to women. Particularly when I can see up their skirts."

"Filthy bugger," said Rose.

The lecherous creep was as slimy and as unshakeable as a sinus infection. One handhold then another, he worked his way up Ella's legs.

A shadow swooped over them, grabbed Inappropriate in one claw and Shitfaced in another and ripped them from the stalk. The ogre-eagle flung them aside.

"I thought being tossed off by a bird would be more fun," cried Inappropriate and was gone.

"Where's Roy?" shouted Ella to the eagle. "Where's Roy?"

THE PROGRESS OF THE HANNAFORD / Whuppie family across the car park to the beanstalk was not without incident. First of all, a dwarf and a shotgun fell from the heavens into the roof of a nearby greenhouse. Then a giant eagle appeared and deposited a startled Roy at Natalie's feet before taking off again. A short while later, a flatulent dwarf made a controlled descent, powered by his own personal booster rocket. Myra had taken aim but the windy one had scuttled round to the far side of the stalk before she could get a shot off.

And now, the sound of an engine revving from the other side of the car park took their attention away from the retreating dwarf. The cement mixer door slammed. A somewhat bruised and tattered Mr Dainty leaned out of the window and shouted over at them. Natalie could indeed see the exotic European passion in his posture and the powerful pride and purpose in his eyes and she was sure that his threats were spoken from the heart but they were, unfortunately, mostly drowned out by engine revs and gusty winds.

"You have all —" *vrmm, vrmm* "— like a fool, and you must know —" *whirl, whoosh* "— mess with me only end up —" *vrmmm, whirl* "— your language contained the richness of cursing that my native —" *whistle, vrmmm* "— and your mother's vagina and —" *swirl, whistle* "— fear the translation does it no justice."

"I'm sorry," hollered Gavin in reply. "We didn't get all of that."

"I said," yelled Dainty, "you treat me like a —" *vrmmmm, swirl* "— curse your mother's vagina and your sister's —" *howl, vrmm* "— shits."

"Yes?" shouted Gavin. "We definitely got the bit about my mother's vagina. My sister's what was it?"

"Are you purposely trying to antagonise him?" said Roy.

"I'm just seeking some clarity," said Roy's nearly but not quite father-in-law.

But Mr Dainty had had enough of talk. He revved the engine, engaged the gear and roared towards them in the giant orange truck. They should have been able to jump out of its path with relative ease but Natalie attempted to herd them all in one direction and Myra in the other and with no time to spare they found themselves exactly where they were. Two dwarfs chose that moment to fall out of the sky and through the front window of the cab.

The truck swerved, banked impressively on fifty percent of the recommended number of wheels and slammed into, and partially through, the beanstalk.

ELLA FELT the impact before she heard it.

"What was that?"

"I would hazard it was a heavy goods vehicle striking the base of the beanstalk," said OCD, gasping for breath as he closed in on Ella.

A low groaning sound could be heard from the beanstalk as it reverberated.

"Are we falling?" called the wolf from above.

The beanstalk leaned... slowly, and ever so slightly, but it *leaned*.

"Yes!" yelled Ella back. She looked for the eagle-ogre. "Get the wolf!" she shouted.

"More importantly," said OCD, "can we talk about the absolute ruin you've made of that lovely dress."

She glared at the crazy dwarf.

"Are you kidding me? This dress is ridiculous and these shoes are killing me!"

"What's a little pain in pursuit of perfection?"

Ella slipped one shoe off and smashed it over OCD's head.

"Indeed," she said, changing her grip as the beanstalk leaned slightly but irreversibly further.

"Reckon it's going over," called Rose. "This would be a really good time for one o' them clever ideas."

"Oh tosswobbling wankgoblin!" called Ella.

"Now then, there's no call for that kind of language," said Rose.

"I need to spunkmaggot twattimasturbankling cunnibasterlate," explained Ella.

"Oh, right," said Rose and cleared her throat. "By all that's flamin' well wrong in life, like... like ready meals and television."

"May need to give it a bit more, Granny," urged Ella, as the beanstalk leaned, quite treacherously now.

"By God. Lancashire cricket! Soft southern water! Herbal infusions!"

Ella's stomach flipped as the stalk began to collapse. Against the green and rapidly approaching ground, a definite rectangle unfurled and raced up to meet them.

IN THE CAR PARK, Gavin, the two loves of his life, two sub-normal bridesmaids and an excusably confused king-in-waiting eyed the creaking base of the beanstalk. Noises that were all kinds of wrong ran up and down the massive structure. Every cell in their bodies was telling them to flee but curiosity held them just for a little longer.

There was a screech from the smashed and partly buried truck cab. The door was forced open and Natalie saw Mr Dainty hobble out of the crippled cement mixer, gun in hand.

"You see!" he cried triumphantly. "Even a crash cannot prevent me from taking my revenge. Amongst my people, revenge is a very serious concept. It is not possible that my displeasure can be sated in any simple manner. No! I will kill you all, for honour, for my teapot, for my sheep!"

"Sheep?" said Roy.

"Yes! Sheep! You see, in my country —"

Then a coil of beanstalk, as massive and as long as a freight train, fell to the ground with a shattering force so powerful that it popped the cement drum off its mounting and threw it across the car park. Every window in the garden centre was smashed by the sudden blast of air, and some near-fatally curious onlookers were blown clean off their feet. Then another loop smashed into the crater of the first, then another and another — throwing out clouds of dust, woody debris and a fair torrent of bean juice.

At some point, the fuel tank of the cement mixer exploded. Fires burned here and there, and smoke and dust filled the air. It was several minutes before Natalie could see well enough to confirm what she suspected to be true: that the falling beanstalk had dug a giant crater with its epicentre at the exact spot where Mr Dainty had been standing.

"Do we think he's a has-bean?" asked Gavin, his face a mask of innocence.

Natalie groaned and Myra thumped him.

"I don't get it," said one of the bridesmaids.

A shadow fluttered above their heads and Natalie looked up to see Ella and Rose coming to land on the magic carpet and, beside them, a not necessarily grateful wolf being carried to earth by a giant eagle. The wolf licked at his hide where the ogre-eagle had clutched him.

"Get your nails cut, hotwings," he said.

The ogre resumed his natural form.

"I can take you back up there and drop you off if you wish."

"Right, lads!" came a shout from somewhere in the ruins of the beanstalk. "Let's get the bastards!"

. . .

ELLA PUT her hand to her forehead to scan the crash site for dwarfs. Through the smoke they came: Psycho, Passive Aggressive, Windy, OCD, Inappropriate, Shitfaced and Disco. They were ragged and scraped but the fact that any of them were still mobile was amazing. In the past week, they had been shot, dropped, cooked, digested, crushed, exploded, sharted, bonked, whacked, eagled and even shoed.

"They're unkillable," said Natalie.

"They're stories," said the wolf. "Ever tried killing a story?"

"Windy! Gas attack!" commanded Psycho. "Shitfaced! Disco! Take down that troll! The rest with me!"

"Troll?" said the ogre, irritated.

With frightening ease, he picked up the giant drum from the cement mixer and emptied it over the charging dwarfs. Viscous cement coated each of them, dragging them to the ground and halting their charge. Undaunted, they struggled to their feet. Psycho raised his hand to wave them on once more.

Ella assumed that what happened next was that the expanding cloud of Windy's gas attack touched upon the dying flames of the burning cement mixer. A powerful whoosh of fire washed over the dwarfs and the ogre and singed the edges of Ella's dress. In an instant, it had burned itself out and there they stood: one uninjured ogre and seven rock-hard dwarf statues.

"Oh, look, they've turned back into garden gnomes," said Lily.

"Yes," said Petunia solemnly. "They are at peace now."

"It's the circle of life," agreed Lily.

"A dance as old as time," Petunia concurred.

"Que sera, sera."

"Machu Picchu."

"Gesundheit."

"You're welcome."

"ENOUGH!"

It was Carabosse's voice, but not as Ella had heard it before.

Carabosse had always had a mother-knows-best voice, quiet smarm and implacable certainty. This voice was the fury of the storm and the dangerous tide, a mother-has-been-at-the-gin-and-is-going-to-tell-some-fucking-home-truths voice.

Ella's fairy godmother hovered ten feet off the ground, wrapped in a sizzling purple nimbus of magic and holding a wand so ancient and so potent Ella could well believe that God had used it to make the world, even the tricky bits.

"Are you all too stupid to know what's good for you?" crackled Carabosse wrathfully. "A happy ending is a simple thing but it is not easy to arrange. There are patterns to be followed, conventions to be observed. What monsters are you to crush my gift to you, more perfect and beautiful than a snowflake?"

"Tha can't tell us what to do," shouted Rose.

"Silence!" said Carabosse. And, with a wave of the wand, Rose fell silent, robbed of speech.

"Each of you will observe your place in the proper order of things," said the fairy. "You two!" She pointed her wand at the ogre and the wolf. "You are wicked creatures and your place is to be punished."

Creepers leapt up from the ruins of the beanstalk and wrapped themselves around arms, legs and chests until the two were bound and immobile.

"I will find a clever pussy cat to put an end to you, ogre," said Carabosse. "And I'm sure a handy woodcutter will soon find you, wolf."

Ella pulled at the creepers around the wolf's body but they might as well have been made of steel.

"Hey, princess," he said grimly, "at least I think I won our bet."

"You don't have to do this," said Natalie.

"You," said Carabosse. "You should either be asleep or dead." A flick of the wand and Natalie collapsed to the ground, lifeless. "Mothers don't last long in the best stories."

Rose was at her daughter's side in an instant, mutely stroking her face and feeling for signs of life.

"And grandmothers only exist to be eaten," said Carabosse.

Magical creepers flew out and dragged her, neatly trussed, to within easy reach of the wolf's jaws.

"And now," declared Carabosse, "there *will* be a wedding and it *will* be perfect."

"My wedding?" said Myra.

Carabosse smiled sweetly.

"Myra Whuppie. You do have an important role to play. After our Ella marries her Prince Charming, your scheming plots will be rightly punished."

"But..."

"Forced to dance in hot iron shoes is traditional. Put in a barrel stuck full of nails and rolled down a hill is an acceptable alternative. As for the vain idiots..." She pointed at Lily and Petunia. Lily looked behind her in case the fairy might be pointing at someone else. "They shall of course have their feet hacked to bits and their eyes plucked out by birds."

Petunia put her hand up.

"Yes?" said Carabosse.

"I don't like the sound of that."

"But it's traditional, dearie."

"Oh. Oh, in that case..." she said with a compliant shrug.

"I refuse," said Ella bluntly.

"I don't care," said Carabosse simply and waved her wand.

Without any input from her brain, Ella linked arms with Roy and together they began walking briskly up the hill toward The Bumbles and the wedding marquee. Lily and Petunia followed, carrying Ella's train, with Gavin and Myra bringing up the rear.

As they progressed, Carabosse waved her wand here and there. Balloon arches repaired themselves or repositioned themselves from wherever they had fallen or flown. And from all directions, the wedding guests returned, walking with all the self-control of zombies (purposeful and well-dressed zombies who had a wedding to get to). Rents in the walls of the marquee re-stitched themselves, chairs righted themselves and all manner of ribbons, decorations and flowers fluttered into place, as though they were part of a jolly video sequence that was being played backwards.

By the time Ella and Roy reached the marquee, all the guests were in place, Ella's dress was mended, the glass slippers were back on her feet and Mendelssohn's "Wedding March" was playing from some unseen source. Up the aisle they walked, towards the now whole and hideous wedding arbour where a registrar (the original registrar, Ella surmised) waited for the happy couple. Carabosse floated alongside Ella, visible to all.

Ahead, beside the wedding arbour was the wedding cake. The little figures on the top no longer depicted a double wedding. There were now tiny representations of Ella and Roy beneath a confectionery arbour, with bridesmaids beside them. It was like the model village Carabosse had trapped her in: real life, shrunk down, frozen, made cute, made perfect.

Ella glanced up at Carabosse. God, she looked so happy. This was what she lived for. Ella could see that. A princess going to her happily ever after. Just this. Just this moment. Ella almost felt sorry for her.

The registrar smiled warmly at them as they came to a stop.

"Are we ready to begin?" he asked.

"Actually," said Ella, finger raised.

Carabosse flashed her a warning look.

"No, no. Not complaining. Just a couple of things."

"And what would they be?" said Carabosse.

"We want this to be perfect, don't we?"

Carabosse narrowed her eyes suspiciously.

"For example, all these people. They're all under your control but, deep down, they all remember the stuff from before. The carnage. The gunfire. The tables coming to life. They're not actually enjoying this wedding right now and they won't with all that in their minds."

"Yes," said Carabosse thoughtfully.

"You do want them to be happy, don't you?"

Carabosse shot off, from person to person, to Roy, to Gavin, to Myra, Lily, Petunia and all the guests. She paused for a split second at each but moved on so quickly that she was a blur of unmeasurable speed, only identifiable by the domino-falling trail of twitches among the guests and the purple afterimage of light she left in the air.

And Carabosse was by Ella's side once more, not even out of breath.

A change in mood had come over the marquee. The guests were still silent, still seated but now they were themselves, zombies no longer, wiped clean of all nasty recollections of the last hour.

"Better?" said Carabosse.

"Oh, yes."

"Good." Carabosse gestured for the registrar to proceed.

"But there is just one more thing," said Ella.

"What?"

"It's the cake," said Ella.

Carabosse looked at the cake.

"It's perfect."

"It's nearly perfect," agreed Ella. "I can see what you were *trying* to do with it."

"Trying?" said Carabosse.

"Yes. It's supposed to be a representation of our wedding day, captured in miniature."

"It is."

"Is it?" said Ella. "Oh. Well. If you're happy with it." She waved to the registrar. "I suppose we ought to get on with this."

Carabosse waved a hand to draw Ella's attention.

"What's wrong with it, dearie? Surely, it's perfect. Isn't it?"

A glimmer of doubt crossed Carabosse's face and Ella knew that she had her.

"Well, there's a couple of missing details."

"What?"

"You'll add them?"

"It's a perfect recreation of this moment. What have I missed?"

"You'll definitely add it?"

"I promise I will sort it out immediately, before I do anything else."

"Thank you," smiled Ella. "It's just that there's no you. You're here but not there."

"Of course," smiled Carabosse in return. "How silly of me." She waved her wand and a tiny fairy godmother in fondant icing appeared on the cake. "There."

"And the wedding cake," said Ella. "There's no wedding cake on the wedding cake."

"Indeed." Another wand wave and there was a miniature cake beside their confectionary selves. "Happy?"

"Very much," said Ella and then frowned. She peered at the cake. "Hang on. That's not the same."

"What's not?"

"The cake."

A magic swoosh and Carabosse shrank down to the same size as the little figurines and peered at her cake on a cake.

"It is the same," she said.

Ella squinted at the miniscule diorama portrayed on the model cake.

"Nope. There's no wedding cake."

"It's here."

"No, on the model wedding cake. There should be a cake on

the cake on the cake. That's if it's to be a copy of what's really here."

"Very well," said Carabosse.

"And a cake on that cake," pointed out Ella. "And a cake on that one. In fact, every cake should have a cake on it. All of them."

"But, you won't be able to see them," reasoned Carabosse.

Was that nervousness in her voice Ella could hear? She hoped it was.

"Yes, but details are important."

"But that's an infinite number of cakes. It would never end."

"You did promise," said Ella. "You promised you would do it immediately, before anything else."

Shrunk though she was, the look of horror and panic on Carabosse's face was unmistakeable.

"Please, Ella. Princess. Dearie. I only wanted..."

"To make me happy?" said Ella. "I know. Get to it."

Ella clapped her hands and the fairy shrank further to create the next cake, shrank further to create the next. When she was too small to make out, she was still visible as a receding mote of purple light, shrinking further and further.

And when the light became too dim to see, Ella still imagined she could hear a faint high-pitched whine, like an insect buzz or a distant scream.

And long, long after the whine had faded, there was a simultaneously clear yet silent...

pop

ROY TOOK hold of Ella's hand.

He blinked several times and shook his head.

"Hello, Ella. Um, what's going on?"

"Well..."

"She's in my place, that's what's going on here!" said Myra sternly.

"I am. That's true and..."

"And what's this?"

"This?"

"Who turns up to a wedding wearing a bridal gown? Only someone who seriously wants to piss off the bride!"

"I'm sure it's all a misunderstanding," said Gavin diplomatically.

Ella began to gesture to the cake. An explanation of what had just happened — with the fairy and the wand and the dwarfs and Roy being next in line to the throne — was already making its way to her throat. And she stopped because she knew that no explanation was needed.

"Just a misunderstanding," said Ella. "Bit of a mix up."

She stepped aside, pulling Roy with her, and made way for the bride and groom.

"Very good," said the registrar. "Ladies and gentlemen. We are here today to join together our friends, Myra and Gavin."

"Mum!" said Ella, abruptly remembering.

"See?" Gavin said to Myra. "I told you she called you mum."

"Sorry," said Ella. "Really, I've got to go."

She hitched up her skirts and ran for the exit.

"That girl!" snorted Myra.

"Sorry!" yelled Ella. "Love you both!"

"Well, come on, Mr Registrar," said Myra. "Get Registraring."

Ella kicked off the ridiculously impractical glass slippers as she ran down the path.

"Ella!"

She turned. Roy had come out after her. There was a buzzing sound in his pocket.

"I can't stop," she said. "I've got to go."

"Is everything alright?" he said.

"I hope so," she said. "Your phone's ringing."

He took it out. "Wilbur? What? Slow down. Ella! Wait!"

"What?"

"You..."

"What?" she said.

"You look beautiful in a wedding dress."

"Ha! Enjoy it while you can," she grinned. And then, "You don't look so bad yourself, Roy."

And she ran on.

"What do you mean, the royals have all come *back*?" she heard Roy say. "I didn't know they'd gone anywhere."

She ran down the path, through the balloon arches, past the hedge into the car park of Diggers and Dreams.

There was no beanstalk. There was, however, a wide but shallow crater in the centre of the car park and the utterly flattened remains of an orange cement mixer which would no doubt cause some head-scratching confusion later. Nearby, was a long row of seven ugly and badly moulded garden gnomes and, on a garden seat next to them, were two women apparently enjoying the afternoon sun.

"Here she is," said Natalie.

"Looking mighty pleased with hersen an' all," said Granny Rose.

"I didn't know what happened to you," said Ella.

"The magic vanished and..." Natalie threw her hands up in the air, for that was as much explanation as she could give.

"The wolf?" said Ella. "The ogre?"

"Gone," said Natalie.

"Where?"

"Where do stories go when they're all told?" said Natalie.

"We-ell," said Rose, who wasn't one for mystical

proclamations. "That big ugly lummox took off across yon fields. An' I reckon I saw t'wolf sniffing around t'sheds a bit back."

Ella smiled. "Are you two going to come up to the wedding?"

"They're getting married? After all this?"

"Carabosse did a mind-wipe on everyone. They've sort of forgotten. So? I'm sure I could squeeze you in at the reception dinner. I'm in charge of the seating plan, after all."

Natalie pulled a face.

"Gatecrashing my own husband's wedding? Might be a bit upsetting."

"Mmm," nodded Rose in agreement. "Is tha having a disco after?"

"Yes, but you don't have to, you know, dance."

"Ah, no. I like a dance now an' then."

"It's been a while," said Natalie. "I might be out of practice."

"What's that one with the 'push pineapple, shake the wotsit'?" asked Rose.

"Agadoo?" said Natalie.

"Aye. I like that 'un."

"I should imagine that one's been long forgotten by now," said Natalie.

Ella laughed. "Welcome to the future, mum. Prepare to be disappointed."

THANK YOU FROM THE AUTHORS

Many thanks to you, the reader for taking the time to read this book.

We'd be incredibly grateful if you could leave a review. Reviews mean so much to authors, and it helps other readers to find our work as well.

We're writing lots of new material, so if you'd like to be kept up to date, sign up to our newsletter here: www.pigeonparkpress.com

The next few pages will tell you about some of our other books.

ALSO BY HEIDE GOODY AND IAIN GRANT

Clovenhoof

Getting fired can ruin a day...

...especially when you were the Prince of Hell.

Will Satan survive in English suburbia?

Corporate life can be a soul draining experience, especially when the industry is Hell, and you're Lucifer. It isn't all torture and brimstone, though, for the Prince of Darkness, he's got an unhappy Board of Directors.

The numbers look bad.

They want him out.

Then came the corporate coup.

Banished to mortal earth as Jeremy Clovenhoof, Lucifer is going through a mid-immortality crisis of biblical proportion. Maybe if he just tries to blend in, it won't be so bad.

He's wrong.

If it isn't the murder, cannibalism, and armed robbery of everyday life in Birmingham, it's the fact that his heavy metal band isn't getting the respect it deserves, that's dampening his mood.

And the archangel Michael constantly snooping on him, doesn't help.

If you enjoy clever writing, then you'll adore this satirical tour de force, because a good laugh can make you have sympathy for the devil.

Get it now.

Clovenhoof

Oddjobs

It's the end of the world as we know it, but someone still needs to do the paperwork.

Incomprehensible horrors from beyond are going to devour our world but that's no excuse to get all emotional about it. Morag Murray works for the secret government organisation responsible for making sure the apocalypse goes as smoothly and as quietly as possible.

In her first week on the job, Morag has to hunt down a man-eating starfish, solve a supernatural murder and, if she's got time, prevent her own inevitable death.

The first book in a new comedy series by the creators of 'Clovenhoof', Oddjobs is a sideswipe at the world of work and a fantastical adventure featuring amphibian wannabe gangstas, mad old cat ladies, ancient gods, apocalyptic scrabble, fish porn, telepathic curry and, possibly, the end of the world before the weekend.

Oddjobs

Snowflake

Lori Belkin has been dumped. By her parents.

They moved out while she was away on holiday, and now, at the tender age of twenty-five, she must stand on her own two feet.

While she's getting to grips with basic adulting, Lori magically brings to life the super-sexy man she created from celebrity photos as a teenager.

Lori learns very quickly that having your ideal man is not as satisfying as it ought to be and that being an adult is far harder than it looks.

Snowflake is a story about prehistoric pets, delinquent donkeys and becoming the person you want to be, not the person everyone else expects you to be.

Snowflake

Printed in Great Britain
by Amazon

29216380R00189